THE FOYLES BOOK

ELAINE ROBERTS had a dream to write for a living. She completed her first novel in her twenties and received her first very nice rejection. Life then got in the way until she picked up her dream again in 2010. She joined a creative writing class, The Write Place, in 2012 and shortly afterwards had her first short story published. Elaine and her patient husband, Dave, have five children who have flown the nest. Home is in Dartford, Kent and is always busy with their children, grandchildren, grand dogs and cats visiting.

THE FOYLES GIRLS

THE FOYLES BOOKSHOP GIRLS AT WAR

Elaine Roberts

First published in the United Kingdom in 2019 by Aria,
an imprint of Head of Zeus Ltd

9 7 5 3 1 2 4 6 8

A CIP catalogue record for this book is available from the British Library.

ISBN 9781788544863

Aria
an imprint of Head of Zeus
First Floor East
5–8 Hardwick Street
London EC1R 4RG

To my husband, Dave,
and my wonderful family.

Chapter 1

June 1916

Molly Cooper tucked her blonde hair behind her ear before picking up the folded newspaper that had been left on the wooden counter in Foyles, the London bookshop. The paper rustled as she unfolded it, causing her to look over her shoulder for old Leadbetter.

'Excuse me.'

A hand tugged at Molly's skirt.

Looking down, a little girl was clutching the black material. She stooped down. 'Yes, little one, what can I do for you?' Molly looked around her. 'Where's your ma?'

The little girl turned and pointed to the rows of shelving, bowed under the weight of the tomes, just as a young woman carrying several books approached them. The child beamed and ran towards her.

The woman smiled apologetically. 'I'm sorry, I lose all track of time when I'm in this shop, and my daughter gets bored.'

'We all feel the same; there are so many to choose from.' Molly smiled. 'I don't think customers get to see half of them.' She looked around, remembering the excitement she felt when she first walked through the doors of Foyles Bookshop, as a young girl.

'I don't know how you manage to get any work done. I'd spend all my time reading the books.' The woman juggled her newfound treasures into her arms and took the little girl's hand. 'Right, we had better go and pay for these, before the shop closes and I have to put them all back.'

Molly smiled as she watched them walk over towards Alice's counter, before going over to the payment booth, where her friend Victoria would take the money for the purchases. She would miss working at Foyles and chatting with her friends, but this wasn't about her. She had to do what was right. As always, Rebecca of Sunnybrook Farm jumped into her head. The story had been with her since she'd read it as a child. Rebecca was a young girl that had to be strong and be herself, no matter what rules were laid down to stop her, and she had won out in the end. Wasn't that what she had to do?

Sighing, Molly glanced around to see if old Leadbetter was nearby. Satisfied there was no sign of him, she turned back to the front page of the newspaper. The picture of Lord Kitchener filled it, along with the news that he had drowned on his way to Russia. Tony's face was suddenly in the forefront of her mind. His smile had captured every woman's heart. Her mind played a rerun of him lighting one of his Players cigarettes as they sat under a tree in Greenwich Park. He showed off, blowing circles with the smoke he had inhaled. She had wanted to be his wife, practising her signature in readiness of his proposal, and giggling at his playful ways. Her eyes blurred as they stared unseeing at the paper. Molly blinked quickly to stop the tears from falling. She had been naïve and her friend, Alice, had been right, although she hadn't listened at the time. Tony hadn't been able to stop himself from chancing his arm with every pretty face he saw. He had never been going to propose to her. She had made a fool of herself over him and now she had to live with the guilt of what she had done. Had she really called him a coward for not enlisting, when all the other men did at the beginning of the war? It was unforgivable. Molly was thankful she hadn't introduced Tony to her parents. They wouldn't have understood the attraction, but now she couldn't talk to them about what was eating her alive.

Now Kitchener's family were going through the same horrors of getting a visit from the telegram boy, telling them they have lost someone they love.

'It's a real tragedy.'

Molly dropped the paper as though it was burning her fingers. There was no need to look round; she knew that voice. She didn't think he would miss her. He had caught her up to no good, on numerous occasions.

'He was a great Field Marshall and I'm sure he will leave a hole that won't be easily filled. Asquith could have a problem there.' Mr Leadbetter's breath brushed against her cheek.

Molly nodded as she looked down at Kitchener's picture. Her nose wrinkled as the strong waft of cheese caught in the back of her throat. 'That's what my father also thought, Mr Leadbetter. He said last night, the prime minister would struggle to replace him.'

He sighed. 'This war certainly has a lot to answer for.'

They both stared down at the picture, each lost in thought.

A girl giggled. 'So many books. It must be lovely to work here. Do you think I could get a job at Foyles when I'm older?'

An older woman laughed. 'You'd never get any work done, and you'd spend all your money on books.'

Molly's lips lifted as she remembered the nervous excitement of her first day working at Foyles. The large sign outside, declaring them to be the largest bookseller in London, shouted at the passers-by, inviting them in. It promised refunds of two thirds of the price, if the book was returned after being read. Once she had walked into the shop, it was like entering another world. The musty smell of the second hand books, stacked along the shelves, had seemed endless. She had been overwhelmed when she realised it spread over six floors and every nook and cranny had been crammed with books.

A lot had happened since that day. Molly crossed her arms, holding herself tight. She bit down on her lip in a bid to stop her chin from trembling. Would she ever love again? The shop doors thudded shut and bolts were drawn across, pulling Molly away from her brooding.

Mr Leadbetter stared at her hunched shoulders. 'Your family must be very proud of you, taking on the challenges that this war has thrown at everyone. The men have an obvious bravery about them, but the women that have been left behind are doing an exceptional job picking up the pieces.'

Molly's grip tightened around her waist. 'Does that mean we might get the vote when this is all over?'

'Who knows, Miss Cooper? Unfortunately, that's not my decision to make.' Mr Leadbetter arched his eyebrows. 'Do you follow the political musings of our government?'

Molly glanced over her shoulder at her manager. 'I must admit, I didn't until the war started, but now I read the news every day.' She looked back at the newspaper.

'That's good.' Mr Leadbetter forced a smile. 'It's important to know what's going on.'

'I suppose, but the news is so gruesome all the time; so many deaths.' Molly sighed. 'Sometimes, I think I'd rather not know.' She gave a little laugh. 'Give me a good book any day.'

Mr Leadbetter clenched his lips tight for a second, fighting the urge to give her a fatherly hug. 'Well, this is it. The time has come for you to say your goodbyes. I suspect everyone is waiting for you.' He chuckled. 'You've worked here for some time and everyone in Foyles will miss you.'

Molly took a deep breath and pasted on her best smile, before she swung round to face him. 'I expect you'll be happy to see the back of me, sir.'

'On the contrary, there hasn't been a day go by when you haven't made me smile, even though you call me "old Leadbetter," when you think I can't hear you.' His eyes sparkled and a smile lit up his normally stern features.

Her rising body temperature told Molly her face was turning a lovely shade of red. She lowered her head slightly. 'Sorry, sir, it was rude of me, but I always thought you didn't like me.'

'Far from it, you have been like the daughter I never had.' Mr Leadbetter coughed. 'Sorry, I shouldn't have said that; most inappropriate.'

Molly smiled at the elderly man standing in front of her. 'On the contrary, there hasn't been a day go by, when I haven't felt I've been working with my father.'

Laughter burst from him. 'I am sorry to see you leave us, but I do understand that young women like yourself are being put under pressure to do war work.'

Molly nodded. 'My mother was thrilled when I started working here. She didn't want me to go into domestic service.' She sighed.

Mr Leadbetter frowned. 'How does she feel about you going to the munitions' factory? It's not just hard work, it's also dangerous.'

Molly lowered her lashes. Should she admit she hadn't told her family yet? Would he think she was a bad person? She sucked in her breath and the words of her half-lie tripped over themselves to escape. 'They'll be fine, once they get used to the idea of it. They don't like change very much.'

Mr Leadbetter nodded. 'I don't think many of us do.'

Molly looked up at him. His upright frame belied his age. She gave him a wry smile. 'It does feel strange to know that, when I come in here again, it will be as a customer.' She stroked the oak counter. 'I've met some lovely people since I began working here, and I have a bedroom full of books that I can't bear to part with.' She looked around at the heaving shelves. 'No more stacking books away. I shan't miss the musty second hand ones, and dusting until it catches in the back of your throat, or fighting the daily temptation to buy books for the children that come into my section.' She took a deep breath.

Mr Leadbetter's eyes crinkled at the corners and a smile played on his lips as she spoke.

Molly glanced up at him. 'You know, I always wanted to sit them down and read to them, help them to become book lovers.'

He frowned. 'I've never heard you mention that before.'

She gave a little scathing sound. 'I never thought anyone, least of all you, would be interested in anything I had to say.'

'What, and yet you are quite outspoken.' His eyes searched her face. 'Rumour has it, you are not to be crossed, although having said that, you appear to be a very popular young lady.'

Molly laughed. 'I don't know about that, sir.' She gave him a wide-eyed look. 'It's not about being popular, but about fitting in and being respected.'

Mr Leadbetter nodded. 'It sounds like I have done you a disservice, Miss Cooper. However, I shall miss you, as indeed will your colleagues, but our loss is the munitions' factory's gain.' He took a deep breath. 'I wish you well there, but please be assured that all the time I am here, there will be a position for you.'

Molly nodded. She stood on the tips of her toes and kissed him on the cheek, taken aback by his deceptively soft skin. 'I shall miss you too, and of course, everyone who works here.'

Thunderous applause and cheers filled the room. Molly spun round to a sea of faces beaming at her. Her friends of nearly twenty years, Alice Leybourne and Victoria Appleton, were at the front, clapping vigorously. Each were battling their demons and trying to survive. Molly fretted about her decision to leave Foyles and whether their friendship might suffer, but this was something she had to do. Their watery eyes told Molly much more than words could ever say. She blinked rapidly, in a bid to hold back the emotions that were in danger of engulfing her.

Alice stepped forward, no longer able to hold the tears in check, as they rolled down her cheeks. She sniffed and wiped her fingers across her damp face. 'Well, Miss Molly Cooper, we have booked tables at Café Monico, for everyone to say their goodbyes and wish you well, so grab your things.'

Molly's eyes glistened, but a ready smile came to her lips. 'I don't know, Alice, since you've had baby Arthur, you seem to shed tears at the drop of a hat. You and Victoria will probably see more of me than ever before.'

'Yeah, well we won't.' A woman's voice came from the back of the room.

Mr Leadbetter blinked quickly and cleared his throat. 'I wouldn't have thought that was possible. I mean, not working in the same place and all that.'

Molly glared up at him. He wasn't helping the situation.

Alice stepped forward, sniffing into her handkerchief. 'It won't be the same as working with you.' She sucked in her breath. Her lips formed a weak smile. 'We won't be able to have lunch together, or go out after we finish here.'

Mr Leadbetter gave the girls a smile. 'Or be gossiping, when you should be working.'

Molly's throat tightened.

'That doesn't sound like us.' Victoria chuckled, attempting to follow Mr Leadbetter's lead to lighten the moment.

His laughter erupted into the store. 'It wasn't you I was thinking of, Miss Appleton.'

Victoria smiled as she took a couple of steps towards Alice, so she could put an arm around her shoulders. 'Shh, everything will be all right. We'll just have to make more of an effort to see each other from now on.'

'Come on, get your things and let's get this party started,' a woman's voice called out. Laughter filled the room, followed by cheers and applause.

Mr Leadbetter held up his hand to bring silence. 'I am unable to come to your party, but I have something to give you.' The room was still. 'We have had a collection and bought you a gift to remember us by.' He handed over a neatly wrapped square package, tied with red ribbon. Molly looked up at him as he nodded his encouragement. He hoped she wouldn't find out he had donated more money than everyone else, but as her manager, he felt he could justify it.

'Open it,' a lone voice called out.

Molly laughed and, with trembling hands, she pulled at the ends of the ribbon. Her heart was pounding as she flipped up the lid, to see a small solid gold heart, hanging from a fine chain, nestling on red velvet padding. 'It's beautiful,' she whispered. 'Absolutely beautiful.' She turned to the women standing around her. 'Thank you, thank you so much.' Molly immediately clipped it around her neck, peering down to admire it. 'I can't believe I'm actually leaving.' Tears pricked at her eyes. 'I shall miss you all so much.' She looked back at her manager. 'Including you, Mr Leadbetter.' The bookstore erupted with laughter.

Mr Leadbetter nodded. 'We will be here, should you need us.'

Alice and Victoria moved to give Molly a hug, quickly followed by others.

Tears streamed down Molly's cheeks. 'I need to get my bag.'

'I have it.' Victoria thrust it in Molly's direction.

'Right ladies, it's time…' Mr Leadbetter walked over, with Molly close behind him, and pulled the bolts across the main doors, letting them swing open. 'It's time you started to enjoy your leaving party.'

The women all pushed forward, eager to escape, but the chatter and laughter died on their lips. A glass, horse-drawn carriage was passing Foyles, slowly making its way along Charing Cross Road. People stopped and stared, before shaking their heads. Some lowered their gaze, murmuring as they made the sign of the cross on their chests. Silence hung in the air, only interrupted by the clip clopping of the horse and the wheels clattering, as they turned. Women wearing beige mob caps, trousers and three quarter length coats, belted at the waist, accompanied the carriage. They marched either side of it, keeping their eyes to the front at all times. The large windows on all four sides made it easy to see the coffin, with the flowers resting on top. Sniffing could be heard as the carriage passed by.

'That must be one of the canaries,' a whisper came from behind Molly.

Molly's throat tightened. Perhaps she should have chosen less dangerous war work. Perhaps her friends had been right. She gulped hard.

A woman's voice murmured, 'Are you sure you want to work in the munition's factory, to be a canary?'

Molly's watery eyes followed the carriage as it slowly drove past. Was that what her future held? Had the carriage come this way to remind her of the dangers that lay ahead? It didn't matter, she had no choice – it was time for her to pay the piper.

Chapter 2

Molly studied the note in her hand. Her heart was pounding. She licked her dry lips. Frowning, she realised her father would be the one reading it. Her mother would have trouble understanding the handwriting. The conversation with Mr Leadbetter jumped to the forefront of her mind. Her conscience screamed that she should have been honest with him and her family. They deserved that. She wished she could say the same, but she wasn't worthy of having an easy life. Molly took a deep breath, hoping they'd forgive her when she plucked up the courage to tell the truth. There was no escape, she felt compelled to do this, and there was no going back. A shiver ran down her spine. The rattle of the wheels and the clip-clopping of the horse's hooves still rang in her head over the hushed silence of the funeral procession outside Foyles Bookshop, the constant reminder of the danger, and why she had to protect her parents and keep her secret. Molly shook her head. She would have to take whatever consequences came her way. She hoped her parents would realise they could all have a better life and her ma could rest up and stop taking in other people's washing. Her slender fingers straightened the bottom of her cream blouse, with its wide black collar, before lifting the black calf length skirt, to slide her feet into the black shoes. The bare floorboards creaked. Molly held her breath and listened for movement in the modest three bedroomed, terraced house, in London's Carlisle Street. The day's greyness emulated her anxiety. Silence reigned.

Squeezing her eyes shut, Molly gave a heavy sigh. Her father would have understood why, if only she'd found the courage to explain. He was always there, fighting her corner, wanting the best for her. A solitary tear trickled down her cheek, its saltiness staying on her lips. She gazed out of the sash window, as the first raindrops sliced across the glass. A draught caused the curtain to flutter. The street and its residents hadn't changed much over the years. The houses all stood tall, their windows and doorsteps scrubbed until they shone. Molly ran her fingers over the damp trail her tear had left behind. A smile played on her lips as she stared at the tops of the trees in Soho Gardens, just visible above the black rooftops. She remembered sobbing as a child, when she'd fallen, trying to climb one of them, with the older boys in the street. Her father had scooped her into his arms and carried her indoors. He'd sat her on his knee, while he wrapped his arms around her, squeezing her tight until the tears had stopped. Her mother had spoken gently to her, while bathing the graze on her arm, and checking her legs for cuts. They had explained then, that little girls didn't climb trees. They learnt to sew and cook. One day, they had said, she would marry well and hopefully have her own cook and domestic help. Molly shook her head. Was that why she hadn't introduced them to Tony? They were still waiting for their proud moment. She bit down on her lip. Her chin trembled. They deserved better.

She carefully placed the crumpled note she'd penned, against the small mantle clock, which stood on top of her chest of drawers next to the treasured bottle of Narcisse Caron perfume. Her friend Alice had given her the scent on her twenty-first birthday, just before the war started. It seemed a long time ago and a lot had happened since then. Molly treasured the expensive gift and only wore it on special occasions, loving its fragrance of rose and jasmine, but today wasn't one of those days.

Molly tiptoed towards her bedroom door. The windows rattled as the wind and rain ganged up, trying to stop her. Pausing, she held her breath with every groan the house made. The clock in the sitting room chimed. Molly waited and was thankful it only rung out once. She glanced over her shoulder towards the chest of drawers. It was time to go. It was five-thirty. Slowly twisting the round wooden door handle, she held her breath with every creak that came with each turn. A frown creased her forehead as a sigh escaped. 'At this rate, I'm never going to get out of the house,' Molly muttered to herself, an uncontrollable urge to giggle bubbling in her chest. 'All the talk of German spies, and being vigilant about what you say and see.' A giggle escaped. 'A spy in the making, I'm not.' She bit down hard on her lip to stop the laughter erupting, wincing at the metallic taste of blood. Pulling the door behind her, leaving it ajar to avoid another creaking session, she listened for the thud of her gran's footsteps downstairs. Molly stared at the steps in front of her, wishing she'd paid more attention to the noise they made. Shaking her head, she mumbled to herself, 'Perhaps making a run for it was the best way forward.' She took a deep breath. 'Or maybe sticking to the sides would cause less noise.' Her head jerked up. Did that thud come from her parents' room? Without hesitation, Molly ran down the stairs, the creaks and groans echoing in her wake. She glanced back up the stairs, as she reached for her coat. It caught the framed photo of her parents on the console table. It wobbled. Molly dropped her coat and just managed to catch the photo, before it crashed onto the red and black tiled floor. She breathed a sigh of relief and glanced up the stairs again, wondering how long she could keep this up. With time running away, she snatched her coat from the floor and opened the front door. Her lips tightened as the hinges squeaked their objection at being disturbed. It was with damp palms that she flung her military style coat around her shoulders, while fighting to force her arms into the sleeves.

Molly frowned as she looked at the front of the house. 'Sorry, Ma.' She shook her head, as guilt coursed through her veins.

A dog barked several times, in the distance. Was that a curtain moving?

Grabbing her bicycle, she pedalled as if the devil himself was after her. As relief spread through her, Molly took a deep breath. She wasn't used to seeing five-thirty in the morning, but had managed to leave the house without being spotted. Could she do it again tomorrow, and the day after, and again after that? She didn't know, but would worry about it then. She was determined she wasn't going to let her parents, or the cool wet start, dampen her spirits. What she was doing was for the best. They'd understand, wouldn't they? *So why did you leave them a note, instead of talking to them?* Her conscience bit back and Molly shook her head. She couldn't think about it now.

It wasn't long before she was cycling past Soho Square Gardens and turning right, into Greek Street. Her bell-shaped skirt wrapped itself around her legs. Her parents had been worried and hadn't hidden their concern, when she followed the modern trend of wearing hems shorter, showing her ankles. Whatever next, trousers? Molly had seen it on their faces; the beginning of the end. The fear of what their daughter might become. They hadn't mentioned the words harlot or strumpet, but they'd hung in the air between them. Molly had shrugged off their concerns and ignored the looks, every time she came downstairs.

Now, as she pushed down on the pedals, she questioned the wisdom of wearing heeled shoes. Her friends, Alice and Victoria, had warned that cycling across London, to the east end's Silvertown munitions' factory every day, would be too much, but as always, she had known best.

Her stomach gurgled with the realisation there was going to be no food until lunchtime. She should have been brave and had breakfast, but hadn't wanted to face the questions. Anxiety tripped down her spine, as she wondered if her note had been discovered yet. *Don't think about it*, the voice in her head shouted. *Just concentrate on what you're doing.* The deed had been done.

'Morning.' An old lady shouted, between wiping the windows of The Pillars of Hercules public house, and wringing her cloth.

Molly took a deep breath. 'Morning,' she gasped.

The lady brushed the back of her hand across her forehead, moving the grey curls that had escaped her mob cap. She stared at the windows as she rubbed vigorously, her voice shaking with the exertion. 'Take care, lovey, it looks like it might be a wet one today.'

Trying to breathe deeply, Molly could only nod in response. She turned left into Shaftesbury Avenue, pausing near the end, to take in the large Victorian building. The Palace Theatre looked intimidating with its domes on the ends. Her fanciful imagination always thought they looked like ears, while the many large windows were the eyes of the building. They listened and stared out at the junction with Charing Cross Road, keeping a watchful eye over London, as the roads became busier. Men in suits hailed taxis, which patrolled the streets, looking for business. Molly gasped as a tram sped past, causing her bicycle to wobble in the breeze it created. She hadn't realised London was so busy, this early in the morning. The noise of engines, along with horses and carts clattering along the street, were gradually building to a crescendo.

A lad stood on the street corner, with newspapers tucked under his arm. He wore his flat cap at a jaunty angle, and his trousers didn't meet his worn down shoes. He yelled out. 'Get yer daily paper 'ere.' He paused. Molly wondered if he'd made a sale. 'Come on gents, let me earn me breakfast. You give me an 'a'penny, and I'll give you a newspaper. It's a fair exchange now, there's no robbery intended.'

Molly smiled to herself. Maybe tomorrow, she would stop and buy her own newspaper. After all, wasn't she striving to be a grown up.

'Get yer paper 'ere.' The boy's message carried along the street.

Molly's slim legs were past aching. They were heavy and each pump of the pedals burnt the muscles in her calves and thighs. As she cycled past Leicester Square underground station, it was tempting to take her friend's advice and forget about saving money and the exercise doing her good. Her initial enthusiasm was already waning and she still had such a long way to go. Molly sucked in her lips and shook her head. Anger gripped her, the flush of her face hidden by the exertion. She had been prepared to give up at the first sign of difficulty. A couple of weatherworn young men, dressed in their army uniforms, were walking towards her. She held their gaze for a second before looking away, wondering if they would now march everywhere. 'You're the reason I'm doing this', she mumbled to herself. "Now get on with it girl.' She sighed. It was a good job the men at the front didn't give up so easily, or Germany would be ruling the world.

Stallholders were setting up their stands and laying out their wares. A flower seller's colourful stand caught Molly's attention, but it was the strong smell of coffee that followed her down the street. Her stomach gurgled, as the aroma of hot pies reminded her she'd missed breakfast. Street vendors shouted to sell their goods, each fighting to be heard above their neighbour, as well as the rattling of the carts being pulled by horses, and the engines that purred past them.

It wasn't long before she was cycling down the Strand, pleased she didn't have to go as far as The Aldwych, where the bomb had gone off in October. It had killed and hurt so many innocent people who were just out for the evening, mainly at the Lyceum Theatre. Alice and her sister, Lily, were sent there as an ambulance driver and police officer. They had told her it was an awful sight, with bodies lying amongst the rubble in the road. It rammed home how everything could so easily be taken away. Her parents immediately popped into her thoughts. She shook her head. It was too painful to think about. She was thankful the zeppelins had stopped bombing London, although damaged buildings and boarded up windows were yet another reminder of the fear they faced, daily.

Molly headed towards the side of the Savoy Hotel, remembering the posh cars and the occupants she had often seen outside. She sighed. One day she would sneak in to see how grand it really was. Her lips formed a smile. Maybe, if she married someone rich, they could stay the night. The clank of metal hitting metal startled her. She wanted to stop and take a sneaky look, to see what was happening at the back of the Savoy. The sound of a man's voice carried over the high brick wall.

'Yer wan another keg?'

'Nah, that'll do,' a deep voice returned.

It dawned on Molly she wasn't going to be the only one up and about, working at this time of the morning. She took a gulp of air and pressed her feet hard on the pedals, fighting the urge to stop and catch her breath, for fear she would never get started again. She was soon pedalling along Victoria Embankment, glancing at the River Thames on her right. Moored boats, large and small, bobbed up and down, while others chugged past, causing ripples in the water. The sun was trying to break through the grey cloud, and rays of light glinted off the water like small stars.

Memories of going to Westminster Bridge with her gran to watch the boats chugging along the river brought a smile to Molly's face. If Alice was visiting her grandparents at the time, then she would join them. The two girls had giggled as they leant into the railings and waved enthusiastically at the men and boys on the boats, and they'd smiled and waved back. In the summer, it had been almost a daily occurrence, but not until her gran had finished her housekeeping duties at Russell Square, and only if she'd been good. Molly would always remember her gran telling her off for staring at the spotless kitchen, with its two ovens. It was large enough to hold a banquet. She had also been wide-eyed, while struggling to carry clean sheets to one of the bedrooms. Alice had walked in on her staring around the room. It was there, at Alice's grandparents' that her friendship with her had begun.

Molly sighed, wondering how she would fare with this journey in the winter, already doubting the wisdom of her decision-making. The tall streetlights no longer lit London at night or in the early morning. With homes mainly in darkness, only moonlight led the way. She often heard her father say if there was a poor moon, there would be no bombs, but if it was a good moon, then head for the cellar. Her jaw clenched and her shoulders tensed under her coat. She stared ahead. Had she thought this through properly?

Molly had recited the journey in her head, trying not to forget the landmarks. She had remembered the two bridges, Waterloo and Blackfriars. The next thing to look out for would be Pudding Lane, where the great fire had started. Then the Royal Mint, immediately wondering if anybody had ever tried to rob it, or if people who worked there ever came out with a stray pound note. She couldn't imagine working with all that money. How did they avoid the temptation, especially when money was so tight?

Molly tried to suck in her breath, but her lungs were on fire. A trickle of perspiration slipped down the side of her face. Her skin was burning. She felt sure she must look a sight. She took her hand off the handlebar to wipe her cheek. The bike gave a dangerous wobble and she made a grab for the metal bar, to steady herself.

'Look at the scenery, such as it is.' She was mumbling to herself, while wishing she'd left her coat at home. 'It's not far, now.' She pushed herself to pedal harder and was soon cycling along Dock Road. The River Thames was still on her right as she passed lines of terraced houses, small two-up two-down properties. They looked tired. The sash windows stared out onto the narrow streets, but tall factories and warehouses blocked their view of the river and all its activities. Smoke billowed out of the thick chimneys, coating everything in its path with dust.

Molly breathed a sigh of relief as the Tate and Lyle sugar factory came into view, knowing the munitions' factory was nearby. It was her first day. Thankfully, she didn't have to report until seven o'clock, but normally, the twelve-hour shifts started at six in the morning or six at night.

Having allowed an hour and a half for the journey, Molly stepped off her bicycle; her legs were weak, and wobbled as her feet touched the ground. Pulling a handkerchief from her coat pocket, she mopped her face before taking a couple of deep breaths. She had done it and made good time. Smiling, she propped her bicycle up against a wall. Her early morning was turning into a day of firsts. *Did that include deceiving her parents for the first time?* The voice in her head was scathing. Molly shuddered. She was beginning to think her father's mother was haunting her.

'Hello, Miss, you early or late? The governor doesn't like it when people are late, yer know.'

Molly physically jumped at the voice behind her. She turned and a bald man, wearing thick black spectacles, smiled at her. He was sitting in a small wooden hut, with the top part of a barn door open, and a newspaper in front of him. Molly smiled as she took in his layers of clothing.

A thickset man, wearing a black suit and a trilby, had his back to her. 'We'll speak later, Frank.' He stepped away, without looking in Molly's direction, lifting a stubby hand

and waving. A gold signet ring glistened on one of his sausage fingers, catching Molly's attention. She couldn't quite catch the initials engraved on it, as he walked away.

'It's no good yer keep coming 'ere. I don't know nuffink and I don't see nuffink.' Frank glared after the man, before turning his smile on Molly. 'It's nippy this early in the morning, innit? At least it is in this blooming coffin I have to sit in all day. Mind you, from what I've read, it's better than fighting them Germans, so I can't complain.' The old man's face beamed at her. 'Now what can I do for you, young lady?'

Molly's gaze followed the man in the suit, wondering who he was, before turning her attention back to the munitions' factory, its dusty walls and tall chimneystacks similar to the other factories around her. No, there was certainly no nine o'clock start here. She was entering another world and she didn't know if she was capable of succeeding in it. Molly had heard stories about the hard work and injuries that went alongside it. Perhaps giving up her comfortable job at Foyles had been a bad idea. Her mind re-ran the funeral outside the bookshop. She shivered, but there was no going back. Rain began to fall. She sighed and hoped she wouldn't regret her decision. 'I'm here to start work.'

Chapter 3

Molly checked her bicycle and took a deep breath, before mumbling. 'This is it.' Her heart was pounding. Sickness washed over her. For as long as Molly could remember, the three girls had always done everything together, particularly the important stuff. Where were Alice and Victoria now, when she needed them the most?

A voice in her head screamed. *It was your decision to leave Foyles, no one else's, and they tried to talk you out of it, but no, you had to be stubborn. As always, you knew best.* She batted away the self-pity that was threatening to act like a shroud.

Molly shook her head, wondering if she was going mad, fighting the urge to get back on her bicycle and ride home, while fleetingly wondering if Mr Leadbetter would give her back the position in Foyles. She pulled back her shoulders and stuck out her chin. No, nothing had changed. She owed Tony. Concentrating on her breathing, in out, in out, trying to stop the pumping sound in her ears, Molly muttered to herself, 'Right, stop this nonsense, you can do it'. She took a couple of steps towards the large wooden barn door. It was framed with thick planks of wood, and another was across the middle, giving it an intimidating appearance. The dents and scratches added to the feel that some had tried but failed to pull open the heavy door, or maybe tried to break in. Molly giggled at the thought of the thieves' mistake, imagining them breaking in to escape with bags of sugar, only to find caustic soda. She used both her hands on the wooden handle and pulled with all her might.

The man shouted from his hut. 'Shall I come and give you a hand?'

Molly groaned under the strain. 'No, I can manage, thank you.'

The door creaked on its rusted hinges, shouting its objections at being disturbed. She stood peering into the entrance of the factory, and the hairs on the back of her neck stood up. With trepidation, she stepped over the threshold.

A slight, tall, dark haired man stopped in his tracks and stared in her direction.

Molly could feel the colour rising in her cheeks as she fidgeted from one foot to the other, under his gaze. The palms of her hands were damp. She prayed she wouldn't have to shake hands with this man, but ran them down the side of her coat just in case.

'Sorry, can I help?'

Startled, Molly looked down at the grey concrete floor.

'You shouldn't just be wandering around in here. It's a dangerous place to be.'

Molly's head jerked up and returned his stare with indignation. 'Thank you for your concern, but I'm not just wandering around. I've just arrived to start work.'

'My apologies. Frank normally...' He eyed her for a moment, colour rising in his cheeks, before looking down at his notepad again and mumbling. 'Let me take you to the office, to complete the necessary paperwork.' He looked across at her again. 'I'm sorry, I didn't catch your name.'

Molly frowned. She wanted to say that's because you never asked for it, but she forced a smile to her lips. 'It's Molly, Miss Molly Cooper.'

'Right, Miss Cooper, follow me.'

Molly followed him. His dark suit hung limply over his narrow shoulders. The back of his white shirt collar didn't completely cover the loosely knotted navy blue tie. She wondered what position he held in the factory. Her mind wandered back to Tony, the love of her life. He had been a snappy dresser. She was doing this for him. Her eyes began to well up. She closed them and shook her head as pity started to rise inside her. She clenched her hands until her nails bit into her palms. There was no point looking back. It was all about moving forward. There was a time she didn't want to, but soon realised she had no choice in the matter. It was all about keeping herself busy. She stared at the man's back, taking in his slim figure and his short-back-and-sides haircut. Was he another one preparing to enlist? Why hadn't he gone already? Was he a conscientious objector? *Stop it, have you learnt nothing at all?*

Molly looked around the bare grey walls. Her heels clattered on the concrete floor, echoing off the walls and high ceiling. The noise in the factory gradually grew louder. People's voices could be heard shouting over machinery. She wrinkled her nose at an unfamiliar odour. At that moment, she had seen nothing to indicate what took place in the factory.

As if he sensed her eyes on him, the man in front turned round. He said nothing at first and she wondered why he felt the urge to check that she was following his instructions. He said something. She saw his lips move, but couldn't hear him. She raised her eyebrows as he turned back to face the front. Again, she wondered what his position was in the munitions' factory. After they walked down corridors and went through doorway after doorway, they climbed a battered metal staircase. Molly gripped the handrail as it wobbled slightly with each step they mounted, each rung creaking and groaning under them. The clanging was soon sucked into the machinery noise that filled the factory. The man came to an abrupt halt outside an office.

Molly glanced through the large window, into a small square room. The soft grey walls were bare, apart from the round, oak-framed clock, sitting fairly high up, telling her it was quarter to seven. She breathed a sigh of relief. There were three desks in there, each covered with paperwork. A blue book with a red spine was on one of the desks, next to a pad of lined paper. Glasses sat open, on top of the pad. Molly fleetingly wondered if they were his. A calendar sat on a shelf over one desk, with a family photograph standing proudly next to it. Underneath the shelf, stood three cream bottles, each of them a different size, but the largest was no more than six inches tall.

The man opened the office door, stood aside and indicated for her to walk in.

Molly nodded and stepped past him, making sure no contact was made. She had no desire to get off on the wrong foot. She shook her head. He had barely spoken to her and she didn't know his name, so how could she do anything to upset him?

'Is everything all right, Miss Cooper?'

The man's deep voice broke into her wayward thoughts, startling her back to reality. 'Yes, yes of course.'

He smiled and immediately his face looked younger. She momentarily wondered how old he was, thirty maybe. There was also the niggling question of why he hadn't signed up to the Great War.

He pulled out a dark wooden chair from under one of the desks and indicated for her to sit down, before quickly pulling out another for himself. 'It can be difficult for people when they first arrive, because it's very noisy, with all the machinery and everything.'

Molly noticed the window for the first time. No sunshine was going to break through the thick dirt that coated it. She tilted her head slightly. Was that a crack that ran down the glass? She squinted as she stared at it. It was hard to tell, but maybe it was the dust locked onto the glass. Her mother immediately jumped into her thoughts and a smile formed on her lips. She would have had a bucket of water and a cloth on it within a blink of an eye. That is, once she got over the fact her daughter was sitting in this dingy office.

'Right, Miss Cooper.' The man shuffled some paperwork around the desk, before opening one of the drawers and slamming it shut again. 'We just have some form-filling to do and then I'll get someone to take you to the lockers, where you can change into the rather fetching uniform of overalls and cap.'

Molly's blonde ponytail bobbed, flicking the back of her neck as she nodded. Her hand went up to smooth it down and she caught her fingers in the bright red ribbon tied around it. It had been gifted to her mother as a child, when she had nothing. She treasured it, claiming it brought her and her husband, Jack, together. Molly often borrowed it, under the threat of death if she lost it. She regretted her ponytail, wishing she'd taken the time to put it in a bun. It would have been more elegant, as well as making her look older than her twenty-three years. Molly realised she was worrying unnecessarily, as he didn't look at her. She sighed. There was a time before the war when she would have enjoyed a little innocent flirting with a man of his calibre, but those days were long gone. They had disappeared with Tony.

The man suddenly looked up at her and gave a little cough. 'When we've finished the paperwork, someone will show where to get changed. It's what we call the dirty area of the factory. You'll remove your clothing and let your hair down. There can't be anything metal about your person, including any material covered buttons or jewellery.' He held out some forms and a pen. 'If you can just read and sign these, then we'll get you settled.'

Molly reached out. Their fingers brushed against each other and she snatched her hand away.

He stared at her for a moment, before dropping the papers on the desk.

Molly picked up the pen and quickly signed the forms.

He coughed again and colour rose in his cheeks as he looked down again at his paperwork. 'If you're wearing a corset, I'm afraid that will also have to be removed. You will be allocated a locker to store your things, then you will cross over to the clean area, where you will put on your overall and mob cap. Your hair must be completely covered by the cap.'

Her hand immediately reached for the gold heart around her neck and she swished it back and forth. Colour rose in Molly's cheeks. Her mind started racing at this unexpected information. Would she have to undress in front of people? Her face was burning at the thought.

The sharp rap on the office door made Molly jump. The man sitting in front of her looked towards the woman behind the glass window of the closed wooden door, and beckoned her to enter.

The woman's slender fingers straightened the off-white mob cap and tucked a stray lock of brown hair under the side of it. She beamed at him. Her eyes held a sparkle and she spoke in a musical voice. 'Good morning, Mr Greenwood. You wanted to see me.'

'Yes, Miss... um... Fairchild. Could you take...' he looked across at Molly. His gaze rested on her and a smile slowly spread across his face. 'Miss Cooper to get changed. Also, don't forget to take her to the medical room for a check-up, and to have her head checked for lice.'

Miss Fairchild pursed her lips as she glared at the pretty blonde sitting at the desk.

Molly scowled at the two of them. 'I can assure you both, I do not have head lice.'

Mr Greenwood raised his eyes heavenwards. 'Trust me, I've heard it all before. It's standard practice.' He glanced up at Miss Fairchild. 'Miss Cooper will be working with you, so I expect you to keep an eye on her and teach her the ropes.'

Miss Fairchild tried to force a smile, but it didn't reach her eyes. 'Yes, Mr Greenwood, it's always good to be working with someone new.'

Mr Greenwood nodded, but didn't look up. His mind had clearly moved on to other things.

Miss Fairchild's eyebrows drew together as she stared at him. Molly noticed her sparkle had disappeared.

A deep-rooted cough filled the small room.

Miss Fairchild took a small step forward, her back bending and her arm outstretched towards him. 'Are you all right, Mr Greenwood, can I get you something?' She peeked under her lashes at Molly, before quickly letting her arm drop to her side and straightening her back.

He shook his head and waved impatiently. His other hand covered his mouth as another cough escaped.

Miss Fairchild swung her head slightly to the right and eyed Molly petulantly. 'Let's go then, Miss Cooper.' Her voice had lost its musical quality.

Molly stood up. She hadn't realised her hands had been gripping each other so tightly in her lap. She fanned her fingers outwards, before running them down her skirt. 'Thank you, sir. It was lovely to meet you.'

Mr Greenwood looked up at her, his dark eyes widening. 'And you. I hope you'll be happy working here, but please make sure you follow the rules, because they are all in place for your own safety, and if you don't, the paperwork is horrendous.'

'Yes, sir.' Molly fought the urge to curtsey.

Miss Fairchild edged towards the door. 'This way, Miss Cooper.'

Molly nodded and followed her out of the office. 'Please call me Molly.'

'I'm Grace, Grace Fairchild.'

Molly followed Grace back down the metal staircase, gripping the banister, each footstep clanging on the rungs. This time, she didn't notice the creaking echoing around her. They walked along a corridor. 'Is Mr Greenwood always so distracted when he talks to people?' A loud grinding of metal on metal seeped through the wall.

'He's a busy man, with a lot of responsibility,' Grace snapped as she waited for Molly, at the bottom of the staircase.

Molly nodded as she stepped off the bottom stair and caught the rose scent Grace was wearing. 'I'm sorry, I didn't mean to speak out of turn.'

Grace turned to walk on ahead. 'What brings you working here then?'

Molly frowned. 'I just wanted to do my bit for the war effort. You know, they keep calling for women to do more.'

Grace raised her eyebrows and gave Molly a sideways glance. 'I bet you've never worked before, have you?'

'Yes, I have.'

'Show me your hands.'

Molly automatically did as she was told, thrusting her hands out in front of her.

'Turn them over.'

Molly did as she was bid.

Grace laughed. 'I don't think you have, at least not serious work. I bet you're one of those posh girls that have played at it, you know, done charity stuff.'

Molly frowned, sensing the animosity coming from Grace. 'Actually, I worked in Foyles Bookstore, in Charing Cross Road.'

'As I said, played at it. That's not what I call hard graft.'

Molly shook her head, wondering what qualified her to know. 'What did you used to do before the war?'

'I had three jobs. I was in domestic service.' Grace gave a disparaging laugh. 'But I guess you'll know about that. I also took in sewing and looked after my family.'

Molly stared up at her. 'Is your husband fighting in the war?'

A bitter sound escaped from her. 'I have no husband.'

Molly blushed at her mistake. 'Of course, I'm sorry. I didn't mean anything by it. I just thought...'

'Yes, yes, I know what you were thinking.' Grace turned left, and in front of them were rows of metal-wired cages. 'These are our lockers, for storing all our personal belongings.' She walked towards one on the end. 'You might as well have this one. Sissy won't be needing it any more.'

'Why?' Molly whispered.

Grace stared at Molly's wide eyes and forced a smile. 'She's moved on to better things.' She pulled open the cage door. 'Right, you need to take off your clothes. How much depends on what you're wearing. You can't take anything into the factory that has got metal in it, no matter how small. That includes hairgrips, covered buttons and any metal in corsets. When you've done, I'll take you over to the clean area, which is just over there, to collect your overall and mob cap. You will also need to change out of your pretty little heels and put on the pumps that have been provided.'

Colour rose in Molly's cheeks. She looked at Grace, noticing for the first time she was clad in biscuit-coloured overalls. The neck did up high under the chin and the long sleeves had buttoned cuffs. There were no frills about it.

'Don't worry, love, you'll soon get used to it. Tomorrow, you'll wear clothes that don't contain any metal, so you won't have to take so much off.' Grace laughed. 'We've all done it.'

Molly's blush deepened as she lowered her eyes, in an attempt to hide her discomfort from Grace, who seemed to be enjoying it.

'Bye.' Alice quickly pulled at the front door of her parent's four-storey house in Bloomsbury Street. The thud was the signal for her tears to flow. She took a deep breath. It was getting harder every morning. Taking the silk handkerchief from her pocket, she dabbed under her eyes.

'Morning, Alice,' Victoria called out from further along the road. She lifted her hand quickly to cover the yawn that was threatening to escape.

Startled, Alice turned round at the unexpected greeting, before smiling and waiting for her friend to reach her, then stepping onto the pavement. The slight breeze lifted the ends of her hair, which sat just above her shoulders. She pulled her lightweight jacket closer, fastening a couple of the buttons down the front. The sunshine was breaking through the early morning cloud. Women held the wooden handles of their parasols, in readiness. Dogs could be heard barking above the birds singing in the trees. Cars spluttered, avoiding the horses and carts as they clattered along the road, laden with their wares.

'Morning, Miss.' The driver of a fruit cart tipped his hat as he drove along the other side of the road.

Alice smiled at the weathered old man. 'Morning.'

The man beamed in her direction, showing his crooked brown teeth. 'Can I interest in you in some fine fruit this morning? You know what they say, an apple a day keeps the doctor away.' His eyes sparkled with mischief.

Alice smiled. 'You're too late, I'm afraid.' She opened her bag and pulled out a red apple, holding it high to show the man.

The old man chuckled. 'You can't blame me for trying.' He gave her a mock salute and carried on his way.

'He was a bit cheeky, wasn't he?' Victoria tucked her arm in Alice's, as they stepped forward together.

Alice giggled. 'He was harmless enough, just trying to make a living.' She glanced across at her friend. Her fine porcelain skin looked paler than usual. 'Sorry Victoria, I was in a little world of my own when you called out. I hadn't seen you walking towards me.'

Victoria's mouth lifted slightly at the corners. 'Let's see, before the saucy old man, you weren't by any chance thinking about baby Arthur, were you?'

Alice laughed. 'No, and believe it or not, he's not the only thing I think about. He is cute though, especially now he's trying to get about more, and it's getting harder to keep leaving him every day.'

'I can imagine. How's Freddie?'

They both automatically turned right into Great Russell Street and headed towards Charing Cross Road. Open windows allowed them to overhear conversations coming from inside the large houses. The malty smell of fermenting hops drifted in the air, from the Horseshoe Brewery.

Alice wrinkled her nose. 'He's fine, thank you. He was telling me how well Daisy and Lily are doing at the station.' She giggled. 'Who would have thought our two sisters would have made excellent police officers.'

Victoria raised her eyebrows, giving a nervous giggle. 'At one time, I thought there was more chance of them breaking the law, than upholding it.'

Alice chuckled. 'I know what you mean. I'm pleased they've both found their place, although who knows what will happen when this damn war is over with?'

'I know.' Victoria shook her head. 'The thing is, Daisy thought she was too good for domestic service before, so now she's had a taste of responsibility, there will be another war to contend with if she's forced into it.'

Alice nodded and squeezed her friend's hand with her arm. 'It's no good worrying about it now. We'll just have to deal with it when, or if, it happens.' Her eyes were transfixed on the two men marching towards them in army uniforms. Their hair was cut in the typical short-back-and-sides that everyone had now come to expect. The men nodded courteously, as they sped past the girls. Alice glanced over her shoulder at them. 'They look like they should still be at school. Do you think they're under age, like those idiot brothers of ours were, when they enlisted?'

Victoria looked over her shoulder. 'Probably, and it's sad because they don't realise what they are going into.' She glanced back and studied Alice's face. 'You look pale. Are you all right? Is Arthur keeping you up at night? Oh my, you're not pregnant, are you?'

Alice frowned. 'Yes, no and no. Thank you for asking. Actually, now you mention it, so do you.'

'It's no good you trying to turn the conversation towards me. It's you we're discussing, and something's clearly bothering you.' Victoria paused for a moment. 'I thought friendships like ours meant we didn't have secrets.'

A faint smile played on Alice's lips. 'We don't.'

'Well something's bothering you.' Victoria let her gaze rest on the dark circles under her friend's eyes. 'Alice, after nearly fifteen years, or whatever it is, I know you better than you know yourself, so you might as well tell me.'

Alice laughed. 'I don't know how I came to get such nosey friends.'

Victoria gave a look of mock horror at her friend's comment. 'Charmed, I'm sure. Actually, I'm only doing what you sometimes do.'

Alice shook her head. 'I don't understand.'

'I'm poking my nose in where it's not required, but I'm doing it from a place of love.' Victoria giggled, giving her friend's arm a gentle squeeze. 'Does that ring any bells?'

Alice gave Victoria a sideways glance and a smile hovered on her lips. 'You're in a cheeky mood this morning.'

'Hah, not really.' Victoria frowned as she looked down at the pavement. 'I've been up most of the night, worrying about Molly and that cycle ride she's taken on.' She took a deep breath. 'The thing is, she's a grown woman and—'

'I've been awake half the night as well, lying in bed worrying about her.' Alice frowned. 'And it didn't end there. Since I got up, I've been wondering whether she made it to Silvertown in one piece, and how her first day was going.' She shrugged her shoulders. 'What I'm most shocked about is that her mother was happy for her to give up her job at Foyles, to work at the munitions' factory, and to cycle all that way, so early in the morning...' Alice shook her head. 'I'm just surprised at Mr and Mrs Cooper, that's all.' She glanced across at Victoria. 'We've both known them for a long time and they've always been so protective of Molly.' She frowned. 'Something isn't right, but I can't quite put my finger on it.'

Victoria tightened her lips as she rubbed her hand up and down Alice's back. 'I know, especially as there was other war work she could have done. I tried to tell her, but she wouldn't listen. It's almost like she has a death wish or something.'

Alice nodded. 'Perhaps we should go and see her this evening, after work. What do you think?'

'I have nothing to rush home for. Daisy is working, so the best I can hope for is a letter from Stephen. It would be good to know that young brother of mine is safe.'

Alice thought about her own brothers, Charles and Robert. 'You have to hold on to the saying "no news is good news". That's all we have.'

Victoria sighed. 'I know.'

Alice turned to study Victoria. 'I hope Molly's all right. Do you think this urge to do such dangerous work stems from what happened to Tony?'

Victoria shrugged her shoulders. 'I don't know, possibly. But I have to say I sometimes struggle to understand what's going on in Molly's head.'

Chapter 4

Molly tugged at her mob cap, as she followed Grace out of the clean area of the munitions' factory and into a large workshop. The pumps they wore deadened their footsteps. The engines, together with the clanging of metal dropping to the floor, drowned out any conversation. Her eyes darted around, trying to take in her new surroundings. The deafening noise frightened her, causing her body to convulse into jerky movements. Could she survive working in such an ear-splitting, chaotic place? She realised she hadn't thought this through.

A young lad came into view and Molly watched him pulling on a lever. The strain on his face showed the effort needed to use the machine.

Grace followed her line of vision. 'That's young Archie. He's only fourteen. He's using the pressing machine, to make copper caps.'

'It looks like it takes all his strength to make one.' Molly stared at the lad as the copper cap fell to the floor and he repeated the process.

Archie suddenly looked up and caught her staring. She quickly looked away, but not before she saw him wave at Grace.

Grace grinned at him and waved back. 'Everybody here works hard. It's important, and no more than our boys at the front deserve.' She glanced at Molly. 'Our job is making sure the firepower we send over is good quality. We pride ourselves on making sure they don't run out of ammunition to bombard the Germans with. It's the least we can do, when they're putting their lives on the line for all of us.'

Molly nodded and took a deep breath, worrying whether she was going to be physically strong enough for what lay ahead.

Grace turned away. 'Come on, you're not working on this section.'

Fear ran down Molly's spine as she watched women and men working on various machines. An older woman was pulling a lever, appearing to make holes in something. She was busy looking around her, not noticing Grace had stopped, and bumped into her. 'Oh, I'm so sorry.' Molly looked from Grace to the women working close by, her eyes wide as she studied them. 'I was too busy watching everyone working and not looking where I was going.'

'That's Nora, she's been 'ere since the war began. 'ard worker she is too, especially for an oldie.' Grace frowned. 'Does it all frighten you?'

For a moment, Molly thought she saw a softening in Grace's expression. 'I'd be lying if I said it didn't, but I'm just as concerned about going deaf. It's so noisy in here.'

Grace laughed. 'You'll soon get used to it, if you stay that is.'

Molly swung round to look at her. 'Why wouldn't I stay?'

'As you said, the noise, and the strength you need to carry out some of this work, is incredible. Although we've all got stronger, the longer we've done the work, so it does get easier.' Grace eyed her up and down with a steely gaze. 'Must admit though, I'm not expecting you to last the week out.'

Molly lifted her chin and squared her shoulders. 'Well, you're in for a surprise then.'

Grace gave her a scathing look. 'Talk's cheap, especially when you don't know what you'll be doing for twelve hours, day in and day out.'

Molly shook her head. 'I can only do the best I can, and hope that's good enough.'

'Huh.'

'You seem to have taken an instant dislike to me, when you don't even know me. Have I said or done anything to offend you?'

Colour rose in Grace's cheeks. 'No. It's your kind I despise.' She turned and carried on walking.

Molly had no alternative but to trot along behind her, doubling her pace to catch up. 'Yeah, me ma always said I was a bit of a princess.' A nervous giggle escaped. 'But there you go, Pa and her raised me, so what can you do?'

Grace gave her a steely look. Her lips pressed tight. Without a word, she carried on walking.

The clatter and clanging of machinery grew louder, making conversation impossible. Molly wanted to question what Grace meant by 'your kind'. Wasn't she the same as the other women here, just trying to make a difference, while the men were putting their lives at risk on the front line?

Grace came to an abrupt standstill and Molly just avoided colliding with her again. She stretched out her arm, taking a couple of steps to stand in the correct position. 'This will be your work area.'

Molly glanced in the direction Grace was indicating, and followed her. There were rows upon rows of torpedo-shaped shells nearby. Noticing a broom handle propped up against a workbench, her curiosity was piqued; surely she wouldn't be sweeping the floor. Drawing level with the small table, she noticed a mallet lying on it. Molly eyed it suspiciously, but kept her hands clasped in front of her.

Grace bent down and picked up a metal bucket, placing it nearer to the workbench. 'Right, your job is to put a small amount of gunpowder into the top of these.' She waved her arm towards the rows of shell cases. 'You use this funnel and scoop, then take the broom handle and press it into the gunpowder, so it flattens it. Then hit the handle a few times with the mallet, to make sure the powder has been squashed down as much as it can be, and then you add some more gunpowder.' Grace paused, resting the funnel in the hole of the shell, before bending down to fill up the scoop. 'Like this, then you repeat the process with the broom handle and mallet. You keep doing it until you can't get any more in. It's called stemming.' She turned and stared at Molly's puzzled expression. 'I can't tell you how important this job is, and I'm not convinced you should be starting on this work, but I'm just doing as I'm told.'

'Have I been put here because this was where Sissy worked?' Molly asked, assuming she was just filling the job the woman had vacated.

Grace scowled. 'Never you mind about Sissy. It has nothing to do with you.' She moved her attention back to the shell in front of her. 'The gunpowder needs to be crammed in, and if you don't do it right, then the shell won't explode properly. Don't give our men cause to worry about the job we do here; they're all someone's father, brother, son or uncle.'

Molly sucked in her breath. 'I do know that, and despite what you may think, I'm here to work hard. I want to support the men on the frontline who are making the biggest sacrifices of all, giving their lives.' She lowered her lashes. 'We all want the same thing.'

Grace lifted her head slightly, raising her eyebrows. 'Well let me see you do it. It's not difficult, but it's physical work and you do need to concentrate on what you're doing.'

Molly nodded. Exchanging places with Grace, she stared down at the shell in front of her, trying to block out the noise. Her hands felt damp with perspiration. Pushing them down her thighs, she took a deep breath. Aware that Grace was watching her, she slowly and carefully placed the funnel into the shell and bent down to fill up her scoop with the fine black gunpowder. Some fell off the edges as it was being lifted towards the funnel. Molly was thankful it had landed back into the bucket and hoped Grace hadn't noticed. With a trembling hand, she poured it into the funnel and waited for it to disappear down the narrow tube, into the shell. While waiting, she put down the scoop and picked up the broom handle, shaking the funnel before removing it, then poking the end of the handle into the hole, pressing hard and moving it around.

She finally picked up the mallet and brought it down hard, several times, on the end of the piece of wood. Molly turned to Grace, her eyes wide, looking for approval.

Grace nodded. 'Well done. The only thing I will say is, don't overfill the scoop. It's better to have to do an extra fill, than to get it all over the floor.'

Molly smiled, pleased with the praise. She had a feeling Grace didn't give it easily. 'I hoped you wouldn't notice my spillage. It wasn't very much, and it did land in the bucket.'

Grace's lips formed a tight line. 'Yes, you were lucky it fell where it did, but be aware that if you spilled that much on every shell, that would be quite a lot of gunpowder lost. It also has to be compacted down as tight as possible, otherwise it won't explode in the way that it should.'

Molly nodded, wondering why Grace had taken an instant dislike to her, and then there was the business of 'your kind'. She shook her head, momentarily wondering about the wisdom of leaving the safety of Foyles and her friends, but she owed it to Tony to carry on. Her guilt had been eating away at her for long enough.

A young girl, wearing the munitions' factory uniform of overalls and mob cap, strolled towards Grace and Molly. She smiled and nodded at various women as they caught her attention, stopping to chat and laugh with others. Her head motioned in their direction, before she carried on towards them. Molly tightened her hold on the broom handle and mallet. Her knuckles were white, as the hard wood bit into her skin. Her cheeks flushed with colour.

Was the new girl under discussion? The heat in her palms began to burn. They throbbed as sharp pains shot through them. She slowly relinquished her hold and wiggled her fingers. Her hands began to tingle as the blood travelled through what had been previously blocked to it.

Grace frowned when she noticed the girl walking towards them. She yelled in her direction. 'Everything all right, Flo?'

Flo smiled at Grace, revealing her yellowed teeth. There was a sprinkling of freckles across her nose. She nodded, before leaning in towards her. 'Yes, I just thought I'd come over and introduce myself to the new girl.'

Grace sighed, before turning to Molly. 'Molly Cooper, this is Florence Attwood, otherwise known as Flo.'

'It's lovely to meet you,' Molly responded with a smile.

Flo eyed her for a moment. 'And you.' She paused for a split second and took a breath. 'Welcome to doing men's work, for half the pay they used to get.'

'Oh god, here we go.' Grace raised her eyebrows and shook her head. 'Give it up, Flo. If you don't like the pay, go and find yourself another job. We certainly earn more than being in domestic service.'

Grace's tone brooked any forthcoming argument from Flo, who just stuck her tongue out at her. Molly tried to hide the ready smile that was forming.

'You'll soon get used to the smell of the sulphur; some days it's worse than others.' Flo sniffed the air like a bloodhound. 'It's not too bad today, but sometimes it stinks like rotten eggs and you can actually taste it in the back of your throat. It makes me feel sick.'

Grace drew in her breath and threw her hands up in front of her. 'Take no notice of her. If she kept her mouth shut a bit more, it wouldn't be a problem for her.' Grace chuckled. 'You may have noticed Flo likes to moan. It's a wonder she still works here.'

Molly laughed at Grace's exasperated expression.

Flo shrugged her shoulders. 'The food's good here, I will say that. There's no break in the morning or afternoon, but we have an hour at lunchtime and we're well fed.' She paused to take a breath. 'The night shift only get a half an hour break at midnight. It's pretty heavy going you know, but we're all in the same boat. What do you think, are you up to it?'

Molly wasn't sure she would ever get used to the endless clattering of machinery and metal, mingled with a strange thudding noise. Something close by hit the floor and she jumped, looking over her shoulder. She noticed several women had a yellow tinge to their skin. How long before she had all the signs of being a canary? Her stomach lurched into her chest as she turned back to face the two women. 'I'm sure, once I get used to the noise, I'll cope.'

'Don't worry, after a while you won't notice it.' Flo chuckled to herself. 'But that might be because you've gone deaf.'

Grace nudged her. 'Behave yourself; Flo's just having a bad day, as usual. It's not that bad.' She smiled at the young girl standing next to her.

Listening to them both, Molly realised Grace, although not much older than Flo, had taken on the role of being her work mother, just as Alice had done for her, years ago at Foyles. 'What do you do here, Flo?'

'I put holes in shells.' Flo gave a brittle laugh. 'Actually, I put holes in the fuses of shells and measure them with a gauge, to make sure they're correct.'

Grace nodded. 'It's an important job, as indeed is all the work we do here.'

Flo raised her eyebrows. 'If the holes don't fit the gauge, boy am I in trouble.'

Molly glanced from one to the other. 'Sounds like a delicate job.' She paused for a moment, fighting the urge to fill the silence, but it got the better of her. 'My friends' sisters have joined the police, but I don't know how much they earn, and I didn't like to ask.' Molly tried to join in their conversation. Both Grace and Flo turned and stared at her, but neither said a word for a moment.

Flo gave a little laugh. 'I suppose someone has to do that job, otherwise we'd be in a right old mess, wouldn't we?'

Grace mumbled, almost to herself. 'It wouldn't do for me to have a peeler in the family.'

'Is everything all right here?'

The girls jumped at the deep voice behind them.

'Yes, Mr Greenwood.' Grace beamed at him.

The man in the ill-fitting suit nodded. 'I trust there are no problems and you are settling in, Miss Cooper?'

'Yes, sir.' Molly nodded in his direction, wondering if he could actually hear her above the din that surrounded them.

'Good.' Mr Greenwood turned and walked away.

Grace watched him until he was lost from view.

Flo mimicked, 'Yes, Mr Greenwood,' and started giggling. She glanced at Molly. 'You're honoured. He actually remembered your name.'

Grace lashed her hand out and caught Flo's arm. She gripped it hard and glared at her. 'Be careful, Flo, be very careful.'

'I hope you girls are playing nicely.' Nora chuckled as she walked past.

Grace let her hand drop. 'Now get back to work, both of you.'

Molly listened to the exchange between the two women. Flo was clearly the younger of the two, Molly guessed around twenty years old. There was a look of innocence about her, yet she was full of mischief. Grace, on the other hand, was probably about twenty-five and quite scary. It was obvious she had been, or was shouldering a lot of responsibility. Molly wondered what a toff had done to cross her while she was working in domestic service, because Grace clearly didn't have time for them. Flo had implied Grace had a thing for Mr Greenwood, and yet he didn't even look at her, let alone show any signs of an infatuation. It was only then, Molly wondered what they thought of her.

Flo straightened her shoulders and rubbed the spot where Grace had grabbed her arm. 'There was no need to be so vicious. I was only messing.' She frowned. 'It's not my fault he doesn't notice you, and actually, it's not that surprising. After all, we all look the same in these damn overalls and caps.'

Grace glared at Flo. 'You're treading on very thin ice.'

49

Molly decided now was not the time to find out.

Alice and Victoria stood in front of Molly's home in Carlisle Street. The black front door, with its pristinely polished letterbox and doorknocker, stood proud amongst the others in the road. The open curtains hung neatly at the sash windows. Darkness was setting in.

Hesitantly, Alice raised her hand to lift the brass knocker. Frowning, she quickly lowered it again and turned to Victoria. 'Do you think we should have checked with Molly first? I mean, it's quite rude to just turn up at someone's house, uninvited.'

'Normally I'd say you're right, but we've known Molly all her life, so surely that alone must relax the visiting rules.' Victoria's gaze darted from the house, back to Alice. 'You didn't worry about that when you just turned up at my house, a few months ago. In fact, you've done it several times.'

Alice smiled. 'That's different, I was worried about you.'

Colour flushed Victoria cheeks as she fidgeted from one foot to the other. 'Well, we're worried about Molly.'

Alice bit down on her lip for a few seconds, before nodding. 'Right, let's do it.' Before she could change her mind, Alice raised her hand, grabbing the doorknocker and letting it thud down.

The door creaked open a little. 'Hello, Alice, Victoria, how lovely to see you both.' Mrs Cooper beamed as she pulled the door open wider and stepped aside. 'This is an unexpected pleasure. Please do come in.'

Alice painted on her best smile. 'Thank you, Mrs Cooper, we're sorry to come unannounced—'

'Oh, don't worry about such things, girls.' Charlotte shut the door behind them. 'Alice, how's your grandfather?'

'He's well, thank you.'

Charlotte nodded. 'That's good news. My mother so enjoyed working for him and your great grandfather. As I'm sure you know, they were very kind to her.' Her hand patted the bun that sat at the back of her neck. 'And your cousin, Emily? I haven't seen her in years. She and her husband are such lovely people and you know, without them, we wouldn't be living here today. They showed Jack and me such kindness when we were young.' She gave a small sigh. 'That will stay with us forever.' Charlotte glanced across at the girls. 'Anyway, you don't want to hear all my nonsense. I'm surprised you didn't come home with Molly. I know she's working late at Foyles for a while, but I assumed you would be too.'

Victoria bit her bottom lip and looked across at Alice, whose hand was resting at the base of her neck. Victoria lowered her lashes, concentrating on the tiled flooring.

Alice frowned, her gaze darting around the hallway.

'Is everything all right?' Charlotte squinted, looking from one to the other. 'You both look a little pale. Come in and I'll make us some tea. Hopefully, Molly won't be long.' She led the way to the best room, stopping to poke her head around the dining room door. 'Ma, Alice and Victoria have come calling.'

'That's nice,' Sophie called out. 'Come in, come in, let me look at you.'

Charlotte moved further into the dining room, to allow the girls to walk past her. 'Ma, I was taking them to the best room.'

A smile slowly spread across Alice's face. 'It's all right, Mrs Cooper.' Alice's hands trembled by her sides. Her legs didn't feel they would hold her upright for much longer. She licked her dry lips.

Victoria stepped forward and gave Sophie a light kiss on both cheeks. Alice wondered if she was showing her thanks for saving them from Charlotte's questions. Victoria stepped back and Alice repeated the process. It only then dawned on her that she didn't know Molly's gran's last name. Alice took a couple of slow breaths. 'Good evening.' She gave her best smile, while wishing she could run away. 'I hope we're not disturbing you.'

Sophie laughed. 'Of course not, it's lovely to have visitors. It's not something that happens every day.' She waved her hand to direct them to the couple of armchairs in the room. 'Take a seat.'

Alice and Victoria did as they were bid. Alice sighed with relief that her legs no longer had the responsibility of holding her up.

'I don't suppose you see much of Emily and George, but when you do, please pass on our love to them, and indeed to your grandfather. Tell them we said hello.' Sophie's eyes lit up. 'They helped set up Jack and my little girl here, teaching them to read and write. Such lovely people.'

Colour flooded Alice's cheeks. 'It's about time I visited them, so I'll pass on your greetings.'

Charlotte frowned. 'It's a shame Jack is still at work. He would have loved to have said hello, but he seems to work later and later every day.' She sighed. 'I'm sure there's a reason for it.'

Alice glanced across at Victoria, who was fidgeting in her chair and keeping her eyes fixed firmly on the floor.

'I shall make some tea in a moment.' Charlotte tilted her head to one side. 'Alice, I understand from Molly that your little boy is delightful.'

A smile spread across Alice's face as her eyes lit up. 'He's wonderful. A bit of a handful now he's moving around though.'

'I'm sure he must be, but little ones bring so much pleasure. I suspect even more so, in these troubled times we're living in.' Charlotte shook her head. 'It would be lovely to have a baby in the house again, but alas, I think we have a long wait.'

Laughter erupted from Sophie. 'She needs to find a man first.'

Colour filled Charlotte's cheeks. 'Right, I'll go and put the kettle on.' She half turned to leave, before turning back again, folding her arms in front of her. 'I don't understand why Molly is working late, and yet you girls aren't. Is it something special she's doing?'

Victoria's eyes widened. She stared at Charlotte. Her palms, hidden in the folds of her black skirt, were clenched. 'I... er... I...'

Charlotte frowned as she looked from one to the other. The thud of the front door broke the silence.

Victoria and Alice both breathed a sigh of relief.

The heavy footsteps grew louder as they got nearer to the dining room. Jack breezed through the doorway, but worry was etched on his face. He glanced across at Victoria and Alice. 'Good evening ladies, this is a lovely surprise.' He stepped nearer Charlotte. His hand reached out and clasped hers as he leaned over to kiss her cheek and whisper in her ear. 'Is everything all right?'

Charlotte blushed and nodded. 'I was just asking the girls why they weren't having to work late, but Molly was. I've also been threatening to make some tea, so now you're here, I'd better get on with it.'

Jack nodded, gently squeezing her hand before pulling away. 'There could be any number of reasons.' He dropped his newspaper down on the table. 'Alice, are your family well? I don't see much of William Gettin these days. He seems to have stepped back from the family business.' He chuckled, almost to himself. 'I never thought I'd live to see the day that happened.'

Alice opened her mouth to speak, but snapped it shut at the sound of heels clattering on the tiled floor of the hallway, followed by the thud of a door shutting.

Charlotte stepped towards the hallway. 'Ah Molly, Alice and Victoria are here to see you. I must admit, I was surprised they didn't wait and come back with you.'

Molly's face quickly turned crimson. 'I'll... Shall I take them through to the other room, so we can chat?' She bit down on her lip.

Charlotte nodded, watching her daughter closely. 'I'll make the tea and bring it in for you.'

'I don't think that will be necessary, Ma. I shouldn't think they'll stay long. We all have work tomorrow.' Molly ran her fingers through her hair.

Charlotte raised her eyebrows, while her fingers intertwined with each other in front of her. 'Regardless of that, it's bad manners not to offer tea and biscuits or something. Have you learned nothing over the years?'

Molly's lips thinned for a moment. 'Clearly not.' She brushed past her mother and strode into the dining room.

Alice and Victoria glared at her as she stood just inside the doorway.

Molly forced a smile to her lips. 'This is an unexpected pleasure. Come through to the other room, where we can sit in comfort.' She caught her father's glare. 'Sorry, Pa.' Molly took the couple of steps to stand in front of him and stood on tiptoe to kiss his prickly cheek. She quickly stepped back and moved to her grandma and gave her a peck on her surprisingly soft cheek. Molly gave her a hug. 'Are you all right, Grandma?'

Sophie smiled up at Molly. 'I am, now you're home.'

Molly giggled before turning to her friends. 'Shall we go through?'

The girls jumped out of their seats as one, both running their hands down their black work skirts.

Alice nodded at Sophie and Jack in turn. 'It was lovely seeing you again and I'll remember to pass on your greetings.'

Molly sucked in her breath. 'Come.'

The three of them walked out of the room in single file. The heels of their shoes clipped the floor, almost in time with each other. Molly opened the door wide and stood back for them to enter first. Once in the room, she clicked it shut.

Victoria couldn't contain herself. Her face flushed with anger as she spat the words across the room. 'What is going on with you? You put us in a terrible situation.'

Molly wrapped her arms around her midriff. 'I didn't put you in a terrible situation at all. You did.' Her lip curled in disgust. 'It's not my fault you chose to visit unannounced. I had no idea you were going to come round today.'

Victoria's face contorted with rage. 'And what would have happened if your mother had popped into Foyles, to see you about something? You're unbelievable, so selfish.'

Molly flounced as she started to pace around the room. 'Selfish? Why, because I want to live my own life, just like your brother and sister did.'

Alice pulled back her shoulders and jutted out her chin. 'Enough, the pair of you. Molly, you spoke out of turn to Victoria and I believe you owe her an apology.' She turned to her friend. 'And you, Victoria, should have taken a couple of deep breaths and counted to ten, before letting your anger get the better of you.'

Victoria shrugged her shoulders. 'We were being pulled into her web of lies. How awkward was that in there?'

Alice nodded. 'Victoria is right. I know I certainly didn't want to lie, and your mother was quite persistent with wanting to know why we weren't working late, and yet you were.' The room was silent for a moment. 'I was under the impression your mother and father approved of your move to the munitions' factory, but that was clearly a lie.'

Molly flopped down on the leather wingback chair. She stared hard at her black shoes. 'I'm sorry. I know I've messed up, but there have been times where one or other of us haven't shared our problems, or been totally honest with each other.'

Alice and Victoria glanced across at each other. 'That's true, but I don't believe we've ever put each other in a position where we've had to lie. At least, not intentionally.'

'I know.' Molly sniffed. 'The thing is, they wouldn't approve of me leaving Foyles, because they wouldn't understand. For them, it's all about finding a husband, a gentleman, and I don't want the fight, the anger, or their disappointment.'

Victoria sunk down into an armchair, her eyes filled with tears. 'But they're going to find out sooner or later. Isn't it better it comes from you, than from someone else?' She tapped her foot on the carpet before jumping out of the chair again. 'If I'm honest, I struggle to agree with what you're doing.' Her face reddened. 'Let's face it, you could have done anything, but not you, no you have to pick the most dangerous job you can find, short of going to the frontline.' She paced around the room, not taking her eyes off Molly. 'You know, Alice and I have been awake all night worrying about you, and this hair-brained decision to cycle all the way to Silvertown and risk your life. I think you need to end it now, before friendships are lost and your parents find out how you've lied to them. Imagine how hurt they're going to be.'

Colour filled Molly's cheeks. 'Just because you disagree, it doesn't make it wrong. You're as bad as them.' She flung her arms wide.

Alice's eyes widened as she stared from one to the other. 'Please stop arguing. The family will hear you if you're not careful.'

Victoria glared at them both. 'Well, maybe that would be a good thing. At least it would all be out in the open. I hate people that lie.' Her face flushed with colour as she spun on her heels and turned her back on her friends.

Molly's anger died away and her voice dropped to a whisper. 'Everyone lies.'

Alice knelt down in front of Molly and grabbed her hand. 'No they don't, Molly, and what's more, they shouldn't because then the trust has gone. You know that really.'

Molly nodded. 'I've had a terrible day.' Her chin began to quiver and the tears rolled down her cheeks. 'The woman who is showing me my job clearly doesn't like me, and I didn't realise how much I would miss our chats. You two are like the sisters I never had.' She swiped her fingers across her cheeks. 'Now I'm working somewhere different, it'll be harder for us to be friends, so things are going to change.'

Alice stroked Molly's arm as she spoke in low tones. 'No, we just have to make an effort, whereas before, we didn't have to.'

Molly nodded, but wondered if that is what they would do, or whether their friendship would fade away. She glanced up at Victoria, not sure if their friendship was already lost.

Chapter 5

Molly tried to block out the constant din as she pushed down hard, holding her broom handle tight. The gunpowder was so tightly compacted, into the head of the shell, it wasn't going anywhere. The responsibility weighed heavily on her shoulders. A horn bellowed out. Molly breathed a sigh of relief. Lunchtime. The machines gradually fell silent and a ringing noise vibrated in her ears. The women's chatter grew in momentum, replacing the grinding and clanging of metal. Several rasping coughs could be heard around the vast room. She looked up, trying to stretch her neck, noticing for the first time the windows up near the roof. Was that the sunshine trying to come through? Molly closed her eyes and sucked in her breath. Pulling back her shoulders, she glanced back at the wooden stick in her hand, before propping it against the workbench and dropping the hammer on top. The stick clattered to the ground. Unable to move, she stood for a moment, staring down at it. The energy drained from her and Molly wished someone would come along and pick it up. She massaged the tops of her arms, through the sleeves of the biscuit-coloured overall. The pain was unbearable. Rolling her shoulders, she wondered if her body would ever get used to the cycling, or the punishing work it was being put through, feeling sure her arms would seize up during the hour break. Still, it was nothing to what the men were going through, as they battled for the ground around the River Somme.

Molly gave a heavy sigh. Things had changed. She was exhausted every day and missed seeing Alice and Victoria at work. Nobody had suggested going to Southend, this coming bank holiday. She smiled as memories of running along the pier with Tony consumed her. His laughter as she paddled in the sea, him splashing her with handfuls of water before she fell into his arms, giggling. Their day had ended sitting on a wall, gazing out to the sea while eating a massive ice cream cone. How quickly things had changed. Her eyes began to well up. Forgetting about her blackened fingers, she rubbed the back of her neck, moving it back and forth, and side to side.

Flo bent down and picked up the broom handle, placing it against the workbench. 'You all right, Molly?'

Molly took a deep breath and swung round. Flo's smile matched her chirpy voice. 'I'm fine. My arms and neck are another thing though.'

Flo laughed. 'You'll soon get used to it.' She looked around her. 'Are you going to lunch, or do you fancy a cigarette first?'

Molly quickly shook her head. 'No thank you.'

Flo chuckled. 'What no lunch, or no cigarette?'

Molly's colour began to rise up her neck. She forced a cough, hoping to stop it in its tracks. 'No cigarette, thanks.'

Flo tugged at her cap, pushing it behind her ears. 'What do you do with yourself, when you're not here?'

Molly laughed. 'Not much these days, I'm exhausted by the time I get home.'

'Perhaps we should go to The Railway, one evening after work.'

Molly frowned. 'The Railway?'

'Ah, you don't come from round here, do you?' Flo chuckled as she watched Molly closely. 'It's a tavern.'

Molly's eyes widened. 'I don't mind going out one evening, but I'd rather not go in a public house.'

Grace stopped as she was walking past, eyeing them suspiciously. 'What are you two nattering about?'

Flo grinned. 'Nothing. You always think I'm up to something.'

'That's because you usually are.' Grace raised her eyebrows, before glancing over at Molly. 'Don't let this one lead you astray.'

'I'm not.' Flo eyes sparkled with mischief. 'I just suggested an evening at The Railway.'

Grace shook her head. 'Don't go there, Molly. It's not a place for a decent lady to go. Flo, on the other hand, thinks she's one of the boys.' She paused for a moment, looking over at the work Molly had done that morning. 'If, and that's a big if, you're staying around, we could try and book to see Florrie Forde at the Music Hall. She's meant to be a great singer.'

'Sounds great.' Flo raised her eyes heavenwards.

'It does sound great.' Molly beamed. Maybe her hard work was beginning to pay off and Grace was starting to accept her. 'We could also get tickets to see Hobson's Choice at the Apollo Theatre. It's meant to be very good.'

Flo looked away from them. 'Lovely, two highbrow friends. Aren't I the lucky one?'

Grace chuckled. 'Right, are you coming to lunch girls?'

'Yes.' Molly answered quickly, wondering if Grace's offer was an empty invitation to save her from Flo.

'I'm having a fag first,' Flo quipped.

Grace raised her eyes. 'Make sure you're well away from the factory. I don't want us all going up in smoke, because you couldn't be bothered.'

'All right, all right,' Flo grumbled. 'I always make sure I'm not too close to it.' She started to walk away.

Grace frowned as she watched her. 'Of course you do.' She straightened her lips for a second, before looking at Molly and jerking her head to the side. 'Come on then, or lunch will be over before we've even got there.'

Molly pulled back her shoulders and fell into line with Grace.

'How are you finding it?' Grace asked.

'It's tiring and my arms are killing.' Molly instinctively rubbed the offending area.

Grace shrugged her shoulders. 'You'll get used to it.'

Molly smiled at the mantra. 'That sounds like you think I'll be staying.'

'Yeah, you're not doing bad.' She glanced at Molly. 'All right, your work's good.' Grace grinned. 'Come on, we've got to wash off this black stuff, before we go into lunch.'

'Ahh, I'm glad I've caught you two.'

Grace spun round, closely followed by Molly, to face the owner of the deep voice. 'Yes, Mr Greenwood.' Grace gave him the benefit of a huge smile.

Andrew Greenwood's eyes darted between the two of them. He looked down at some paperwork he was carrying, before returning his attention to them. 'I want Molly, Miss Cooper, to work with you and Miss Attwood this afternoon, and until further notice.'

'Yes, sir.' Grace's colour began to rise.

'What about the large shells I've been working on this morning?' Molly ventured quietly.

Grace glared at her.

Andrew looked at Molly for a moment, before giving a little cough. 'Apparently, we need to up our game and produce more of the smaller ones that Miss Attwood and Miss Fairchild work on.' He looked across at Grace. 'I'll leave you to organise it, after the lunch break.'

Grace nodded. 'Yes, sir.'

Andrew walked away, his head bent down, reading his paperwork.

Molly's lips parted slightly, as she watched him march away. 'He's always reading something.'

Grace didn't take her eyes off him. She folded her arms in front of her midriff and tightened her jaw. 'He's a busy man.' She paced on ahead, in silence.

Molly ran a couple of steps, to catch her up.

'No running,' Grace snapped, without looking her way, before pushing open the door to a washroom.

Molly silently followed her in and made her way to an empty sink. She glanced at Grace, her face etched with tension. Molly shook her head, not noticing the lukewarm water splashing onto her uniform as she rinsed her hands under the tap. She reached for the carbolic soap and rubbed it hard against the palms of her hands. The soap lathered, but all Molly could think about was what had happened to suddenly change Grace's mood towards her.

'Get a move on; lunch will be over at this rate.'

Molly jerked. 'You don't have to wait for me. I'll catch you up.' She quickly rinsed her hands, before reaching for the towel to dry them.

'That would be lovely, but Mr Greenwood said I had to keep an eye on you.'

Molly forced a smile. 'I won't tell him if you don't.'

Grace glared, opening her mouth to speak, but then thinking better of it. She turned and opened the washroom door.

Molly quickly followed Grace along the corridor. There was no chatter this time. Molly kept her eyes fixed on the way ahead.

Finally, Grace pushed open a wooden door to rows upon rows of wooden tables and benches. Women were filling every available space. The laughter and chatter bounced off the walls and ceiling, filling every crevice in the long room.

'Hi, have you two only just got here?' Flo shouted.

Molly jerked round at her, as they edged forward towards a seat. 'Mr Greenwood stopped us on our way here.' She turned back to face the front, wrinkling her nose and swallowing hard, trying to remove the stale smoke that clung to Flo, spreading its tendrils around her. Tony had always smoked Players cigarettes and the smell had always delighted her, but those days had gone. Molly shook her head. Her fingernails bit into the palms of her hand.

'Why?' Flo gasped.

Molly frowned as she glanced back.

Flo's shoulders were hunched over as a hacking cough ripped through her. Her blackened hand came up and covered her mouth. She fought to catch her breath, just as another was wrenched from her body.

'You all right?' Molly frowned, turning round to give her a pat on the back, wondering why she hadn't washed her hands. 'You don't sound too good.'

Grace pushed round and rested her hand on Flo's back. 'It's them damn cigarettes. It's about time you gave them up.'

An older lady tried to press a glass of milk into Flo's hand, but she waved it away. Grace reached for it. The tips of her fingers were red raw, her nails bitten down to be almost non-existent. 'Thanks, Ivy.'

Molly watched the scene in front of her and wondered if it was the cigarettes, or if Flo was actually sick.

As she ran down the stairs at home, Molly couldn't help thinking about Flo. Her cough hadn't been as hacking as the afternoon wore on, but it did sound like it came from her boots. She wondered if Flo would be well enough for work tomorrow. Molly checked her hair in the hall mirror, before shouting out, 'Ma, I'm popping out to see Alice and Victoria.' She reached for the front door handle and turned it. The squeaking shrilled out in the silence. Hanging in the air was the overpowering smell of beeswax that her mother liked to use liberally on the wooden furniture.

Her gran's shrill voice came from the dining room. 'You haven't been in long. Don't you see enough of them at work?'

Molly's lips tightened. She stopped and let go. The screeching filled the space around her.

Her mother appeared in the dining room doorway. 'Take no notice of your gran. Just go out and enjoy yourself.'

Molly lowered her eyes. Her arms wrapped around her midriff, hugging herself tight, clinging onto her silk blouse. Her shoulders hunched over as she stared hard at the floor. This was the time to come clean. 'It's really busy at work these days, so we don't have time to chat,' she heard herself lie.

'Stand up straight.' Charlotte pulled herself upright as she admonished her daughter. 'Is that why you've been going in so early and working late for the last couple of weeks? We've hardly seen you.' She frowned. 'I suppose there's a shortage of people wanting to work in shops, especially with girls taking jobs elsewhere. I hear they can earn more at the munitions' factory, or doing other work that the men used to do, before this dreadful war ripped them away from us...'

Colour crept up Molly's cheeks. The moment had gone. She wanted her mother to stop talking, and tried not to listen. Every word twisted the knife of guilt in her stomach.

'What are you doing out there?' Sophie's voice startled them both.

'I'm coming, Ma.' Charlotte frowned. 'I'll be glad when it's over and life can get back to normal,' Charlotte continued. 'Still, at least you've been sensible and kept your job at Foyles. I know someone has to do the work, but some of them are putting their lives at risk. I've seen the girls with their yellow skin. Goodness knows what working in the munitions' factory is doing to the poor things. I suspect it's slowly killing them. They might get paid a lot more money, but it's not worth losing a child for, none of it is. It must be such a worry for their families. I'm so glad you aren't one of them.'

'We all have to do our bit, Ma.' Molly paused, before mumbling, 'And follow our own consciences.'

'Yes well, no good will come of it, you'll see, and prices keep going up as well. Goodness knows how some people are managing.' Charlotte paused, tightening her hold on the heavy wooden door. 'You know, Mrs Grainger had a telegram. The poor woman is beside herself. She's a widow now, with three young children. It's terrible. I'll be glad when this damn war is over.'

'I know, Ma, the whole country is suffering.' Molly stepped towards Charlotte and wrapped her arms around her, squeezing tight. 'I love you, Ma. Please don't ever forget that, whatever happens.'

Charlotte patted her daughter's hand that was resting on her shoulder. 'I just worry about everyone, that's all.'

'I know, Ma, and we all worry about you. It would be lovely if you could stop going round doing everyone's chores for them, let alone taking in washing and sewing. It would please me to see you relax a little.'

'That ain't gonna happen anytime soon.' Charlotte smiled. 'Now stop worrying.'

Molly shook her head. 'No, I'm sure it won't'. She smiled at her. 'How about I'll stop worrying when you do.' Molly gave her mother a hug, before leaning back to look at her. 'Hopefully, everything will work out right in the end. I'll give Mrs Grainger a knock over the next couple of days and see if there's anything we can do.'

Charlotte nodded. 'You're a good girl, but her life, and those children's lives are changed forever. It's not going to end well for them.'

Guilt washed over Molly. 'I haven't seen Pa this evening. Is he home to keep you company?' She hoped the change of subject would help to clear her conscience.

'Not yet.' Charlotte frowned. 'I don't know what's going on, but he's spending more time at work than he is at home these days.'

Molly took a step back so she could watch her mother's reaction. 'Have you asked him?'

Charlotte gave a brittle laugh. 'It's not for me to question him; that's not my place.' She turned her back on Molly. 'Have a good evening with your friends and tell them I said hello.' She looked back over her shoulder for a moment. 'Ask Alice if she passed on my greetings to her cousin Emily and her husband George.' She gave a faraway look. 'They're such a lovely couple.'

Frowning, Molly knew better than to try to continue the conversation about her father, but she was keen to know what kept him away from home in the evening. 'I will, Ma.' She stepped towards the front door and reached for the metal catch. 'Are you sure you wouldn't like me to stay in with you? Alice and Victoria won't mind.'

A chuckle could be heard coming from the dining room. 'No, no, you go off and enjoy yourself. I'll be fine. I've got your gran to chat to. Just take care.'

Molly hesitated, wanting to tell her mother the truth about her job. She was swamped with guilt as the need to follow her own convictions got the better of her.

The grandfather clock chimed. Alice looked round at it standing half hidden by the green foliage of an exotic plant, its woody stem rooted in a wide roll-edged pot. Victoria followed her gaze, as they sat waiting patiently at Café Monico, in Regent Street. The usual excitement of the plush surroundings was lost on Alice as her anxiety began to grow. The clock was striking half past eight.

'Do you think Molly's forgotten she's meeting us here after work?' Alice frowned. Her fingers twisted and turned the cameo pendant that hung loosely around her neck. She glanced towards the entrance, as the timber door opened for the umpteenth time, into the large room filled with round wooden tables and matching chairs. Arched mirrors on the wall gave the illusion of space, while the white Roman pillars gave it grandeur. The panelled ceiling was edged with scrolled mouldings and large potted palms were strategically placed around the room.

Victoria shrugged her slim shoulders. 'No, I shouldn't think so. I expect she's just running late. Stop worrying. Don't forget, she has that long cycle ride now. Goodness knows how long it takes her to get to Silvertown every morning, and then to do that journey again after a hard day's work is… well I think she's expecting too much of herself.'

Alice looked back at Victoria, her eyes darting between her friend and the door. 'I think you're right. It's certainly not as convenient as working at Foyles, and it must be considerably harder work.' She paused for a moment. 'I wonder how her parents took the news that she'd left Foyles.'

Victoria shrugged her shoulders. 'I suspect we'll hear all about it tonight, if she's listened to us and told them, but I do hope it wasn't as bad as Molly thought it was going to be.' She studied Alice for a moment, before continuing. 'If I'm honest, I'm struggling to understand why she insists on putting her life at risk. I don't know if I can stand by and watch her kill herself.'

Alice bit down on her lip for a moment. 'No, I don't understand it either, or why she felt the need to go all the way to Silvertown to work.' She brought up her hand and smoothed out the white tablecloth. 'But I suppose we have to respect her wishes. I know she wanted to do something for the war effort, but apparently there are lots of things to be done. I've heard there's a shortage of men in most areas of work, so there would have been plenty of jobs to choose from.'

Victoria nodded. 'I would have thought going over the water to Woolwich and working in the munitions' factory there might have been a shorter, or at least an easier journey.'

Alice glanced back at the clock. 'The journey might be easier, I don't know, but it is the other side of the river. I guess, if the bridges were bombed, she would have a problem getting home. I've heard said the Germans dropped over twenty bombs in Woolwich last October, probably trying to hit the factory. Although a few fell on the army barracks there as well, so I don't think she'd be any safer over the other side of the water.'

Victoria stared down at her pristine white napkin as she fiddled with the corner. 'I don't think any of us are safe anywhere, but at least they seem to be leaving London alone at the moment. Perhaps we should be trying to persuade Molly to come back to Foyles, you know, tell her how much she's missed by everyone.'

Alice beamed. 'It's certainly worth a try, although Molly can be very strong willed when she has a mind to.'

Victoria sucked in her breath and looked around. 'Ain't that the truth.' The aroma of freshly cooked food surrounded them and she tried to peer discreetly at what people were eating. There was no evidence that a war was going on, or of any food shortages. She ran her tongue over her lips, almost tasting the meals, but knew, as tempting as it was, she certainly could never afford to eat a proper meal in Monico. 'The food here smells delicious.'

Victoria chuckled, resting her hand on her tummy. 'My stomach is making embarrassing noises.' Looking back at Alice, she sighed. 'How long shall we give her, before we order our tea?'

Alice glanced at the clock again. 'What shall we say, another five or ten minutes?'

Victoria nodded. 'That seems fair, especially as she's already half an hour late.' She smiled. 'Knowing Molly, she's probably had a better offer and hasn't given us a thought.'

Alice laughed. 'You could well be right.' The clatter of heels on the tiled flooring echoed around the room, above the murmurs of conversation. Her head jerked up. Men looked in their direction. The blonde girl was beaming as she walked across the floor. Smiles formed on their lips.

'Sorry I'm late, but my mother kept me talking.' Molly pulled out a chair between them and flopped down.

'Hello, Molly,' the girls answered in unison, smiles lighting up their faces.

Alice leant forward and kissed her friend on the cheek. 'We were getting worried.'

Victoria followed suit.

Molly's chest heaved with breathlessness. 'While I think of it, she asked me to check whether you'd passed her love on to Emily and George.'

Alice smiled. 'Not yet, but I will when I get round to visiting them. They go back a long way.'

Molly picked up her napkin, shaking it loose onto her lap. 'Don't I know it.'

Victoria watched her friend closely. 'How's the new job going?'

Molly ran her fingers down her long blonde hair, leaving it to nestle on her shoulders. 'That cycling is a killer, I can tell you. I ache from head to toe.' Her lips tightened for a brief moment, before breaking into a smile. Her eyes scanned the crockery-free table. 'I thought you'd have ordered by now.'

Victoria laughed at her. 'We've been waiting for you.'

'Well let's order then.' Molly's lips lifted at the corners as she glanced between her friends and beckoned the waitress over. 'How's Foyles?'

'Just the same, you haven't missed anything, apart from being surrounded by books, which you've always loved.' Alice paused. 'Everyone keeps asking after you. I think they're missing your laughter and mischievousness.' She forced a smile as her fingers toyed with the edge of her blouse, under the table. 'I don't think they've replaced you yet.' She didn't take her eyes off Molly. The dark skin under her eyes was evidence of lack of sleep.

Molly chuckled. 'I never thought I'd say it, but I miss trying to avoid old Leadbetter.'

Victoria laughed. 'I think he misses keeping an eye out for you too. Maybe you should come back and do war work that fits in with working at Foyles, like Alice does, then you wouldn't have that long cycle ride every morning and night.'

Molly's lips tightened.

The waitress hovered in the background, waiting to be beckoned into the circle, to take their order.

Molly looked over her shoulder at the woman dressed all in black. Her frilled white apron straps draped over her shoulders. Her black hair was scraped into a bun and hidden underneath a white cap. She waved the waitress to come forward. Her mind was immediately invaded by Grace's view of her. She shook her head. 'Can we have three teas and three slices of chocolate cake, please?'

Alice sighed. 'Are you all right? I do worry about you cycling all that way, twice a day. It'll be murder in the winter.'

Molly laughed. 'I'm sure I'll get used to it.'

Victoria screwed her eyes up, squinting at Molly. She glanced over at Alice, who frowned for a split second before looking at Victoria. Molly's laughter had a ring of loneliness to it.

'Is everything all right, Molly? You look very tired.' Victoria leant forward and rested her hand on her arm. 'Is your new job not what you'd hoped for? If that's so, Mr Leadbetter said there would always be a job for you at Foyles, and, as Alice said, everyone misses you.'

Molly gave a shrill laugh. 'It's fine. It's just about getting used to the journey and being the new girl.'

Alice nodded. 'That's always difficult, especially when you're taking on something new as well.' Her thoughts were transported back to her first days of meeting the trains and the injured soldiers at Victoria Station, and how terrified she had been. She remembered being in a permanent hot flush. Alice rested her hand on Molly's arm. 'Are you finding the work very difficult?'

Molly's chin jutted out a little. 'It's not easy. I'm stemming, so I have to concentrate, otherwise I could make a mistake. By the end of the day, my arms are in agony, but it can only get easier.' She paused, looking down at her sore fingers. 'It's just about getting used to the work. It's very physical. Between that and the cycling, it's all quite exhausting.' She laughed, but it wasn't a joyful sound.

The waitress carried a tray to the table, balancing the china crockery, along with a silver teapot, milk jug and sugar. She carefully placed the items onto the table, before retreating to collect the slices of cake.

Alice nodded. 'I'm sure you'll soon fit in and forget about us at Foyles.'

Molly's eyes clouded over. 'Hmm, I don't think there's any likelihood of that happening.' Her lips lifted slightly at the corners, as she stared at the girls she'd known all her life. They appeared to be studying her. 'Why would it? I loved my time there. How's baby Arthur? It seems ages since I last saw him.'

'He's wonderful.' Alice's face lit up. 'He's just started crawling, so nothing is safe now. He tries to get into everything.'

Victoria and Molly giggled.

'Aw, we'll have to come round and see him.' Victoria lifted the lid off the teapot and stirred the hot steaming liquid, lost for a moment, as she watched the tealeaves spin in the whirlpool she was creating.

Alice's eyes darted between the two of them. Victoria was clearly lost in her own thoughts, and Molly had lost some of her sparkle.

'Vicki, are you trying to stir a hole in the bottom of that pot?' Molly smirked over at Alice, before returning her gaze to Victoria.

Alice closed her eyes and shook her head. Some things never change.

Victoria's head jerked up. 'How many times, don't call me Vicki or Vick. My name is Victoria, after the great queen.' She glared across the table at Molly.

Molly tugged at her imaginary forelock. 'Yes your majesty, sorry your majesty.' The girls giggled at her exaggerated head bowing.

'Now that's what I miss.' Alice smiled from one to the other.

Victoria shook her head, giving Molly a stern look. 'Yeees, I'm not so sure.' A smile crept across her face, just as the laughter bubbled to the surface.

'Ah miss, yer know I luv yer right?' Molly's eyes sparkled with mischief as she reached out and took Victoria's hand in hers.

Victoria chuckled. 'You are incorrigible. It's a good job you don't have any brothers or sisters, or it would be a war zone in your house.'

The waitress appeared, carefully placing three tea plates on the table, in front of the girls, laden with large slices of chocolate cake.

'Hmm.' Victoria licked her lips. 'Don't you think it's strange that every time we come here, we only ever have chocolate cake?'

Molly picked up her fork. 'That's because it's the best thing they sell.' She stabbed at the thin end and scooped it up. 'Not that we know that for sure, but it would take some beating.' She giggled, before placing the cake into her mouth. Her eyes closed as she savoured the rich sweet taste.

Alice and Victoria laughed as they watched the pleasure skip across her face.

'How are Freddie and Charles?' Molly asked, between mouthfuls, the crumbs gathering on her lips. Her tongue popped out to wipe them away.

'Freddie is doing really well, but it's going to take some time for him to recover properly. He's most concerned about his eyesight. He tells me that although his leg is painful, he can live with it.' Alice smiled. The love she had for her husband was there for all to see. 'Mother was over the moon when she received a letter from Charles last week. That brother of mine knows what to say, to keep her happy.' She grinned. 'I'm pleased he's grown into a fine, considerate young man. I write to him every day. Are you still writing to him?'

Molly nodded. 'Yes, but I haven't heard from him in a while.'

Alice splashed a little milk into her cup and reached for the teapot. She began pouring the hot brown liquid into the cups. 'You can add your own milk and sugar.' She put down the pot and picked up the teaspoon to stir her tea. 'So, Molly, what do your mother and father think about you changing jobs? Was telling them as bad as you thought it was going to be?'

Molly eyed Alice under the cover of her lashes. 'You know, I think I could live on this cake. It's absolutely wonderful.'

Victoria poked her cake with the fork. 'It is lovely.'

Alice shook her head. 'Molly, why are you avoiding my question? I've known you practically all your life, so do you think I don't know when something is bothering you. Do you regret leaving Foyles? It's not too late, I don't mind speaking to Mr Leadbetter for you.'

Molly placed her fork on the side of her plate. She studied the half eaten cake for a moment. 'No, it's not that. It's hard work and we earn every penny of our wages.' She paused and looked up. Her gaze darted between her two friends. 'Please don't think badly of me.'

Victoria's eyes widened, her loaded fork poised in mid-air.

Alice patted Molly's hand. 'Nothing you could do would make us think badly of you, so just tell us. We know something is bothering you.'

Victoria lowered her fork back onto her plate, all thought of the scrumptious chocolate cake forgotten. 'What is it? What have you done?'

Molly placed her hands in her lap and lowered her gaze. She took a deep breath, before looking up again. 'It's more about what I haven't done.' She paused for a moment. 'They still think I work at Foyles.'

'What?' Alice and Victoria said in unison, their voices both rising an octave.

Diners frowned, as they turned to stare at them.

Molly's gaze darted between them. 'I don't know why I can't tell them, but now it just feels like it's gone too far.'

Victoria scowled at her friend. 'Remember, you said the only reason you hadn't told them was because you knew they wouldn't have wanted you to leave the book shop. You have to tell them. We went through this two weeks ago. Remember the lies and trust conversation we had?'

She shook her head as her anger took hold. 'I can't believe you still haven't told them.'

Alice placed her hand over Victoria's. 'Victoria is right. You were brave enough to make the decision to leave, so now you have to be brave enough to tell them. How long do you think it will be before someone else tells them? I can't believe it hasn't come out before now. As hard as it is, it will be better coming from you.'

Molly's hand reached up under her hair and rubbed the back of her neck. 'I know, I know.' Tears began to prick at the back of her eyes. 'They just won't understand why I have to do it, and then I'll have to face their disapproval.' She paused. 'I nearly told her tonight, but I chickened out.'

Victoria shook her head. 'Bearing in mind the shop doesn't open until nine, doesn't she wonder why you are leaving at five thirty in the morning and getting home so late?'

A hint of a smile played on Molly's lips. 'She thinks the shop is short staffed, because the girls are taking on the men's better paid work. I just couldn't tell her I was one of them.'

Disbelief flew across Victoria's face. 'It's not funny. You need to tell them. I can't believe your mother is so gullible, but trust me when I say, that will all disappear when she finds out you've lied. Is that what you want?' She took a deep breath. 'They're going to be devastated, but they would feel worse if they heard it from someone else. I know I would.'

Alice nodded, before turning to Molly. 'You need to listen to Victoria. She's had the experience of being both a mother and father to her brother and sister, so she knows what she's talking about.'

'I know. I know she's right. I'm just frightened, that's all. They don't know about Tony and won't understand that I need to do something to help the men that are risking their lives for us, like Charles, Stephen and Robert. They come back broken, like Freddie did, that's if they come back at all. When I read Charles' letters it's heart breaking.' Molly shook her head and focused on the white tablecloth. 'My parents probably won't even realise they could stop working so hard because I'm earning more money. I want to do what's right, but I know that means seeing them disappointed in me.'

Alice and Victoria glanced at each other with troubled eyes. So they had been right; it was all about Tony, and Molly's guilt. Alice frowned, wondering if Molly would tell her what was in Charles' letters. Was he telling her how it really was?

Victoria reached out and took Molly's hand in hers. 'They won't be.' She sighed. 'None of us understand why you are putting yourself through this, but Alice tells me we have to respect your wishes. If I'm honest, I don't know if I can stand by and watch a dear friend slowly killing herself.' She paused for a moment. 'But we'll see. When Stephen decided to enlist with Charles, when they were both under age, I was angry. I knew he had to do what was right for him though, and that was for me to accept. Your parents know they can't protect you all your life, but they still want to.'

Molly's throat tightened as she squeezed Victoria's hand.

'Take it from someone who knows.' Victoria looked at her friends, each with a look of wonderment. She released Molly's hand and smiled. 'Right, let's eat cake. We can't let it go to waste.'

Chapter 6

July 1916

Molly gazed around the small dining room of her parents' home in Carlisle Street. The room hadn't seen any grand dinners. The rectangular dark oak table and four chairs dominated the room, leaving very little space for anything else. It had come from the much grander home of Alice's grandparents. The mantelpiece at the end of the room held family photos. Her two grandmothers were each holding the baby version of her. Molly could remember how distraught her parents had been when her father's mother had died of tuberculosis. She had only been a young child, but the raw emotion had left its mark.

The fire grate was in pristine condition; she couldn't remember a fire ever being lit in it. A standard lamp stood in the corner of the room, tassels nestling into the scalloped edging of the thinly gathered, tangerine fabric of the shade. Her father didn't like to spend on their home and, consequently, it was filled with other people's things. Her lips pinched together. She thought of Alice's family home in Bloomsbury Street and the lovely colourful fabrics used for the curtains and chairs. The soft rugs were probably bought from Liberty's in Regent Street. Her mother and father worked so hard, and yet there was no luxury in the house. She gave a heavy sigh.

'Everything all right, Molly?' Charlotte startled her.

'Yes, of course.'

'You were frowning.' Charlotte studied her daughter.

Molly knew now was the time to follow her friends' advice, but as usual, something held her back.

Sophie waved her spoon in the air for a moment. 'My dear, don't let your egg get cold.'

Molly's blonde hair flicked at her cheek as she shook her head. She tucked it behind her ears. 'Don't worry, Gran, it won't go to waste.' She topped up her cup of tea and added a scraping of butter to a slice of bread, before picking up a teaspoon and tucking into her boiled egg. Frugality had been the order of her parents' life. Wastage was frowned upon, even before the war. As she spooned the yellow egg yolk into her mouth, she thought again about telling her parents about her change of employment. There was no pleasure in eating, as it stuck to the roof of her dry mouth. Her tongue loosened it and she swallowed hard. It formed a soft ball and gripped the sides of her throat on the way down. Panic started to rise as the constriction took hold. She wanted to retch. Molly picked up her cup of tea and took a mouthful, gulping it down. Relief flooded through her when she felt able to breathe again. It was no good; she would have to tell them after breakfast. She closed her eyes and took a couple of breaths, before placing her cup back on its matching saucer. Molly pushed aside her half eaten egg and glanced surreptitiously at her father, seated opposite her at the vast dining table. He hadn't spoken since he came in from buying the Sunday Pictorial newspaper. He'd placed it next to him and glanced over at the front page a couple of times. The pictures showed the British in France and Flanders. At the top of the page, it announced to readers 'Mr Winston Churchill Writes in Next Issue'.

Charlotte half smiled as she busied herself, pouring out her husband's tea and moving his boiled egg in front of him.

'Everything all right, Pa?' She forced a smile as he glanced over at her. She shrugged her shoulders. 'You're not very talkative this morning.'

'I'm fine, don't you worry about me.' Jack spoke quietly, as his attention went back to the newspaper. 'It'll be interesting to read what this Winston Churchill has to write next week. I quite like him. I've read somewhere he was popular amongst the soldiers when he was fighting at the front with them. They say he wants to get back into politics, so it will be interesting to see how far he goes in the future.'

'Ahh, these politicians are all the same if you ask me.' Sophie scowled at Jack.

Charlotte nodded knowingly. 'He might do well, if he's popular.'

Molly smiled, wondering if her mother and gran knew what her father was talking about.

Jack moved his hand on top of hers and gave it a gentle squeeze. 'You could be right, Charlotte, you could be right.'

Sophie peered over at the pictures, as she sipped her hot tea. She put her cup down and lifted her hand, to pat the grey bun at the nape of her neck. 'I wonder when this mess will be over with, Jack.' She sighed. 'If I remember rightly, they said it would be over by Christmas, and that was nearly two years ago.'

Jack glanced across at his mother-in-law. 'It's certainly gone on for a lot longer than they expected, but I suppose it has to be done.'

Sophie raised her eyebrows. 'Yes, but I wonder how many innocent people have lost their lives. How many sons, brothers, fathers and uncles won't be coming home, and those that do won't be the same.'

Jack focused on his boiled egg. 'I know it comes at a high cost, but it has to be done.'

Charlotte glared at her mother as she opened her mouth to continue the conversation. 'Ma, enough, let's just have a relaxed breakfast. We don't seem to eat together very much these days.'

Sophie opened her mouth to protest, but thought better of it. Picking up her teaspoon, she dipped it into her egg. She had learnt many years ago not to bite the hand that feeds her.

'Now. Now. Now.' A voice screamed in Molly's head. *Now.* 'I… I… er.' Her stomach lurched. 'I have something to tell you both.' Her throat tightened. She tried to swallow, but it was painful.

Charlotte and Jack were staring at Molly.

Sophie squinted as she stared at her granddaughter. 'You're not pregnant, are you?'

Charlotte's eyes widened as she shifted her gaze over to her mother. 'Ma.'

'Well, from what I hear, the young girls these days are even going into public houses unaccompanied.' Sophie leant forward. 'And I can tell you, that wouldn't have happened in my day, unless you were a woman of the night.'

Flo's invite to The Railway Tavern threw itself to the front of Molly's mind. She fidgeted in her chair, wishing she hadn't started the conversation with her gran in the room. Heat filled her face. 'No, Gran, I'm not pregnant. Thanks though, for the confidence you clearly have in me.'

'I'm sorry, sweetheart. You just looked so troubled, so I automatically thought the worst.' Sophie placed her hand over Molly's and gently squeezed it. 'As my daughter's always telling me, I need to learn when to keep my thoughts to myself.' She smiled, belying her true feelings.

Jack sucked in his breath. 'Yes, you do.'

Charlotte returned her gaze to her daughter. 'Don't get upset.' She tilted her head to the side. 'It can't be that bad.' Frowning, she studied her daughter's troubled expression. The deep red in her cheeks was beginning to fade.

Molly's heart pulsated in her ears. 'I don't think it is, but…' She paused and looked down at her hands.

Her father stared hard at her, before whispering. 'But what?'

'I think you're going to be disappointed in me.' Her words tripped over each other, in a bid to explain. Tears pricked at her eyes as she slumped down in her chair, staring at nothing in particular. How she wished she hadn't started this conversation.

Charlotte frowned, before enveloping Molly's hand in hers. 'Whatever it is, we are your parents and we love you.'

Her mother's calm voice washed over her. Molly's hands were clammy. She took several deep breaths in a bid to calm her pounding chest. 'I no longer work at Foyles.' She heard her mother's sharp intake of breath, but she was relieved to say the words out loud. 'I'm sorry. I left about a month ago.'

Sophie took a deep breath and opened her mouth to speak, but caught Jack's ominous look.

Charlotte whispered, almost to herself. 'I never thought you would lie to us in such a way.'

The dark cloud of their inevitable disappointment was gathering. Molly looked through her lashes at her mother. What little colour there was had disappeared. She was ashen. Molly whispered, 'I haven't lied, Ma. I just didn't tell you.'

'Don't split hairs, Molly,' her father growled. 'You never told us. You've been going out early and coming home late, all the time claiming to be doing extra hours at Foyles.'

'Wait, a month? The girls have been here in that time and they didn't say anything, when I asked why they weren't working late.' Charlotte's eyes hardened as she shook her head. 'You've made us look like fools.'

Molly could feel herself shrinking into her chair, trapped by their tight-lipped, pained expressions. How she wished, just for once, they would shout at her and get it over and done with. 'You're right. I'm sorry, I just—'

'Just what?' her father barked.

Molly pulled herself upright and jutted out her chin. 'I didn't want you to be disappointed in me, that's all.'

Charlotte shook her head. 'And why would we?'

'I know you think working in Foyles is a good job, and it is, but I wanted to do something more, for the war effort.'

Charlotte's eyes widened, fear racing across her face. Her head jerked towards Jack, before swivelling back to stare at her daughter. 'What… What are you doing?'

'I'm working at the munitions' factory in Silvertown.' A deathly silence followed Molly's announcement. She couldn't look at any of them.

Sophie cleared her throat and looked up, surprised to see all eyes were on her. 'Well, that's been a long time coming.' She nodded at Molly. 'I think it's a good thing. Good for you.'

Charlotte's mouth dropped open for a few seconds. 'What?'

Sophie ignored her daughter. 'Just be careful. From what I hear, they're dangerous places, but it's a good thing you've done, and don't let anyone tell you otherwise.' She stood up. 'I shall take my leave now, because I'm sure your ma and pa will have something to say.' She rested her hand on Molly's shoulder as she walked past, giving it a gentle squeeze. 'I'm proud of you.'

'Why, Molly? I don't understand. Why would you want to put your life at risk?' Charlotte put her hand up to her throat. 'You know how I feel. We were only talking about the canaries recently, yet you have chosen to ignore my feelings. Let alone how I looked in front of your friends. You've made me look a fool.'

Jack stared at his wife who was clearly close to tears. He glared at his daughter, his eyes holding a spark of steel. 'Molly, you must leave the factory immediately. I will not have you causing this embarrassment to us, let alone upsetting your mother like this.'

Molly pulled herself upright and dared to look her father's anger in the eye. 'I can't, Pa. This is something I have to do. I knew you wouldn't approve, that's why I haven't told you before now, but what was it you said earlier? "I know it comes at a high cost, but it has to be done." If I was a man, I would have been on the frontline and you would have accepted that, because it would have been embarrassing to you if I hadn't gone. I'm compelled to do this and I had hoped you would support me in my efforts, but if not...' Molly stood up, shrugged her shoulders and strode away from the tension that filled the room.

Molly's parents were proud people, who had worked hard all their lives. She'd known they'd wanted something different for their only child. It had been ingrained in her from birth. Her grandmothers had filled her head with stories about them meeting as children in a woman's refuge, and how Jack was always looking out for Charlotte. George and Emily Wyatt, nee Gettin, had helped their mothers rebuild their lives. Emily's father, Henry, and Uncle Arthur had taken her father under their wing and given him a job in the family accountancy firm, although nobody talked about why that was the case. They had always impressed on Molly how honesty and working hard had given the three of them, and their mothers, a good life. They were forever grateful for the chances they had been given, and constantly reminded her of where she came from. At twenty-three, Molly was tired of hearing their mantra 'if it wasn't for Alice's family, the Gettin's, we wouldn't…' Nausea crept into her stomach and she shuddered as it steadily climbed into her throat. She had heard it all her life. Her parents were so grateful, they didn't seem to realise they could have so much more. Their silence over the last couple of days, about her working at Silvertown, had been unbearable. The disappointment and anger were tangible. No words needed to be said. She had wanted them to shout at her, get it over and done with, but that hadn't happened. Their silence had been much worse than any argument. Molly had wanted to offer an explanation, but hadn't. For once in her life, she had to stick with what she believed to be right. She wondered if they would ever forgive her for messing up their plans for her to have a better life.

Charlotte yawned as she stepped into the dining room. 'Morning. Sorry, I meant to be up earlier to prepare your breakfast.'

Molly looked across at her mother's slim frame, before shaking her head. 'Ma, it's about time I took care of myself. It's only just after five. I told you last night not to get up. Go back to bed.'

'Whenever I haven't been working, we've always had breakfast together, and today won't be any different,' Charlotte whispered. Glancing over her shoulder towards the doorway, she pulled out a chair, giving her daughter a wry smile.

There was no excitement in her eyes, as there had been when Molly started at Foyles bookstore. Although nothing had been said, she always assumed her parents had hoped she would meet a nice young man in such an establishment, but that hadn't happened.

Charlotte perched on the edge of the seat, pulling the edges of her cotton dressing gown closer. Her hands looked years older than her face, weathered by many years of domestic service. The heavy eyelids and the dark rings under them told Molly she had spent a sleepless night, no doubt worrying about her. Her mother had never asked too many questions of her, but Molly knew she wouldn't understand why she had given up a good position in Foyles, for a much harder life.

Molly lightly brushed the crumbs off the wide, blue striped collar and the loose tie that was clipped by a silver brooch to the front of her white, sailor-inspired blouse, a birthday present from her friend Alice. 'Yes, I know that, and I must admit it did feel strange sitting here by myself every morning, but it's far too early for you to be up.' She watched her mother bite down on her lip for a moment, guessing what had really caused her to rush downstairs in her nightwear.

'Your father and I are worried about you cycling all the way to Silvertown, particularly as it's so wet.' Charlotte wrung her hands on her lap, hidden under the table. 'If you insist on doing this job, why don't you travel on the underground? I've looked into the journey.'

Molly looked away from her mother, before shaking her head, fighting the urge to correct her. She picked up her cup and briefly stared down at the dark brown liquid, before taking a sip. 'I'm sure it will brighten up, especially as the bank holiday weekend has been such a wash out. There can't be much more up there to come down.'

Charlotte trained her gaze on her daughter. She was like her father in many ways, and his stubbornness had been in evidence since the day she was born. She wasn't going to win, but something drove her to keep trying. 'There's a train from Oxford Circus or Tottenham Court Road to Liverpool Street, where you would have to get another one to West Ham or Canning Town.' A smile tugged at the corner of her mouth. 'It would be much quicker, so you wouldn't have to get up so early and you could read one of the many books that are piled high in your bedroom while you travel to work.'

Molly placed the cup on its saucer and gave her mother a smile. 'You have been busy. I do appreciate what you're saying, but I'm going to cycle to Silvertown. It will do me good, and I don't want to spend the extra money I'll be earning on the trains.' She gave her mother a broad smile. 'Besides which, if it works out all right, you can stop working yourself to death for the toffs, Ma. You're better than that.'

Colour crept into Charlotte's cheeks and her normally soft brown eyes had a hint of steel about them. 'It's the "toffs", as you put it, that have helped to provide us with our home.' She frowned as her voice took on an angry tone. 'You best remember your father and I came from nothing. We had nothing, but we've worked hard. It's honesty, loyalty and hard work that has given us what we have today, and don't you forget it, young lady.'

Molly sighed as the voice in her head shouted, *and rich people's hand me downs.* She reached out and stroked her mother's arm. 'I know, Ma. I didn't mean anything by it. I just don't want you working yourself into an early grave. It's bad enough we have the Germans to worry about.'

Charlotte's eyes softened. 'I know. You're a good girl, but there's a lot worse off than us, as you well know.' She took a breath. 'Anyway, the way these prices are going up, who can afford to give up work? That loaf of bread cost ninepence, and the sugar, well let's not talk about the sugar prices.'

'I know, but I want more for you, that's all.'

Charlotte studied her daughter. 'And I did you, but there you go, we can't always have what we want.'

Molly shrugged her slender shoulders. 'We all deserve more, that's all.'

Charlotte jumped up out of her chair and gave Molly a withering look. 'When your father and I encouraged you to spend time with Alice and Victoria's family, it wasn't meant to make you ashamed of us.' She ran her hand over her cheek.

Molly lowered her gaze as her face flushed with colour.

Her mother sucked in her breath. 'It was so you'd realise there's more out there than slaving away in domestic service. We hoped, by mixing with the right people, you would meet a good man and have a gentler life than us.'

She pushed back her chair. 'We've tried to do what's right, but instead, we've raised a spoilt child.'

'No, Ma, that's not true.' Molly paused before whispering, 'You've raised someone that doesn't fit into either world.'

Chapter 7

August 1916

In the dead of the night, the constant ringing of the bell on the policeman's bicycle fought to be heard over his bellowing voice, as he furiously pedalled along Carlisle Street.

Sophie woke to the repeated shouting outside, and the ringing noise echoing in the stillness. She glanced over at the pendulum clock as its musical note struck one.

'Take cover, take cover.' His voice kept repeating the same words, as he trundled further along the street.

Sophie tried to move quickly. She pushed back the blankets to gingerly swing her legs out of bed, stopping for a second to listen for movement upstairs, but the house was in silence. She had to raise the alarm, and valiantly pushed herself off the bed. Pain shot up her legs, keeping her rooted to the spot. Her mouth clenched shut, momentarily holding her breath. 'Damn these old legs of mine.' Pulling down her nightdress and pushing her arms into the sleeves of a long woollen bed jacket that her daughter had knitted for her, she forced herself to take a step. 'Come on legs, stiff or not, you have to work. My family are not going to die because I can't get to the bottom of the stairs.' Sophie gripped the top of the armchair and dragged her legs forward. She sighed, before shaking her head. 'I'm too old for this malarkey.'

The stairs creaked as Molly ran down them. Not stopping to think about anything, she ran into the partitioned off part of the back room. Sophie's watery gaze greeted her.

'Thank goodness you're up. These damn legs of mine take a while to start working, once I've been to bed.' Sophie moved to sit in the armchair.

Molly lunged forward to grab her arm. 'No, Gran, come on, we have to get you into the basement.'

Sophie shook her head. 'I'll be all right sitting here. You three go downstairs. I just want you to be safe, and that's all that matters to me.'

Molly frowned. 'And all that matters to me is that my family, including you, are safe.' She clenched her lips into a straight line. 'We don't have time to waste talking about this, so come on.'

Jack and Charlotte came stumbling into the room.

'Come on, Ma.' Jack stepped towards Sophie. 'Molly, take your mother downstairs and I'll carry your gran.'

Molly nodded and moved towards her mother. 'Come on.'

They watched Jack lift Sophie's frail body into his arms, as they stepped into the hall and headed towards the basement.

Charlotte lit some candles and strategically placed them around, where the four of them would be sitting. The small flames danced as the draughts whipped around them.

Jack carefully placed Sophie into an old green armchair. It had seen better days, but they were both glad it was there.

Sophie adjusted her bed jacket. 'You're getting too old to be lifting me and carrying me down those narrow stairs.'

Molly wrinkled her nose. The air was stagnant and the mustiness of it hit the back of her throat. She shook open a single-sized coarse grey blanket and tucked it over her grandmother's legs, pulling it high up her body. 'Hopefully, that will help to keep you warm.'

Jack looked around him at the shelves and racking, lining the walls. They had never used the space for storage, or had wine to savour and keep for special occasions. He shook his head. A small low sigh escaped. He had never really thought of it as home, even though they had lived here for over forty years. Despair grabbed him as he wondered if he'd done wrong by his wife and family. With a despondent look, Jack sat down on an armchair. 'Well, we might as well get comfortable. We could be here for some hours.'

Charlotte nodded, before forcing a smile. 'At least we're all together.' She passed him a blanket, to cover his pyjamas and dressing gown.

Molly followed suit and wrapped a blanket around her. 'I hope Alice and her family heard the policeman.'

Charlotte tried to give a reassuring smile. 'I'm sure they will be fine, and Victoria.'

Molly chuckled. 'I think Victoria and her sister, Daisy, have been sleeping in the basement since the war began.'

Jack frowned at Molly. 'It sounds like they're being sensible to me.'

'Indeed, Pa.' Molly paused before whispering, as a heavy rumbling noise carried into the basement, 'Everything's going to be all right.'

Charlotte leant over and squeezed Molly's hand. 'It will be, Molly. All that matters now is we're all together.'

'Your right, Ma. I don't want to drag everything up, but I'm sorry for not telling you and Pa, and I didn't mean to make a fool of you.' Molly shook her head. 'If it's any consolation, Alice and Victoria were angry with me because I hadn't told you, so you're not a fool in their eyes.'

Charlotte's chin trembled and she bit her lip for a moment. 'None of it matters. My family is my world and what's important is that we are here together.'

Molly stood up and gave her mother a hug and kissed her cheek. 'I am sorry though, I've been a fool.'

Sophie gave a little cough.

Molly pulled away from her mother and looked over at her. 'Are you all right, Gran?'

Sophie gave a wry smile. 'Yes, I was just thinking you brought several books down here and it reminded me of when you used to read to me when your ma was at work.'

Charlotte nodded. 'She used to read to us in the evening too, and put on different voices for the people she was reading about.'

Molly laughed. 'That was a long time ago.'

'But we loved it.' Sophie paused for a moment. 'Maybe you could pick one of the books and read to us now, take our mind off what's happening outside.'

Molly stepped towards the books sitting on a table and looked at the covers. She giggled. 'Ah, The Railway Children. That used to be one of my favourites.' She moved the book to one side. 'What about Anne of Green Gables? I loved Anne. She was smart and not afraid to speak her mind.'

A roar of laughter filled the basement. Molly spun round and looked at them. 'What?'

Jack raised his eyebrows in surprise, as he looked at his daughter. 'If anyone thought books didn't make a difference, they need to come and live in this house for a day.'

Charlotte and Sophie giggled at Molly's confusion.

Molly propped her bicycle against the wall of the factory. She pulled at the collar of her coat.

'Morning, Miss Cooper, I think winter's coming early this year.' Frank Reynolds was huddled inside his wooden hut, with his coat pulled around him.

'Please, call me Molly.'

The security guard shook his head. 'I'm old enough to be your father. We don't want people getting the wrong idea now, do we?' The idea made him chuckle.

Molly smiled. Father? More like grandfather. 'No, we certainly can't have that, but I'm sure we could weather any storm that people wish to throw our way.'

His eyes crinkled as he smiled at her kindness. 'That we can, Molly, that we can. You go careful in there.'

She nodded and waved, as she made her way inside, heading for the changing rooms. The dirty room was full of women in various stages of undress. 'Morning.' Molly weaved between them, towards her locker. She was a quick learner and after that first day, made sure she only had to remove her outdoor wear, dress and shoes, before making her way over to the clean area for her overalls.

'Have you heard?' Grace followed Molly to collect their work wear.

'Heard what?' Molly frowned, glancing across at her.

'I think most of south of the river was bombed last night. From what I hear, Blackheath, Greenwich, Deptford and Plumstead took the brunt of it, with Eltham also copping a few.'

Molly's eyes widened and her jaw dropped as Grace spoke. 'Oh no. It'll be a miracle if nobody died.' She shook her head. 'I heard the warning and spent a sleepless night in the basement, but that's nothing to what those poor people were going through.'

'Blooming Germans.'

Molly frowned. 'Are you sure? I passed the paperboy on the way in, and I don't remember him shouting out those kind of headlines.'

Grace's lip curled under Molly's questioning. 'Obviously not, I wasn't there, but one of my neighbour's friends works at the Arsenal in Woolwich and she was telling me this morning.'

Molly placed her hand over her mouth, as she tried to stifle a yawn. 'Well we don't need any further motivation than that. Come on, let's make sure our men have enough bombs to put an end to this damned war.'

Grace patted Molly on the back. 'It looks like you're thinking like one of us now. Let's go.' She turned to the other women. 'Come on girls, let's get this day started.'

'Gawd, you're eager today.' Nora's shrill voice echoed around the hall.

Laughter competed with the chatter that followed Grace and Molly into the workshop, their pumps silent on the floor.

'Where's Flo this morning?' Molly asked, as she took up her position opposite Grace. She looked around at the crates of empty shells that needed filling with gunpowder. She sighed. It seemed endless.

Grace shook her head. 'I expect she'll be late. She often is. She spends…' Her voice ebbed away into silence for a moment. 'Come on, let's get started. I'm sure Flo will be here soon enough.'

Molly nodded her agreement, but was curious about what she'd been about to say. 'Have you got any men folk away fighting?'

Grace gazed at the wall behind Molly. 'My brother, I don't know where he is, but just keep hoping and praying he's safe.'

'I'm sorry. It's a dreadful war. I wish it would just end.' Molly picked up her scoop and loaded it with gunpowder. 'I write to my friend, Alice's brother. I think he looks forward to receiving letters, and I send the odd parcel as well.' She emptied the scoop into the shell.

Grace mumbled to herself, 'He's lucky then.' She looked down at the shell in front of her, before picking up her scoop.

Molly studied her for a moment. 'I suppose he is.'

'Is he your sweetheart?'

Molly laughed. 'He's a sweetheart all right, but he's not *my* sweetheart. Do you not write to your brother then?'

Grace kept her eyes fixed on the task at hand. 'He knows what I'm like and he wouldn't expect me to.'

Molly raised her eyebrows and opened her mouth to speak, but thought better of it.

Grace poured the gunpowder into the top of the shell and picked up the half-size broom handle and hammer. 'You do exactly the same as you did on the larger shells.'

'Morning people.' Flo was breathless as she took up a position next to Molly.

'I don't want to state the obvious, but you're late again.' Grace glared at her. 'If you're not careful you'll end up getting the sack, and then where will you be? Four or five pounds worse off each week, and doing somebody else's dirty washing.'

Flo frowned at Grace. 'I'm sorry. I'm trying to do better, and I will, I promise, but I'm struggling to shake off this cough.' She quickly moved a shell into position and loaded her scoop with gunpowder.

Molly looked under her lashes at Flo, wondering what was going on in her life. She was clearly flustered. Molly shrugged her shoulders. It could be just because she was late.

The sun was beating down, burning her fair skin, while reflecting from the shop windows Charlotte strode past. Slowing down, she glimpsed sideways, admiring a Milliner's colourful shop window. One day, Molly and her would go in there and have fun trying on all the different hats. She remembered Emily telling stories about doing such things with Alice's mother, when she was a young girl. She frowned as sadness swept over her. There was no time for frivolous nonsense, no time to admire window displays. She quickened her pace, purposefully striding forward, remembering her mother was at home by herself. Beads of perspiration formed on her forehead as she weaved her way along Charing Cross Road. Her pace slowed again as the large white lettering on the sign of the Foyles Bookshop came into view. She smiled as she read 'Novels 3d Each, 2d Given On All Returns'. She was entering what was once Molly's world. She stepped through the shop doorway and her eyes widened as she looked around.

'Good morning, Madam.'

Startled, Charlotte spun round. A tall, grey haired man was smiling at her.

'I'm sorry, I didn't mean to make you jump.' He offered his hand. 'Welcome to Foyles Bookstore. I'm Mr Leadbetter, the Floor Manager here.'

Charlotte returned his smile and shook his hand, which was surprisingly soft. 'I have never seen so many books in one place before. How does anyone ever find what they are looking for?'

Mr Leadbetter laughed. 'Once we get a customer in the shop, we don't like to let them go.'

Charlotte giggled. 'I can believe that; no wonder the girls love working here. It's a wonderful place for book lovers.'

Mr Leadbetter gave her a curious look. 'The girls?'

A smile played at the corners of Charlotte lips, as she shook her head. 'Sorry, I was talking about Alice, Victoria, and my daughter, Molly.'

'Ahh.' Mr Leadbetter chuckled. 'So Miss Cooper is your daughter?'

Colour filled Charlotte's cheeks. 'From your tone, I'm not sure whether that's a good thing or not.'

'I'm sorry. She was a delight to work with, but she did keep me on my toes.'

Charlotte shook her head. 'Then I should be the one saying I'm sorry.'

Mr Leadbetter threw back his head and laughed. 'Most definitely not, I was sorry to see her leave, but I do know there's a lot of pressure on young women these days.'

Charlotte frowned, wondering if that was why Molly had left the safety of the bookshop. She became aware that Mr Leadbetter was watching her. 'There is, but I'm sure she could have found less dangerous war work, like delivering the post.'

Mr Leadbetter raised his eyebrows, secretly agreeing with Mrs Cooper, but felt the need to defend her daughter. 'I'm sure she just wants to do something worthwhile.'

Charlotte stepped further into the shop and cleared her throat. 'Molly used to say there was a smell around the bookshop that she would struggle to explain to someone, but I think I'm beginning to understand.' She sniffed the air. 'It's a musty, smoky type smell, isn't it?'

Mr Leadbetter smiled. 'It can be, or it could be a different smell, one of a new book.'

Charlotte shook her head. 'I don't understand why Molly had to leave; she loves books. In fact, I'm here because I wanted to buy one for her, but I have to say I wouldn't know where to start.'

'I'll take you to Mrs Leybourne. She'll probably be more of a help than I could be.' Mr Leadbetter swept his arm out, indicating they move forward.

'Thank you, that is very kind of you. Alice would be helpful. I'm afraid I don't have much time to spend, searching for something.'

They both stepped forward towards Alice's wooden counter, waiting while she served a customer.

Alice looked up. The colour drained from her face as anxiety immediately ran across it. Her pen clattered onto the floor. She immediately looked over at Victoria, who seemed oblivious as she served a customer. Had Mrs Cooper popped in to see Molly? Had her friend told her parents she no longer worked at Foyles? Had something happened to Molly at the munitions' factory? Gripping the edge of the counter for support, Alice looked back at

THE FOYLES BOOKSHOP GIRLS AT WAR

Molly's mother. 'Mrs Cooper... Mrs Cooper is... er... is everything all right?' Alice kept her fingers on the table top as she walked around it.

Charlotte smiled and reached out to Alice, kissing her on both cheeks. 'Everything is fine. I'm sorry; I didn't mean to worry you. I love the perfume you are wearing. Is it rose or jasmine, or maybe both?' She giggled. 'Perhaps you'll tell me what it's called later.'

Alice nodded and forced a smile.

Mr Leadbetter stepped forward. 'Mrs Leybourne, can you please help Mrs Cooper. I'll get someone to cover your counter, while you are away from it.'

Alice looked over at him, taking several deep breaths. She glanced back at her friend's mother. 'Of course, what do you need help with?'

Charlotte frowned. 'It's silly really. I wanted to buy Molly a book, but' she looked around her, 'I don't know where to start.'

Alice beamed. 'Well you've come to the right place, if we don't have a book, it doesn't exist.'

The three of them laughed.

'Well, I'll leave you in Mrs Leybourne's capable hands.' Mr Leadbetter turned to walk away.

'Thank you for your kindness, Mr Leadbetter.'

Mr Leadbetter looked over his shoulder and smiled, before nodding in their direction.

'Right, Mrs Cooper, do you know what type of book you're after?'

Charlotte looked anxious, as she stared at the rows and rows of racking. 'I'm not sure this was a good idea. It's going to take me ages to find something suitable amongst all of this.' She waved her arm around. 'I have to get back for my mother.'

Alice frowned and pursed her lips, wondering if she could come up with a title, before Mrs Cooper asked to see where Molly worked. 'Hmm.'

Charlotte glanced back at Alice. 'What?'

Alice's finger came up to tap her lips. 'I was just thinking, we've had some books brought back today, and if I remember rightly, there was something there that may be of interest to Molly.' She turned on her heels, walked back to her counter and started rifling through the many books behind it. 'Ah, here it is.' Alice held up a paperback. 'Sense and Sensibility, it's by Jane Austen. She wrote it before Pride and Prejudice, and I know Molly loves that book.' Alice passed the book over to Charlotte. 'It's about the Dashwood sisters having to move from the home they grew up in. I haven't read it, but I understand it's very good.'

Charlotte took the book and looked at the plain cover, before handing it back. 'I don't know. What if she doesn't like the story?'

Alice smiled. 'I'm sure Mr Leadbetter would let Molly change it.'

Charlotte frowned for a moment. 'All right, I'll take it.' She unclasped her handbag and pulled out a small purse. Her fingers twisted it open, before rooting around for the required three large copper coins.

Alice bent down, picked up her pen from the floor and started writing the book details on her pad. 'I'll write you out a payment slip, then you take it over to Victoria in the payment booth and she'll take your money. Then bring the slip back to me and I'll give you the book.'

Charlotte gave a nervous giggle. 'It sounds quite complicated.'

'I'm home, Ma.' Molly's voice carried along the hall. A tired sigh escaped as she removed her jacket. She took a deep breath and wrinkled her nose. The sweet, but overpowering smell of lavender hung in the air.

'We're in here,' Charlotte called back.

Molly smiled to herself. They only ever used the dining room. The sitting room was for guests, which they never had. Pushing open the door, the squeaking hinges announced her presence. She flopped down on one of the dining chairs. 'Hello, Gran, Ma. Have you two had a good day?'

'We've been busy.' Charlotte smiled. 'Your gran has been darning your father's socks and sewing on buttons, while I've been making rags out of some old bed sheets.'

Molly yawned. 'Good.'

Charlotte leant over the arm of her chair, to pick something up off the floor. 'I popped into Foyles today and bought you a present.'

The colour drained from Molly's face. Alice and Victoria would have been worried sick at the sight of her mother.

Charlotte beamed, stretching out her hand to Molly. 'Alice assures me it's very good, but she said if you don't like it, Mr Leadbetter will probably change it for you.'

Molly grasped the book and stared hard at the cover. 'Did you have a chance to talk much to Alice and Victoria?'

Charlotte shook her head. 'Not really. I thought Alice in particular looked strained, mind you, it was busy in there.'

'Foyles always is.' Molly forced a smile. 'People clearly like to read, or send books to the soldiers on the frontline.'

Charlotte frowned. 'Is it not what you'd read? To be honest, I was in a hurry because I'd left your gran on her own so didn't have time to look around. Mind you, there are so many books in that shop, I'm surprised anyone finds anything.'

'I know, but when you work there, you get used to where the different types of books are.' Molly looked up. 'Don't look so worried, Ma, it's a lovely present. Thank you.' She turned the book over. 'I've not read Sense and Sensibility before, so it was a good choice.'

'Good, I did worry about it.'

Molly stood up and gave her mother a kiss on the cheek. 'It's a wonderful present, thank you.' She chuckled as she sat back down, waving the book in the air. 'You can't have too many books, you know.' A sigh escaped as she leant back in the armchair.

Sophie's head tilted to one side. 'Been a long day, dear?'

'Every day is a long day, Gran. It's hard work too.' Molly sighed. She wanted to talk about it, but didn't want to give her mother a chance to say 'I told you so'.

'I'm sure you'll soon get used to it.' Sophie's eyes clouded over.

Molly forced a smile. 'Yeah, that's what the girls at work say.'

Charlotte jumped up from one of the two small armchairs that sat either side of the fire grate. 'You chat to Gran and I'll make you a cup of tea.' She put her hands on her hips and leant back, arching and stretching.

Sophie nodded, picking up her needle and thread with one hand, and a sock with the other. 'What are the girls like?'

'I don't know, Gran. They seem quite nice, but I don't think Grace likes me. She's a bit older than me and I think she's in charge. If she isn't, she's very bossy.' Molly gave a wry smile. 'Flo's a bit younger than me and seems a happy person to be around.' She sighed. 'I just don't like being the new girl.'

Sophie chuckled. 'I'm sure you won't be the new girl for long. Don't worry. Everyone's suspicious of people they don't know, but things will soon settle down.'

Molly smiled. 'I hope you're right, Gran.' She paused and glanced over at the doorway. 'Grace thinks I'm too posh to work there, and that working at Foyles wasn't a real job, not like being in domestic service.'

Sophie frowned. 'Well in a way, she's right, lovey. Being in domestic service can be tough.'

Molly's jaw dropped a little; she'd thought her gran would defend her.

'That's not to say you didn't work hard at the bookshop.' Sophie's eyes darted from side to side, as she searched for the words to help her granddaughter. 'It's just a different type of work, not so physical, or as your mother would say, more ladylike.' Sophie gave a throaty chuckle, resting the sock on her lap.

Molly laughed. 'You're being mischievous, Gran.' Her hands clenched on her lap and she could feel the tears pricking at her eyes. 'I know ma is disappointed in me, but it was something I had to do. Although she never said it, I think she hoped I would meet Mr Right there, or through Alice, and marry into gentry or something.'

Sophie threw her head back with laughter. 'How smart you are little one, you know, there are plenty of war effort jobs you could've applied for, to keep your ma happy. I understand there are even office jobs. Now, working for the Government would've made your mother very happy.' She giggled. 'I'm just being mean now.' Sophie paused. 'You know, she just wants what all parents want.'

Molly frowned. 'What's that? To see me married off, with children?'

Sophie's lips tightened for a second. 'Maybe, but I was thinking more about wanting you to have a better life than she had. That's what all parents want.'

Molly pursed her lips for a moment, staring at the potted lavender plant that had been placed in front of the fire grate. 'But what about what I want?'

Sophie glanced thoughtfully at her granddaughter. 'What do you want? Did you seriously want a job in Silvertown?'

Molly closed her eyes for a moment and pulled her lips inwards. 'Probably not.' She sighed. 'But I earn more money now, and ma could stop working. They could have a better life. You know, have some finer things around them.'

Sophie nodded. 'Maybe your ma doesn't want to give up her job. She's a good woman and I expect she'd wonder what to do with her time.'

Molly shook her head. Her jaw tightened for a moment. 'She could go shopping, spend some time finding things for her home, that she actually loves, instead of making do with second hand stuff all the time.' She saw the glint appear in her gran's eyes and knew she'd gone too far. 'I'm sorry. It's just that I don't understand how pa can have a good job, and them be so poor. It doesn't feel right.' Her head jerked round as the soft footsteps from the hallway drew nearer.

Sophie cursed under her breath. 'Open the door wider for your mother. That tray will be heavy.'

Molly did as she was bid.

'Thanks, Molly.' Charlotte stepped through the doorway and placed the tray on the dining table. 'I expect you're gasping for a cuppa.' She proceeded to pour the tea, adding a splash of milk into each cup.

'I must admit, it'll go down a treat.' Molly sat back on the chair she'd just vacated.

Charlotte frowned. 'You look tired.' She passed the cup and saucer over to her daughter. 'Drink this, while I get you a bowl of vegetable stew.'

'No thanks, Ma, I'm too tired to eat. Save it for Pa.'

'Well, you have to eat, especially now you're doing such long hours. You need to keep your strength up.' Charlotte eyed her daughter with concern. 'Oh, I almost forgot, this will cheer you up. You have a letter.' She reached for the brown envelope that was sitting on the mantelpiece. She studied the spidery handwriting, before passing it over to her daughter. 'It looks like it could be from Alice's brother, Charles.'

Molly pulled herself upright, beaming at her mother as she reached out to take it from her. She looked at her name and address, instantly recognising his handwriting. 'You're right, Ma.' She put down her cup and tore open the seal. Pulling out the single sheet of paper, she unfolded it and began to devour the words scrawled across the page.

Dear Molly,

Thank you for your letters. They do cheer me up, so please keep them coming. As always, I'm up to my ankles in water in a trench somewhere. I'm not allowed to say where, just in case everyone wants to join us in this much sought after holiday destination. Seriously though, it's dreadful here, but I can tell you it's a different trench to the last time I wrote to you. Not only are we accompanied by rats galore, we also have weird insects descending upon us. They drop on to your hair, from nowhere it would seem. The days are long, as there is a lot of waiting around. We usually get the call to go over the top at about three in the morning. Apparently, the darkness will help save our lives, but I can tell you that's not working. But still, we wouldn't be able to sleep anyway. The machine guns are blooming noisy at night, I can tell you, and you'd have to be deaf to sleep through that racket. I hope all is well back home. I'm getting letters from the family and I've even received a photograph of little Arthur. Alice tells me he'll be walking

soon. Haha, that'll keep them all on their toes. How's the new job going? Have your family forgiven you yet? I think Alice misses seeing you around Foyles and worries about you working in Silvertown, but we all thank you for your efforts. It's raining here now and I've run out of paper, so I'll sign off for now. Take care of yourself old girl, stay safe and please write soon with all your news.
 Your dear friend
 Charles.

A tear rolled down Molly's cheek.

'Is everything all right, lovey?' Sophie rubbed the back of her neck, as she took in her granddaughter's pallid features.

Molly's lips and chin trembled as she swiped her hand across her cheek. She nodded. She reached out, picked up her cup of tea and gulped it down. The tepid liquid made her shudder. 'He's safe for now, but I'd be lying if I said his letters didn't frighten me.' She glanced down at Charles' scrawl. 'I think he tells me stuff he doesn't feel able to tell his family.'

Charlotte nodded. 'I suppose he doesn't want to worry them.' She took a deep breath. 'But then, it's a lot for you to take on.'

Molly jumped up out of her chair. 'He has to tell someone, Ma.'

Her mother sighed. 'You're worrying about him, as I worry about you.'

'I know.' Molly wearily flopped back down on to the chair. 'The difference is, even if he survives, his life will never be the same again.

Chapter 8

September 1916

Molly lowered her head and tried to pedal faster. The cold rain lashed onto her face and dripped off the end of her nose. The small yellow light on her handlebars was lost in the downpour. Water splashed up the pavement, as the wheels turned in the puddles and muddy rivulets raced along the road, ahead of her. Her shoulders were damp under her coat. Men and women were half running along the street, their umbrellas giving them little protection. There was no sign of dawn breaking or the rain stopping. The birds weren't giving their usual early morning chorus. Molly turned down the side of the Savoy Hotel, but there was no time for daydreaming. The Thames soon came into view. The pounding rain was swallowed up by the swell of the river. There was no romantic tinkling of water hitting water. She continued to pump her pedals and, crossing the mouth of Waterloo Bridge, she became aware of a heaviness. The front wheel seemed to be hitting everything in its path, causing her to jolt. Reluctantly, she stopped and jumped off, groaning as water immediately splashed up her legs, but glad she'd made the decision to wear her ankle boots.

Holding the handlebars, Molly bent down to inspect the bicycle. She jumped up as it wobbled. Her boots squelched as she slowly bent down again, holding the bicycle firm. She shook her head and pinched her lips together. She did the expected, pressing her fingers into the muddy tyre. She shook her head again, glancing down at her dirty fingers. 'Great, a flat tyre, now what?' Frowning, she glanced along the riverbank. 'This day couldn't get any worse.' She stared down at the wheel, wondering if she dare ride any further.

'You all right, lovey?' An old man hobbled over to her. 'You're soaked through and you'll catch your death, if you stay out in this too long.'

'I've got a flat tyre.' Molly tried to muster up a smile, but failed. The temptation was to turn around and go home.

'Well you don't want to be out fixing it in this weather.' The man spluttered into a handkerchief.

Molly frowned. 'Why are you out in this awful rain?' All thoughts of getting wet were forgotten. After all, how wet could one person get? She was already soaked through.

The man gave a frail laugh. 'I always walk along the river at this time of the morning.' He pushed his flat cap up slightly, revealing deep brown eyes and wispy grey eyebrows. 'I see you most mornings, cycling for all you're worth.'

Molly lowered her eyes, wondering how she'd not noticed him before. Rain trickled down the back of her neck. 'I'm sorry, I'm so intent on surviving my journey.'

'Where have you got to get to?' His wizened eyes crinkled at the corners, as he watched her.

'Silvertown. I work at the munitions' factory.'

The man nodded. 'Ahh, you're one of the canaries.' He gave a toothless smile. 'There's an underground station up the road, Temple it's called, about a five minute walk. If you're nice to the old guy in there, he might let you leave your bicycle there, until you've finished later.' The old man chuckled to himself. 'Tell him Fred sent you.' He pulled down his cap and turned to walk away. 'Take care, young lady. These are dangerous times we live in.' He raised his hand and carried on down the road.

'Bye, thank you,' Molly called out.

The old man waved, without turning round.

Molly took a deep breath and retrieved a damp handkerchief from her coat pocket. She ran it over her wet face before grabbing both handlebars and pushing her bicycle forwards, towards Temple station.

It wasn't long before she was standing on the train. She took off her hat and gave it a gentle shake. She held it by the narrow brim and turned it on its side, as she gripped the pole with the same hand. She ran her hand through her flattened hair. A puddle was forming at her feet, slowly spreading outwards.

'Here love, have my seat.' A young lad spoke from behind her.

Molly turned and smiled at him. 'No, no thank you, I'm soaked through and I'll make the seat wet for the rest of the day. Thank you though, I appreciate the offer.'

The lad gave her a warming smile. 'If you're sure, miss.'

Molly nodded. 'Thank you.' She wondered how much of a mess she looked. Her hair felt wet and lank, and her face was burning now she was out of the rain. At least she didn't have the bicycle to worry about until later, thanks to the kind gentleman at the station. He'd chuckled gleefully at the mention of Fred.

The train slowed down as it pulled into Blackfriars and, two minutes later, it continued on its journey to Mansion House. Molly wasn't sure how far it was to Canning Town, so she had to pay attention to the stops.

Andrew Greenwood stared at the white feather. A young girl had handed it to him when he was putting his key in the front door, last evening. She ran off with an older woman, as soon as she'd rested it in his hand. 'Coward. You should be ashamed.' He'd gone indoors without a word and dropped the feather on the hall console table. It was left there as a constant taunt of his shortcomings. Their words had shouted themselves in his head all night, as he tossed and turned in his single bed. He glanced in the hall mirror. His black hair had grown a little, but it still reminded him of what had been. The dark circles under his pale blue eyes jumped out against his ashen skin. His face had taken on skeletal features, with the weight loss. He ran his tongue over his thin lips and the residue of his morning coffee still lingered there. He ran his finger along the edge of the feather, enjoying the softness against his skin, forgetting for a moment what it stood for. It came from a beautiful elegant creature that was a picture of innocence, yet now the plumage screamed cowardice. Is that what everyone thought of him, just because he wasn't on the frontline, risking his life?

Andrew gave a heavy sigh and snatched his black umbrella out of the stand, by the front door. He opened the door and groaned, as he battled to put it up against the rain. The wind caught the front door and slammed it shut behind him. He walked briskly towards New Oxford Street and turned left. The rain ricocheted off the umbrella and he was thankful it was only a short walk from Bury Street to Holborn Underground Station.

'Buy yer paper 'ere sir, just a 'a'penny will do it,' a weatherworn lad shouted out.

Startled, Andrew jumped. He looked around, but the voice seemed to be in the air.

'I'm over 'ere sir, in the shop doorway.' The boy stuck a worn down shoe out into the rain. 'It's too wet for me papers today.' He laughed, pulling his foot back into the dry. 'And for me.'

Andrew took in his threadbare jacket, and the flat cap that was far too big for him. His trousers had a rip near the pocket that was beginning to fray. Andrew thrust his hand into his pocket and pulled out a crumpled pound note. 'There you go.' He smoothed it out and thrust it forward for the boy to take.

The smile faded from the lad's face. 'I can't change that, sir.'

Andrew let a rare smile light up his eyes. 'I don't want you to change it. You can keep it.'

The boy's jaw dropped, as he stared at the money being offered to him. ''Ere, I don't know what your game is, mate, but I'm only selling papers.'

Andrew's laughter burst from him. 'I'm glad to hear that, mate, but I don't want a paper. It'll be soaked through before I get two steps down the road. You keep it. And keep the quid as well.' He proffered the pound again. 'Go on, you're gonna have a rough day if this rain don't stop.'

The boy's face lit up. 'That must be more than I earn in a year.' He snatched the pound note, before Andrew could change his mind. 'Thank you, sir, make sure you have a good day. You're a kind man.'

Andrew nodded. 'And you.' He turned to walk away. 'Make sure you spend your money wisely, or even save it. Put it in a bank somewhere.'

The boy laughed. 'Not much point in saving it; the Germans might get me tomorrow.'

Andrew waved, but his lips tightened at the sadness of it all. This so called Great War had a lot to answer for. He shook his head and stepped into Holborn Underground Station. He lowered his umbrella and shook it outside, the drips catapulting out into the darkness.

An old lady limped towards him. 'You don't want to sell that to me, do yer? I can offer you thruppence.' She grinned, showing a row of brown teeth. A strong waft of stale tobacco assaulted him. 'I ain't got nuffink else to offer, apart from me body.' She cackled loudly.

What did it matter if he got wet? Who would care? He shook his head, trying to shake the melancholy that had gripped him since he'd woken up. 'I can't let you have it, I'm afraid. I've a long walk, once I get off the train.'

'That's all right, lovey, I was only chancing me arm wiv yer.' She turned to hobble away. 'You 'ave a good day.'

Guilt surged through his veins and, without a thought, he heard himself shout across the station. 'You can have my coat, it'll keep you warm.' He slipped his arms out of the coat, before taking the couple of long strides towards her and handing it over.

The old man at the kiosk smiled and nodded his good mornings. Andrew mimicked his action, without stopping. He swerved to avoid the many people hovering around, hoping the rain was going to stop, and carried on down the steps to the platform.

Dread filled Molly's being, as she headed towards the exit of Canning Town Underground Station. This was going to be a long walk. Her clothes now clung to her, with the stench of dampness following her around. She pulled at the ends of her hair, now sitting lank and dull on her shoulders. Molly twisted several strands together, squeezing the water from them, fighting the urge to find a mirror and run a comb through it. She stood at the exit of the station, looking out at the moon casting its silvery light on the rain lashing down. Perhaps she should wait to see if it stopped, or at least eased off. Taking a step back under the cover of the station, she immediately felt someone's foot under hers.

'Oh, I'm dreadfully…' Molly swung round to see Mr Greenwood staring back at her.

'Morning, Miss Cooper.'

'Mr… Mr Greenwood.' Molly's gaze darted back and forth. Colour began to fill her cheeks. 'I didn't mean to step on your foot.' His eyes bored into her. She reached to straighten her hair. 'I'm sorry, I should have looked before… I'm sorry, I'm not having a very good morning.' She was rambling, but couldn't seem to stop.

'So I see.' He raised his eyebrows. 'You're looking rather damp, to say the least.'

Molly pulled back her shoulders and jutted out her chin, as fire coursed through her veins. 'Yes, well at least I haven't been stupid enough to come out without a coat.'

'No, just without an umbrella.' Andrew paused, taking in her appearance. 'I wonder which is worse.'

She scowled, turning her back to look outside. 'That's a long story, and not one I'm in the mood to get into right now.'

Andrew stepped forward and peered out at the rain. 'Well, we're going to need something to talk about on the way to the factory, if you're going to share my umbrella.'

Molly wanted to jump up and down with delight, at not having to get a further soaking, but stared silently out into the darkness, listening to the splashes of water hitting the puddles.

Andrew glanced across at her. 'I assume by your silence, it's a tough decision to make.'

Molly lowered her gaze. 'No, sir, it isn't a tough decision. It's just…'

'You're worried what people will think, if you are in such close proximity to me.' He sighed. 'You have nothing to worry about, Miss Cooper. Your virtue is safe with me.'

Molly frowned. She'd had no problems snuggling up close to Tony, but this was different. 'You're my boss, remember.'

'And you're soaked through, remember.' Andrew took a step forward and pushed open his large umbrella, holding it high above his head. 'If the thought of sharing my umbrella is so abhorrent to you, I'll be on my way.' He turned to walk away.

Molly watched him step further into the darkness, before shouting out to him. 'Wait.'

Andrew turned back and glanced at her.

'It's not abhorrent, or whatever you said.' Molly's voice gradually faded. 'It's just.' She shrugged her shoulders. 'I don't know you.'

Andrew stepped back towards her. His eyes held a steel-like quality. 'You'll be perfectly safe with me.' A smile hovered on his lips for a moment. 'And, you have a half an hour walk to get to know me, should you wish to.' He lifted the umbrella a little, inviting her to step under it.

Molly hesitated, but took a step towards him.

Andrew pushed out his elbow. 'Put your arm in mine, so you're in tight.'

Molly looked up at him, wide-eyed and unsure, but did as he bid. Her fingers sunk into the softness of his woollen jumper and she felt herself snuggling in and enjoying his woody scent.

Andrew gazed down at her. 'Ready?'

Molly stiffened. The moment had gone. She nodded and they both stepped forward, as one. Silence stretched before them as her mind frantically searched for something to say.

Andrew cleared his throat. 'How are you settling in at the factory?'

'It's hard work, but I'm fine with that.' Molly paused for a moment. 'Grace is a little bit scary though.' Biting down on her lip, she immediately regretted mentioning her.

Andrew gave her a confused look. 'Grace?'

Molly chuckled in disbelief. 'Miss Fairchild.'

'Ah yes, Miss Fairchild. I can't say I've noticed a scariness about her.' Andrew's grip tightened around the handle of the umbrella, as the wind threatened to whip it away. 'Why do you think that?'

Molly's hand tightened around the flex of his arm muscles, thankful for the dark morning, as colour flooded her cheeks. She took a deep breath. 'I… I don't know.' She paused for a moment. 'It might be because I'm not used to such directness.' Molly lowered her eyes, as her mother's words screamed in her head. *Honesty and hard work, that's how you get on in life, and above all else, you never lie.*

They walked on in silence, every step causing their hips to brush against each other. Molly sucked in the damp air and gazed down at their feet, concentrating on the splashing and the ripples that followed along the narrow pavement. The fresh smell of rain had long disappeared. Molly's heart thumped, as though it was trying to escape from her chest. The dull thud pounded in her ears. Her mind searched for something to say.

'Why did you decide to leave Foyles?'

Molly tensed at the unexpected question. She heard his sharp intake of breath.

'Sorry, I didn't mean to startle you. I shouldn't have asked. It's none of my business.'

'No, it's fine. I was in my own little world.' Molly chuckled. 'Trying to take my mind off this horrible weather.' Another lie.

'Yes, it's pretty wet.' Andrew grinned. 'I hate to think how wet you'd have got, if you hadn't joined me under the umbrella.'

Molly pulled back her shoulders and lifted her chin. 'Once you're soaked, you're soaked. You can't get any wetter than that.'

A joyful laugh escaped from Andrew. 'That's very true, and you certainly looked soaked when I first saw you.'

'Thanks for that,' Molly quipped, impatiently.

'I didn't mean to annoy you. Are you always so touchy, first thing in the morning?'

'I'm not touchy.' Molly scowled. 'But I am soaked through, and finding this whole thing more than a little embarrassing, thank you.'

A deafening silence followed her outburst.

'So, at the risk of getting my head bitten off again.' Andrew paused for a moment. 'I thought you usually cycled to work.'

Molly let out a deep sigh, wondering how he knew. 'I do.'

A smile played on Andrew's lips. 'Ah, you're a fair-weather cyclist then, are you?'

Molly sucked in her lips, fighting the strong urge to hit out. 'No, I'm not. For your information, I had a flat tyre this morning and left it at Temple Station, under the protection of a man that works there.'

'Ahh, hence no umbrella.'

Molly nodded. 'And why I'm soaked to the skin, looking a mess.'

Andrew laughed. 'You don't look that bad. Trust me, I've seen worse.'

Molly laughed. 'Thanks, I think.' She felt his head jerk round at her, but said nothing.

Chugging alerted them to cars approaching. They trundled through the puddles, causing waves on the pavement. Andrew and Molly moved in as far away from the road as they could, but the muddy water splashed across their legs and feet. They both sighed at the same time, which gave Molly the giggles. 'For once, I won't be sorry to change into those awful overalls.'

'What do you mean awful?' Andrew chuckled. 'They're quite flattering. I might even find a pair for myself today.'

Molly's hand rested on her chest, as the giggles took hold. 'Oh don't. I can't imagine you wearing them.' She gasped, taking a deep breath.

Andrew chuckled at her laughter. 'Yeah, you could be right. It might cause a bit of a stir.'

'A bit.' Molly shook her head, the laughter gradually fading. 'How long have you worked at the munitions' factory?' She glanced up at him and saw something flick across his face, not sure what to make of it. 'I'm sorry, I shouldn't have asked.'

Andrew gave a tight smile. 'That's fine. I asked you questions, which by the way, you still haven't answered.'

'I have.'

Andrew shook his head. 'No, I asked you why you left Foyles, and you've conveniently ignored it.'

Molly's grip tightened on his arm, as she lost her footing. Andrew immediately squeezed her hand tight to his body. Her stomach churned. She took several deep breaths. Slipping would finish off any decorum she had left.

Neither spoke as they carried on walking.

Molly looked up at Andrew. 'I left Foyles because I wanted to do something for the war effort. Something meaningful.'

Andrew nodded. 'That's very commendable, but there were lots of other meaningful jobs you could have done.' He paused and turned to look at her. Their eyes locked for a moment, before Molly glanced down at the pavement. 'And yet you chose a dangerous occupation. You're clearly trying to prove something to someone.'

'No,' Molly snapped. 'I've nothing to prove to anybody.'

'Except yourself, maybe.'

Molly shivered.

'Are you cold?'

She nodded. 'It's probably where I'm so wet.'

'I have nothing to offer you, except body heat.' Andrew moved the umbrella to his other hand and lifted his arm, placing it around her. 'Don't worry, I shall move it when the factory is within sight.'

Molly tensed as the weight of his arm lay on her shoulders.

He pulled her in close.

She found herself relaxing and enjoying him. Molly cleared her throat. 'So... you haven't answered my question.'

'What question?'

Molly gave a little laugh. 'How long have you worked at the factory?' She could feel his body tense next to hers.

'I don't know, a few months.'

Molly waited for him to expand, but he remained silent for a few minutes. She wanted to know what he did before that, and whether his short hair meant he was enlisting. Determined not to say anything, she bit down hard on her tongue. After a few minutes, it began to throb and blood seeped into her cheeks.

'I'll er...' Andrew cleared his throat. 'I'll come back to the station with you after work, and help with your bicycle... if that's all right.'

'Thank you, Mr Greenwood.' Molly felt his body tense, but couldn't stop herself from continuing. 'That would be appreciated.'

Andrew dropped his arm and held out his hand. 'I think it's stopped raining now.' He lowered the umbrella and gave it a shake, before closing it. 'Just as well, especially as the factory is just ahead.'

Molly felt bereft without his arm around her. He was back to being her manager, and she was a canary.

Chapter 9

Grace pulled at her mob cap, tucking her hair under it. 'I'm glad to see you made it on time for a change, Flo.'

Flo beamed. 'I'll have you know I was very good this morning. In fact, I was early, and it was quite enjoyable despite the terrible weather. I saw everyone arrive; soaked through, they were.' Her eyes held a glint of something unfathomable to Molly. 'I might even try and get here early more often.' Flo winked in her direction.

Molly forced a smile. 'I didn't see you. Mind you, I was too busy trying to get out of the rain.'

Flo laughed. 'Oh you were busy all right.' Her gaze didn't stray from Molly. 'Frank invited me into his security hut and made me a cuppa. He showed me the newspaper headlines. Seems we've shot down one of those zeppelin fings, near Enfield.' She grinned, before turning to face Grace. 'The headlines made me proud to be British; you should ask him if you can read it.'

Grace turned away. 'Nah, I don't read newspapers. If you ask me, you can't believe a word they say.'

Flo shrugged her shoulders and leant in towards Grace. 'I have something juicy to tell you.' Flo looked over her shoulder. 'According to Frank, the peelers are hanging around, so we've got to be careful.'

Grace chuckled. 'You might have to be careful, but I don't. I'm a law abiding citizen, I'll have you know.'

Flo laughed. 'Yeah right.'

'So why are they hanging around then?' Grace looked thoughtful for a moment. 'There's nothing for them to hang around for, unless someone here has got something dodgy going on.'

Grace turned to stare at Molly.

'Don't look at me.' She raised her eyebrows. 'I'm also a law abiding citizen.'

Flo giggled. 'Nah, I don't think, on this occasion, it's Molly. From what Frank said,' she leant in and lowered her voice, 'it's meant to be a secret, so keep it to yourself. It's something to do with some thieving from the docks. He said it's gone on for over forty years or summink.'

Grace shook her head. 'Forty years? I wonder what's happened, for them to be investigating it now.'

'We will probably never know, unless Frank tells us.' Molly smiled, glancing down and began fiddling with the sleeves of her overall, wondering if that was who the man in the suit was. 'I tell you one thing, I'm glad to be out of the wet clothes, and in the dry.'

Grace smiled. 'It's certainly a miserable start to the day, that's for sure.'

Flo laughed. 'Only for some.'

Grace glanced at her. 'What's got into you this morning?' She leant forward and sniffed the air. 'Have you been drinking already?'

'No.' Flo scowled at her. 'Of course I haven't. What do you take me for?' She bent down and fumbled with her shoes. 'It's nothing, honest. All's good.'

Grace stared at her for a moment. 'Come on, ladies,' she yelled, without taking her eyes off Flo. 'Let's get started.' She turned and made her way to the workshop, where they would begin making up the shells again.

Molly jumped as the roar of machinery came to life. She took up her normal position opposite Grace and Flo, before reaching out to grab a shell, to start the stemming process. It would be the first of many that day. Staring at the shell, she concentrated on loading it with gunpowder, always aware that Grace didn't miss a thing. Her mind wandered to Mr Greenwood and the secret he was obviously keeping. She shrugged her shoulders. He was probably going to the frontline soon and would never be seen again, at least not by her. Her stomach churned as she thought about his muscles under his jumper. Without realising it, she tilted her head to one side. Why wasn't he wearing a coat? She frowned, hammering the stick down into the shell. Surely his secret isn't about money; perhaps she should offer to buy him one. A smile hovered on her lips.

Flo interrupted her meanderings. 'What are you smiling at?'

Molly immediately looked up, to find two sets of eyes staring at her. 'Nothing.'

Flo laughed. 'It didn't look like nothing to me.' She nudged Grace in the arm. 'Don't you think she looked a little gooey-eyed?'

Grace laughed. 'Leave her alone. If she's got something to be gooey-eyed over, then good luck to her.' She turned and looked over at Flo. 'Get on with your work.' She waved her arm towards the end of the table. 'We've got to get all these done today.'

Flo rolled her eyes heavenward. 'All right, all right, stop moaning.'

The chatter stopped for a few minutes as they all filled their shells with the loose black powder. Molly no longer noticed the noise that surrounded her, but her voice seemed to be permanently hoarse from shouting above it. At least now, she had an excuse not to talk. Her mind wandered back to the journey to work. She sighed, not understanding why Mr Greenwood brought out the worst in her. She wasn't proud of herself. Molly looked up and caught Flo staring at her.

'So, Molly, have you found the man of your dreams? Is it looove?' Flo threw her arms around herself to imitate cuddling.

Colour rushed into Molly's face. 'No.'

'Are you sure? You can tell us, can't she, Grace? We could do with a bit of gossip to liven up our day.'

Grace laughed at Flo. 'Just leave her alone. I don't know what's got into you today.'

Nora stopped by their workbench. Her gravelly voice startled Molly. 'Grace is right, Flo. Leave the poor girl alone. Everyone knows you're picking on her. She's one of us, working hard to help our boys, and that's all that matters.' She patted Molly's back as she carried on walking by.

Molly's gaze followed her, wondering if Nora was sickening for something, as she made her way back to her own heavy piece of machinery. She wanted to give her a hug but knew that wasn't appropriate.

Flo shrugged her shoulders. 'Sorry, Molly, I was just having a bit of fun.'

'That's all right.' Molly gave a weak smile.

Flo didn't take her eyes off her. 'Although, now I think about it, I didn't notice your bicycle in its usual place, out the front.'

Molly straightened her lips. Her tongue stuck to the roof of her mouth. 'I got a flat tyre.'

Flo put her hand to her ear. 'Sorry, I can't hear you with all this racket in here.' She waved her arm around.

Molly yelled. 'I said, it has a flat tyre.'

Grace looked up. 'That's bad luck. You come a long way as well.' She pushed the small wood hard into the shell, bashing the end with a hammer.

Molly breathed a sigh of relief and caught a familiar woody scent.

'Did you come by train then?' Flo gave a smirk at the clatter of Molly's stick hitting the floor.

'How are we all getting on this morning?'

A tingling ran down Molly's spine as the voice behind her confirmed she was right. She didn't turn around. No good was ever going to come of thinking too much about him.

'Very nice, Mr Greenwood, love the ankles,' a woman's voice rang out with laughter. 'You going to come down 'ere and work with us?' She started clapping and it got louder, as the idea took hold.

There was a smattering of laughter and the applause gathered momentum. The temptation got too much for Molly. She turned round to take in the spectacle of Mr Greenwood wearing overalls. She grinned at his ankles showing, where the trousers didn't meet his shoes. Flo joined in, her laughter ringing out above the machinery. It got caught in her throat and she was suddenly choking.

'All right, all right.' Mr Greenwood frowned as he stepped forward. 'You've had your fun; now get back to work.' Gradually, the laughter and clapping faded, under the noise of the machines. He bent down and picked up the stick.

Molly reached out to take it. Their fingers touched for a second. Her stomach lurched up into her chest. She felt breathless.

Mr Greenwood dropped his hand and looked across at Flo. 'Is everything all right?'

Grace dropped the tools and slapped her on the back a few times, until the coughing slowed down. She finally looked past Molly. 'Are you becoming one of us, Mr Greenwood?'

Flo took a couple of gasps of air. 'The overall certainly suits you.' She grinned sheepishly.

'Yes, well needs must and all that. I got soaked this morning.' Mr Greenwood glanced at Molly for a few seconds before looking away. 'Anyway, are there any problems here today?'

Grace looked from one to the other. 'No, everything's fine, thank you, sir.' She picked up the hammer and hit the wood into the shell with great force.

Mr Greenwood eyed the three of them before walking away, between the shells and a large machine, stopping to talk to Nora along the way.

Molly frowned. 'Is everything all right, Grace?'

'You tell me.' Grace whacked the stick again. 'Is it?'

Molly swallowed hard. 'As far as I know, it is.'

Grace looked at Molly's wide-eyed expression. 'That's all right then.'

Flo's gaze darted between the two of them. A smile was dying to escape her sealed lips.

There was no doubt Flo was up to no good. Had she seen her arrive with Mr Greenwood? Molly hadn't noticed her. Flo wouldn't keep her waiting for too long. It would get too much for her. Molly just had to get through the rest of the day. She shook her head. She hadn't done anything wrong, had she?

The bell bellowed out, marking the six o'clock finishing time. Women cheered and sighed. Molly was relieved it was over. She just had to get changed, and leave as quickly as possible.

In record time, Molly was pushing open the factory door, shouting her goodbyes. 'Goodnight, Frank,' she shouted and waved across at him sitting in his shed, as she half ran up the road.

He waved. 'Goodnight, Molly, you're in a hurry this evening. Got a date?' His laughter carried in the evening air.

She looked back and waved, noticing the man in the dark suit striding towards Frank's cubbyhole. Something told her she should stop, in case Frank needed support, but the need to avoid Mr Greenwood won the argument.

'Take care going home,' Frank shouted after her.

Molly turned back and paced it out. Her shoes slipped and skidded along the muddy path, as she stepped over puddles. Her body objected to the smoke and dust, filling her lungs from the many chimneystacks. She coughed hard as her breathing became laboured.

'Miss Cooper.'

She quickened her pace. Instinct told her Grace already thought something was going on between them, and he was the love of her life, even if he wasn't. Molly knew she would have to come clean, before Flo added fuel to the fire that was already smouldering away.

'Molly.' His authoritative tone carried.

How long could she keep ignoring him? More importantly, how long could she keep up this pace? She slowed down, gasping for air and turned to face her nemesis.

'I did shout out.' Mr Greenwood smiled. 'You were going at a pace though. I don't think I've ever seen anyone speed up the road like that before.'

'Sorry, Mr Greenwood, I didn't hear you.' *Another lie*, a voice screamed in her head. It was fast becoming a habit. 'I'm afraid it's going to take me a while to get home this evening, and my mother will start fretting.'

'Please, outside work, call me Andrew.' He smiled at her wide-eyed expression. 'I can't be doing with all this Mr Greenwood nonsense.'

Molly nodded before whispering. 'Yes, sir.'

Andrew laughed. 'That also includes sir.'

Colour flooded Molly's cheeks. 'I'll try to remember, sir… Andrew.'

'Right, let's get this bicycle, so it can be fixed.' Andrew placed his hand on Molly's elbow, guiding her to turn and move forward.

They stepped forward in silence for a couple of minutes. 'The overalls caused a stir, didn't they?' Andrew laughed at the memory of everyone's reaction to him, earlier on.

Molly couldn't resist the smile that readily spread across her face. 'They certainly did.'

Andrew chuckled. 'Still, they saved me sitting in wet clothes all day, and brightened up a dull day for everyone else.'

'I think it's fair to say that's true.' Molly giggled. 'At least it's stopped raining, at long last.'

Andrew nodded. 'So, we have to collect your bicycle from your saviour at Temple Station, and look at how we can get it home and repair it.'

'Thank you for the offer, but I'm sure I'll manage. I'll just take it home on the train.' Molly paused. 'My father should be able to help.'

Andrew sighed. 'Far be it for me to take away a father and daughter moment, but I don't think it would be gentlemanly of me to leave you to struggle home with it.' He looked across at her, trying to read her expression. 'You don't like me very much, do you?'

Molly jerked round to face him. Was he joking with her? 'Like doesn't come into it, as I told you this morning, you're my boss.'

'Not when we're outside the factory.' Andrew paused, trying to absorb the silence, but it got the better of him. 'Why can't we just talk to each other?'

Molly took a deep breath. Grace's face immediately popped into her mind. Was she finally beginning to accept and respect her, despite not liking "her kind"? 'You're my boss.' She repeated it continually in her head.

'I know that, and I'm unlikely to forget it, especially when you keep telling me.' He chuckled. 'What I don't understand, is why we can't have a normal conversation.'

Molly clenched her hands by her sides. 'Oh, you mean like this morning, when you clearly didn't want to answer any questions about yourself, and yet you told me off for doing the same thing.'

Andrew's mouth tightened. A sigh finally escaped from him. 'You're right.'

Molly stopped dead in her tracks. Her mouth dropped open a little and she was immediately consumed with guilt. 'You don't have to tell me anything you don't want to,' she mumbled, as her anger ebbed away.

Andrew frowned at her. 'What would you like to know?' He reached for her hand and gently squeezed it. 'Let's see, well, my father…' He stopped talking and took a deep breath. 'His life was spent looking after other people's money, at the London County and Westminster Bank.'

Molly left her hand in his as they stepped forward, enjoying the softness of his touch. She pushed shoulders back and gave a satisfied smile. 'My father also looks after other people's money, only he works for accountants.'

Andrew shook his head and forced a smile to his lips. 'So, we have that in common.' He paused. 'Let's see, what else can I tell you? I was born in London, thirty years ago, and I have lived in the same area for most of my life.'

'Me too, well not thirty years ago.' Molly giggled, relaxing into their conversation.

'I still live in my parents' home.'

'I do too.' Molly frowned as she looked up at him. 'I didn't realise you still lived with your family.'

Andrew's lips straightened as he studied her. 'Would that be horrific?'

Molly shrugged her shoulders. 'No, just unusual, I think.' She hesitated for a minute. 'I mean, for a man to be your age and still living with his parents.' Her lips tightened as she realised she'd said too much.

Andrew nodded. 'Well, I don't live with my parents. I live in their home.'

'Sorry.' Molly looked up at him. 'I obviously misunderstood.'

'No, I'm probably being deliberately misleading.' Andrew sighed, before taking a deep breath. 'My parents died last year.'

'Oh my goodness, I'm so sorry.' Molly stopped walking. Her eyes welled up. 'I should learn to be more careful with what I say. My friends, Victoria and Alice, are always telling me off for not thinking properly before I speak.'

Andrew clasped her hand in both of his. He carried it up to his lips and gently left a lingering butterfly kiss, enjoying the warm taste of her skin.

Molly's stomach somersaulted.

'You have nothing to be sorry about.' Andrew lowered her hand, keeping it clasped in one of his. He turned and stepped forward, keeping his eyes staring straight ahead of them. 'My parents were seeing a show at The Lyceum Theatre.' He sucked in his breath. 'They went outside during the interval, just as a German bomb landed. They didn't survive.'

'Oh my goodness, that was October last year. I'm so sorry.' Molly blinked rapidly in a bid to keep her emotions in check. 'My friend Alice is an ambulance driver, and her sister is a police officer. They were called to that explosion and I believe they worked through the night trying to rescue people. I'm so sorry your parents were among those killed.'

Andrew nodded. 'It makes you realise a few things.' He gave a little laugh, but it was a hollow sound. 'You know, I gave some money to a newspaper boy and told him to save it, and even he said what's the point, because the Germans might get him tomorrow.'

Tears suddenly spilled over onto Molly's cheeks. 'Is that what happened to your coat?' She quickly wiped them away.

Andrew gave a hearty laugh. 'Yeah, I gave it to some old woman. Her needs seemed greater than mine at the time, although I suspect it would have been far too big on her.'

Molly fought the urge to wrap her arms around him and hug him tight.

'Gosh, I need this cup of tea.' Alice sighed as she sat down on the padded wooden chair in Café Monico. 'My feet are killing me.' She closed her eyes for a second. The grandfather clock chimed twice behind her. A cold draught brushed her legs, as laughter came from the doorway, quickly followed by a thud, as the voices faded away. She opened her eyes again, looking around at the diners in the busy restaurant. 'I could do with an afternoon nap.'

Victoria giggled. 'Me too, we've walked miles in and out of shops, up and down Oxford Street, but we've all bought some lovely things.'

Alice nodded and turned to Molly. 'I love those lovely silver earrings you bought for your mother. The scrollwork on them looks so delicate. I'm sure she'll love them.'

Molly laughed. 'I've really enjoyed it, especially Liberty's in Regent Street. That shop sells such beautiful things.'

Victoria picked up the menu. 'That it does. You could spend a fortune in there.'

Molly raised her eyebrows and nodded at the menu her friend was holding. 'Does this mean you're considering having something other than chocolate cake?'

Alice and Victoria laughed at Molly's astonishment.

'I might consider it.' Victoria's eyes sparkled with mischief. 'The food always looks and smells so wonderful in here.' She looked around her, trying to peer at other diners' plates. I know we always have tea, but I'm tempted to have coffee.' She lifted her head slightly, as she noticed a waitress walking in their direction. Her silver tray was laden with several cups and saucers. A little white hat was perched precariously on her dark curls, which telegraphed her approach. She was dressed in the traditional ankle length black dress, covered with a long white apron with frilled straps. The material rustled as she pushed between the large fronds of the potted palms and edged between chairs, trying to reach her destination. Victoria sniffed the air as she walked past their table, taking in the strong aroma. 'Hmm, I can almost taste it. Maybe it'll be coffee for me today.'

Molly's eyes widened. 'Oh wow, things must be on the up, Victoria, for you to be even considering it.'

Victoria grinned at her friends. 'Things haven't been too bad lately. Stephen has been promoted, so he's sending money home, which I'm trying to save for when the war is over. Daisy has been generous with her housekeeping money; thankfully, the police pay well, and I've been doing extra hours at Foyles.'

Molly nodded. 'It all sounds good. I'm pleased about your brother's promotion. Make sure you tell him to keep his head down.'

Alice eyed her friend. 'What about you, Molly? You seem to have more of a spring in your step, since the last time we saw you. I'm assuming you've told your parents about your change of job.'

Victoria gave Molly a steely stare. 'Yes, we had that scary day when your mother came in to buy you a book as a surprise. I was terrified she was going to ask to speak to you.'

Alice nodded. 'So was I. I'm surprised I didn't faint, when I saw her walking towards me with Mr Leadbetter.' Her eyes widened. 'I was convinced they were going to ask me about your new job.'

Molly fiddled with her cutlery for a moment. 'Yes, I'm sorry I put you through that. I had no idea she was going to pay the shop a visit. I don't think she's ever been in there before.' She rested her chin in the palm of her hand. 'Anyway, they know, and predictably it didn't go well, but they appear to have either got over it, or have decided to keep their thoughts to themselves. It suits me either way.' She smiled. 'You know, I think they were hoping I'd find someone from the landed gentry to marry, working at Foyles.' She giggled. 'As if.'

Alice reached out and touched her arm. 'They only want what's best for you.'

Molly's lip curled. 'So I keep being told, but what about what I want?'

Victoria laid the unopened menu on the table in front of her. 'I don't think you appreciate how much you're putting your life at risk, that or else you don't care. Either way, it's worrying. I'm worried for you, so I hate to think what your parents are going through.' She paused. 'I think you're risking losing everything, but I don't understand why.'

The three of them sat in silence, each lost in their own thoughts.

Victoria sighed. 'I want you to think about what I've said, Molly. I don't want to lose a friend because you cannot bring yourself to talk about what is going on inside your head, to bring about your decision to work in such a dangerous place.'

Molly shook her head. 'I had hoped, as my friend, you'd support my decision to do something that would have an impact on the war, but you're no different to my parents.'

'We all care about you and it's because I'm your friend that I'm speaking out. I don't understand the reasoning, and trust me when I say I've thought about it over and over again. I can only put it down to your guilt over Tony, but you putting yourself in danger won't bring him back.'

Molly sniffed as a tear tripped over her lashes and rolled down her cheek.

Alice placed her hands on Victoria and Molly's hands simultaneously. 'Everyone just wants what's best for you, that's all. Have you settled into your new job now? It's been a couple of months.'

'It's repetitive and hard work, let alone the horrendous journey, but it's working out all right.' Molly smiled.

Alice gave her a knowing look. 'You certainly look happier than I've seen you in a long time, so if you're happy, we are too.'

Victoria turned to glare at Alice. Her lips were firmly closed.

Molly looked from one to the other of her friends. 'The pay's good. I wanted mother to take more housekeeping from me, so she could stop working, but she's having none of it.'

Alice shook her head. 'If I recall, your parents are proud and strong minded people. They must be, to have survived what life has thrown at them. It couldn't have been easy for them, growing up with nothing.' She paused. 'It doesn't bear thinking about.'

Molly sighed. She was tired of the sympathy that always surrounded her life. 'Yes, it must have been difficult, but they could have an easier life now, if they chose to take it.' Anger flushed her cheeks. 'As you can probably tell, I'm finding it frustrating that they won't accept my help.'

'Don't get angry with them.' Victoria could feel her eyes pricking with unspent tears. 'Enjoy them while you have them, and they have you.'

Molly looked up at Victoria's watery eyes. 'I'm sorry, don't get upset. I know having lost your parents means you see things differently, and I do love them to bits. I just wish they'd let me help them.'

Alice gave a little smile. 'Just be there when they need your help, that's all you can do.'

Molly nodded. 'I will, and I'm saving what I can.' She picked up the menu. 'I'm still writing to Charles. I thought I'd send him a parcel of goodies, if you don't mind, Alice?'

Alice laughed. 'Why would I mind? I'm sure that young brother of mine is grateful for any parcels or letters he receives. I think it's all that keeps the men on the frontline going.'

'Yes, I must admit it sounds horrendous.' Molly frowned. 'You know, Grace in work doesn't write to her brother.'

'What?' the girls answered in unison.

'I know. It's odd isn't it?' Molly paused. 'She doesn't read a newspaper either, so I did wonder if she couldn't read or write, but I don't know how you ask a question like that.'

Alice looked thoughtful. 'Would she be offended if you asked?'

Molly laughed. 'Oh without doubt. I'd probably be lucky not to be skinned alive.'

Victoria grimaced. 'It's a difficult one. As you both know, my pride would stop me from asking, or accepting help.'

Alice laughed. 'Oh yes, we're very much aware of that.'

A waitress hovered near the table. 'Are you ready to order?'

Victoria looked at her friends. 'Can we have three teas and three slices of chocolate cake please?'

Laughter burst from the girls.

'You and your, "I might order something different."' Molly giggled and shook her head.

Alice looked around the restaurant. 'It's always busy in here.'

Molly followed her glance around the room. Her smile faded and the laughter disappeared, as she noticed Andrew sitting at a table with five other people. All of them were couples. A slim brunette sat next to him and leant over to say something, before resting her hand on his arm and letting out a melodious laugh, which filled the space between them. She couldn't take her eyes off them. Was that his girlfriend, or even worse, his wife? There appeared to be an intimacy between them. Her heart lurched into her mouth. She'd been a fool to allow him to flirt with her. Tony's flirting jumped into her head. How she pretended not to notice the looks and smiles he gave to other women, including Alice. The girls had been right about him, but she hadn't listened. Molly had let herself get carried away, thinking he loved her, but he hadn't. Was she falling for another Tony? She must never allow that to happen again. It was time she protected herself from the pain and heartbreak, which she couldn't let go of. She would never again be someone's plaything, to pass the time until something better came along.

Victoria glanced around her. 'Yes, it's certainly popular. We were lucky to get a table.'

Alice nodded. 'Perhaps we should think about going to the theatre for a change. I love it and don't go very often these days.'

'That sounds good to me.' Victoria looked across at Molly, before turning to follow her line of sight. 'What do you think, shall we make it a date?'

'Molly, you all right?' Alice tapped her arm. 'You've gone quite pale.'

'Sorry, what were you saying?'

Victoria shook her head. 'Nothing, at least nothing important. Who is that man?'

Molly lowered her eyes as tears pricked behind them. She forced a smile as she looked up. 'What man?'

They stopped talking as the waitress appeared, carefully placing the tea service and cake on the table. Nobody moved.

Victoria watched the waitress move away, before whispering to Molly. 'The one who caught your eye over there, the man who made the colour drain from your face.'

'No one important.' Molly forced a laugh. 'He's my boss, Andrew Greenwood. I just didn't realise he was married.'

Alice and Victoria looked in his direction. As he looked over at them, they both quickly looked away. 'They certainly seem close,' Victoria mumbled.

'Watch out, I think he's coming over.' Alice straightened her shoulders and lifted her head slightly.

Molly knew that stance. Her friend was preparing to do battle.

Andrew stood tall, next to Molly, sitting at the table. 'Good afternoon, ladies.' He nodded, glancing down at the cake sitting in front of them. 'Don't they do the best chocolate cake you've ever tasted here?'

'That they do.' Victoria looked up at him.

'Molly, aren't you going to introduce me to your friends?' Andrew's eyes lingered on her pale features. 'Are you unwell?'

Molly cleared her throat. 'I'm fine, thank you.' She couldn't bring herself to look at him. 'Alice, Victoria, this is my boss, Mr Greenwood, Andrew Greenwood.'

Andrew nodded at them in turn. 'It's lovely to meet you.'

'It's lovely to meet you too.' The girls spoke as one.

'I'm sorry to disturb you. I just wanted to say hello and introduce myself to Molly's friends. I'll let you get on with eating your cake.' Andrew nodded and weaved his way back to his table.

Molly watched the willowy brunette turn and look at them, before laughing at something he said.

Alice glanced at Victoria and shook her head slightly.

Chapter 10

September 1916

The black material, behind the curtains up at the dining room windows, shut out all daylight. There was no clue to the weather outside. The standard lamp cast an orange glow in the corner of the room.

Molly squinted as the knitting needles clicked against each other. She pulled at the dark brown ball of wool, trying to wrap it around her fingers, like Alice and her mother did. The wool tightened as she tried to thread it through the needles. 'I'm never going to get these socks finished at this rate, and I wanted to send them in the parcel to Charles,' Molly half mumbled to herself.

Charlotte put down her sewing and smiled at her daughter's concentration. 'I'm sure he'll love them.' She rubbed her eyes and gave a yawn.

Molly giggled, dropping the needles on to her lap. 'That shows how little you know him. Charles won't be able to resist ribbing me to death over them, but that's fine. He'll appreciate the gesture and be grateful for them, but I'd never be surprised to hear he wore them as gloves.' She laughed. 'Mind you, they do look more like mittens than socks.'

Sophie smiled at her granddaughter's frustration. 'Did you have a good day with Alice and Victoria?'

'It was lovely. When you get a chance, you and Ma should have a wander around Liberty's in Regent Street; they sell such beautiful things.' Molly smiled.

Charlotte grimaced. 'A bit out of our price range.'

'Ma, they sell all kinds, and if nothing else, it's lovely to just go and have a look. You don't realise such beautiful things exist in the world.' Molly sighed as a voice whispered in her head. *A bit like the woman on Andrew's arm; she's a cut above you girl. Who was she? Was she his wife, girlfriend, and why didn't he bring her over and introduce her? Why was he flirting, if he was already married? Did he think he could have his pick of the hired help? Was that what he did with Grace, and he's pretending he doesn't know her first name? Is that why Grace doesn't like 'her kind?* Molly shook her head, trying to stop all the questions rattling around.

'Don't shake your head.' Charlotte's words stopped the voice in her head. 'I know you get frustrated with me, but I can't help the way I am.'

'I know, Ma, sorry, I didn't realise I'd done it.'

Charlotte frowned. 'Those earrings you bought for me were beautiful and probably expensive, let alone the perfume you got for your gran. You shouldn't be wasting your money on us.'

'Huh, you speak for yourself.' Sophie chuckled. 'I loved the rose scent; mind you I don't know where I shall ever go to wear it. I don't leave the house very often these days.'

Molly giggled. 'Just wear it indoors. It's for you, not anyone else.'

The clock in the sitting room could be heard chiming six.

Charlotte shook her head. 'I know you mean well, but if you ask me, it all seems a bit wasteful.'

Molly decided it was best to keep silent. She was never going to get her mother to spoil herself, if she didn't want her doing it. She picked up her knitting needles again and gazed down at the most unlikely looking sock she'd ever seen. The rustle of the newspaper made her look up. She'd forgotten her father had carried in another armchair and squeezed it under the standard lamp, in the corner. The paper rustled as he shook it out, to turn the page. His eyes skimming the content, before he turned it over. Curiosity suddenly got the better of her. 'How's work, Pa? You seem to be working longer hours than you used to. Are you short staffed?'

Charlotte sucked in her breath and glared at her daughter. 'Molly, you shouldn't be asking your father such questions. He works hard, and that's all you need to know.'

Jack dropped the newspaper and rubbed his eyes. 'It's all right, Charlotte.' The rustle screamed in the silent room, as Jack closed it before folding it in half and resting it on his lap. 'There's nothing to tell. Naturally, most of the younger men have joined up, but we're managing. It's just a busy time.'

Molly watched him closely. His eyes closed for a second, but not before she'd seen the troubled look he was trying to hide. 'Is it anything you want to talk about?'

Jack took a deep breath, before opening his eyes and folding his arms in front of his chest. 'No, it's just work.'

Sophie glanced across at her son-in-law. 'You look very tired. Be careful you don't overdo it.'

Jack smiled. 'Don't worry, Ma, it's all in hand, and it'll be over soon.' He glanced down at the neatly folded newspaper, lifting his hand to rub his chin.

Molly studied her father. His smile hadn't lit up his face in the normal manner. A quiver ran down her spine. She was certain there was something he wasn't telling them. Two raps in quick succession at the front door saved her father from further questioning. Molly smiled to herself. More like it saved her from getting into further trouble.

Jack looked up from his newspaper and glanced at the clock sitting on the mantelpiece. 'It's ten past six. Are we expecting someone?'

Charlotte shook her head. He got to his feet and took the couple of steps out into the hall. The hinges of the door gave their usual squeak at being disturbed.

Molly stopped knitting. Charlotte sat upright, trying to hear the mumbling from the hall. Sophie half turned in her seat, waiting for Jack to reappear. Molly looked at them both and had to stifle the giggle that was rising inside her.

The screech told them the front door was being closed. Molly smiled as she remembered her first day at the factory, and trying to sneak out of the house. Listening to it now, she wondered how she'd managed it.

Two pairs of footsteps strode down the hall to the back room. Only the odd squeak of their soft soles on the disinfected chequered floor tiles, gave them away. Molly raised her eyebrows. It must be serious. She couldn't remember the last time anyone, outside of her friends, had gone into the sitting room, except to clean it. Charlotte pulled herself out of the armchair. She ran her hands down her black, ankle length skirt and pulled at the bottom of her white blouse, before patting the bun at the nape of her neck. The creaking of the doorknob made them all look round.

Jack stood in front of them, his shoulders back and his chin slightly raised. 'We have a visitor, or maybe I should say, Molly has a visitor.'

Molly frowned and dropped her knitting. 'I'm not expecting anyone.' She took a deep breath. 'I only saw the girls today, and they never said anything about popping round.'

Jack nodded. 'Charlotte, you might want to put the kettle on, after you've met our guest. He's in the back room.' He stretched out his hand for his wife.

She frowned, before taking a deep breath. 'Should I be worried?'

Jack smiled at her and patted her hand in his. 'No, it's definitely nothing for you to worry about.' They stepped forward, before Jack turned round and glanced at Molly and Sophie in turn. 'Come on you two, it would be rude to keep our guest waiting.'

Molly followed her family into the best room of the house, wondering who could be so important they all had to be there. Perhaps there should be a trumpet fanfare to welcome this gentleman, whoever he was.

The best room wasn't grand. One end had been screened off and was being used as Sophie's bedroom. Candles were casting flickering shadows around the room. Thin tendrils of smoke escaped through the glass funnel that covered the flames of the oil lamps. The smell of the burning oil was warming to Molly, reminding her of childhood days and the games they used to play together. When had the shame of the way they lived taken that away? Was it when her father started trying to pronounce his 'h's' and when they started to correct the way she spoke. When did that happen? Was it when his mother had died? She shook her head. When had things changed? When had the laughter died in their home?

Molly could hear her father's deep meticulous tones reverently introducing her mother and grandmother. Her hands clenched by her sides as she stretched her neck, trying to see if he was bowing as well. The familiar voice hit her. What was he doing in her home? She swallowed hard as a lump threatened to block her airways. Her stomach churned. Her palms became damp as her finger nails bit into them. She ran her hands down the side of her skirt.

Sophie stepped aside, slowly lowering herself into the nearest armchair, smiling up at the tall dark haired man.

There he stood, smiling at Molly, like butter wouldn't melt in his mouth. The willowy figure of the mystery woman jumped once again into her mind. What was he playing at?

'Obviously, you know my daughter, Molly.' Jack smiled at Molly. He stood tall and proud, clearly pleased this stranger had knocked on his door.

Andrew nodded. 'Good evening, Miss Cooper.'

Jack beamed. 'Charlotte, make us some tea please.'

Charlotte nodded and turned to leave the room.

'No, please, I have not come to disrupt your evening. I came to return Miss Cooper's bicycle.'

Molly remained silent. She had no desire to be part of this game.

'I insist.' Jack waved his hand at Charlotte. 'And please, call my daughter Molly. After all, it sounds as though you were her knight in shining armour.'

Colour started to rise in Molly's face. Lowering her eyes, she concentrated on the red swirl pattern in the brown carpet. She hoped he hadn't noticed how old and shabby her home was.

'It was nothing.' Andrew's glance bounced between Molly and Jack. 'You have a lovely home.'

Was he laughing at her parents and the way they lived? Molly tried to picture what his family home would be like, and then she remembered his father worked in a bank. Stop it. She pulled herself upright, straightened her shoulders and jutted out her chin. She didn't know why he was here, but she was going to put a stop to it right now. 'Thank you for returning my bicycle, Mr

Greenwood. It was very kind of you, but an unnecessary waste of your time.' Molly gave him a sugary smile, one that she had often used on customers in Foyles Bookstore. 'Pa, we must not hold Mr Greenwood up. I'm sure he has a lot to do.'

Andrew narrowed his eyes as he stared at Molly. 'Please, call me Andrew.' He paused and glanced across at Jack. 'Mr Cooper, I would like to ask your permission to take your daughter out for the evening.' He glanced over at Sophie and gave her a smile, before looking back at Jack. 'I promise no harm will come of her.'

Jack seemed to grow another couple of inches as he stood there. 'Well, Mr Greenwood.' Jack turned and glanced at his daughter, who gave him a wide-eyed stare. 'I would take my hat off to you, sir.' He chuckled. 'If I was wearing one. I admire the old fashioned morals and ways of doing things, so as long as you bring Molly home safe and sound, then I don't see why not.'

Molly's eyes widened. 'Pa…'

Jack held up his hand. 'It's all right, Molly, I'm sure Mr Greenwood is a man of his word and all will be well.'

'But…'

'Please take a seat, Mr Greenwood.' Jack indicated the wingback armchair, next to the fire hearth.

'Please, call me Andrew.' The soft seat of the chair gathered around his legs as he sat down.

'What about work?' Molly blurted out, forgetting all about decorum and social etiquette.

'Tomorrow's Sunday.' Andrew paused. 'Of course, if you don't wish to…'

'Molly.' Jack scowled at his daughter. 'Go and help your mother bring in the tea things.'

Her face flushed with colour as Molly turned on her heels and marched out of the room. Her jaw clenched, as anger surged through her. How dare he just turn up at her home, without an invitation? And as for her father, he hadn't spoken to her like that in years.

'Ah Molly, can you take this for me please.' Charlotte held out a silver tray.

Startled, Molly took the tray from her. 'The best china; he's truly an important guest.' She looked down at the homemade biscuits, haphazardly placed on a plate. 'We are obviously honoured to have such a man in our home.'

'Stop it.' Charlotte frowned at her daughter. 'I don't know what's got into you, but it's always important that we display the best of ourselves.'

Molly lowered her eyes and nodded. She would have to bite her tongue tonight. 'I'll take this in.'

Charlotte's gaze followed her for a moment, before she turned and went back to the kitchen.

Molly forced a smile as she entered the sitting room and placed the tray on a small console table. 'Mr Greenwood, would you like milk and sugar with your tea?'

Andrew's troubled eyes stared at her for a moment. 'Just a splash of milk please.'

Molly poured the brown liquid into the cups. There was a repeated ringing sound as she placed a teaspoon on each of the saucers, before passing them out.

Charlotte came in and placed a Victoria Sponge on the tray. 'Who would like some cake?'

Andrew licked his lips. 'It looks delicious, so I'll try and squeeze in a small piece please.'

Charlotte beamed and started to cut the sponge.

'Molly, I was just telling your father, I have two tickets to see Hobson's Choice tonight, at the Apollo Theatre in Shaftesbury Avenue.' Andrew smiled at her, before moving his glance to take in everyone in the room. 'I understand it's a very good show.' He took the tea plate from Charlotte, along with the cake fork.

Molly frowned. Where did the cake forks come from? She forced a smile and looked over at Andrew. 'Yes, I've heard that too. I mentioned going to see it with Grace and Flo.' She chuckled. 'Although I don't think Flo was that keen.' She sat on the edge of her chair and sipped her tea, pulling back quickly as the hot liquid burnt her top lip. Molly fought the urge to giggle, as she watched Andrew juggle balancing the plate on his lap with holding his cup and saucer, while trying to cut into the cake.

Molly pulled up the collar of her coat. The wind whipped around her and Andrew as they stepped it out in silence, past Soho Square, before turning right into Greek Street. The darkness of the evening wrapped around them. There was no moonlight or stars guiding their way along the road. The shafts of light that used to seep through the curtains of the terraced houses, no longer lit the pavement. No one wanted to help the Germans. A couple of young boys in short trousers were outside the Pillars of Hercules public house, playing war games, waving sticks at each other and shouting 'bang, bang.' As Molly and Andrew walked past, the youngsters could be heard arguing over who was going to be German and who was going to be English.

Andrew shook his head, but remained silent.

A ray of light appeared from a window, as someone was fiddling with the curtains. A man's voice roared from the house. 'Shut those curtains. 'Ow many times do you 'ave to be told? You'll be the bloomin' death of us.'

Andrew took a deep breath. 'It'll be a good thing when this war is over. Everyone is so fearful, although they hide it well.' The children shouted behind them. 'Boys think going off to fight is heroic, and no one corrects them.'

Molly shot him a sideways glance. She wanted to agree with him, but held her silence.

Andrew stared ahead for a moment, before shaking his head. 'You're angry with me.'

Molly stared into the darkness and shrugged her shoulders.

Andrew hesitated, before taking a deep breath. 'You might as well get it over and done with. I can't abide sulkers.'

Molly's hands formed balls by her sides. 'How dare you? I'm not a sulker.'

The sound of his laughter carried in the air. 'Well, I suppose it depends on your definition of a sulker. In my mind you are, so you might as well have your say before you ruin the whole evening.'

Molly sucked in her breath. 'I didn't ask for this evening out, nor did I ask you to just turn up at my home, uninvited.'

Andrew chuckled. 'Ahh, spoilt and ungrateful.'

Colour flushed Molly's cheeks. Her nails bit into the palms of her hands. 'I am not spoilt or ungrateful.' She shook her head. His words echoed those of her mother. 'It's just bad etiquette to come round, when one hasn't been invited.'

Andrew glanced across at her. 'I returned your bicycle, so you can get to work on Monday, or have I spoilt your plans to meet me at the station?'

Molly loosened her collar as her temperature rose. 'I wasn't planning anything. In fact, I hadn't given Monday a thought.'

'Just as well I had then.' Andrew smiled. 'Mind you, a thank you would be nice.'

Molly clenched her lips together, angry with herself at being caught out. 'Yes, you're right, it was very rude of me not to extend my thanks.' She frowned and took a deep breath. 'Thank you.'

Andrew laughed. 'That hurt; I can feel your pain.'

Molly remained silent.

'If I'm honest, I don't understand why you dislike me so much.' Andrew paused for a moment. 'I think you should tell me what I've done to bring about such anger. I don't believe for one minute it's because I turned up at your home unannounced, or because I'm your boss.'

Molly sucked in the cold air and lifted her chin. 'All right, I don't understand why you've asked my parents if you can take me to the theatre tonight.'

Andrew frowned. 'I thought it was the right thing to do.'

Molly's eyes hardened. 'What you don't understand is, you've raised their expectations on something that's going nowhere.' Her mouth clenched into a thin line.

'How do you know it's going nowhere?' Andrew shook his head. 'It sounds like you've written off our friendship, before it's begun.'

Molly could almost feel the steam coming out of her ears, as her anger reached boiling point. 'What about your wife or girlfriend? Won't she have something to say about you taking me out tonight? You know, I'm not part of the hired help that you can pick up and put down. I'm not your plaything...'

'Hold on, hold on.' Andrew lifted his hand to draw an end to her tirade of accusations. 'What wife or girlfriend? Who said I had either?'

Molly glared at him. 'I saw you, remember?'

Andrew eyes darted from side to side, before giving her a blank look.

'Café Monico remember? You came over and met my friends,' she burst out impatiently.

'That was today but—'

'The tall willowy brunette that was obviously very close to you.' Molly lowered her voice to almost a whisper. 'I saw her look over at us.'

Andrew stopped and grabbed her hands, pulling her close to him.

She closed her eyes as his familiar woody scent embraced her. Butterflies danced around her stomach. Her hands rested against the roughness of his woollen coat.

His breath tiptoed across her cheek. 'Are you jealous?'

Molly was silent for a second, trying to control her body reacting to being so close to him. 'No,' she whispered.

'Then why are you so angry with me?'

'I won't be used.' Molly straightened her shoulders and looked up at him for a second, before lowering her eyes again. 'I've heard stories of the rich using their authority over people that work for them. I know women who have done stuff just to keep their jobs.' She let out a low sigh. She was getting proficient at lying.

Andrew jerked his head back slightly. He placed his finger under her chin and gently pushed it up. 'Look at me.'

Molly wanted to shield herself, but she had no choice but to look at him.

'I am not the person you describe. In fact, that's the last person I would ever want to be.'

His voice felt like silk as it wrapped itself around her. Her body softened into his. Her mouth parted but no sound came out. She was unable to take her eyes off him.

Andrew slowly lowered his head and their lips touched lightly. His lips were soft against hers. The bristles on his face rubbed against her skin, adding to the intimacy as their passion grew.

Chapter 11

October 1916

'Good weekend everyone?' Grace called out to the girls, all in various stages of dress, as they changed into the biscuit-coloured overalls.

Flo smiled. 'Just the usual, what about you?'

'Not bad. As you say, just the usual.' Grace looked across and watched Molly tying her hair back with a blue ribbon. 'Very nice, although I don't know who you're trying to impress.'

Molly lowered her lashes. She pulled the soft, silky material into a bow. 'No one, I'm doing it for me, to keep my hair out of the way.'

Flo stepped towards Molly. As usual, she had a look of mischief about her. 'I see your bicycle's fixed.'

Molly looked away and wrinkled her nose as the stench of stale alcohol and cigarettes wafted her way.

'Yeah, I noticed it was out by Frank's shed.' Grace's eyes pinched at the corners as she stared at Molly. 'Did your father fix it for you?'

Molly hesitated. 'No.' She bent down and put her feet in the pumps provided. 'A friend did.'

A bell rang out in the clean area. It was time. They all stepped forward, heading towards their workbenches. One of the older ladies, Nora, bumped into Molly. 'Sorry, lovey, seem to 'ave lost me footing for a moment.'

'Don't worry, I'm fine.' Molly looked at her bloodshot eyes, ringed with dark lines. 'Are you all right?'

Nora cackled. 'Yeah, I'm always all right. I just feel a little wobbly this morning.'

Molly rested her hand on Nora's arm. 'Take care.'

'Don't you worry about me, lovey, I'm fine.' Nora grabbed Molly and Grace's arms as she lost her footing again.

The grip tightened on Molly's arm. She fought the urge to take away Nora's hand, but clenched her lips together, holding in the yell that was itching to be heard.

Grace stared at Nora. 'You do look pale; maybe you should go home and rest.'

'Nah, trust me, I'd rather be 'ere than at 'ome.' Nora grinned, letting go of them and wobbling as she stepped away.

Flo giggled. 'You need to stay off the sauce, Nora.' She made hand gestures of sipping from a pint glass.

'Get away wiv yer.' Nora giggled.

'Come on ladies, less chat,' Andrew shouted into the crowd. 'It's another day and there's no time for talking. Let's get the machines fired up.'

Grace immediately swung round to gaze at him. She stepped forward, but her focus was on him.

'Morning, Miss Fairchild, Miss Cooper.'

'Morning Mr Greenwood,' they answered in unison.

Andrew focused on his notepad. 'Er, Miss Cooper, there's a form I forgot to give you, so if you'd like to follow me.'

Grace eyed them both. 'Do you want me to come as well, just in case Miss Cooper can't find her way back?'

Andrew scribbled on the paper he was holding. 'I don't think that will be necessary, thank you. I'm sure Miss Cooper has been here long enough to understand the lay of the land.'

Molly stared down at her pumps, fidgeting from one foot to the other, wishing the ground would open up and swallow her. What was he playing at?

Grace stared at Molly. 'I'm sure she has.' She marched off to her workbench, closely followed by Flo.

Molly looked around her, before glaring at Andrew. 'What are you playing at?' Her words drowned in the noise of the machines coming to life.

'It's simple, Miss Cooper, you haven't signed a form, so if you could come with me.' Andrew turned on his heels and walked away.

Colour flushed her face. She looked around and saw Grace staring at her. Molly pulled herself up to stand tall, before meekly complying with his instructions. She could feel the women's eyes following her as they weaved in and out, past their workplaces. An older man she hadn't seen before stood next to Nora, who appeared to be gripping her machine, while the man was wagging his finger at her. Molly strode past them and hoped she wasn't in trouble.

Molly chewed on the inside of her bottom lip and kept her eyes forward. Something told her this wasn't going to end well.

'You been a naughty girl?' a shrill voice carried to her.

Molly shrugged her shoulders and smiled in the direction she thought it came from.

'More like going up there to be a naughty girl,' another voice shouted out. 'Perhaps wearing the blue ribbon under that lovely bonnet is to impress the boss.'

Molly's pale face turned crimson, under their scrutiny. Screams of laughter followed her out of the workroom.

Andrew looked over his shoulder at her. 'Take no notice of them. They've nothing better to think about.'

Molly frowned. 'I'm sure that's not true. Most of them have men off at the front, fighting for their lives.' She shook her head at his coldness.

The metal staircase creaked under their feet as they climbed to the office, the same one she had followed him to, just four months ago. Andrew pushed open the door, holding it for Molly to enter first.

Molly physically jumped as the door slammed shut behind them.

'Right.' Andrew stepped towards one of the desks and a pile of papers that were sitting to one side. They rustled as he rifled through them, before finally pulling one out. He scanned the form. 'I need you to read and sign this. It just states that you agree to medicals, as and when required.'

Molly nodded, reaching out and frowning, as her eyes scanned it. 'I thought I'd already done this.'

'Well if you have, I'm sorry.' Andrew sighed. 'I appear to have mislaid it.'

Molly stared at him for a moment, wondering what was going on inside his head, and what this was really all about. 'It's not a problem, I'll sign it.' Picking up the pen that was lying on the desk, cold against her warm fingers, she scribbled her name at the bottom of the form. 'Is that it?' she asked without looking up.

'Yes,' Andrew mumbled. 'Yes thank you.' Keeping his eyes fixed on the paperwork. 'I'll walk back down with you, because I need to speak to a couple of the other women as well.'

'That's all right, I can find my own way.' Molly turned and reached for the door handle.

Andrew smiled. 'Don't you want to be seen with me?'

Molly laughed, letting go of the handle. 'Oh yes, that went so well when we came up here, don't you think?'

Andrew laughed. 'They're just messing. That's what it's like, working in places like these.'

Grace stopped dead, halfway up the stairs, as Molly and Andrew's laughter rang out. Tension ran through her veins. A low growling noise escaped from her throat. She pursed her lips and turned tail, to go back to her workplace. She had what she came for.

Charlotte cut into her meat and potato pie and placed a small piece on the end of her fork, before glancing up at her family around the dining table. 'I hate this time of year. It's getting colder now and the nights are drawing in.

I think it's safe to say winter's on its way.' She placed the fork into her mouth.

Molly looked across at her mother sitting opposite her. 'Ma, that was lovely.' She looked down at her empty plate and pushed her knife and fork together, straightening them like soldiers standing to attention. Molly dabbed the white napkin on her lips, before folding it into a square and placing it on the matching crisp tablecloth. 'You make the best meat and potato pie.'

'Thank you.' A smile spread slowly across Charlotte's face until her eyes were sparkling. 'Mrs Tyler gave me some apples she'd got hold of, so we have a pie for afters.' Charlotte clapped her hands with excitement.

Sophie put down her fork. 'I can't remember the last time we had apple pie.' She rubbed her stomach. 'It's always been our favourite, hasn't it, Molly?'

'Most definitely.' Molly smiled. 'With lashings of custard, of course.'

Sophie chuckled. 'Mind you, I'm not sure I've room for a piece right now, but give me half an hour.'

'I know what you mean.' Molly gulped from the glass of cold water next to her, letting it remove the last pieces of pastry from around her teeth.

The front door slammed shut and several footsteps clip-clopped rhythmically down the hall. They all looked to the doorway. Muffled voices could be heard going into the back room.

Charlotte frowned as she glanced over at the clock; half past seven. 'Perhaps your father has brought someone home from work.' Her hand reached up and smoothed her hair back into the bun, sitting at the nape of her neck.

The beat of Jack's familiar footsteps sounded along the hall. They all looked expectantly at the dining room door. He removed his overcoat. 'Molly, Victoria Appleton is here to see you. I've put her in the back room.' He turned round to hang it up.

Molly frowned as she stood up to leave the table. 'I didn't hear a knock on the front door.'

Jack stepped back into the room. 'No, I met her outside. We arrived at the same time.'

Molly smiled. 'Sorry, Ma, my slice of apple pie will have to wait.' She pushed her chair back under the table; wondering if now would be a good time to talk about Andrew. He never seemed to be out of her thoughts. She longed for him to hold her hand and for his lips to kiss her so tenderly again, yet she knew it was wrong. She didn't become a canary to fall in love. With a sigh, she stood up. 'I best go find out what's brought her here.'

Sophie gave a small smile. 'I hope everything's all right.'

Molly stepped away from the table. 'I'm sure it will be, but I must admit it's unusual for Victoria to be out visiting at this time of night, especially on her own.' Walking out of the room, she ran her hands down her navy blue skirt, while her curved heels clipped on the floor. Molly took a deep breath and pushed open the door to the best room, not noticing the lack of objection from it. Victoria came into view, pacing around the room.

Molly's heart raced and she was momentarily stunned into silence. 'Victoria, is everything all right?' Her stomach lurched into her throat. 'It's not Stephen, is it?'

Victoria stopped pacing around and gave Molly a watery stare. Her hands held on to each other as though her life depended upon it. 'What? Sorry no, as far as I know, my brother's fine.' She held up crossed fingers. 'I have no wish to tempt fate by saying that.'

Molly sped towards Victoria, frowning as she wrapped her hands around hers. 'What is it? You look like you've been crying.'

Victoria's chest lifted as she took a deep breath. 'I do have news, but you need to sit down.'

Fear gripped Molly. She stood rooted to the spot. 'It's not the baby, is it?'

'No.' Victoria shook her head. 'No, Arthur's fine.' She sighed and looked down at her feet, before taking another deep breath. 'I fear Alice's parents are going to need their little grandson more than ever right now.'

'What's happened? It's not Charles, is it?' Molly's eyes began to fill up. She dropped into the nearest chair, as her vision became blurry.

Victoria knelt down beside her and clasped her hands.

A yelp escaped from Molly. Her chest became tight as she tried to hold it all together.

'You have the wrong brother. It's Robert.'

'Oh, thank God.' Molly covered her face with her hands, as the tears cascaded down her pale features.

Victoria gave her a hug, while making comforting noises.

Molly pulled back and dropped her hands onto her lap. 'I'm sorry. Thank goodness Alice didn't hear my reaction.' She shook her head. 'Thank goodness she isn't here.'

Victoria gave her a squeeze. 'Alice is looking after her mother, who collapsed when the telegram boy arrived.'

Molly nodded. She remembered seeing the telegram boy in her own street, dropping his news and cycling off. Everyone knew it was bad when he didn't wait for any reaction. Women had been seen screaming and collapsing on their doorsteps. 'How long has Robert been missing?'

Victoria sighed and stood up. 'He's not missing.'

'Oh God.' Molly jumped up, her legs wobbling under the sudden movement. 'Mr and Mrs Taylor must be in a terrible state.' Her bottom lip quivered, while her voice moved up a pitch. 'We must go and see Alice. She'll need us now, more than ever.'

Placing her hand on Molly's arm, Victoria whispered, 'I think they need to be left alone to grieve.'

Molly nodded and dropped back into the armchair. 'Do they know how or when? Not that I suppose that matters.'

Victoria shrugged her shoulders. 'Apparently he died a hero, saving lives, but I don't think that's making Mrs Taylor feel any better. He was somewhere near the River Somme, which I believe is in France, although I'm not sure that's right.'

'That poor family.' Molly shook her head and frowned. 'It's everyone's worst nightmare.' A light knock on the sitting room door interrupted her meanderings.

The door slowly swung open and Charlotte's head poked around the corner. 'Can I interest anyone in a cup of tea, and maybe a slice of apple pie?'

Victoria forced a smile. 'Thank you, Mrs Cooper, just tea for me, but only if it's not putting you to too much trouble.'

Charlotte's gaze darted from one girl to the other. They had clearly been crying. She drew her eyebrows together. 'Molly?'

'Just the tea for now, Ma, thank you.'

Charlotte lingered, before nodding and leaving the room.

'I don't like feeling so helpless.' Molly stood up and walked around the room. 'Is there nothing we can do for them?' She glanced across at Victoria.

'I suppose we just have to keep an eye on them from a distance, and be there when required.' Victoria shrugged her shoulders. 'I don't know what else we can do.'

'That's all very well, but I don't see much of Alice, now I'm not working at Foyles, and I don't want her thinking I don't care.' Molly clenched her hands by her sides.

Victoria shook her head, but remained silent for a few minutes. 'Alice knows you care. We all worry about each other.' She took a deep breath, wanting to change the subject. 'You know, we worry about you in your new job.'

Molly raised her eyebrows. 'Why?'

Victoria shrugged her shoulders. 'You know why. We also get a sense that there's something you're not telling us.'

Colour began to fill Molly's pale skin. 'I don't think there is.'

A smile played on Victoria's lips. 'How come you've gone a delicate shade of pink then?'

Warmth invaded Molly's body. 'I don't know what you're talking about.'

Charlotte, carrying a silver tray, pushed open the door with her elbow. 'You all right, Molly? Have you got a temperature?' She quickly sat the tray down and looked nervously at her daughter.

'No, Ma, I'm fine,' Molly snapped, before taking a deep breath and forcing a smile. 'Sorry, I just felt a little hot for some reason.'

Victoria smiled as she walked over to the tea tray. 'I'll pour it, Mrs Cooper. You go and put your feet up.'

Charlotte nodded and left the room.

'You should be kinder to your ma. One day, she won't be here, and then you'll be sorry for everything you ever did wrong, no matter how small it was at the time.' Victoria added a splash of milk to each cup, before lifting the teapot.

Molly sighed. 'You're always telling me that.'

Victoria looked across at her friend. 'Then it's about time you started listening to me.' The teaspoon clinked against the side of the cup as she stirred the tea, then clattered as she dropped it on the saucer, before handing the drink to Molly. 'So what's going on?'

'What do you mean, what's going on?' Molly raised her eyebrows. 'Nothing's going on.'

Victoria laughed. 'You never were any good at hiding things, so you might as well tell me now because I'll only nag and get on your nerves, then we'll have a falling out.' She walked over and sat down on the chair near the fireplace.

'You don't know everything, you know.' Molly curled her lip. 'There's nothing to tell you.' She put her cup down on the side table, next to her chair.

'See that.' Victoria pointed her finger at Molly, waving it around in a small circle. 'That thing you do with your lip. That tells me you're hiding something.'

'Oh shut up, little miss know it all.' Molly fidgeted in her chair, before picking up her cup of tea again. She sipped the hot liquid, searing her mouth in the process. Damn Victoria, and her superior attitude. Her tongue ran along her sore lips.

'I'm sorry, Molly. Don't be cross with me.' Victoria paused. 'I shouldn't have asked, especially after the news about Robert, but I was just trying to help.' She lowered her eyes and stared at her tea.

'It's terrible news about Robert, and I feel for Alice and her family, but if I'm honest, I didn't know him like I do Charles.' Molly looked down, studying the cup in her hand. 'You know, Robert never really spoke to me.'

Victoria nodded. 'I know what you mean. Alice admits that Robert didn't get involved in their lives, except to tell them what to do, but maybe that's what first-borns are like.' She laughed. 'After all, I'm a first-born.'

Molly looked over and giggled. 'Yes, you have a point there, but what does that make me, because I'm a first and last born.'

Victoria rolled her eyes. 'Confused.' She laughed. 'You're bossy, but you have no one to order around.' Both girls laughed and the tension between them was broken. 'You don't have to tell me tonight, but I know something is wrong, and whatever is going on in our worlds, we are there for you.'

'I know, and I'm there for you too.'

Victoria glanced sideways at her, under the guise of drinking her tea. 'It's something to do with your boss, isn't it?'

Molly closed her eyes for a second, as the tell-tale heat rushed into her face.

'I knew it.' Victoria laughed triumphantly. 'Has he taken your fancy? He's not making your working life difficult, is he?'

'No, no, it's not what you think.' Molly caved in.

'Then tell me what it is.'

Molly sighed. 'I can't. It's too complicated.'

Victoria sucked in her breath. 'Oh god Molly, you're not...'

'No, I'm not pregnant.' Molly slammed her cup and saucer onto the side table. 'You know, whenever I have a problem, you always ask me if I'm pregnant, and I always tell you I'm not that sort of girl, but you seem to have a problem believing that.'

'I'm sorry. You're right, I do ask that a lot and I don't actually know why.' Victoria bit down on her bottom lip. 'Do you have feelings for him?'

Molly sat still for what seemed an eternity. Only the ticking clock on the mantelpiece broke the silence in the room. 'I don't know. He seems to bring out the worst in me, and yet I long to be in his arms at the same time.'

Victoria smiled at her friend's troubled expression. 'Sounds to me like you're smitten.'

'Yes, well, I can't be. Grace loves him.' Molly frowned, jealousy rushing at her from nowhere. Her eyes welled up.

Victoria put down her cup and stood up. She rested her hand on Molly's arm, giving it a gentle squeeze. 'Does he love her?'

A frustrated sound escaped from Molly's lips. 'He said he didn't even know who Grace was when I mentioned her. He only knows her as Miss Fairchild, but...' She shook her head. 'But Grace melts every time he's anywhere near her.'

'But if he doesn't feel the same...'

'You don't understand.' Molly fiercely shook her head and took a deep breath. 'Grace already hates 'my kind', whatever that is and for whatever reason, which is definitely unclear to me. I don't want to add to it.' Her voice dropped to a whisper. 'Also, I don't want anyone in my life after Tony. Why would I want to put myself through that again?'

Victoria squeezed Molly's hand. 'Don't you think you should ask what her problem is with 'your kind', and then maybe tell her how you feel about him?'

Molly fought the urge to scream. If only life was that simple. If she knew what her feelings for him were, then life might become simpler.

Chapter 12

Molly's arms ached as she lifted the broom handle, ready to stem the black powder into the nose of the shell, shuddering as the sulphur hit the back of her throat. She wrinkled her nose. Would this taste and smell of rotten eggs ever go?

She'd slept fitfully, blaming the rain lashing against her window in the early hours. Thoughts of Alice and her family jumped into head, quickly followed by Tony. Her eyes tightened and her nostrils flared. If she'd still been working at Foyles, she'd have found out how Alice's family were coping. Molly shook her head. Her hours were long and, thanks to her job, she felt their friendships had suffered, and Victoria hadn't hidden her disapproval about her working at the munitions' factory. She sighed, knowing she also wouldn't have met Andrew and all the turmoil that came with him, but whose fault was that? Frowning, she wondered what could be done to rectify it, short of giving up her job.

'What's your problem?' Grace stared at Molly.

Molly jerked as the voice invaded her thoughts. 'What?'

'I said, what's your problem?' Grace's eyes narrowed as she studied her.

Molly rammed the broom handle into the shell, before mumbling, 'No problems here, Grace, no problems here.'

Grace sneered. 'Oh, I think you have lots of problems.'

Flo glanced from one to the other. Her eyes sparkled with excitement.

Molly's head jerked up. Fear ran down her spine. She looked around and the women close by were staring her way. 'What's going on?'

'You tell us.' Grace's lips thinned into a straight line. 'You tell us what gossip you've been passing on to the man in your life'

The clatter of the broom handle hitting the floor alerted Molly that it had dropped from her hand. Her eyes widened. 'I don't understand.' She pinned back her shoulders. 'I don't have a man in my life.' Aware that a couple of the women had stepped closer to her, she lifted her chin. 'I have no idea what's going on, but whatever it is you think you know, you're wrong.' Her fingers twitched by her sides.

Flo's lips lifted at the corners. She stared at Molly from across the worktable. 'Did you notice Nora's not in today?'

Molly glanced round to the machine Nora normally worked on, but another woman was standing there. 'No, I didn't. Is she all right?'

Flo snarled. 'She came in this morning, but Mr Greenwood sent her home, because she was unsteady on her feet. There's even talk that she came in drunk.' She took a deep breath. 'I can't help wondering how he knew about Nora in the first place.'

Molly frowned. 'Well don't look at me. I didn't even notice she wasn't in today.'

Grace glared at her. 'No, but you went up to his office to sign a form, remember?' She paused, studying Molly closely. 'I came up to the office and heard you laughing, so maybe you told him then that Nora had problems.'

'Yeah,' someone shouted from behind her.

'No. No. I signed the form and came out.' Molly could feel panic rising in her chest. 'I've nothing to tell him, and anyway, why would I?'

'It's not how we work here. We stick together.' Grace pointed at her. 'This is exactly why I don't like your kind. You're all the same.'

Flo smiled at Molly, before glancing across at Grace. 'I'm sure Molly wouldn't have said anything. She's one of us now.'

Molly and Grace both stared at her. Molly was thankful, if not suspicious of Flo's reasons for defending her. Grace had disbelief written all over her face.

'What's going on here?' Andrew's voice rang out above the din of the machinery. 'There's no time for gossip. Remember, the boys on the frontline urgently need these shells.'

Flo looked to Grace to say something, but there was a gooey look in her eyes. 'Mr Greenwood.' Flo hesitated. 'We were just wondering where Nora is today.' She stared at him. 'I saw her earlier, but she's not here now.'

He held her gaze. 'Nora?'

Flo lifted her chin. 'She worked the machine over there, where that new woman is.'

Andrew nodded. 'You don't need to worry about Nora. Your job is to fill shells and let me worry about everything else.'

Grace pulled her body up, straightening her shoulders. 'So there is something to worry about then?'

Andrew stared round at all the women. His expression gave nothing away. 'You need to worry about the men on the frontline, suffering under the constant bombardment of the Germans. And that's all you need to worry about while you are in this factory.'

The women lowered their heads, as they slowly turned back to their jobs. Mumblings could be heard over the machinery. 'Nora wasn't drunk; she doesn't drink any strong stuff,' a voice shouted out in defiance.

'That's right,' another voice joined in.

Molly looked around at everyone as they suspiciously eyed up Andrew and her. She couldn't let the women think she was a snitch. Nora deserved more than that, as indeed did she. Molly licked her dry lips. 'Mr Greenwood, sir.' She hesitated for a moment, looking around, taking in the expectant faces eagerly waiting to hear what she was going to say. She knew this was going to sink any relationship she had with Andrew. What relationship? Molly shrugged her shoulders. She didn't want a relationship, with him or anybody else, or all the heartbreak that went with it. 'If Nora has been sent home, let alone sacked, she will lose money, and that's something she can't afford to do. None of us can.'

Murmurs travelled around the room. Molly even thought she heard someone clap.

Andrew glared at her. 'Miss Cooper, Nora will not be losing money, and I'd appreciate it if you'd all get on with your work and stop worrying about other people's business.'

Her name was cold on his lips. So this was how it was all going to end. Molly's eyes held a spark of steel about them. 'People care, sir, and it's that caring that makes this country great.'

The women cheered and clapped around her. Molly dared to look across the table to see Flo clapping and cheering, while Grace nodded in her direction, remaining stony-faced and silent.

Andrew opened his mouth to say something, but quickly closed it again. He turned away and marched out of view.

Flo jumped up and down on the spot and clapped her hands. 'Well done, Molly. That certainly told him. Hah, he'll think twice about coming down here and throwing his weight around again.'

Colour seeped into Molly's face. Her heart sank.

Grace turned and glared at Flo. 'Mr Greenwood's right. The men need these shells, so stop messing about and get on with your work.'

Molly nodded at them both. She lowered her eyes and stared hard at the black powder waiting to be pushed down into the shells in front of her. Bending down to pick up the broom handle, a sigh escaped from her as she wondered how she got caught up in this mess. The last thing she'd wanted was to take Andrew on at work. Was their friendship now over? She had to go back to thinking of him as Mr Greenwood, the boss. Molly had to stop thinking about his butterfly kisses and his arms wrapped around her. The question remained though, did he ever see her as anything other than a worker he could use as a distraction.

Andrew marched past the women, weaving his way through the machinery, oblivious to the overpowering smell of sulphur that never seemed to leave the factory. Their clapping and cheering followed him, echoing in his mind, standing above the usual daily grinding of the machines and metal.

Why had Molly taken him on like that, trying to belittle him in front of everyone? Hadn't he always been kind to her? He shook his head. After all, he'd fixed the tyre and returned the bicycle to her home. *She didn't ask you to*, his conscience argued. *You weren't being kind at all. You had an ulterior motive, because you wanted to see her again*. His chest heaved as he raced along, wanting the refuge of the office, away from prying eyes.

His father's voice bellowed in his mind; *I told you to never mix business with pleasure*.

Andrew straightened his lips and shook his head. 'I know, I know.' He should have known better and listened to Molly. She'd tried to keep him at arms' length, by constantly telling him he was the boss, but something had driven him on. He'd always kept a distance between himself and the people that worked there, until now. It had to stop. She had thrown down the gauntlet, but he had chosen to walk away. The lines had been drawn. He needed to make sure, in future, he didn't step over them, and put her out of his head.

The metal staircase to his office creaked as the toes of his soft-soled shoes touched each step. Flinging open the door, he stepped in, before slamming it shut behind him. The door shook and rattled when the catch caught in the lock. He threw his papers onto the desk and paced around the office. His face flushed and his hand clenched by his side. Damn her. He should never have allowed her to get under his skin. He dragged out his wooden chair, too angry with himself to notice or care about the legs scraping across the floor. Andrew threw himself down on the seat and pressed his fingers to his eyes, before leaning back against the hard slats that offered support. He ran a hand through his hair and let out a sigh. What a fool he'd been.

Andrew took a deep breath and began scanning the paperwork sitting in front of him. He sighed as he picked up his pen to scribble notes and sign documents. It felt heavy as it balanced awkwardly between his fingers. His frustration took over as he threw it back down on the desk. Damn her. How had she managed to get under his skin? He jumped up, making a grab for the chair, as it fell back towards the floor. His head and heart were pounding in time with each other. The need to escape the self-imposed prison was great, but it was out of the question. Andrew paced around, wringing his hands, stopping only to massage his painful forefinger, which was stiff and unyielding.

A sound escaped from him, similar to an injured animal. How had he managed to get himself into this situation? He would stay away from her from now on. That was all he could do, wasn't it? Perhaps trying to talk to her would be the answer. Maybe explain his feelings towards her. Stunned, he flopped back down on the chair. He murmured into the empty room. 'Feelings, what feelings?' He ran his hand through his short hair. 'What feelings? Who knew I had any feelings?' Perhaps the doctors had been right. Maybe he did have a self-destruct button.

The brass knocker thudded onto the front door in Carlisle Street. Molly looked out of the dining room window and gasped. Her hand automatically lifted, to fiddle with her gold heart necklace. She heard her mother's heavy footsteps in the hall.

Sophie frowned as she glanced up at her granddaughter. 'Is everything all right?'

Molly nodded in silence, her fingers combing through her hair, unable to peel her eyes away from the window. The winter sun was trying to break through the grey clouds that threatened to rain on them. The squeals of children could be heard, as they jumped in the puddles created overnight. Women's high-pitched voices shouted at them, only to be followed by more squeals of delight. The Saturday morning weather hadn't deterred him, as he stood tall in his grey winter coat. His black shoes, although wet, were polished until a reflection could be seen in them. He looked round, as though sensing someone was watching him. She took a step back into the room, before turning round and catching her grandmother staring at her.

'You look lovely dear. Perhaps it's time you gave him a chance.' Sophie lowered her eyes and ran her fingers down the material she was holding.

Colour seeped into Molly's face.

'This old shirt of your father's should have been used for rags a long time ago.' Sophie pulled a tiny white button away from the fabric and wedged the small sewing scissors under it, before closing them. The button dropped and chinked into an old tin, nestling on her lap. Lowering the scissors, she fished out the button, so the thread could be pulled from it.

Molly concentrated on the button tin, mesmerised by the various colours and shapes. Where had they all come from? She had no memory of anyone wearing the more flamboyant colours, but did remember playing for hours with them, when she was a girl. Life was simple back then. How she would love to have those days of innocence back again.

Sophie looked at her granddaughter. Her young face had become ashen as she stared at the buttons. 'You need to let it out.'

Molly jerked back, her memories snatched away. 'There's nothing to let out.'

Sophie opened her mouth to speak, but the door opened, stopping her in her tracks.

'Molly, you have a visitor.' Charlotte lowered her voice. 'It's Mr Greenwood. I've shown him into the best room.' She smiled. 'He seems a very nice man; so polite.'

Molly raised her eyebrows. She'd have to watch her parents. They'd have her married off before she knew it. Hard working, honesty and manners was everything to them. A smile formed on her lips; what more could she ask for? 'Thanks, Ma. Did he say what he wanted?'

Charlotte frowned at her daughter. 'No, and I wouldn't be so impertinent as to ask.'

Molly sucked her lips in for a moment, before taking a deep breath.

'Go on,' Charlotte whispered, waving her out of the room. 'It's rude to keep a visitor waiting. You should know that.'

Molly let her breath out slowly, before breathing in again. Her heart was racing. She could swear it was trying to jump out of her chest, and that was before being in the same room as him. Her heels clipped rhythmically along the hall, to the back room. She paused, taking another deep breath, before pushing the door open.

Molly forced a smile. 'Good morning, Mr Greenwood.'

His eyes held a flint-like quality. 'I thought we had established you would call me Andrew, when we're out of work.'

Molly nodded slowly. 'I'm not sure it's appropriate.'

Andrew's lips tightened. 'I see.'

There was a knock on the door and Charlotte stepped into the room. 'Mr Greenwood, may I offer you a cup of tea?'

Andrew forced a smile in her direction. 'Thank you, Mrs Cooper but, if I have your permission, I would like to take your daughter out for a walk.'

Molly gasped. 'Unfortunately, that's not possible, Mr Greenwood. I'm helping my mother with some sewing.'

Confusion ran across Charlotte's face as she glanced at her daughter. 'That can wait. The fresh air will do you good.' She frowned at Molly, before turning her best smile on Andrew. 'Let me wrap up some cake for you to have later.' Charlotte turned away from them. 'I'll fetch your coat, Molly.'

Andrew opened his mouth to speak, but Charlotte was already out of the room.

Molly glared at Andrew. A smile slowly spread across his face. Instinct told her he knew what he was doing.

Five minutes later, they were leaving the house, with Charlotte's voice trailing after them. 'Have fun; there's no need to rush back.'

'Thank you for the cake, Mrs Cooper, it is most generous of you.'

Charlotte beamed. 'You are most welcome. Enjoy yourselves.'

Mrs Taylor was on her knees, scrubbing her doorstep. She stopped and smiled as they walked past. Molly could feel the colour rising in her cheeks as she fell into step, next to Andrew. She was relieved the pungent smell of disinfectant didn't follow them down the road, into Sutton Street.

Andrew chuckled, his breath a white vapour in the cold air. 'I think your mother likes me.'

A disparaging noise escaped from Molly's throat. 'Don't read too much into it. They would like Jack the Ripper if he was polite, hardworking and honest.' She pulled up the collar of her coat as the cold air licked around her neck.

Andrew threw back his head, as a deep belly laugh filled the air around them. He gasped for breath. 'Are you trying to say I'm nothing special?' He chuckled. 'But she gave me cake.'

Colour flooded Molly's cheeks, the heat burning against the cold air. 'When you put it like that, it sounds as though I was being impolite. I just meant...'

'Oh I know what you meant.' Andrew let out a little sigh, before smiling. 'You do like to keep me on my toes, but I like that.'

Molly looked up at him. His normally stern features were transformed when he laughed. His eyes sparkled, and crinkled in the corners. Whatever haunted him at work seemed to disappear when he relaxed in her company.

'Actually, if you don't mind, I'd like to drop this slice of cake home before we go anywhere. It's not far and it would be a shame for it to get crushed in my pocket.'

'Of course.' Molly sighed. 'I don't understand this need to feed everyone, especially with the food shortages, but she won't listen.'

Andrew lowered his eyes. 'My mother was the same; apparently, it's the done thing.'

Without a word, they both turned left into Charing Cross Road.

Molly frowned as she stared straight ahead. 'Why have you manoeuvred me into this outing today?'

Andrew's mask was back in place. 'I wanted to talk to you, and you wouldn't have come out with me if I hadn't just turned up.' The corner of his lips lifted. 'I must admit, your mother was an added help.' He chuckled. 'I think she'd be quite happy if we were to marry.'

Molly stopped dead in her tracks. 'Marry?'

Andrew took in the fear that ran across her pale features. 'Don't worry, that wasn't a proposal.' He chuckled as Molly stepped forward, guiding her into New Oxford Street. 'It was just an observation.'

They ambled in silence for a few moments, each lost in their own thoughts. Andrew grasped Molly's hand and threaded it under his arm.

Molly's fingers curled into the softness of his sleeve, gently rubbing the woollen material between her thumb and forefinger. She looked up at him, as he looked down. Their eyes locked. Her heart pounded in her chest, trying to escape its confines, while butterflies flitted around in her stomach. She took a deep breath, in an attempt to slow the overwhelming urge to hold him in her arms again. His woody scent tingled in her nose. There was no doubt she was falling headlong in love with him. This was the man who brought out the worst in her, every time they had a conversation.

Andrew cleared his throat, breaking the tension that hung in the air. 'Was your father not at home this morning?'

Molly lowered her eyes, momentarily unable to form a sentence. She took a moment, taking slow, deep breaths in and out for a few seconds. 'He's at work. I don't know what's going on, although I'm certain something is, but he's not talking about it.' She frowned and looked ahead. 'He works so hard, and yet they don't seem to reap the rewards for it.'

'If I remember correctly, he works for the Gettin family, or I should say their firm of accountants.'

Molly nodded.

'I believe my father used to deal with them at the bank.' He paused for a moment. 'From what I remember, I got the impression there were quite a lot of under the table deals going on at the Gentleman's Club old Henry Gettin used to attend. I think people used to call him The Accountant.' Andrew chuckled to himself.

Alarm bells rung in Molly's head. Frowning, she looked up at him. 'You seem to know quite a lot about them.'

Andrew laughed. 'It's just stories. Men are worse than women when it comes to gossip.' He looked at her troubled expression and squeezed her arm close to his body. 'Don't worry, it's probably a busy time for them.'

She hoped he was right, although she couldn't shift the niggling doubt, which told her otherwise.

Chapter 13

Andrew and Molly turned into Bury Street. Black ornate railings framed the front of the six-storey, red brick houses. The many large sash windows had decorative scrollwork above them. The black front doors stood proud and imposing.

Andrew's keys jangled together as he pulled them out of his trouser pocket. 'Here we are.' He turned to her and smiled. 'My guess is, there's no point offering you a cup of tea.'

Molly raised her eyes heavenward. 'That's correct.'

Andrew laughed as he pushed open the heavy door. 'It's a shame, because I have some delicious cake, made by someone I know. It won't be of interest to you, but she has a wonderful daughter. She's feisty and gives me a hard time, but lovely all the same.'

Molly shook her head at him, despite the smile creeping across her face.

'Come in.' Andrew waved the piece of wrapped cake. 'I'll just put this in the kitchen.'

Molly closed the door behind her, shutting out the cold breeze. Turning round, she stood transfixed, watching a white feather float softly back down to the hall table. Was this Andrew's? Was he a conscientious objector, a coward? Tony's face jumped into her mind. She shook her head. Molly caught sight of her reflection in the mirror, above the table, telling herself it was nothing to do with her. She couldn't go through it again. Determined to ignore it, Molly ran her fingers through her hair, smoothing it out. She tweaked at her small black earrings. Her attention was drawn to a framed photograph of a couple gazing at each other, clearly in love. Were they Andrew's parents? Her eyes were drawn back to the feather. Should she ask him, or ignore it? Did it matter? She had made that mistake before. Andrew's soft footsteps on the pristine black and white tiled floor alerted her to his presence. She wondered how long he'd been standing there. His face looked grim as she jumped away from the table, hoping he hadn't noticed her staring at the feather. 'I…er…I was just admiring the photograph.' She paused, but didn't meet his eyes. 'They look a lovely couple. Are they your parents?'

Andrew stared at her for a moment, his lips set in a grim line. When he spoke, his tone was void of any emotion. 'Yes. Shall we go?'

Molly's throat tightened, as his familiar mask slipped into position. She turned and opened the front door. The cold air rushed in, causing her to shiver.

Andrew stepped forward and glanced down at Molly. 'I know it's cold and damp, but I thought we could take a walk to Hyde Park; take in some fresh air.' He tucked her arm in his.

Molly sucked in her white wispy breath. Her heart missed a beat. Was he intending to spend all day with her? 'That would be nice, after being shut inside the factory all week.'

Andrew placed his hand over hers as they walked on in silence, towards New Oxford Street.

Despite the cold, warmth coursed through Molly and a smile spread across her face.

Andrew stepped aside to avoid a child that had abruptly stopped in front of him. 'Sorry.' He looked back at the child, who was now making shooting noises at another boy. 'They think it's all so heroic.'

Molly immediately thought about the white feather. Should she ask him about it? She followed his gaze, before taking in his troubled expression. 'They're children. They don't know any better.'

'I know.' Andrew sighed. He watched the boys enjoying their game for a moment. He opened his mouth to say more, but closed it again.

They turned into Oxford Street and were immediately caught up amongst the crowd of shoppers. Wooden carts cluttered the footpath as the sellers tried to sell their wares. The waft of hot pies and jacket potatoes tickled at Molly's taste buds. Men and women walked past them, cradling cups of hot soup in their hands. The steam of the hot food clashed with the cold air. It was normal to see men in army uniforms, enjoying the atmosphere of the London streets. Molly often wondered whether they were home on leave, or new recruits, but as she got closer she could tell which were the battle-weary, trying to hide their pain behind smiles and laughter. Women police officers mingled with shoppers and sellers alike, sometimes shaking a pointed finger at individuals, but always giving a ready smile to all.

Andrew nodded at a nurse as they walked past her. 'Anyway, what made you give up your job at Foyles? I can't think of anything better than working with books.'

Molly laughed. 'You make it sound like a glamorous job.' She looked up at him. 'Although I did love it.'

Andrew gazed at her smiling face for a moment. 'So why did you leave?'

Molly shrugged her shoulders. 'I believe you've asked me that before.'

'Have I?' He grinned. 'I obviously wasn't happy with your answer then.' Chuckling to himself, he steered her around a group of old men standing on the street corner, puffing on their cigarettes.

Molly coughed as she breathed in the smoke; the acrid taste hit the back of her throat.

Andrew frowned as he gazed down at her. 'Are you all right?'

The men's raised voices followed them along the street as they argued their views about the war.

Molly nodded, clearing her throat at the same time.

Andrew studied her for few seconds, before carrying on with their conversation. 'You still haven't told me.'

Molly smiled up at him. 'There's nothing to tell. I just wanted to do my bit for the war effort.'

Andrew glared down at her. 'That's nearly a really good answer. You do know you're putting your life at risk every day, working at the munitions' factory?'

'I've heard stories.' Molly concentrated on not bumping into people, randomly stepping out of the shops.

Andrew let out an exasperated sigh. 'Stories? Did you know Nora died?'

Tears immediately pricked at Molly's eyes. 'No, everyone thought—'

'Yes, I know everyone thought I'd been mean to her, because the assumption was made about her drinking.' Andrew glared ahead of him. His fingers tightened into a fist. 'None of that is true. Apparently, half of her throat had been burnt away by the sulphur, but she had no idea and passed away, the day I sent her home.'

The tears began to roll down Molly's cheeks. Was that what happened to Sissy? Was that what was going to happen to her? Fear gripped her heart and the pain formed a band around her chest. Everyone's words of warning filled her head, but once again she hadn't listened to them. Did she want her family to go through the grief of losing their only child? Her gran's words, as she lay dying, suddenly bounced into her head. 'Be brave little 'un, this is the right order of things'. Molly took a couple of slow breaths, trying to relieve her pain and heartache. Was she intentionally trying to change the order of things? Was her life so worthless to her now?

Andrew squeezed her hand. 'Are you all right?'

Startled out of her soul-searching, Molly stared straight ahead. 'Everyone thought you'd fired her.'

Andrew half shook his head. Dismay ran across his face. 'Everyone has such a high opinion of me.'

With her free hand, Molly swiped away her tears, while her fingers squeezed his arm tight to her. 'I'm sorry, I didn't realise.'

Andrew raised his eyebrows. 'No, but it doesn't stop me being the bad person, does it?'

Molly remained silent for a moment. 'That poor family; how will they pay for the funeral? I got the impression they didn't have much.'

'Don't worry, it's been taken care of.' Andrew sighed as his grim features stared ahead.

Molly nodded, wondering how it had been taken care of, but didn't like to ask. 'Do the others know?'

Andrew shook his head. 'You're the only person I've told.'

Molly's eyes fixed on the arches, just ahead of them. 'I'm sorry for misjudging you.'

Andrew grimaced. He continued to stare ahead of them, oblivious of the people around him. 'I'm getting used to it.'

Molly sighed. 'I deserved that.' She lowered her lashes and her tone dropped to a whisper. 'Poor Nora.'

They remained silent as they reached Marble Arch, slowing down to admire the carvings. The magnificent gateway towered above their heads, as they walked alongside it. Hyde Park was just ahead.

'This park is beautiful; we're lucky to have it in the middle of London.' Molly gazed around her. The rain had given the grass a new lease of life and it was a luscious green.

'Shall we head for the lake?' Andrew smiled. 'Have you ever been here on Christmas Day?'

Molly raised her eyebrows quizzically. 'No, why?'

'Apparently, you can watch people swim in The Serpentine. It happens every year on Christmas Day.'

'Really.' Molly frowned. 'That water must be freezing.'

Andrew laughed as he gazed down at her. 'I think that's the whole point of it.'

Molly shook her head. 'They must be mad.'

'You don't fancy giving it a go then?' Andrew chuckled.

'I assume that isn't a serious question.' Molly looked at him as if he was mad, before sighing. 'No I don't.'

Andrew's eyes sparkled with mischief. 'You say no to me quite a lot, you know.' A chuckle escaped. 'Perhaps one day, we could go on an organised date, one where I'm not forcing myself upon you.'

As always, Molly's hackles rose to the occasion. 'For that to happen, you would have to ask me, instead of just randomly turning up at my home.'

Andrew smiled at the anger glinting from her eyes. 'Are you always so tetchy, or am I just the lucky one?'

Molly's anger fled as quickly as it had arrived. 'You seem to bring out the worst in me.'

Andrew gave a hearty laugh. 'And despite that, here I am. Hmm, I'm not sure what that says about me; perhaps I'm a glutton for punishment.' He chuckled to himself. 'If I'd have asked you, would you have said yes?'

Molly looked up at his knowing expression. Her lips lifted at the corners. 'No.'

Andrew threw back his head with laughter. 'Hence why I randomly turn up at your home.'

'You need to know, Mr Greenwood—'

'Look, if we are going to spend the day together, I insist you stop this Mr Greenwood nonsense and call me Andrew.'

Molly sighed. 'That's all very well, but you are still my boss and what's more, I'm not the hired help that will be your beck and call girl.'

Andrew stopped dead, pulling Molly round to face him. He stared at her in disbelief, before he spluttered. 'What?' He shook his head and stepped forward again. 'What kind of man do you think I am?'

Molly stayed silent as her thoughts ran wildly around her head. His distaste for what she'd said wrapped around her. She had overstepped the mark with him.

Andrew shook his head. 'I knew you had a low opinion of me, but yet again, I can't believe you think so little of me.'

Molly blinked rapidly as her vision blurred. She stared hard at the wet ground in front of her, before whispering to him, 'It's not that I think so little of you. I just—'

'Just what?' Andrew squeezed her arm close to his body. 'Think all men want to take what they can get from the hired help, as you put it, and if they don't agree, they lose their jobs, is that it?' He stopped and pulled her to him. He shook his head as he stared at her.

Molly's heart pounded as she tried to pull away, but he held her close.

Anger glinted from his eyes. 'Do you mean like this?' He lowered his head.

Molly gasped. His heart was pounding against her chest, matching her own. His lips brushed hers. The people and the noise around them fell away as his musky smell filled her being. Their breaths mingled as their lips parted. All common sense forgotten, she pulled him closer until there was no space between them. Her lips met his. It was no longer an innocent tease, but a fiery passionate kiss. Her hands caressed his back. All control was lost. She had no desire for the kiss to end. Andrew pulled his head away. His rasping breath told her he felt the same, but was it real?

Andrew cleared his throat. 'I think we need to walk, before things get out of hand in the middle of the park.'

Colour flooded Molly's face. He took her hand and placed it back under his arm. 'Sorry, that wasn't meant to happen.'

Molly stared at the ground as she fell into step with him. Embarrassment flooded through her veins. She felt sure the heat from her body would stop winter from arriving, for at least a couple of months. Hired help or not, he clearly regretted their kiss.

Molly and Andrew walked on in silence through the park, which Molly was thankful for. Shame threaded through her. She was sure her cheeks were crimson in colour, yet there was nothing she wanted more than to be in his arms again. She had to stop thinking about it, about him. Molly shook her head and forced herself to concentrate on her surroundings. She looked around, as if seeing everything for the first time.

The green grass was barely visible in places, littered with the various shades of red, amber and gold of the autumn leaves, which had swirled down from the trees. The bare branches reached up into the grey skyline, as they began their winter sleep. The breeze lifted the leaves to dance at their feet, paying homage to the already forgotten summer.

'It's a beautiful time of year isn't it?' Molly murmured as her head twisted and turned, taking in the array of colour that lay at their feet. 'I truly hate the greyness of the season, but these colours are beautiful.'

Andrew allowed his gaze to follow hers. 'Indeed it is. We're quite fortunate to have this on our doorstep.'

Molly nodded. 'It's almost an end of something, and the promise of new things to come.' She looked up at him. 'Do you think this war will ever end?'

Andrew nodded. 'We have to hold on to the hope that it will end soon.' He paused for a moment. 'There's talk that Lloyd George could soon be our Prime Minister, so that should give us some encouragement that it will soon be over.'

Molly frowned and tightened her lips. 'My father has said something similar. I just want it to end. It's ripping families apart and I don't know anyone that isn't affected by it.'

Andrew nodded.

'My friend, Alice, lost her older brother recently. He'd enlisted just before the war began and was somewhere near the Somme when he died. I need to see her, but don't wish to intrude on the family's grief. I know her mother will be distraught. It's hard to know what to do for the best.' Molly's mind drifted back to Tony. 'It's an awful situation to deal with.'

Andrew remained silent.

'Of course, me being me, I encouraged someone to enlist.' Molly paused, before carrying on in a whisper. 'He was my boyfriend at the time and didn't want to, but I told him there was shame that goes with not doing so.' Molly blinked rapidly, sucking in the cold air for a few moments. 'I was a fool and have to live with the fact I sent him to his death. I've done a lot of growing up since then.'

'Don't be hard on yourself.' Andrew paused as he glanced down at her. 'It's what you are meant to believe. You only have to look at the posters that are pasted on every available surface.'

Colour drained from Molly's face, as a tear rolled down her cheek. 'Yes, I know, but if I'd known then what I know now, I would have done things differently.' Her fingers ran over her damp face.

Andrew's gaze had a steel-like quality to it. 'Did you love him?'

Molly pulled her lips in for a few seconds. 'I thought I did at the time, I was heartbroken when I found out he'd died, but I don't think I really knew what love was. It would never have worked. He was a womaniser, lovely and charming, but still a womaniser. Looking back, I think he only wanted to be in my company because he fancied my friend, Alice. He saw her as a challenge, because she wasn't interested in him.' She took a deep breath. 'Having said all of that, it doesn't stop the overwhelming feelings of guilt about sending someone to their certain death.'

Andrew nodded and squeezed her arm close to him. 'It's awful for everyone.' He paused, before taking a deep breath. His voice was low and devoid of all emotion. 'The men at the front are concerned about their families back home, while the families get very little news about what's going on, so they worry about their men.'

Molly's head jerked up. She hadn't heard him speak in such dead tones before. 'It sounds like you're speaking from experience.'

Andrew stared ahead.

Molly remained silent, hoping he would offer something of himself to her, but the silence hung heavy in the air between them. She sucked in her breath. Her hand swung by her side, clenched into a ball. 'When I first met you, I thought you were going to be called away to the front. I mean, you had the typical army haircut that's seen on new recruits.'

Andrew stayed silent as he continued to stare straight ahead. His body tightened.

Molly, oblivious to his change of stance, carried on. 'It's a wonder you haven't been called up, with conscription I mean, but perhaps your job's too important for that to happen.' She looked up at him. 'Although, you say you've only worked there for a few months.' A pulse throbbed at the side of his temple, and his jaw clenched tight. He didn't look at her; his gaze darted around. She waited for a few moments, before continuing. 'Have I spoken out of turn?'

A bitter sound erupted from Andrew. 'No, you have made the same assumptions that everyone seems to.'

'I'd say I'm sorry, but if you aren't prepared to talk about things, that's what happens. I won't be pussy-footing around you. Since I've met you, life seems to have become so difficult and complicated. My friends always say I speak before I've thought things through, but—'

'Hah, tell me about it.' Andrew's eyes crinkled at the corners, as he looked at her. 'I have never known anyone to be as difficult as you.'

'Difficult?' Molly spat. 'You're the one that doesn't give an inch, and what's more, you seem to ignore everything I say. I know nothing about you, except you're the boss at the factory, and you tragically lost your parents in the bombing last year.'

'Which is more than I know about you.' He paused for a split second, as he took a breath. 'Let's see, you have issues, lots of them and—'

'No I don't.' Molly's hackles were up.

'Yes, you do. You think everyone wants to take advantage of you—'

'Not everyone. I just won't be someone's plaything.' Molly lowered her voice. 'I will not give my love away to just anyone. I've done that before and it hurts too much.'

Andrew pulled her round to face him. 'Is that what I am, "just anyone"?' He wrapped his arm around her, pulling her in close. 'You are the most frustrating person I have ever met.'

'But I thought—'

Andrew's mouth crashed down on hers, pressing hard to silence her. Molly's eyes closed as she became lost in the warmth of his lips bruising hers. Her annoyance ebbed away. His scent enveloped her and her temperature soared as breath was ripped from her lungs. She didn't notice their cold noses brushing against each other. His lips softened as they began to caress hers. A groan escaped from her as his hand moved into her hair, while the other pressed into her back crushing her to him. Her hand moved over his back, enjoying the touch of his taut muscles, hidden under the soft texture of his coat.

He slowly lifted his head. The cold air clashed against the warmth of her lips, jolting her back to reality. Her eyes opened slowly. His eyes stared back at her, smouldering with passion. She knew he had felt the same ravaging abandonment that made you want to carry on, regardless of the rights and wrongs of it.

Molly tried to make sense of what was happening to her, but her mind and body weren't co-operating. She just ached for his kisses and his touch. He slowly lowered his head again. Their lips touched lightly, giving the butterflies permission to gently flutter their wings in her stomach. Andrew's hand moved to her face and his thumb caressed her cheek. Her body trembled and her back arched as she pulled him closer, never wanting it to end.

Andrew pulled away from her.

Molly felt bereft of the warmth of his touch, and slowly opened her eyes, to stare into his. His smouldering look told her he didn't want it to end, but she knew, like he did, they had to walk on before they got arrested.

*

They walked in silence. Molly struggled to understand how someone she was always at odds with, could bring her body to life with such passion. The world, and the people around her, had fallen away with the sparks he had ignited within her. Shame flowed through her veins as she realised she would have given her all to him there and then, had he not pulled away when he did.

'Mr Greenwood,' a young woman's voice called out behind them. 'Hello, Mr Greenwood.'

Without looking round, Molly snatched her arm away from his.

Andrew narrowed his eyes, staring at Molly before he spun round. 'Good afternoon, Miss Attwood, isn't it?'

'Yes, sir, I didn't mean to disturb you, but I thought it would be rude of me to see you and not say hello.' Flo gave a beguiling smile, before turning to Molly. 'Hello, Molly, this is an unexpected pleasure.'

Colour flooded Molly's cheeks. This was rapidly turning into her worst nightmare. She painted on her smile, before turning round. 'Hello, Flo, what brings you to Hyde Park?' Her eyes darted around, looking to see if she had anyone with her.

'I'm just out walking.' Flo paused, as her eyes darted from Molly to Andrew. 'I like to get out at the weekend, you know, get a bit of fresh air after being cooped up in that factory all week.'

Panic swept over Molly. How long had she been there? Had she seen them kiss? Would she tell Grace or the others? What would it matter? Grace didn't like her anyway. She cleared her throat, wishing she could remove her coat, as her temperature was suddenly soaring. 'Yes, it's a little damp, but a lovely day all the same.'

Andrew frowned at Flo. 'You appear to have come a long way for your walk. Are you on your own?'

Flo gave an innocent smile that didn't reach her eyes. 'Yes, sir, some people seem to be finding a lot of pleasure in the day.' Her eyes fixed on Molly.

Colour flooded Molly's face, as she realised Flo had seen them together. Fear wrapped itself around her heart. She could feel the beads of perspiration forming on her forehead.

Flo nodded at them both. 'It's a bugger working Sundays, but I'll see you there tomorrow.' Before either of them could answer, she had turned and was walking away.

Molly's eyes widened and her voice wavered, as reality hit her. 'She saw us.' She clenched her jaw, jumping when a dog barked, somewhere behind them. Her gaze followed Flo until she was out of sight, then it bounced around, but nothing registered. 'What am I going to do?' She took a deep breath, continually moving her weight from one foot to the other. 'I need to calm down. Everything will be all right.' She lifted her hand and rubbed her forehead, frowning as she did so. 'That's it, that's what I need to do, calm down.'

Andrew pursed his lips together as he watched her. He stood tall and rigid, his neck muscles pushing out against his skin. He turned and strode away.

Molly followed him, having to run a couple of steps to keep up. 'Doesn't it bother you?' she called out. 'I suppose it doesn't, because you're the boss, so it's always a feather in your cap.' She collided into his back when, without warning, he stopped dead.

He turned, his face contorted with rage. 'Will you please stop with the boss allegations? I have never taken advantage of anyone. Yes, maybe I shouldn't have forced my company on to you, and that could be something I shall live to regret, but that's it. There's nothing else, that's it.'

Tears tripped readily down Molly's face. 'She saw us kiss.'

Andrew pulled her towards him, wrapping his arms around her, before speaking in a low whisper. 'You don't know that.'

Molly snuggled into the safe haven of his arms. She gulped, trying to catch her breath. 'I'm pretty certain, and she'll tell the others.' She paused, before looking up at him. 'And then there's Grace; she loves you so much.'

Andrew shook his head. 'You must have that wrong. I have never done anything to encourage her, or anyone else for that matter.' A wry smile spread across his lips. 'Well, except you that is.' He squeezed her tight. 'That's why you think so badly of me, because you have the perception that I've done it to all the workforce. Well, I can assure you I haven't.'

Molly wiped away the dampness from her face.

'Come, there's a seat over there, let's sit down.' Andrew clasped her hand in his and led her to the wooden bench that was nestled under a tree, with colourful leaves surrounding it. 'Be careful, some of the leaves are slippery underfoot.'

Molly pulled a handkerchief from her coat pocket as she sat down on the damp wood. Her fingers rested on the seat, but immediately pulled away from the slimy residue of the rainfall. She blew unceremoniously into the lace-edged, cotton square. The waft of lavender, from the flowers her mother placed in her drawers, immediately calmed her. 'Sorry, my mother is always saying I'm not very lady-like, although it's not through her lack of trying to teach me.'

Andrew laughed as he sat down beside her. 'You are your own person, and I like that.' He pulled her hand into his and rested them both on his leg. 'Why does it bother you so much?'

Molly wondered if she would ever tire of the softness of his touch. Colour immediately began to fill her cheeks. 'Oh, it doesn't bother me at all.' She brushed the handkerchief across the end of her nose. 'On the other hand, my parents have grand ideas that I will marry well, and to do that, you have to act like a lady.'

Andrew threw his head back with laughter.

Molly frowned as she watched him. 'I know it's funny, but it's not that funny. I can act like a lady when I want to.'

The laughter gradually died on his lips. 'I wasn't talking about your manners.' He shook his head in disbelief. 'I was talking about Flo Attwood seeing you with me.'

Molly shrugged her shoulders. 'I don't know. They think I'm something I'm not. Grace thinks my "kind" whatever that is, can't be trusted. Someone, somewhere, has wronged her and when she finds out we've spent time together, it will prove her right. I'm sure they think I'm a spy for you, or have you in my sights for a husband.' She closed her eyes for a moment. 'Right from the beginning, Grace thought I was too posh to work at the factory, but now there's a little respect for the work I'm doing. I'm proving her wrong.' Her hand screwed up the handkerchief, her fingers continually kneading it. 'Grace adores you, so if she gets wind of this, my life will be hell.'

Andrew gave her hand an extra squeeze. 'I'll talk to her. There'll be no bullies where I'm in charge. If she can't behave, she'll have to go.'

Panic gripped Molly. 'No, no you can't do that. Don't you see? That will make matters even worse.' She stared down at her feet. 'Besides, Grace had three jobs before coming to work at the factory. She shoulders a lot of responsibility, looking after her father and the rest of the family.' Molly paused, before lowering her voice. 'If anyone goes, it should be me. I'm the one that doesn't fit in. I don't fit in anywhere.'

'I think you should just wait and see what happens. Running away never solved anything.' Andrew rubbed his chin. 'Perhaps ride the storm and see where it ends up. After all, if we are going to be together, they're going to have to get used to it.'

Molly took a sharp intake of breath. 'Be together?'

Andrew turned to look at her, the passion lighting up his eyes. 'You can't deny what you feel, after today.'

Molly lowered her eyes as her vision became blurred. 'No I can't deny it, but life isn't as simple as that. Haven't you been listening? It's not just about you and me.' She snatched her hand away as she stood up and started to walk towards Marble Arch.

Andrew yelled, 'Wait, you can't just walk away.' He rushed towards her, pulling at her arm.

Molly swivelled on her low heeled ankle boots. Her eyes welled up and her tone was low. 'That's exactly what I must do. I'm sure you'll thank me, one day.'

Andrew loosened his grip on her arm.

She couldn't look at him. Molly refused to think about the passion, and the love she was throwing away. This wasn't what she wanted, but she had to think about Grace, even if she hadn't thought about that other woman. Guilt stormed at her from all directions. What had she become? She needed to avoid him at all cost. As she fled, tears streamed down her face. There was no stopping to admire the wonderful arches, and she didn't notice the inquisitive stares as she strode past people. There was no looking back; she just had to keep going. Loneliness wrapped itself around her, like a shroud. She marched along, not really knowing where she was going, and refusing to look back. She could hear her father's words in her mind. *Only look back to remember where you've come from, and when things go wrong, learn from it.* How she wished she could talk to him. He was a wise man, but he wouldn't understand this. She wasn't sure she did. Molly swiped away her tears. Anger gripped and squeezed at her heart. Once again, she had been a fool with her love, except this time it was different. He wasn't good for her, and what about the woman she saw him with at Café Monico? Why hadn't she asked him about her?

Chapter 14

'Molly, what on earth's the matter? You look dreadful.' Alice dropped the book she was holding and rushed round the wooden counter to her friend, wrapping her arms around her. She didn't notice the customers and staff in Foyles were stopping to stare in their direction.

'Oh Alice, I've been such a fool.' Molly fell into her arms and sobbed.

Alice sucked in her breath as she saw Mr Leadbetter approaching them. He pulled out his fob watch and checked the time, as he strode towards them.

'Mrs Leybourne.' Mr Leadbetter frowned, his eyes full of concern, as Molly's body wracked with sobs. 'Miss Cooper is clearly upset, so would you like to take her somewhere to give her comfort.' He wanted to ask questions, but didn't relish getting caught up in a woman's delicate problems that could lead to embarrassment. 'The shop's due to close in five minutes, so you might as well leave for the day.' He looked towards the payment booth and saw Victoria craning her neck. He sighed. 'I'm not going to get any work out of you or Miss Appleton now, so she may as well finish as well, what with the three of you being as thick as thieves.' He hesitantly lifted his hand to pat Molly's arm, but thought better of it.

Alice patted Molly's back; her shoulders shook with each tear that fell. Her body gulped for air as her hands gripped on to her. 'Thank you, Mr Leadbetter.'

He nodded at Alice, before turning to walk towards the payment booth.

Alice could feel her friend's heartbreak. She lowered her voice to almost a whisper. 'Come on Molly, let's go out the back, so I can collect my things.' She hoped and prayed nothing had happened to her parents. She steered Molly to the back of the shop. Customers and staff turned to give sympathetic looks.

Molly kept her head down as she shuffled along, her body ravaged with pain. She was certain no one would understand how someone she had known for barely six months could mean so much to her. He had crept into her heart while her back was turned.

Victoria ran over, almost colliding with them as they took a step forward. 'What's happened?'

Alice shrugged her shoulders and whispered, 'I've no idea.'

'Let's get her out of here and find somewhere we can talk.' Victoria ran ahead, to collect their belongings and clock them both out. Two minutes later, she was clad in her winter coat, and handing Alice her things.

Molly looked up. Her face was red and blotchy, but her desolation was confirmed in her puffy, bloodshot eyes. 'I'm sorry.' She sniffed, wiping her damp handkerchief across her eyes. 'I shouldn't have come here, but I didn't know where else to go.'

Victoria shook her head. 'I don't know what's happened, but you listen to me, Molly Cooper, we're your friends so you always come to us, anytime, day or night. That's what friends are for, and don't you forget that.'

Molly gave her a watery smile. 'Yes, mother.'

Victoria grinned. 'That's better, that's the Molly I'm used to, not the quivering wreck that's standing in front of me.'

Alice shook her head. 'Let's go somewhere we can talk.'

The three of them turned round and left the shop, Molly, flanked by Alice and Victoria. They walked on in silence. Without a word, Alice opened the door of a small tearoom. A bell rang out at the same time, letting everyone know there were customers. Victoria gripped the door handle, letting it gently close behind her. The chiming continued until it gradually faded away. An elderly waitress shuffled over to them. A white-netted hat covered her grey curls, but the black dress had seen better days.

'Good afternoon, ladies.'

Alice smiled at the waitress. 'Good afternoon, we would like a table for three please.'

The waitress' gaze slipped over the three of them. 'Of course, would you like one near the window, or can I interest you in one tucked away, with more privacy?'

Alice cast an eye over her friends, before looking back at the waitress. 'I think we'll have the one with more privacy please.'

The waitress nodded and led the way to the corner of the room, before pulling out the dark oak chairs. 'I shall be back shortly, to take your order.' She smiled and wandered over to another table.

Victoria looked around. It was no Café Monico, but it was clean. Several of the tables were being used, mainly by older people, but she recalled her mother saying many years ago that, where you see older people eating will be good value. She removed her coat and untwisted her woollen scarf from around her neck, while watching Molly do the same. Victoria glanced across at Alice, raising her eyebrows and shrugging, before sitting down at the table.

Alice frowned as she looked across at Molly, staring at the white tablecloth. She watched her rub the gold heart that hung around her neck; the gift the staff at Foyles had given her the day she left. She placed her hand on Molly's arm, feeling her jump at her touch. 'What is it, Molly?' She waited, but there was no response. 'Are your parents and grandmother all right?'

Molly's eyelids shot open wide, but when she spoke her words were barely audible. 'Yes, yes, they're fine.'

Victoria forced a smile. 'Everyone at Foyles has been asking after you, even Mr Leadbetter.'

Molly's lips thinned for a moment. 'I should never have left. I've been an idiot.'

Victoria leant forward to say something, just as the waitress returned to take their order. She sighed, eyeing her with frustration.

Alice forced a smile. 'Can we please have three teas and three portions of chocolate cake?'

The waitress nodded as she scribbled it on her pad, before moving away from their table.

Molly took a deep breath, trying to stop the wobble she felt sure would be in her voice. 'Good old chocolate cake.'

Alice glanced at her and Victoria. 'It's almost become our own little tradition. Whatever's happening in our lives, good or bad, chocolate cake marks the occasion.'

Molly twisted her handkerchief in her lap. She felt a fool for going to Foyles in such a state. She blinked rapidly as the pinpricks hit the back of her eyes again; surely there couldn't be any more tears to come out.

Alice blindly fiddled with her napkin. Her gaze didn't move from Molly, she had never seen her in such a state, except when Tony–

'So, Molly, what's going on?' Victoria interrupted Alice's musings.

The waitress sidled up to the table and placed a china tea service in front of them. A large white teapot and a small milk jug were centred on the table, along with a sugar bowl. Laden tea plates were placed in front of them, each serving of cake looking like it could feed a small family.

Victoria watched the waitress move to clear another table. 'Well? Come on, what's going on?'

Tears rolled down Molly's cheeks. No words came. She flicked her fingers across her cheeks as the saltiness rested on her lips.

Alice grabbed her hand. 'Molly, you do know you can tell us anything.'

Victoria lifted her eyebrows and half smiled at Molly. 'If you don't tell us, I will have to ask if you're pregnant, despite promising never to ask you again.'

Alice chuckled.

Molly groaned. 'I've fallen in love.'

'Gosh,' the girls said in unison.

Molly couldn't help but smile at their shocked expressions.

'I don't understand.' Victoria frowned. 'That's a good thing, isn't it?' She turned to look at Alice for confirmation. 'Isn't it?'

'Molly, you're clearly not happy about it, so does that mean he's not free to love you in return?'

Molly silently shrugged her shoulders.

Victoria looked around, before whispering across the table. 'Is he married?'

Molly sniffed. 'I don't think so.'

'Does he love someone else?' Alice asked, wishing Molly would just tell them everything.

Victoria gasped. 'Why don't you just tell us everything, so we don't have to keep asking questions?'

Molly sighed. 'You saw him in Monico's.'

Alice and Victoria's eyes darted left and right, as they tried to remember.

'Ah.' Alice lifted her hand. 'You mean your boss, the one with the stunning lady on his arm.'

Molly nodded. 'That'll be it.' She sighed. She picked up her fork and prodded at the cake in front of her. Then there's also Grace to throw into the mix, she thought. Perhaps eating chocolate cake is not a good idea. She let the fork fall onto her plate, unable to look up at her friends, as colour flooded her cheeks.

Victoria let out a heavy sigh. 'I might have known.' She quickly scanned the tearoom before whispering. 'I thought we discussed this some time ago.'

'Wait.' Alice frowned at Victoria. 'I don't remember talking about this.' She put her fork back on her plate. 'When was it?'

Molly shook her head. 'Does it matter?'

'Obviously not, sorry.' Alice lowered her eyelashes.

Molly closed her eyes for a moment. 'I'm truly sorry. I've been so wrapped up in myself, I haven't even asked you how the family are coping with the news about Robert. They must have been devastated; it's the wrong order of things.' Molly stood up, her chair scratching along the wooden floor. Customers turned to stare at them. 'I'm sorry; I shouldn't have come to you, particularly when you have enough on your plate to deal with. I don't know what's happening to me.'

Alice grabbed Molly's hand and squeezed it tight. 'Molly, you should always come to us. It's what we're here for.' She paused. 'You're right, it is the wrong order of things, but I suppose we've been expecting the telegram since the war began. I'm thankful my mother is improving every day. The baby is a godsend and he gives her such pleasure.'

Molly nodded. 'Alice, you've been a good friend to me over the years, picking me up when I fall. I'm ashamed not to have returned the favour, but there's no doubt we come from different worlds.' Molly pulled her arm to walk away, but Alice's grip tightened. 'I need to go.'

Alice shook her head. 'We might have started off in "different worlds" as you put it, but you've been part of my world for as long as I can remember. We're as good as family, and I'm not going to let you just walk away from us. We're better than that, and what you don't realise is, underneath it all we're all the same.'

Victoria blinked rapidly as she stared at what was unfolding in front of her. 'Molly, sit down.' She reached inside her skirt pocket for her handkerchief. 'We all come from "different worlds" but, thanks to the war, we all need each other more than ever now. And actually, what's more important, we've always been there for each other, no matter what.' Victoria sniffed and dabbed at her eyes. 'Now look, you've made me cry.'

Molly flopped down in the chair. 'I'm sorry, I didn't mean to. I've felt quite lonely since I left Foyles. Life has got so complicated. I love a man that is out of bounds to me because Grace loves him, and I can't talk to her about it because she doesn't like "my kind", whatever that is? He just turns up at my home unannounced, and they all seem to love him. Then there's the white feather in his hall. Flo is just out to cause trouble, but I don't know why. Today, she saw us kissing in Hyde Park, so goodness knows what she'll have to say about that when I go into work. It's all such a mess.'

'Take a breath, Molly.' Victoria reached over and held her hand. 'We need to talk all this through and see what we can come up with.'

Alice nodded. 'I never realised.'

Molly gave them both a watery smile. 'It's easier to hide stuff when you don't see each other every day.'

Both girls nodded.

Victoria picked up her cake fork, letting it swing up and down in her fingers. 'I think this could be the most important piece of chocolate cake we may ever eat in our entire lives.'

Molly and Alice both smiled at the dramatic statement.

'We need to drink our tea, while it's still warm.' Victoria's hand rested against the outside of the pot. 'My mother, and I'm sure all our mothers, think a good cup of tea solves everything, so let's put it to the test.'

Molly forced a smile. 'It would have to be one helluva cup of tea to sort this mess out.'

Victoria placed her fork back down on her tea plate and picked up the teaspoon, to give the pot a stir. 'It does need to be a strong cup, that's for sure.'

Alice smiled her thanks to Victoria, before turning to Molly. 'Did your boss say anything to Flo? When she saw you, I mean.'

Victoria carefully pushed the full teacups nearer her friends, before wrapping her hands round her own and taking a sip.

'No.' Molly shook her head. 'It doesn't seem to bother him, but then, he's not working with them like I am.'

'Is that why you were in such a state when you came into Foyles?' Victoria took another sip. 'Don't let your tea go cold.'

Alice did as she was bid and picked up her cup.

'I don't know why I was in such a mess.' Colour flooded Molly's cheeks. 'I hadn't wanted his kisses to end, so when I heard Flo's voice, it was like a bucket of cold water had been thrown over me. Panic set in and I just ran.' Molly picked up her cup. 'I feel so stupid now.' She held the cup tight to her body and sipped the warm, dark brown liquid.

'You shouldn't feel stupid.' Victoria replaced her cup on its matching saucer and gave Molly a wry smile. 'God, I can tell you about stupid, over and over again.'

Alice smiled. 'Can't we all? Molly, have you thought about talking to Grace about what she means by "your kind"?'

Molly shook her head. 'She used to be in domestic service and, I don't actually know why, but I got the impression something happened to her.'

'You could be right.' Victoria sighed. 'I've heard stories of what it used to be like for some young girls in that situation. I've even wondered if that's why Daisy hated it so much, but I haven't asked her, as there seems little point now. But as far as Grace is concerned, unless you ask her, you'll never know and even if something did happen, it's not your fault.'

'I know.' Molly gave a little smile. 'To be honest, she scares me a little.'

Both girls glanced at each other, before giggling. 'Sorry, what have you done with Molly?' Victoria gasped.

'What?' Molly arched her eyebrows. Her gaze darted between the two girls.

Alice dabbed her napkin at her eyes. 'Oh you do make me laugh, Molly. What is it Mr Leadbetter said to you on your last day at Foyles... let me think... oh I know, "rumour has it you are not to be crossed" and that's the Molly we all know and love, so what have you done with her?'

Molly's lips tightened into a straight line, as she recalled that conversation. 'If I remember rightly, I told him it was all about fitting in and being respected.' She glanced from one to the other of her friends. 'And, I guess, yet again, I just don't feel as though I fit in there. It feels like I have to keep proving myself to them every day.'

'Then you need to stop doing it.' Victoria picked up her fork. 'I'm determined to try this cake.' She pushed the prongs of the fork into the end of the sponge. 'If you think about it, you're trying hard but you aren't getting anywhere, so stop trying and just be yourself.' She lifted the fork with a small piece of cake balancing precariously on the end. 'Think about it, what's the worst that can happen?' The cake disappeared into her mouth and she closed her eyes as she chewed, making noises to indicate it was lovely.

'I hate to say it but Victoria's right.' Alice glanced across at Molly, before looking down at her plate. 'If they don't like or trust you, at least you'll be happier with yourself.'

Molly nodded. 'I suppose you're right. It's hard work trying to fit in with people all the time.'

Victoria waved her fork in Molly's direction. 'That's because you either don't know or understand, what they want from you. That's why it's more important to be yourself. Let them all get on with it. Eat your cake, I'm not getting fat on my own.'

Molly giggled and prodded at her cake. 'Is it as nice as Monico's?'

The girls laughed before speaking as one. 'Nothing is as nice as Monico's.'

Molly looked around the small tearoom for the first time. It wasn't fancy, but it was clean and apparently, most important of all, the chocolate cake was good.

Victoria raised her hand to the waitress. 'Excuse me, could we have another pot of tea please.' She looked back at the girls. 'It seems our mothers are right.' She glanced across at Molly, wanting to ask about the white feather, but decided now was not the time.

Molly stopped to look down Carlisle Street. The houses were all standing to attention. Proud people lived in this street, always cleaning their front door steps, shining up their letterboxes and doorknockers. There were no lights shining out from the houses, no street lanterns to light the way. No one wanted to help the Germans. Standing in complete darkness gave an eerie feel to the street. For the second time that day, Jack the Ripper jumped into her mind. Molly shuddered and pulled at her soft woollen coat collar. Taking a deep breath, she dragged her feet towards her front door. There was a lot to think about, but exhaustion had wrapped its cloak around her and she had trouble holding herself upright. Molly wanted to sit quietly and escape her mother's barrage of questions. Her mother was going to be excited about her spending so much time with Andrew. Should she tell her the truth? Her lips thinned, her mother would be horrified. A giggle rushed to the surface as she wondered what she would be most horrified about, the kiss, or her running away from him and sobbing all over Alice. Molly shook her head. Her mother wouldn't understand. She didn't understand. Perhaps she should try and talk to her gran.

A child screamed. Startled, Molly swung round and watched a young woman gather a small girl up into her arms. The screaming gradually subsided. Molly shook her head, wondering why they were outside after dark. What she wouldn't give to be a child again, to be carefree.

Molly sighed. Had she created this situation? Opening her bag, she fumbled for her front door key and had just wrapped her fingers around it when the creaking of the front door caught her attention. Molly forced a smile. 'Hello, Ma.' Molly frowned. She was sure her mother hadn't been wearing the blue ankle length skirt with the white lace, high collared blouse when she left earlier.

Charlotte beamed as she pulled the door wide. 'I thought I'd save you looking for your key. I must say you've had a long day with Mr Greenwood. It shows the pair of you must have been having fun.'

'Yes, Ma, it was fun.' Molly stepped into the hall, not meeting her mother's gaze.

The only light was from a candle, dancing as the breeze caught it. It should have flickered with vulnerability, but the blackened wick stood steadfast in its pool of melted wax, unafraid as it filled the hallway with the scent of beeswax.

Charlotte's eyes sparkled as her excitement grew. 'Does this mean you're going to start being nice to him? After all, he's quite a gentleman.' The hinges screamed in the silence, as she pushed the door closed.

Molly sighed. 'Do you mean he's quite a catch, Ma?'

Colour rose in Charlotte's cheeks. 'I meant what I said, Molly. I don't think you understand how important it is to us, to know that you'll be looked after once we've gone.'

Molly's eyebrows shot up her forehead. 'Don't talk like that, Ma. If the German's don't get us, we have plenty of years left.' She frowned. 'Have you changed into your Sunday best, in case he came back with me?'

'Of course, we don't want him to think we're poor now, do we?' Charlotte picked up the candle to carry it back into the dining room, when a knock on the front door stopped her in her tracks. She stood the candle back on the console table.

Molly sighed, before turning to open the door. A thickset man stood in front of Charlotte and Molly. His dark suit blended into the night, along with his black trilby. His face was partly shielded by the darkness and his hat.

The man tipped the brim with his sausage fingers. 'Good evening, ma'am, I'm looking for Mr Cooper.'

Charlotte cleared her throat. 'Well, he's—'

'Who are you?' Molly asked, wondering what he wanted with her father. Her stomach churned, anxiety sweeping away her tiredness.

The man leant in. Molly wrinkled her nose as the stench of ale wafted over her. His tight clean-shaven pudding face broke into a smile, which didn't reach his flat cold eyes. 'It's nothing to worry about, miss, but I do need to speak to him.' He pulled out a red square handkerchief and dabbed at the beads of perspiration that were leaking out in full force, on his forehead.

Molly gripped the door handle and put her body in front of the entrance, ensuring her mother was tucked in behind her. She didn't know who he was or what he wanted, but something told her it wasn't good news, despite his polite tone. 'Might I suggest you come back when it's daylight, then you can introduce yourself to my father in the correct manner.'

The man's eyes took on a steely quality. 'I can assure you miss, Mr Cooper and I have already spoken, several times in fact.'

'Well, he has never mentioned you, so I'm afraid we only have your word for that, and I don't think he would want us to let a strange man into the house, in his absence.'

The man raised his bushy eyebrows and nodded. 'I would certainly advise my wife and family the same.' He paused for a moment. His eyes darted between Molly and Charlotte. 'If you could just tell him I would like to speak to him, I would appreciate it.'

Molly stared at him. There was something familiar about him, but her mind was racing as she tried to work out why he was at their front door, so late in the evening.

The man lifted his trilby and a gold signet ring became visible in the candlelight. He nodded. 'Good night to you both.' He placed it back on his head and turned to walk away.

'You haven't given us your name,' Molly shouted after him, but he didn't turn round. 'Have you seen him before, Ma?' She watched him waddle up the road until he was out of sight.

Charlotte shook her head. 'No.'

The hair rose on the back of Molly's neck. Something told her this man didn't want to give her father good news.

Chapter 15

Molly concentrated hard on threading her arms into the sleeves of her biscuit-coloured overalls. Her head was foggy. Her eyes were gritty and bloodshot, where sleep had evaded her. A gusting wind had crashed against her bedroom window, encouraging the rain to hammer on the glass pane, before it ran away down the road, like children playing knock down ginger on people's front doors. It had been a long night. Andrew had filled her thoughts. Had she been wrong to walk away from him? Had she been wrong to put Grace first, let alone the mystery woman she had seen him with? Or had she been a coward? Was she frightened of getting hurt again? A hollow laugh escaped. Her heart was already breaking. Could it get any worse?

Alice and Victoria had tried to give comfort, but nothing wiped away the feeling that she had lost something precious. Molly was convinced she saw disappointment in Alice's eyes. Perhaps she'd been thinking about someone else falling in love with her husband, but don't they say you can't help who you fall in love with?

Victoria's words bounced into her mind from nowhere. 'Have you asked him who that woman was?'

Molly only managed a shake of her head.

'Have you asked him whether he's married or not?'

Again, Molly shook her head.

Victoria lifted her arm up in frustration. 'Well don't you think you should have asked him, before you ran away and broke down like that?' She'd glanced across at Alice for support.

'Victoria's right, Molly, that woman could have been anybody or nobody.'

Molly pulled at her sleeves, straightening the cuffs. She sighed. They were right of course, but that moment had gone. She'd allowed Flo to worry her so much; she'd run away from him.

Grace looked over at Molly. 'You're quiet this morning, everything all right?'

'I'm fine.' Molly forced a smile. 'The rain kept me awake, that's all.'

Flo raised her eyebrows. 'Are you sure you're not worried about something?'

Molly couldn't meet her gaze. 'No more than anyone else.'

Grace turned her attention to her pumps, putting them in position before sliding her feet into them. 'From what I can gather, most women are wondering how they're going to put a Christmas dinner together, what with the food shortages and prices going up.' She moved from one foot to the other. 'Still I suppose you won't have that problem.'

Molly wanted to ask why not, but realised she couldn't be bothered with the tirade of assumptions Grace would make about her. Her conscience suddenly came forward, *oh you mean like you did with Andrew?* Alice and Victoria's words were ringing in her ears. She had nothing to lose. Molly lifted her head and pulled back her shoulders. Her chin jutted out in defiance and her eyes took on a steel-like quality. 'Grace, I don't know what your problem is about me and "my kind", but I can assure you my family will have the same problems as everyone else when it comes to food at Christmas.'

Flo giggled. 'Ooh, she bites back.'

Grace and Molly both glared at Flo.

Casting her gaze back to Molly, Grace shrugged her shoulders. 'The rich don't seem to suffer in times like these. They can afford to eat out, and they certainly don't work in places like this.' Her arms flayed around her. 'They can read about what's going on in the newspapers and write to their men. I can't afford to go to the theatre to watch Pathé News.' Grace sniffed and quickly turned her back on the girls.

Molly stepped forward and rested her arm around her shoulders. 'Grace, I'm sorry, you can tell me to mind my own business, but I have to ask.' She looked around before lowering her voice to a whisper. 'Can you read and write?'

Grace shook Molly's arm off and took a step away.

Molly stepped nearer to her. 'I can teach you. I'm not a teacher, but I don't mind giving it a go.' She paused, waiting for a response, but her offer was greeted with silence. 'I want to help, if you'll let me. We don't have to tell anyone, it can be our little secret.' Molly waited, but again there was nothing. She stepped back. 'Well, it's up to you, but I'm happy to try if you are. Please don't let your pride get in the way.' She paused before taking a deep breath. 'My father once told me it's a fool that lets a good opportunity pass them by. Grace, please don't be that fool.'

Grace swung round. 'Why? Why would you do that for me?' Her colour had drained away, along with her forthright manner.

Molly took in her grey pallor and smiled. 'You know, I met my friends yesterday and they told me I was trying too hard to fit in, and to just be myself.' Her arms lifted from her sides and dropped back down again. 'Well, this is me just being myself.' She laughed. 'I like to think, despite popular opinion, I'm quite a nice person really.'

Grace lowered her lashes. 'I want to write to my brother. He writes me letters all the time, but I can't read them.' She sucked in her breath. 'I don't think I'll be able to learn.'

Molly smiled. 'None of us can until we are taught how.' She paused for a moment.

Grace wrung her hands together. 'He knows I can't read, but I recognise his handwriting.' She gave a hollow laugh. 'I expect it's his way of letting me know he's all right.'

Molly nodded. 'Let me tell you, Grace, if you don't try, you will never know whether you could have learnt or not. Also, it could open up a whole new world for you.'

Grace looked up and nodded. 'If you don't mind trying, I'm happy to give it a go.'

Molly nodded, before taking a deep breath. 'I hope you don't mind me asking, but how come your brother can read and write, but you can't?' Colour flushed Molly's cheeks. 'You can tell me to mind my own business, I'll understand.'

Grace gave a hallow laugh. 'It's the usual. Boys are more important than girls. My pa thought it was a waste of time teaching girls anything outside of domestic chores, and when my ma died…' She shrugged her shoulders, matter of factly.

Sadness wrapped itself around Molly. 'I'm so sorry, Grace.' She rested her hand on Grace's arm. 'This evening, I'll write the letters down for you to copy, and we can find a quiet spot tomorrow, to go through the sounds they make when you're reading.'

'I hope I can do it.' Grace paused for a moment. 'I can't believe you'd do this for me.' She frowned. 'I don't want you wasting your time.'

'Learning to read and write is never a waste of time.' Molly smiled. 'No matter how long it takes.'

Flo wandered over and stared at them suspiciously. 'What's going on? What's all the whispering about?'

Grace glared at her young friend. 'There's no whispering going on, it's called a private conversation.'

'Well, don't get taken in by miss proper, over here.' Flo waved her hand in Molly's direction. 'She's not all she seems.'

Grace shook her head. 'Oh give it up, Flo, none of us are as we seem. We all have secrets.'

Colour filled Flo's face and neck. She nodded, before biting back. 'Trust me, some secrets are worse than others.' She turned to face Molly. 'Isn't that so?'

Molly could feel her cheeks burning. 'The trouble is, Flo, some people get a little information and they think they then know the whole story, but they are usually wrong.'

Flo stared at Molly before shrugging her shoulders. 'That's not the case this time.'

Grace looked from one to the other. 'What's going on? I can't help feeling I'm missing something important.'

'Nothing stays hidden forever.' Flo's nostrils flared. 'I can wait and enjoy my moment.' She smiled at them both, but her eyes were hard, before she turned her back on them.

Molly couldn't shake the feeling that Flo was going to take them both on, in a great showdown.

'Come on, ladies. As always, we have a lot to do today.' The familiar deep voice could be heard from the other side of the wall.

Molly stiffened.

He sounded distracted. How she longed to see him, tell him she was sorry for being a coward, but she couldn't see that as an option open to her. Molly blinked quickly to stop the tears from falling, rubbing her hands over her face.

'Are you all right?'

Molly let her hands drop to her sides, not realising Grace had been watching her. 'Of course, as I said earlier, just lack of sleep.' She'd spent all night trying to work out why she had given up so easily. Did the passion he unlocked in her, frighten her? Every time her eyes closed, she was back in his arms again. His scent was so strong;

she could be forgiven for thinking he was lying next to her. Molly could feel the strength of his arms holding her tight, while his hands caressed her body. In the darkness of her bedroom, she had curled up and the tears had fallen freely, leaving a salty residue on her lips. Her mind battled hard to block him out of her thoughts, but her wet pillowcase told of her failure.

Molly blinked rapidly, trying to prevent the tears from falling again. What a fool she'd been, but as her gran used to say, 'you made your bed, so lie in it.' There was no way to turn back the clock. Pressing her eyes shut, she wished she'd stayed at home, but had been scared of the questions that would have raised. Taking a deep breath, Molly tried to block out the laughter and chatter around her, wondering how she was going to get through the day, and whether ignoring Flo was even an option.

Grace frowned, following Flo's gaze, which appeared to be settled in Molly's direction. 'You all right, Flo?' Her voice carried, over the chatter that filled the room.

A strange noise escaped Flo's throat and she coughed to clear it, forcing herself to smile and give Grace her undivided attention. 'Oh yes, I've never been better.'

Grace frowned, scratching her cheek, her gaze darting between Molly and Flo. 'That's good. Did you have a good day off yesterday?'

'It was quite a day. I went for a walk in Hyde Park. It's amazing what you can see there, even at this time of year.'

Molly's heart leapt into her throat as Flo's eyes bore into her back, but she didn't turn round to face her. She wasn't ready for that. Nausea travelled at speed, from her stomach. Holding her breath, she waited for the bombshell to drop.

Grace chuckled. 'Like what?'

'Oh Grace, you'd be surprised. Wouldn't she, Molly?'

Molly's fingers fumbled with the overall buttons, her eyes not shifting from them. 'That's right, it's quite beautiful.'

Grace shook her head. 'You two are mad, there's nothing beautiful about this time of year.'

Flo laughed. 'You know, Grace, love isn't just in the air in the spring, it's all around us, sometimes closer than we think. Isn't that right, Molly?'

Molly took a deep breath; she wouldn't be able to cope with this all day, but had no idea how she was going to deal with it all. She pulled her shoulders back and forced a smile to her lips, before turning to face Flo and Grace. 'I don't know about that, but the colours of autumn are wonderful.' She picked up her mob cap and placed it over her blonde hair and the blue ribbon that held the ponytail in place. 'Time must be getting on. Are you ready to go in?'

'Does anyone know how Nora is?' a woman shouted above the early morning chatter. 'I haven't seen 'er since she was last 'ere.'

Molly gasped, wondering when Andrew would tell everyone about Nora. She avoided looking at them as she fought the urge to speak out, knowing it would raise too many questions and confirm to them that she was a spy for the manager.

Murmurs travelled around the clean area, as the women shook their heads.

The klaxon bellowed out. Groans filled the room, confirming it was time for the talking to end. They all stepped forward; the stench of sulphur hit them. The continual ringing herded them, like a sheep dog would its flock, moving slowly and in single file to their pens.

'Morning, ladies.' Andrew's voice greeted everyone with a smile, as they walked through the doorway.

Molly took several deep breaths. The putrid smell caught in the back of her throat; it would be her turn soon. One by one, they filtered through. A voice shouted in her head, *now, but no eye contact*. She forced a smile and looked straight ahead. 'Morning, Mr Greenwood.'

Flo was ahead of her and turned to watch, but shrugged her shoulders when there was nothing to see. She took a couple of steps forward, before coming to an abrupt standstill. A smile slowly spread across her face. She turned to face Molly, smiling before letting her eyes settle on Mr Greenwood. 'Mr Greenwood, I just wanted to ask, did you have a good day off yesterday?'

Andrew thrust his chest out, but kept his eyes fixed on his clipboard. 'Lovely, thank you.'

Flo's lips tightened as she lowered her head. Her shoulders slumped for a few minutes.

'Come along, Miss Attwood, there's work to be done.' Andrew's jaw tightened as he scrutinised her for a moment. 'Your country needs you.'

Flo smirked. She pulled herself upright and jutted out her chin. 'Yes, sir.' She moved her gaze and fixed it firmly on Molly. 'Only I thought I saw you in Hyde Park with a lady friend.' She paused for affect, noticing Molly blush as she stared at the floor ahead of her. 'Of course, I could be mistaken.' She smiled innocently.

'Oooh sir, yer got a lady friend, 'ave yer?' A high pitch cackle came from the throng of women waiting to get to their workplaces.

Andrew frowned at Flo, before turning his head and smiling at the women. 'Of course I have, and she's delightful.' He laughed, keeping his gaze on the women. 'I don't know why you are all so surprised. Am I not a good catch?' He chuckled, returning his attention to the clipboard.

'I'm not surprised, sir. Yer can leave your shoes under my bed, anytime you like.'

Raucous laughter followed. 'You should be so lucky, Maud.'

Andrew chuckled. 'I'll bear that in mind.'

Flo backed away, shaking her head. Her arms hung limp at her side, but her cheeks were burning. She caught sight of Grace; there was no sign of a smile or any laughter on her face. Grace squinted in Flo's direction, while wrapping her arms around herself. Flo blinked quickly, holding back the tears, as she realised she might as well have punched her friend, Grace, in the stomach.

'Mr Greenwood, sir, we were wondering if you knew how Nora was?' Maud stared up at her boss. 'Only none of us have seen her since that day she left here with the wobbles.'

Andrew clenched his jaw, drawing in his lips. 'Unfortunately, I'm afraid it's not good news.' He coughed to clear his throat. 'Nora passed away on the same day. It appears she was very sick, but nobody realised it.'

The laughter and chatter faded away. Sobbing could be heard as the news filtered through to everyone.

Maud ran a hand over her eyes. 'She has to have a good send off, like Sissy did, the carriage, the guard of honour and all that stuff.'

Murmurs of agreement travelled around the women.

Mr Greenwood nodded. 'I agree. It's all in hand.' He paused. 'I know it's a difficult time for you all right now, which is why I was delaying telling you until all the information was available, but I'd like you all to try to focus on the job at hand.'

The women nodded, wiping their eyes, as everyone moved to their areas and work began.

The girls took up their positions at the table. Molly picked up her half size broom handle; she ran her hands down the smooth wood. Coming to work here had caused more problems than she needed. Her parents had long given up trying to persuade her to get her job back at Foyles but she was beginning to wish she had never left. Life seemed so simple back then.

Flo's high-pitched tone broke through Molly's meanderings. 'So, Molly, you haven't told us what you got up to yesterday.'

Here it comes. It was her turn. Colour rose in Molly's cheeks. She bent down to fill her scoop with the black gunpowder, deciding to pretend she hadn't heard Flo. She sighed. She wasn't going to get through the whole day like this; a plan was needed.

★

Alice fidgeted on the wooden chair, as she sat down at the small table in the corner of the staff area, to the rear of Foyles Bookstore. Steam spiralled up from the cup of tea she'd stood on the table. She looked up and smiled as Victoria stepped towards her, carrying her lunch and a cup of tea. She placed them on the table, sitting down opposite her. The chatter in the room got louder as it began to fill up with staff. The clang of the clock repeated every few seconds, as everyone pushed their card in to clock off for their break.

A shiver ran down Alice's spine. She rubbed her arms vigorously, through her white cotton blouse.

Victoria rubbed her hands together. 'It's definitely got colder, hasn't it? At this rate, I reckon we'll probably have snow before Christmas.'

Alice grimaced, picking up her cup and wrapping her hands around it. The warmth of the tea slowly filtered into her fingers and spread across her hands. 'I love looking out at the snow. It's beautiful, until children mess about in it and it becomes treacherous.' Alice sipped the hot liquid, gasping as it burnt her mouth. She ran her tongue over the sore area of her lips and put the cup back on to the table.

'Yes, I know what you mean.' Victoria laughed. 'I find myself walking with very stiff legs.'

They both giggled at the thought of it.

Screeches of laughter came from the other side of the room. Alice tilted her head to see what was going on, at the same time as Victoria spun round on her seat.

Alice couldn't help giggling. 'It sounds like someone is having a good day.'

Victoria smiled as she turned back. 'Hmm.' She looked pensive, dragging her lunch nearer. 'How do you think Molly is today?'

'I don't know, but I'm assuming she didn't get much sleep last night.' Alice unwrapped the sandwiches, the crinkled paper rustling as her hand ran over it, smoothing it out so it could be used again. She lifted the corner of the soft, thick white bread to see the pink fish paste filling. 'She was in a terrible state, wasn't she? I haven't seen her like that since Tony—'

'No, I know what you mean, we all get ourselves so worked up in the name of love.' Victoria pulled at the paper wrapped around her sandwiches. 'Me included.'

Alice nodded. 'Have you heard from Ted?'

Victoria beamed. 'I get a letter every week, sometimes two, and I write to him and Stephen every day.' She bit into the bread and butter, frowning. It wasn't as fresh as she thought. 'Although that brother of mine isn't so great at letter writing, I'm always pleased to get one.'

Alice laughed. 'I know what you mean. Charles isn't great either, but he does write to mother regularly, so that's the main thing. I suspect they have other things on their minds.'

Victoria picked up her cup, wrapping her fingers around it, sipping at the hot tea. 'Hmm, that's a good cuppa.' She smiled, placing it back on the table. 'I also send parcels to him and Stephen every week. You know, the usual stuff, paper, chocolate and cigarettes.' Her eyes sparkled. 'He has asked if he can come and see me when he next gets leave, although he doesn't know when that will be.'

Alice watched her friend closely, so animated, just talking about Ted. She lowered her lashes, fearful for what could happen in the future.

'Don't worry about me, I'm no longer the fragile child trying to be an adult to two children.' Victoria sighed. 'I know Ted may not make it back, but by writing to him and getting his letters, I know I'm giving him something to live for. That's all that matters at the moment.'

Alice cleared her throat. 'You're right. I'm sorry, I can't help but worry.' She glanced across at her friend and swallowed hard. 'You've been through so much already and I'm frightened he will break your heart all over again.'

Victoria leant forward and rested her hand on Alice's arm. 'He might.' She shrugged her shoulders. 'But I love him as much as ever, so I have to try, no matter what happens.'

Alice nodded. 'I can see that, but please remember I'm here for you, as is Molly, should you need us.'

'I know.' Victoria smiled. 'I think we're very lucky people.'

Alice chuckled. 'I don't think Molly feels like that at the moment.'

Victoria groaned. Her jaw tightened and her hands went up in a dramatic fashion. 'No, I don't suppose she does, but what I don't understand is why Molly hasn't asked him about the woman in Café Monico, or whether he's married or not. As for this Grace, he doesn't even know her, so why worry about her.'

Alice nodded. She didn't have the answers, but knew Molly must have her reasons. 'It's no good getting frustrated with her. I think she's just trying to fit in and be liked, and that means not treading on people's toes. We have to respect her wishes, whatever they are, just like we do yours about Ted.'

They both sat in silence for a few minutes, each lost in their own thoughts.

'I know you're right, I just don't know how to help her that's all.' Victoria gave a heavy sigh. 'I wanted to ask her about the white feather in his hallway, but it didn't seem the right time.' She sighed. 'Mind you, I'm not sure when would be the right time to talk about such things.'

'I know what you mean, it's a sensitive subject.' Alice held her sandwich in mid-air, immediately recalling how she'd messed up trying to help Victoria and the arguments they'd had.

Victoria frowned and slumped back in her chair. 'Do you think he's a conscientious objector?'

Alice shook her head. 'Who knows?' She bit down on her sandwich. The soft white bread and the strong fish paste clung to her teeth.

Victoria sighed. 'I'll tell you this though, nothing about Molly is straightforward.'

Alice moved her tongue over her teeth. 'No. Do you think she's frightened to love again, after Tony I mean?'

'Possibly. That could be why she ran away from him.' Victoria shrugged her shoulders. 'I think it's too late for that; Molly's well and truly smitten. I also think she's lost her way, it was clear in the tearoom she felt she didn't fit in with us or the canaries, and I think that's the crux of the problem. She's looking for something that is right under her nose.' Wrinkling her brow, she bit down on her lip.

Alice frowned. 'What is it?'

'Nothing really.' Victoria paused, pinching her lips together. 'I've been thinking lately how you and Molly have put me to shame.'

Alice put down her sandwich and stared at her friend. 'I don't understand how we could have done that. It certainly wouldn't have been intentional.'

'No and that's not what I mean.' Victoria clenched her lips together. 'I mean you both do outstanding war work, as indeed do both of our sisters. Daisy is like a different person now, as I imagine is Lily, but all I do is knit.'

Alice smiled and reached over to Victoria. 'That's as important as anything else.'

Victoria shook her head. 'Molly's made me realise I should be doing more, but I haven't figured out what yet.'

They carried on eating their sandwiches in silence.

'You know, when I take the wounded soldiers from Victoria train station to the local hospitals, they are always crying out for another pair of hands.' Alice paused for a moment. 'I don't think you need to be trained as such, and you could probably fit it in around your work here, unless you want to leave as well.'

'No, I'm not leaving here,' Victoria insisted. 'I love working at Foyles and who knows what the work situation will be like when the men return for good, but I'll definitely ask about working in the hospitals.'

Alice shook her head. 'It's a shame we can't convince Molly to come back here where we could keep an eye on her.'

Victoria nodded.

They both fell silent, lost in their own thoughts.

It dawned on Victoria how much she missed Molly every day. The realisation came as a surprise to her. Things had changed between the three of them, and it wasn't for the better. Molly was the missing link and they had to find a way to bring her back into the fold.

Chapter 16

December 1916

Molly hammered down on the broom handle, while casting furtive glances at the other women working around her. She had noticed that some of them had yellow streaks of hair where it had escaped the safety of the mob cap, and their skin was turning the same colour. She hoped that wasn't happening to her. Fear ran down her spine at the thought of her life ending like Nora's had. She shook her head. She had to be brave; Tony was.

Grace's voice shrilled out above the noise, jolting Molly back to the task at hand. 'Apparently we have The Right Honourable David Lloyd George to impress now. My Pa thinks with him as Prime Minister there's hope for us yet.'

Flo glanced across at Grace. 'Does your pa talk to you about stuff like that then?'

Grace laughed. 'Of course not, I heard him talking to the next door neighbour.'

The high-pitched bell rang out for a few minutes, indicating it was the end of the shift. The machines in the munitions' factory gradually ground to a halt and the women's voices echoed around the room.

Flo's stick clattered on to the table. 'I'm going out for a smoke before I get changed.' She brushed her hands against each other, gunpowder dust silently dropping next to the stick. Smiling at the others before she stepped away. 'I don't suppose you two want to join me outside?'

Molly shook her head.

Grace frowned. 'It's too blooming cold out there and I'm not going to encourage you.'

Flo giggled. 'Get off yer high horse, Grace.' Flo ran her fingers through the fine particles of dust on the table. 'Do yer not think this stuff is gonna kill us, just like it did Nora, and Sissy and no doubt many before them?' She brushed it away from her fingers. 'Anyway, it's good enough for the stars in the films, so it's good enough for me.' Flo shook her head and started walking towards the door.

Molly's eyes pricked with tears. Was it Sissy's funeral she had seen outside Foyles on her last day?

Grace stared after Flo. 'She's going to come a cropper one of these days.' She sighed and glanced across at Molly. 'I was wondering if you would help me. I know I have a cheek to ask but—'

'What is it?'

Grace's eyes sparkled; her lips broke into a huge smile. 'I have a letter from Sam.' She paused taking in Molly's frown. 'Sorry, he's my brother and I wondered if you'd help me read it.'

Molly blinked quickly and smiled at Grace. 'Of course I will, it would be an honour to, and I don't mind helping you write a reply to him.'

Grace's face lit up. 'That would certainly surprise him.' Colour began to fill her cheeks. 'Don't tell anyone, but I've been practicing the letters you wrote down for me and I try to sound them out like you told me to.' She giggled. 'I don't remember all the letters when I sit in bed doing it.' Her laughter faded. 'I haven't told anyone I'm learning, so no one can laugh at me. That's why I practise it in bed.'

'They shouldn't laugh at you anyway.' Molly frowned, brushing the dust from her hands.

'I wonder if I'll ever be able to read Sam's letters by myself.'

Molly smiled. 'You will, trust me.' Forgetting about the black dust, she put her finger to her chin. 'I think I still have some books at home, from my childhood days, like The Tale of Peter Rabbit by Beatrix Potter.' She laughed at Grace's confused expression. 'I can't bring myself to throw any books away, so I'll have a look. If I'm honest, I haven't seen it for years.'

Grace frowned. 'Why would you read a book about a rabbit?'

'You'll see. It's wonderful. I'll be able to bring you some of my books to read soon and then you'll wonder how you managed without a good book in your life.'

Grace's melodious laugh carried around the large hanger. 'I can't imagine that will ever happen.'

Molly giggled. 'That's because you haven't read Pride and Prejudice by Jane Austen. I've read it at least four times.'

Grace shook her head. 'It's one of your favourites then.'

'Favourites? Trust me when I say we all need a Mr Darcy in our lives.' Molly giggled as her face filled with colour. 'I have it at home and when you're ready I will lend it to you. You're not allowed to keep it because I love it.' Molly paused. 'No, I'll tell you what, I'll buy you your own copy. I'll have a look in Foyles.'

They walked away from their table together. Grace stared straight ahead. 'I can't imagine ever being able to read a book.'

'You will, Grace, especially if I have anything to do with it.' Molly paused for a brief moment. 'I love books, they take you into another time and place.'

Grace frowned as she looked across at Molly. 'Why did you leave Foyles Bookstore then?'

A hollow laugh escaped from Molly's lips. 'That's a good question, and one I've been asking myself over and over again.' She looked around at the women chatting and laughing, as they got changed into their own clothes. 'I suppose I wanted to do my bit. My friend Alice drives an ambulance most days to Victoria train station, taking the wounded to hospitals all around London.' Molly sighed. 'When she's not doing that, she's on the tea and cake stall at the same station, so soldiers see a friendly face when they return home.'

Grace's lips thinned as she rested her hand on Molly's arm. 'I bet your friend doesn't work for a living though, does she?'

'Oh she does, part time in Foyles, and she has an adorable little boy too.' Molly laughed.

'Blimey, she sounds too good to be true.'

Molly chuckled. 'It does make me feel I'm not doing enough, but Alice is a good friend and would be horrified if she knew that's how I felt.' She paused for a moment. 'I can't imagine not having her or my friend, Victoria, in my life. They're like sisters to me. I think I've been looking for something I already had, but was too wrapped up in myself to realise it.'

Grace nodded. 'Would you try and go back to Foyles?'

Molly smiled. 'I'd love to go back and help the small children learn to read and appreciate books, so I suppose maybe, if they'd have me.'

Flo came rushing over to them. 'I'm going for an ale. I know I'm wasting my time asking, but do either of you want to come?'

Sophie's words bounced into Molly's mind. Surely Flo wasn't a woman of the night, as her gran had suggested. Coughing, she shook her head as the cigarette fumes engulfed her. 'No, but thanks for asking.'

'You know it's not my thing and it shouldn't be yours.' Grace scolded Flo, before shaking her head.

'See you then.' Flo turned on her heels and strode outside, waving her hand in the air as she went.

Molly looked around. The changing room was empty. She sat down glancing back at Grace. 'Have you got the letter on you?'

Grace's face lit up like the street lights glowing in the dark before the wretched war had put them out. 'Yes, can we read it now?'

A smile made its way across Molly's face as she nodded.

Grace pulled a brown envelope from her bag and passed it to Molly, before dropping down next to her. Her hand delved into her bag again and pulled out a wad of letters tied together with red ribbon. A giggle escaped as the excitement bubbled away inside her. 'I have quite a few letters to read.'

Molly raised her eyebrows and laughed. 'We could be here for some time.' Her gaze dropped to the letter she was holding and she turned it over in her hands. The writing was spidery, quite similar to Charles'. 'Are you sure you want me to read it?'

'Yes, yes, yes.' Grace momentarily forgot herself, jumping up, clapping her hands. She stopped and looked around her, before shrugging her shoulders.

Molly lifted the flap to the envelope, the paper rustling as the sheet was pulled free. She unfolded it and rested it on her lap, before placing her finger under the first word, and slowly moving it along the mud splattered page.

Grace's eyes followed Molly's hand as it moved across the page, committing each word to memory.

Dear Gracie,

The best sister a man can have, haha, do you like that? I'm writing it because I know you can't read my letters. Joking aside, I hope you're looking after yourself because when I finally get away from these rat infested, water-filled trenches I'm going to take you out somewhere posh.

Grace chuckled as tears rolled down her cheeks. She sniffed. 'Carry on.'

Molly was glad to be home, as the long cycle rides in the dark evenings and the cold weather were getting her down. The wind ripped the front door out of her grasp. She reached out to grab it before it hit the wall, but failed.

The thud brought Charlotte rushing into the hallway, the flame of the candle she was holding dancing under the fierce breeze that had rushed in. Her hand came up to shield the flame. 'Oh it's you, Molly, I wondered what the noise was.'

Molly shook her head, grabbing the edge of the door and quickly pushing it shut. 'Sorry, Ma, the wind whipped the door out of my hand. It's freezing out there.'

Charlotte nodded, taking in her daughter's rosy cheeks. 'Maybe you should consider getting the train this time of year.'

Molly laughed. 'I do love you, Ma, you never give up.' She removed her hat and coat and hung them on the wooden coat hooks. 'Actually, I'm not cold when I'm cycling, it's hard work, it's when you stop you notice it.' Molly stepped forward to follow her mother into the dining room. The warmth of the house wrapped itself around her, causing her to sniff. She pulled her handkerchief out of her pocket and blew her nose. 'Can I smell coal burning?'

'I don't think you understand.' Jack's voice bellowed out from along the hallway. 'You keep asking me the same thing and I can only tell you what I know, which is nothing.'

Molly stopped short and her gaze followed the voices. 'Who's Pa talking to?'

Charlotte stepped nearer to Molly and looked towards the best room, before whispering to her daughter. 'It's that man that came here the other night. I don't know what he's doing here, but they've been in that room for ages.' She tucked her arm in her daughter's. 'He hasn't asked me to make them a cup of tea either.'

Molly looked across at her and patted her mother's surprisingly soft, wrinkled hand. 'Something must be wrong then, Ma.' She frowned before whispering, almost to herself, 'I can't remember when I last heard Pa raise his voice.'

'Let's get you in the warm, Pa's lit a fire tonight.' Charlotte pulled her daughter forward.

'I thought I could smell a coal fire burning, but assumed it was coming from the neighbours.' Molly's lips lifted in the corners, but the smile didn't reach her eyes, which were concentrating on the voices coming from down the hall. 'Gosh, it must be cold tonight.' She shook her head. 'It's an evening of firsts.'

'I think you should leave.' Jack's voice carried down the hall. 'I have nothing more to say to you and would appreciate it if you don't come to my home again.'

A deep voice replied, but not loud enough for Molly to hear the words spoken.

'Ma, shall I go in there? I could ask Pa if he's all right or offer a cup of tea or something.' Molly's gaze didn't move from the other end of the hallway.

'No,' Charlotte snapped. 'Your Pa would be furious if either of us interrupted his meeting.'

'But, Ma, it doesn't sound like it's going well.' Molly clenched her jaw. 'We could throw the man out.'

Charlotte shook her head and grimaced. 'I don't know what I've done to have such a headstrong daughter, I really don't.'

Molly grinned and looked at her mother, as both the men's voices were just a mumble to her. 'I only want to protect you both.'

Charlotte pulled at her daughter's arm. 'You need to realise me and your Pa were bought up in a man's world and it weren't like it is today. You did as you were told back then. It took a strong woman to take on, let alone leave, their menfolk in those days.'

'You mean like my grandmothers did.' Molly squeezed her mother's arm close. 'I've got news for you, Ma, it's still a man's world. They're still in charge.'

Charlotte's eyes became hooded as she looked at her daughter. 'I don't know about that; you youngsters are quite headstrong.'

'Ma, we might be headstrong but we have no say in how we live our lives. Remember, we can't even vote.' Molly paused to take a breath. 'Remember the suffragette movement?'

Charlotte shook her head and sighed. 'As I said, headstrong.'

'Flo in work is right.' Molly sighed. 'She talks a lot of nonsense most of the time and I don't expect you to understand but it'll be interesting to see how things will be when the men return from the front.'

The door to the best room flew open and the man stepped through the doorway. Jack's voice could be heard clearly. 'Anything you wish to ask about the company you can make an appointment and come to the office where Mr Gettin, the owner of the company, can speak to you.'

It puzzled Molly why she thought the man looked so familiar. She stared hard at him. Her lips tightened and her gaze darted around trying to remember.

The thick set man placed his trilby on his head, a signet ring glinted in the candle light as he stepped towards the front door before turning to Jack. 'You know it's in your best interests to co-operate with me.'

That was it. It was the ring. He was the man talking to Frank on her first day at the munitions' factory. What had Frank said… he was investigating theft from the docks or something like that, but what did that have to do with her father?

Jack threw up his arms. 'Please God, how many times do I have to say it, I don't know anything. You're talking to the wrong person.'

The man shrugged his shoulders. What little neck he had seemed to disappear. He stepped nearer to the front door. 'Don't let it be said I haven't given you an opportunity to come clean.' He sniffed and rubbed his red bulbous nose.

Molly turned and opened the front door.

The man nodded in her direction. 'Miss.'

Molly slammed the front door shut before the man was off the step, shutting out the ale fumes that emanated from him.

'What's going on out there?' Sophie's voice travelled to the hall.

'Come, we best get into the warm, your grandma will be fretting.' Charlotte dropped her hand from Molly's arm and walked towards the dining room. She glanced back at them both, raising her eyebrows. 'We have cheese and potato pie for dinner, if it's not burnt that is.'

Molly gazed up at her father and studied his pale features, noticing for the first time the dark rings under his eyes. 'Are you all right, Pa?'

Jack forced a smile. 'It's nothing for you to worry about.' He rested his hand on Molly's elbow and guided her towards the dining room. 'Let's not keep your mother waiting, dinner is already late.'

Molly moved forward before stopping to turn and look up at her father. 'Pa, who is that man?'

Jack frowned. 'I've told you, it's nothing for you to worry about.'

Molly shook her head before an exasperated sigh escaped. 'Pa, he's been at the munitions' factory.'

Jack's body stiffened. Anger was etched in every line on his face.

'Sorry, Pa.' Molly lowered her lashes before taking a deep breath. 'I don't mean to question you, but when he came the other evening, it was quite scary and had Ma been here with just gran… well it just worries me that's all.'

'Come with me, I don't want your mother worrying about things.' Jack turned around and headed towards the best room.

Molly followed him down the hall, her heels tapping on the tiled floor. 'I think it's too late for that.' She stepped through the doorway and turned to see her father shutting the door. The carriage clock on the mantelpiece chimed one light musical note.

'I shall talk to her.' Jack bit down on his lip. 'Sit down.' He thrust his hands into his trouser pockets and began pacing around the room. 'I could do with a whiskey right now.'

Molly gasped. 'It must be bad, I don't think I've ever seen you drink anything other than tea and coffee.'

Jack tried to laugh but it was a feeble, hollow sound. 'I don't know if I've ever told you before but my father was a drinker, which is why I don't indulge.'

Molly shook her head. Her hands gripped each other in her lap. 'You've never mentioned your father before.' Her eyes welled up. 'Gran told me years ago how you and she had run away from him in the middle of the night. She said you both owe George Wyatt everything for finding a room for you both at the women's refuge he ran with his sister.'

Jack stopped pacing and raised his eyebrows. 'Did she now?' His lips thinned and his brows pulled together. 'My father used to beat us when he'd had a skinful.' His tense features softened and a smile crept across his face. 'Me ma used to tell me every day, yer not a fief, it's all about 'ard work and 'onesty.' He laughed as he mimicked his mother. 'She was a good soul and I always believed she was right.' The laughter died on his lips. 'Until now that is.'

Tears were pricking Molly's eyes. 'What's happened for you to think your ma was wrong after all these years?'

'I seem to be caught up in something I know nothing about.' Jack sighed, colour draining from his face as he began pacing again. He stopped to pick up the photograph of his mother that sat on the mantelpiece. 'She worked so hard. Life had treated her badly but she was still a good woman.'

Molly stood up and walked over to him, resting her hand on his arm. 'Gran was very proud of everything you'd achieved.' She smiled, staring at the photograph in his hand. 'She didn't even mind when you started to pronounce your h's.'

Jack gave a hearty laugh and replaced the picture. 'She was so proud when I was offered employment at the Gettin accountancy company and saw that as a necessity for me to talk to people in that world, a challenge to be accepted.' He sighed as he looked around the room. 'You know I've never understood why I was allowed to live in this house as part of the job but I never questioned it because it meant we all had a roof over our heads and after being in the women's refuge it was like moving into a palace.'

'It must have been horrendous for you, I can't begin to imagine.'

Jack sighed. 'It wasn't that bad. Emily and George changed all our lives; they were always fighting our corner. She taught your mother and me to read and write. It took them a long time to realise they loved each other, they were always arguing.' He smiled at his daughter and wrapped his arms around her. 'The one thing to recognise as important is I always knew I was loved and hope you know you are too.'

Molly breathed in his musky scent. The roughness of his jacket scratched her cheek as she moved her face. 'Of course I do, Pa. I know you and Ma are disappointed I left Foyles and haven't taken up with someone rich, but I want to marry for love, and that person needs to love me like you love Ma.'

Jack pulled back from Molly and stared down at her. 'You need to know I'm never disappointed in you, I just want what's best for you.' He hesitated for a moment. 'Your ma and I have heard you crying at night.'

Molly gasped and moved to pull away, but her father's arms tightened their hold.

'We first became aware of it about a year or so ago but it stopped until we heard you again the other night. Is it Mr Greenwood? Has he said or done something?'

A tear rolled down Molly's cheek. 'No, Pa, he's a gentleman.'

'Then why are you crying?'

Molly shrugged her shoulders. 'I don't know.'

Jack shook his head. 'I think you do, but you don't have to tell me.'

'I do love him, but I've thrown it all away.'

'Does he love you?'

Molly shook her head. 'I don't know.' She sniffed. 'He's the boss and I don't want to be his plaything for a while, before he moves on to someone else.'

Jack pulled back his shoulders. 'Is that how you see him then? Is he that sort of man?'

'No, I don't think he is.' Molly paused for a moment. 'We went to his house to drop off Ma's piece of cake and he had a white feather in his hallway.'

'Did you ask him about it?'

Molly shook her head. 'No.'

Jack sighed. 'Maybe you should. Things aren't always what they seem.'

'I expect you're right, Pa, I'm just too scared.'

'This world isn't a nice place to be at the moment, and it certainly isn't kind to women. He seems a good man to me, but having said that, there's no pressure for you to marry anyone. I just don't want you ending up in a refuge, or worse, on the streets. I want to leave this world knowing you'll be looked after. I've always tried to do my best, since the day you were born, to make sure you'll be taken care of after I'm gone, and things are set in place for when that happens.'

'Don't talk about leaving, Pa, I can't stand it.' A tear tripped over her lashes. 'What has this man said or done to have you thinking like this?'

Jack stepped away from Molly, his face ashen. 'He thinks I know something, which I don't.' He paused and turned away before turning back again to give his daughter a wide-eyed stare. 'Wait, you said he had been at the munitions' factory. He hasn't tried to speak to you as well, has he?'

Molly shook her head. 'No, Pa, why would he?' She frowned and took a tentative step forward. 'I believe he was talking to Frank, he's like the security man there.' She gave a faint smile. 'Not that he could do much to stop any trouble, if there were some. Anyway, your man with the trilby was talking to him about things going missing from the docks. Apparently, it's been happening for years. Frank said he doesn't know anything about it but I get the impression the man doesn't believe him and keeps coming back.' Molly paused. 'I didn't recognise him as being the same person until tonight.' She sunk down onto the armchair. 'Surely he can't think you are part of it, can he?'

Jack shook his head. 'I don't know what he thinks, I just know he keeps asking me the same questions over and over again. I keep saying I don't know, but he clearly doesn't believe me.'

Molly jumped up, as anger pumped into her veins. 'Perhaps you should pay Emily a visit and tell her you're being hounded by this man.'

Jack gave his daughter a faint smile. 'Emily has nothing to do with the company. It's her brother William that owns it.'

'Of course, well maybe I'll go and see him. If you won't, I'm not going to stand by and watch some man bully you into some kind of admission.'

Jack smiled at his daughter's outrage. 'I'll sort it out, don't worry yourself, and please don't speak to your mother about it.'

Andrew's words suddenly popped into her head. 'I've heard that the Gettins had a reputation for doing things under the table, so to speak.' Molly hesitated before going on, unable to face her father. 'Apparently, a lot of business took place at the gentleman's club, where Henry Gettin was known as The Accountant.' She glanced up at him. 'Do you think that has anything to do with it?' She held her breath, waiting for her father's anger to explode.

Jack dropped slowly onto the wingback chair sitting by the fireplace. His gaze darted from side to side. 'Has my life been a lie?'

Molly dashed over and knelt at his feet. 'No, Pa, don't think that. Everyone is proud of you, and you have never knowingly done anything wrong. I'm sorry, I shouldn't have said anything, it's just rumours.'

Jack shook his head and brought his hand up to stroke his daughter's soft blonde hair. 'You're a good girl, Molly and whatever happens, don't forget I love you.'

Molly wandered aimlessly up Oxford Street, not noticing the cold breeze that whipped around her, or the shop windows advertising their Christmas merchandise. The street traders were out in force, each voice fighting to be heard, as they tried to sell their goods. She inhaled deeply. The aroma of warm, fresh bread immediately smothered her taste buds. Her breath was visible in grey, smoky tendrils as she breathed out. People stood around, clasping large cups of warming soup and chunks of bread in the cold, damp air. Hot potatoes and pies beckoned her towards the crowded food barrows, but she carried on weaving in and out of the sellers and their customers, side stepping her way along the street. The dark rings under her eyes told everyone she wasn't sleeping. Her skin had a yellow pallor that wasn't there six months ago. People turned and stared at her as she walked by, but she didn't notice. All she could think about was her father and the man in the trilby hat.

'You all right, lovey?'

Molly turned to see an old lady wearing a headscarf and a thin coat. Her lips had a blue tinge to them.

'You don't look like yer've slept for a week.' The old lady gave a toothless smile. 'Ye're one of them canaries ain't yer? You girls do a wonderful job, putting yer lives at risk and all.'

Molly lifted her hand to her face. The cold from her frozen skin seeped through her woollen gloves, gradually freezing her hand. She let her arm drop to her side, wriggling her fingers inside the glove. 'Thank you.'

The old lady patted Molly's arm. 'Take care lovey, yer don't look too good.'

Molly nodded, before carrying on along Oxford Street. Her mind jumped between her father and what the woman had just said to her. Molly shook her head. She hadn't been told before that she looked ill. Perhaps it was the sleepless nights.

Molly gasped as the Christmas tree in Selfridges' shop window caught her attention. She stopped and peered at the display. The tree must have been about ten feet tall, beads and decorations hanging from the pine branches. It was certainly a magnificent display. Two mannequins, dressed in their Sunday best, stood either side of it. Molly stood and stared at the scalloped silk curtains that hung from the top of the window display, and the sculptured doves holding the tinsel in front of the oval shaped windows, that had been painted into the scene. A smile slowly spread across her face. Maybe it was time she started her Christmas shopping. She took the few steps to one of the many grand entrances and walked into the world of Selfridges. It wasn't a shop she visited normally and she gasped, taking in the shining glass baubles, floating in mid-air. Molly felt her spirits lifting, as she took in the gentle chatter and laughter all around the shop. The shop assistants, dressed in their black skirts and white blouses, looked quite serene, with not a hair out of place as they served their customers. Molly immediately ran her fingers through her hair, which hung loose under her black narrow brimmed hat. The chink of coins dropping into the tills echoed around the huge store, only just heard above the rustling of paper, wrapping the many purchases being made. She looked around at the many sparkling glass cabinets, wondering whose job it was to remove all the finger marks that would be added during the course of the day. She smiled as the scent of Lily wafted her way. Maybe she would buy her ma something nice from here.

'Isn't it wonderful?' A deep familiar voice came from behind her, startling her out of her meanderings. 'It's another world, you would never guess there was a war on.'

Molly's stomach somersaulted. She took a couple of deep breaths, before turning to face him. She forced a smile. 'I agree.' Her eyes sparkled. 'But isn't it lovely to have the chance to escape the worry of it all for a few hours?' She turned back, her eyes widening, to take in the wonderment of everything around her.

Andrew stood watching her for a moment, before smiling. 'Indeed it is.'

Molly could feel Andrew's eyes burning into her back. Her gaze darted around the shop, while her mind ran around in circles. She had to get away, before he questioned her about Hyde Park. 'Well, I have presents to buy, so I must get on.'

Andrew lifted his arm and pulled back his sleeve before looking down at his wristwatch. 'It's just mid-day and this store doesn't close until ten o'clock tonight, so we could do our shopping together, unless you're in a hurry of course.'

Colour flooded Molly's cheeks. 'I don't know if I'm buying anything.' She gave a faint smile. 'The window display enticed me in.'

Andrew raised his eyebrows. He smiled, lighting up his face. 'It's done its job then, hasn't it?'

Molly laughed. 'That's very true.'

Andrew took her gloved hand and tucked it under his arm. 'You're not running away from me this time.' He smiled, squeezing her hand with his arm. 'Shall we have a coffee and something to eat, before we wander around together? The crepes here come highly recommended.'

Molly breathed in his musky scent and was immediately transported back to Hyde Park. Her body temperature began to rise. She tried to think of something else, to stop her cheeks turning crimson. Her father should do it.

Andrew stepped aside, to let a woman pass them. He gazed at Molly for a moment. 'If the weather had been warmer, we could have gone up to the roof garden and looked across London.' He wrinkled his nose as they approached the perfumery. 'But maybe we can do that in the summer.'

Molly gasped.

Andrew kept hold of Molly's hand as they weaved in and out of the customers and staff. He guided her to a table dressed with crisp white linen, pulling out a chair for her, before moving to sit opposite her. 'We need to start again, so perhaps we could pretend we are meeting here for the first time.' A chuckle lit up his eyes. 'I'm an acquaintance, I'm not your boss.' He gave a little cough. 'We don't work together and we've certainly never exchanged passionate kisses.' Andrew's eyes sparkled with mischief. 'Do you think you could do that? Do you think you could pretend to like me?'

Molly lifted her chin slightly. 'If I do that, it means you can't tell me what to do at work.' Her eyes shone to match his.

Laughter burst from Andrew. 'I'm not sure you listen to me anyway, so that's a small price to pay.'

A waitress approached their table, dressed in the traditional black uniform with the white apron, donned with frilled white straps, sitting neatly on her shoulders.

Andrew looked across at Molly. 'Would you like to try a crepe or would you prefer something else?'

Molly's stomach somersaulted once again; she wasn't sure if she'd be able to eat anything. 'A crepe would be fine, thank you, and a cup of tea please.'

Andrew nodded. 'Do you like mushrooms, or as they call them here, champignons?'

Molly began to undo the buttons on her coat. 'I'm not sure I've had them before, but if you recommend them, I'm happy to try champignons.'

Andrew looked back to the waitress. 'We'll have two the same please.'

The waitress didn't move her attention from Andrew. She bobbed and reluctantly walked away from the table, looking back over her shoulder at him.

Andrew undid his buttons and removed his coat. 'So, what are you planning to buy while you're here?'

Molly shrugged. 'I don't know. I'd like to buy my parents something nice. They never spoil themselves and they deserve to experience some of the good things life has to offer.'

Andrew nodded, before a smile crept across his face. 'Have you experienced the good things in life?'

'Are you laughing at me?' Molly frowned.

'No, I'm just trying to find out more about you, that's all.'

Molly's tense features began to relax. 'I have, but only in the sense that my friend comes from a reasonably wealthy family, so it's given me a taste of what could be.'

'So money is important to you then. Is that why your parents want you to marry well?'

Molly laughed. 'Money isn't important to me. When I marry, if at all, it will be for love and no other reason.' She shook her head and frowned. 'My parents worry that after they've gone, I will at best be in a refuge, at worst on the street. They just worry.'

Andrew nodded, his eyes never leaving her face. 'That's understandable. I think that's the sort of thing all parents worry about, especially for their daughters. Unfortunately it's a cruel world, particularly for girls.'

Molly raised her eyebrows, but stayed silent for a few moments. 'Don't you think it's odd that we found ourselves here on the same day, let alone at the same time?'

Andrew shook his head. 'Have you been following me then?' He grinned, before squeezing her hand across the table.

Molly's colour immediately became heightened.

Something flitted across Andrew's face, but she wasn't quite sure what it was. He laughed. 'You are so suspicious. It's nearly Christmas and we both have shopping to do.' He waved his hand outwards. 'As indeed do many other people, just look around you. I'm starting my shopping early, because I don't have a clue what to buy, although, I have been given some heavy hints about some diamond earrings.'

The smile faded from Molly's lips and her eyes clouded over. Was this the woman from Café Monico, or was it someone else? One thing was for certain; the earrings were definitely not for her. *Ask him, ask him* a voice screamed in her head.

'Your parents are nice people.' Andrew sighed.

The moment was lost.

His eyes clouded over. 'They remind me of my own.'

Molly reached out and clasped his hand with both hers, not caring that her chance had gone. 'They are good people, but I think I must be a disappointment to them sometimes.'

Andrew studied her for a moment. 'That's not how they come across. I think they want the best for you, whatever that may be.'

Molly couldn't help being drawn to Andrew, despite him bringing out the worst in her. Her father's story of George and Emily arguing, and not realising they were in love, jumped to the forefront of her mind. They are very happy. Maybe it could work. Maybe she had misjudged him. Maybe he wasn't the boss, looking for a plaything. But there was still the woman in Café Monico, and the earrings, but she wasn't going to let them spoil a good day.

Chapter 17

'Ma, I've asked Alice and Victoria round this evening, so we can wrap our presents together, as well as exchange Christmas gifts.' She smiled at her mother. 'I know you like to see them, but if you don't mind, I'd like to take them into the back room. We don't get much time to catch up since I stopped working at Foyles.'

Sophie looked up from the previous day's newspaper, adjusting the position of the beeswax candle on her side table. The flame flickered, casting its shadows, and the scent escaped from the melted pool of wax at the base of the burning wick. 'It's nice that they want to come round here and be polite to us old folk.' She looked across and chuckled at Charlotte's wide-eyed expression.

Charlotte pushed herself forward in her chair and waved her hand in her mother's direction. 'Less of the old folk, Ma.' She patted the bun at the nape of her neck. 'I may not be as young as Molly, but I'm not old folk yet.' She leant back until the armchair was supporting her again.

Sophie chuckled, returning her attention back to the newspaper. There was a faint rustle as she smoothed out the crumpled lines that interrupted the print on the pages.

'That's fine, Molly.' Charlotte fidgeted in her chair and stretched her legs out in front of her. 'I'll bring in some tea and biscuits for you all. I only ask you don't leave it a mess.'

Molly pummelled the soft embroidered cushion on a chair, before sitting down. The clock in the hall chimed eight times. 'As if I would, Ma, do you not think I know you well enough? You know, even on my first day at the munitions' factory, I was thinking of you.' Molly chuckled. 'There was a really filthy window in Andrew's office and I remember smiling to myself while I was sitting there, terrified, thinking how you would have been up there scrubbing it clean.'

Colour poured into Charlotte's cheeks. 'It's the way I've been brought up. Me ma was always saying 'cleanliness is next to godliness', ain't that right, Ma?'

Sophie glanced up, frowning at them both, before returning to the paper. 'It's how it should be.'

Molly smiled at her mother. 'Some things never change, Ma.'

Charlotte raised her eyebrows. 'I wouldn't say that's true. You seem to have more of a spring in your step these days. Could that be Mr Greenwood's doing?'

The thud of the doorknocker startled them both; Molly breathed a sigh of relief. 'I'll get it.' She jumped out of her chair, running her hands down her navy blue, calf length skirt, and took the couple of steps towards the hallway. She caught her reflection in the small mirror, turning her head one way, then the other. Molly hadn't noticed the change in her skin, and no one had mentioned it until the woman in Oxford Street had told her. Now she found herself constantly staring in the mirror.

Charlotte levered herself out of the armchair. 'I'll go and put the kettle on.' She pulled at the frill of her off-white, high neck blouse and straightened her ankle length black skirt.

Sophie didn't lift her eyes, but smiled down at the newspaper. The creaking hinges and the girls' voices had saved her granddaughter for now.

'Hello.' Molly stepped aside. The wind whooshed around the hall, sneaking into all the nooks and crannies. 'Come in out of the cold.'

'Hello, Molly.' Alice and Victoria spoke in unison, as they stepped over the threshold. A couple of dogs barked, some distance away; Molly whimsically wondered if they were talking to each other.

Charlotte smiled at the girls as she stepped into the hall.

Alice returned the smile. 'Mrs Cooper, I hope you and Mr Cooper are well.'

'Indeed we are, thank you for asking. I was so sorry to hear about your brother, Alice. It's a terrible time we live in.'

Alice's smile faded. 'Thank you, my mother has been quite distraught. It's been difficult to leave her at times. While she is subdued, I don't think she has any more tears to cry. My son, Arthur, gives her so much joy and it's hard not to smile around him.'

Charlotte nodded. 'Yes, I can imagine that must help at these difficult times.'

The hinges screamed in the silence that followed. Molly cleared her throat and indicated to the console table, near the front door. 'Why don't you both leave your bags here and we'll just go in and say hello to Gran, before we disappear into the back room.'

Victoria forced a smile. 'That sounds like a good idea.' She carefully placed her carpetbag next to the leg of the table, and Alice followed suit.

Molly led the way into the dining room. 'Gran, Alice and Victoria are here.' Molly stepped aside so they could follow her into the small room.

Sophie smiled. 'Hello, girls, it's lovely to see you again.' She frowned as she glanced at them. 'Alice, I was so sorry to hear about your brother and hope your family are coping. Please let them know my thoughts and prayers are with them.'

Alice blinked quickly. 'Thank you, that's very kind of you.'

Sophie forced a smile. 'Anyway, I expect you girls have got a lot of gossip to catch up on, so don't waste your time with me, go on, off with yer.'

Molly smiled her gratitude to her grandmother and ushered her friends out of the room. 'Let me hang up your hats and coats.'

The girls unbuttoned their coats, removed their hats and unwrapped the woollen scarves from around their necks. They picked up their bags and followed Molly down the hall, the heels of their shoes clipping the tiles as they went.

'Take a seat.' Molly waved her arm around the room. 'I think Ma is going to come in with some tea and biscuits in a minute.'

'How's things with you, Molly?' Victoria asked, as she emptied her bag of ribbons, paper and gifts.

'All good.'

'And Mr Greenwood?' Victoria pushed, studying her friend closely. 'Has it moved on since Hyde Park?'

Molly frowned, her mind rushing back to the lovely time she had with him in Selfridges, but then there were the earrings. 'I don't really want to talk about him. Let's talk about other stuff.'

Alice glanced at Victoria, before shrugging her shoulders. 'Have you finished all your Christmas shopping?'

Molly beamed at her friends. 'I bought some lovely bits from Selfridges.' She developed a faraway look in her eyes for a moment. 'The decorations in there are lovely. You should go and have a look.'

Victoria shook her head. 'I don't think it's a shop I've ever been in.'

'You should go.' Molly's eyes widened and her smile broadened. 'I had a lovely mushroom crepe there too. I think the menu was written in French, but I'm not sure about that.'

Alice squinted at her friend. 'Who were you in there with? It wasn't Mr Greenwood by any chance, was it?'

Colour flooded Molly's face. She lowered her eyelashes. 'I walked in the shop by myself, the window display looked lovely and enticed me in.' She told herself she wasn't lying, as she did walk in alone. Molly had no desire to talk about Andrew. She knew she had to talk to him about this other woman. She knew she loved him more than life itself. It was just finding the right moment to have that conversation.

The table was laid with Charlotte's best china. A small tree stood in the corner of the room, its fresh pine smell greeting you at the dining room door. Under her gran's supervision, Molly had decorated it with shiny glass baubles and tinsel, just like she had every year for as long as she could remember. Neatly wrapped presents stood under the tree, waiting for eager excited hands to tear the paper and ribbon away.

Charlotte glanced across at Molly. She had lost weight, but then she supposed, thanks to the war, so had most people. 'Christmas isn't the same without the excitement of a child running around.'

Sophie laughed. 'Molly used to get so excited. Do you remember how she used to want to feel and shake all the presents under the tree?'

Charlotte and her mother laughed.

Molly forced a smile, as they both roamed down memory lane. It dawned on her that she was their life. All their expectations of having grandchildren and great grandchildren rested with her. She lowered her lashes and rubbed the back of her neck. 'Maybe one day, when this war is over, there will be children in this house again.'

'Maybe, time will tell.' Sophie smiled, but it quickly vanished as she studied her granddaughter. 'You look pale, and you've lost weight. Is everything all right?'

'Yes, I'm just tired.' Molly's voice dropped to a mumble. 'It's been a hard month.'

Jack lowered the previous day's newspaper he was reading. It rustled on his lap, as he stared at his daughter. 'You do look pale, maybe you should see a doctor.'

'I'm fine, Pa.' Molly studied her father. The dark circles around his eyes seemed to be getting worse. She sighed; guessing the man with the trilby hadn't gone away. 'There's no need for that extra expense to be spent on me.'

Jack shook out the creases in the paper before closing and folding it, the rustling filling the silence. 'It might be expense to you, but you're working in a dangerous place and I don't want anything happening to you.'

'Don't worry, Pa, I'm sure I'm as healthy as you are.' Molly smiled. 'Shall we start Christmas and open some presents?' She clapped her hands together. 'I'm very excited about the gifts I've bought for you all this year. I hope you like them.'

Charlotte laughed at her daughter's enthusiasm. 'Go on then, you're the youngest, so you can hand them out.'

Sophie clapped her hands. 'Aww, I wonder what we have, they're all beautifully wrapped, it's almost a shame to open them.' She giggled as Molly handed her a box with a large bow tied in red ribbon. She studied it, before giving it a gentle shake. 'Maybe not.' Sophie chuckled as she pulled the end of the ribbon and the bow unravelled. The paper unfolded, revealing a large box. She carefully pulled off the lid and moved the paper covering the contents. Sophie squealed. 'Oh it's beautiful.'

Charlotte leant towards her mother. 'Come on, let's see it.'

Sophie glanced across at her daughter. 'It's beautiful. Thank you, Molly.' Sophie pulled the silk nightdress, with its fine lace and embroidered flower detail out of the box. 'It's wonderful to touch, so soft.'

Charlotte gasped. 'It is beautiful, Ma.' She turned to Molly and frowned. 'I hope you haven't spent this kind of money on all of us.'

Molly sighed. 'Ma, don't spoil it. I want you all to experience some of the lovely things that are out there.' She reached over and clasped her mother's hand. 'You want the best for me, but I want the best for you too.'

Charlotte's eyes became watery. 'I know. I just worry, that's all.'

Molly smiled and gently shook her mother's hand. 'But not today.'

'No, not today.'

Sophie looked up from the nightdress. 'Molly, thank you, I've never seen anything so beautiful. I shall save it for best.'

Molly laughed, before moving to wrap her arms around her gran. 'You're the best gran a girl could ask for, ever.' She gave her a gentle squeeze, before sitting on the floor next to the Christmas tree. 'Ma, are you next?' Not waiting for an answer, she pulled out an oblong shaped package, again wrapped with red ribbon, with a magnificent bow on the top. Smiling, she passed it to her mother.

'You've spent a lot of time wrapping your presents. Your gran is right, they do look too good to open.'

Molly bit down on her lip, as she watched her mother follow her gran's actions. She twisted and turned the package, giving it a gentle shake before pulling at the end of the ribbon.

'Oh my, what a beautiful bottle.' Charlotte tweaked the thin green ribbon that was tied in a bow around the neck. 'Look Ma, it has lily of the valley painted onto the glass.'

Molly smiled. 'Open it, Ma, and have a smell of the perfume.'

Charlotte shook her head. 'Oh no, I know I shall love it, and besides, it'll go off.'

Molly threw back her head and laughed. 'Ma, just open it. It'll last for ages.'

Charlotte carried on twisting and turning the bottle, before she finally did as she was bid. She pulled the stopper free and the floral perfume wafted around the room.

They all, as one, sniffed the air.

Sophie smiled. 'It's a lovely smell.'

Jack laughed. 'That it is. It's a good job the men are all away at war, I can tell you.'

The women laughed as Charlotte blushed.

'Your turn, Pa.' Molly reached under the tree and pulled out a flat parcel, tied with the same red ribbon. She tweaked the bow, before passing it to her father. 'There you go, Pa.' She smiled. 'When it came to buying yours, I couldn't make up my mind, so I hope you like it.'

Jack smiled. 'I'm sure it will be fine.' He pulled at the ribbon and the paper fell away, revealing a white shirt. He held it up for everyone to see. 'Excellent, Molly, I could do with some more work shirts.'

Molly smiled. 'Pa, it's not like your usual shirts.' She paused as she watched him examine it. 'Look at the cuffs.'

Jack dropped the shirt on to his lap and lifted the cuff of a sleeve. 'What? These are lovely, they look quite luxurious.' He held the sleeve out, to show Charlotte and Sophie. 'Look at the blue enamel, against the gold swirls. They're wonderful cufflinks.' He looked over at Molly and reached out to squeeze her hand. 'Thank you, I think you've spoilt us all today.'

'I'm pleased you like them. I spent ages wondering whether to buy them or not.'

A loud thud at the front door prevented the conversation going any further. Charlotte turned in her chair, to look in the direction of the hall. 'We don't usually get people knocking on Christmas Day?'

Jack stood up, dropping his present onto the seat of the armchair, along with the newspaper he'd been reading. 'I'll go and see who it is.' He pulled at his waistcoat and strode out into the hall.

The women bent their heads in the same direction, trying to pick up snippets from the disjointed voices. Molly gasped and quickly ran her fingers through her hair, letting it fall onto her shoulders. She smoothed the blue skirt of her dress, before pulling her black cardigan across her body. She looked up to see her mother and grandmother smiling at her. 'You brought me up to always be presentable.'

'Of course, dear.' Charlotte smiled. 'I'm pleased you've listened to us about that.'

Jack's heavy footsteps were quickly followed by a second pair, but before anything could be said, he walked through the doorway, closely followed by Andrew.

Jack announced with a flourish. 'We have a visitor.'

Andrew smiled and nodded as he walked further into the room. 'I hope you don't mind me disturbing your Christmas afternoon, but I wanted to drop off these small gifts for you all, and wish you all a happy Christmas.'

Molly couldn't look in Andrew's direction, but was so tempted to feast her eyes on him. She closed her eyes and breathed deeply, allowing his scent to assault her senses. Memories of their day in Selfridges made her smile. The kiss they had in Hyde Park quickly flooded her mind; she worried that the colour in her cheeks would give away her thoughts.

'That is too kind of you, Mr Greenwood.' Charlotte pulled herself out of her chair. 'Please let me get you a cup of tea, and maybe something to eat?'

'No, please, I haven't come to burden you.' Andrew gazed across at Molly. 'I'm on my way to have a late dinner with my sister.'

Molly's eyes flew open. *Sister? He had never mentioned a sister before. Was that who he was with at Monico's? If so, why didn't he say? Why didn't you ask?* A voice screamed in her head. She was desperate to know and opened her mouth to speak, only to quickly shut it again.

Andrew looked away and smiled at Charlotte. 'I would never be forgiven if I couldn't eat the feast that she probably has planned.'

Sophie and Charlotte laughed and nodded their understanding.

'Surely you can stay a few minutes?' Sophie tilted her head in his direction.

Molly's chance had gone. She almost burst out laughing at the irony of the situation. Was her grandmother flirting with him?

Andrew laughed. 'Maybe just a few minutes.' He handed Jack the bag containing the four presents. 'It is only a little something for each of you.'

Jack delved into the bag, pulling out the exquisitely wrapped presents and handing them out. 'My word, sir, did you wrap these yourself?'

Andrew laughed. 'Definitely not, the lady in the shop took pity on me.'

Sophie giggled, ripping open the small present she had been given. 'This is exciting; I do love Christmas.' She held up four cotton and lace embroidered handkerchiefs. 'These are beautiful, thank you.' She spread one out on her lap and studied it. 'Such exceptional needlework, thank you so much.'

Andrew smiled. 'I'm pleased you like them.'

Charlotte carefully opened her present, as always hoping to use the paper and ribbon again. She gasped as she pulled a blue floral silk scarf from the wrappings. 'It's lovely, thank you. I shall treasure it.'

Andrew nodded. He glanced over at Molly, studying her hands, clasped tightly in her lap.

Sophie and Charlotte stared at Jack, in anticipation. Sophie chuckled. 'Come on, Jack, I'm dying with excitement here.'

As he ripped open the paper, Jack felt everyone's eyes on him. He released a navy blue tie from the decorative trimmings and held it up. 'This is wonderful.' Jack nodded in Andrew's direction. 'Thank you, I can never have enough ties.'

Andrew grinned. 'I thought it might match the cufflinks Molly bought for you.'

Jack hesitated for a split second and glanced over at his wife, who was staring wide-eyed at him. 'I think they will be a good match, don't you think, Charlotte?'

'Indeed I do.'

Jack turned to look at Molly. 'It's your turn now.'

Charlotte looked at her daughter, before turning her attention to their guest. 'It's very kind of you, sir, but we have nothing to give you in return.' Colour flooded her cheeks as she realised she should've had something wrapped up for just such an occasion.

Andrew smiled. 'I didn't mean to cause embarrassment, Mrs Cooper. I was brought up to believe you don't give to receive, so my gifts are just something I wanted to do.'

Jack pulled his shoulders back. 'Indeed that is true. We have also instilled that in Molly.' He frowned at his daughter. 'Molly, are you not going to say hello to our guest? We don't wish him to think you have no manners.'

'My apologies, Mr Greenwood.' Molly bent her head slightly. 'It's kind of you to take time out of your busy day to visit us. To bring us presents as well is truly the action of a wonderful person.'

Jack and Charlotte stared incredulously at Molly.

Molly squirmed. She knew she was in the wrong, but couldn't help herself. Andrew had no idea the trouble he'd caused her, by coming to the house and revealing he knew about the cufflinks. A good match indeed, were they talking about them, or the tie and cufflinks? She had to put a stop to this runaway train, before it was too late.

Sophie giggled. 'Forgive my granddaughter. I have a feeling you are not her favourite person right now. She has never been very good at hiding her feelings.'

Andrew smiled and cast his gaze from Sophie to Molly. 'Oh I can assure you, I have come a cropper from Molly's tongue, on more than one occasion.'

Molly's eyes blazed with anger. 'Please don't talk about me as though I'm not here.'

Sophie turned to Molly. 'Whatever your issue with Mr Greenwood is, you need to remember it's Christmas, and that's a time for love and forgiveness.'

Andrew fidgeted from one foot to the other. 'Please don't argue on my account. I shouldn't have come.'

Molly stood up. 'No, you shouldn't have done.'

Confusion ran across Jack's face as he scowled at his daughter. 'Molly, I don't understand what's going on, but I will not allow you to treat Mr Greenwood this way.' He looked over at Andrew. 'Maybe, if you have the time, sir, you should spend some of it with my daughter, to sort out whatever it is that has happened.'

Andrew bowed his head slightly. 'I would gladly do that, Mr Cooper. Your daughter is very important to me.'

'Molly.' Jack's eyes pleaded with his daughter. 'Please take Mr Greenwood into the back room and talk about what's bothering you, once and for all.' He looked at Andrew. 'Good luck.'

Molly did as she was bid, escorting him to the best room. Once they were in there, she slammed the door.

'How dare you come here and make me look like the bad person, in front of my family. Let alone bringing presents, when they, or I, have clearly not bought you anything. My mother will feel guilty for weeks now.'

Andrew shook his head. 'I'm sorry about your mother. I thought I was just doing something kind, that would please them, and of course, I love giving presents.' His eyes hardened, showing a steel-like quality. 'You, on the other hand, left me very little choice.' He sighed. 'You almost ran for your life out of Hyde Park and, despite having what I thought was a good day Christmas shopping, you avoid me after work. What am I supposed to do?'

Molly's lips straightened into a thin line. 'Move on to someone else. Isn't that how it works?'

Andrew took a step nearer and pulled her into his arms. 'Damn it, you're the most frustrating person I know. Don't you realise I love you?'

His mouth smacked against hers, bruising her soft lips. Her breath was ripped from her lungs, but instead of objecting, her body moulded itself tight against his. A groan escaped as his tongue delved inside her mouth.

Andrew suddenly pulled away from Molly, ripping away the strength of his arms and the passion of his kiss.

Her head was spinning. She slowly opened her eyes. Her love was shining through, but he was gone. Tears filled her eyes, as the thud of the front door resounded along the hall, letting her know he wasn't waiting for her reaction. That moment had gone.

Chapter 18

January 1917

Alice sighed, running her hands down her charcoal grey skirt, before straightening her navy blue blouse. The usual busy day at Foyles was coming to an end. She picked up the feather duster that was lying on a shelf underneath the counter and slowly flicked it over the books that had been waiting patiently for her attention, holding her breath when the particles of dust floated in the air. She rubbed the end of her nose with the top of her hand, as the smell of cigarette smoke wafted up. There was mustiness about second hand books. The pages of some had curled corners, where they had been well thumbed, while others were in pristine condition and the spines hadn't been cracked, indicating they had never been opened. Sadness wrapped itself around her at the thought of these, sitting alone somewhere, with no one wanting to open them. Alice shook her head. Her emotions seemed to be all over the place. She didn't understand what had got into her lately.

Molly had filled Alice's thoughts, since she came weeping into Foyles, and there had been no talk of Mr Greenwood when they were wrapping their presents. The trouble was, Alice didn't know how to help her friend. She glanced over at Victoria, sitting in her usual position in the payment booth. Since Hyde Park, Victoria had been deep in thought and her eyes carried a despondent look. Without asking her, Alice knew Molly's situation had resurrected memories for Victoria that she would rather have forgotten. As a friend, Alice felt unable to cope and didn't know how to help either of them.

Victoria looked up and caught her eye, giving a small wave.

'Everything all right, Mrs Leybourne?' Mr Leadbetter's deep voice jerked her out of her thoughts.

Alice swung round to face her manager. 'Yes, sir.' She forced a smile, picking up her notepad and pen, but not really knowing why.

'Miss Cooper was quite distraught when she came in here, before Christmas. Are her parents in good health?' Mr Leadbetter frowned. He straightened his black jacket. His fingers delved into the small pocket of his waistcoat and pulled out a fob watch. He pressed the small button, allowing the lid to fly open. He stared down at it, but didn't register the time. He'd spent weeks wondering whether he should ask after Molly Cooper, and it had got the better of him in the end.

Alice fidgeted from one foot to the other, wondering what she should say. 'Her family are fine, sir, and I shall let her know you were asking after her.'

Mr Leadbetter nodded. 'I obviously don't want to intrude, but please let her know if it's anything to do with her new employment. I will be happy for her to come back here. I quite like her idea of encouraging young people to read. After all, they are our future.' He flipped down the watch lid with his thumb and put it back in his pocket.

Alice nodded and gave him a smile. 'I'll pass on your message. I know she misses working here, yet still feels the need to do something for the war effort.'

'Hmm, she's not alone in those thoughts. There's a lot of pressure on women to pick up the jobs that the men have left behind.' He paused, before shaking his head. 'In a way, I quite miss her. She kept me on my toes.' Mr Leadbetter smiled as his memories took over. He sighed and frowned as he looked across the counter at Alice. 'In my limited experience with the female of our species, when a woman is that upset, it usually involves a man.'

Alice lowered her eyelashes. 'It was a personal problem she was wrestling with, and I believe it all got too much for her.'

'As I said, I have no desire to intrude, but whatever it is, you and Miss Appleton are clearly concerned, because your bubbly natures seem to have disappeared since that day. In fact, Miss Appleton appears to have returned to the maudlin person she once was.'

Alice knew he was right and they had to do something to sort the mess out. 'I'm sorry, Mr Leadbetter, if I'm honest I don't know how I can help my friends at the moment. Consequently, I keep going over things in my head.'

Mr Leadbetter nodded. 'I can understand that, but let me give you some words of wisdom from this old man.' He paused for a moment. 'There's often nothing you can do, but be there to listen and pick them up when they fall. It's about keeping the faith that everything will work out in the end.' He patted the counter and turned to walk away, looking back over his shoulder. 'It will be enough that your friends know you are there for them.'

Alice nodded; he wasn't as harsh as he made out.

The shop doors banged shut, jolting Alice out of her thoughts. She slipped around the counter and strode towards the payment booth.

Victoria glanced up. 'I saw you talking to old Leadbetter. Is everything all right?'

Alice frowned at her friend. 'How do you feel about meeting Molly from work?' She paused for a moment, waiting for a response from Victoria. 'Look, we need to snap out of it and be there for her if she needs us.'

Victoria took a deep breath, before a faint smile played on her lips. 'What are you suggesting?'

Alice shrugged her shoulders. 'If I'm honest, I don't know. She isn't opening up about what's on her mind. In fact, quite the contrary, she clearly didn't want to talk about any of it when we went round there. We need to find her, or are we just fair-weather friends that will just leave her to it?'

Victoria stood up and the lock clicked as she turned the key, opening the booth door. 'You're right, I've allowed myself to be dragged down by it, instead of finding solutions for her.'

Alice nodded. 'Even Mr Leadbetter has noticed we're preoccupied.'

Victoria's eyes widened. 'We must have been bad then.'

Alice laughed. 'Why don't we meet Molly from work? If we go on the underground, hopefully it will only take half an hour or so. We would have to look at a map though, because I don't have a clue how to get there.'

Victoria's eyes darted from side to side. 'We could walk to Tottenham Court Road and look at the map there.' A glimmer of hope sparked in her face. 'I think Molly said she'd have to get the train to Canning Town, although I'm not entirely sure about that.'

'It's a start.' Alice smiled at her friend, her spirits lifted, at the prospect of doing something to help Molly. 'The shop's shut now, so shall we grab our coats and go?'

Victoria nodded, stepping through the doorway of the booth.

Molly sighed and glanced around at the women busy doing their bit for the war. She finished stemming the shell she was working on and rested her broom handle on the table. It was no good. It was now or never. She took a deep breath and walked away from the table.

'Where are you off to?' Flo's voice rang out, over the noise of the machinery.

Molly didn't look back, quickening her pace as she weaved in and out of the different pieces of machinery.

'Are you all right?' someone shouted.

Molly nodded, but didn't stop walking. Her breathing was laboured when she finally reached the rickety iron staircase that led to Andrew's office. As soon as she stepped onto the bottom rung of the stairs, the creaking started, announcing that someone was on their way up. Molly took comfort in the fact she would be the last person he expected to see, especially after the Christmas fiasco. She moved onto the second step and was convinced it moved more than usual, so sped up the remaining ones. Molly stopped at the top and waited, gasping for air, trying to slow her breathing, but her lungs were burning. Her chest tightened. Molly shook her head. Surely all the cycling she was doing should be adding to her fitness, not taking it away. The office door sprung open.

'Oh, hello.' Andrew's eyes widened as he stared at her. 'Er, do you want to see me?'

Molly nodded, sucking in her breath, despite finding herself unable to breathe. She coughed as the stench of sulphur hit the back of her throat.

'Come.' Andrew reached out and put his arm around her. 'Are you all right, you look very pale.'

Molly wasn't sure if her legs would carry her the few steps into the office. Gingerly, she stepped forward.

'Lean on me.' Andrew was grey when he lifted her into his arms and carried her to the chair in his office. Gently disentangling himself, he got her a glass of water. 'Here, sip this.' He held the glass to her lips.

Molly let the cold liquid fill her mouth; grateful to wash away the bad egg taste.

Andrew perched on the edge of the desk and stared at her. 'Have you had a medical lately?'

Molly stayed silent. This wasn't how it was meant to be.

'Well, we clearly need to sort one out for you.' He lifted the glass again. 'Would you like some more.'

Molly nodded, grateful for the shaking to be subsiding and the tightness in her chest loosening its grip. She took another sip, before speaking in a soft whisper. 'I'm sorry, I don't know what came over me.'

'I must say you look pretty dreadful. Maybe you should go home.' Andrew raised his eyebrows. 'Is that why you came to see me, because you wanted to go home?'

Molly shook her head. 'I wanted to talk to you.' She gasped, resting her hand on her chest.

Andrew raised his eyebrows. 'Really, about work I take it?' His lips lifted slightly. 'After all, I am your boss.'

'I deserved that.' Molly lowered her lashes. 'I'm sorry, but I need to talk to you about my father.'

'Is he in bad health?' Andrew frowned. 'I have money, if he needs a doctor.'

'No, no, no, nothing like that, but thank you for your kindness.' Molly took a deep breath. 'There's a man that has been coming here and speaking to Frank, and now he's bothering my father at home. I think it's all to do with where my father works. This man thinks he knows something, but he doesn't—'

'Wait.' Andrew grabbed Molly's hands. 'I don't understand, go back to the beginning.'

Molly closed her eyes, taking a breath, and then another, in a bid to slow her breathing down. She opened her eyes and momentarily saw the panic in his. 'Remember you told me that Henry Gettin was rumoured to do some

THE FOYLES BOOKSHOP GIRLS AT WAR

under the table deals at the gentleman's club, well I think it's all connected to that. My father is an honest man and the thought of him being accused of anything illegal will break his and my mother's hearts.'

Andrew looked thoughtful. 'I don't really know what I can do to help.' He tapped his fingers on the desk for a moment. 'I can talk to the man, if he returns, and try to find out what's going on.' He paused. His gaze darted back and forth. 'My father may have kept some papers at home, although that is highly unlikely. I can have a look, but I would have thought someone from the bank would have come knocking for them by now.'

Molly nodded. 'I'm sorry. I shouldn't have burdened you with my problem. It's just that my father looked dreadful when I spoke to him about it.'

Andrew nodded. 'I must admit, he did look tired at Christmas, but I didn't like to say anything.'

Darkness was like a shroud wrapping itself around Alice and Victoria, as they stepped out of Canning Town underground station. Victoria pushed her arm through Alice's, as they both peered into the blackness, waiting for their eyes to adjust. There was an eerie feeling to the night, with no moon or stars lighting the way. The biting wind whistled around them. Alice pulled her woollen hat over her ears, glad she had wrapped her scarf around her neck. They both took a deep breath and stepped further into the darkness, straining to see where pavements started and ended.

Victoria's gloved hand squeezed Alice's arm, as they both stepped forward. 'Is it my imagination, or is it darker around here?'

Alice studied the road ahead, willing herself to ignore the ominous shapes on either side of the road. Her voice wobbled as she spoke. 'We mustn't let our imagination get carried away. It's just trees and bushes.'

Victoria shuddered. 'I don't know how Molly does this every day. I don't think I could.'

'No, but I expect it's like everything, you get used to it, especially as she does it twice a day.'

'She's definitely braver than I am.' Victoria forced a laugh. 'I suppose we should get going.'

'We probably should have walked this in the daylight. After all, neither of us know where we are going.' Alice frowned. 'All we can do is head for the docks and hope for the best.'

Victoria nodded. 'Perhaps we should sing, to help keep us calm.'

Alice laughed. 'What do you suggest, Onward Christian Soldiers or All things Bright and Beautiful?'

Victoria giggled. 'Yeah, it was a stupid suggestion. If anyone heard us, we would be locked up in a lunatic asylum.'

'We need to hurry. At this rate, we'll miss Molly.' Alice quickened her step. 'I think we probably spent too long in that tea room, planning what we were going to do and say.'

The girls jumped at the foghorns sounding ahead of them, indicating the docks were close by. Dark shapes of the various factories came into view. The ground shook under their feet, as an ear-piercing explosion filled the night sky. A fiery ball of orange and red flames licked up, high above their heads. Black dust mingled with the flames, billowing out in all directions. The girls screamed as they hung onto each other. They huddled together as shards of glass and dust rained down on them. Another explosion quickly followed. It reverberated around them. Fireballs fell down to earth, breathing flames wherever they landed. People rushed out of their burning homes, screaming the names of their loved ones. Slates from roofs crashed down on the ground, some causing injury along the way. Bells rang out, in the distance at first, but gradually getting louder as the fire engines got nearer.

For a moment, Alice and Victoria clung to each other, stunned and rooted to the spot. Groans carried towards them. A young girl screamed for her mother.

Alice and Victoria jerked out of their stunned silence and screamed. 'Molly.'

Alice ran forward and picked up the little girl, carrying her away from the house and handing her over to Victoria. 'Can you look after her until help comes?'

Victoria nodded.

'I'm going to see what help I can give, but I'll be back in a moment.' Without stopping to think, Alice turned and ran towards the flames that were engulfing the sky.

Victoria could hear Alice shouting Molly's name, but nothing came back. She wanted to help look for her friend. A woman covered in dust staggered towards her. 'Silly question, but are you all right?'

The woman nodded.

'Mam.' The girl held out her arms to the woman.

'Jeanie, thank god you're safe.' The woman turned to Victoria. 'Thank you for keeping my little girl safe.' She swept Jeanie into her arms and sobbed as she squeezed her tight.

'Don't cry, Mam.' Jeanie hugged her mother.

Victoria felt her eyes prick with unshed tears. She stroked her on the back, before turning away. She took a step forward; fear held her where she stood. The thought of the men she loved dealing with this and worse, on the frontline, brought shame on her and she rushed towards the groans that were fighting to be heard. Victoria shouted out as loud as she could. 'Alice, Molly.'

'Over here,' Alice's voice came back.

Sophie clutched the wooden arm of her chair. 'Did you feel that?' She paused. 'The ground vibrated.' Her face distorted with fear. 'Was it a bomb?'

Jack jumped up and pulled a small amount of the soft black material away from the window. He peered up and down the street. 'I can't see anything.' He turned back to look at his mother-in-law. 'Whatever it was, it's not close by.' He returned his attention to the street.

'The ground definitely moved Ma, I felt it shoot up my legs.' Charlotte frowned. 'If it wasn't close by, then it must be a big bomb of some sort.' Her hands clasped each other tight. 'Do you think Molly's all right?'

A mushroom cloud of yellow and orange flames lit up the sky.

'Oh my goodness, look at that.' Jack ran out of the room. 'Stay indoors.'

The winter's cold air rushed into the hallway, and through into the front room. Sophie pulled at her woollen shawl, wrapping it tighter around her.

Charlotte's stomach churned. She jumped out of her chair. 'What's going on?' She took up Jack's position at the window. Her chest tightened as she let out a gasp.

Sophie's face crumpled with worry. 'What is it, Charlotte? Please tell me.'

'I think the ground moving was an explosion.' Charlotte stared out at the flames licking high in the sky, trying to reach up to heaven. 'It's unbelievable. I can't tell where the fire is coming from.' Her hand fiddled with a necklace sitting at her neck. 'I'm not even sure which side of the river it's on.'

The cold draught died away, as the front door thudded shut. Jack ran his hand through his hair as he walked in the door. 'It looks like it's further along the river, somewhere. It's hard to tell exactly where.'

Charlotte's eyes filled with tears, fear written all over her face. 'Can you tell how far? Is it this side, or the other?'

Jack shook his head, but remained silent for a moment. He sighed. 'I think it's this side.'

Charlotte dropped like a stone. Jack just managed to catch her, before her body hit the floor. He lifted her into his arms, carrying her effortlessly into the best room, and rested her on the sofa. 'Sit tight, I shall light the fire, fetch your mother and then make you a cup of sweet tea.'

Sophie's voice came from the doorway. 'There's no need. I'm here.'

Startled, Jack turned to face her, before looking down at his wife.

Charlotte's voice was barely a whisper. 'Molly?'

'Shh.' Jack stroked a stray strand of hair away from her face. He smiled, before leaning forward to gently leave a butterfly kiss on her forehead. 'I'm sure she will be fine.'

Charlotte's lips lifted slightly in the corners. 'I don't know what I would have done without you, Jack Cooper.' She took his hand in hers. 'You have looked after me since I was a girl. You're a good husband and friend.'

Jack rested his hand on top of hers. 'I love you, Charlotte, and I have done since the day we met, so don't you forget it.'

Sophie stood tall in the doorway. A tear was threatening to have its day, but she squeezed her eyes shut. She wanted to move away, but didn't want to break the spell their love had created. The door creaked as she hobbled from one foot to the other.

Jack's head jerked up at the unexpected sound.

'I shall go and make the tea.' Sophie's gaze travelled between her daughter and her beloved son-in-law. 'You stay and look after Charlotte. She needs you.'

Charlotte tried to sit upright. 'I don't think...'

'You can just do as you are told, for once.' Sophie's smile belied her words. 'I want to help.'

Charlotte looked up at Jack, before nodding at her mother. 'Please be careful. Jack can always carry the tray in.'

Sophie nodded, accepting the compromise. She frowned as she left the room. Without a word being said, she knew exactly what her daughter was thinking about. Did the explosion come from the munitions' factory? Was Molly safe? Her eyes welled up. She couldn't outlive her granddaughter. Please God, don't let that happen. Sophie rested her hand against the wall, as she took slow steps towards the kitchen, praying hard that she would be taken instead of Molly. She could hear Jack's soothing voice, as he spoke to Charlotte.

'Molly will be all right. You have to stay positive.'

Charlotte's tears rolled down her cheeks. 'But she might not be.' She sniffed and took a deep breath.

Jack stood up straight and began pacing around the room. His hand rubbed the back of his neck. 'You know, families are going through this every day, not knowing whether or not their sons, fathers or brothers are alive, and they have been for years now.' He took a deep breath. 'Now it's our turn. We have to keep our faith and pray she'll come home to us, that's all we can do.'

Charlotte sniffed, before finally nodding. 'It might not be there.' She paused, her eyes searching for reassurance, as they darted from side to side. 'Would it be worth trying to go to Silvertown, to find out?' She looked up at Jack, with a little bit of hope in her eyes.

Jack took a couple more steps, before stopping to pull back the black material at the window. The sky was bright. It looked like a bright morning, if you glanced in the right direction. 'I don't think you'd get close enough to it, besides the time it takes to get there, Molly could be home.' He let go of the material and it sprung back tight to the window frame.

Charlotte stared up at him. She took a deep breath. Her voice faltered, despite her best efforts. 'Isn't… isn't there anything we can do?'

Jack paused, before shaking his head. 'Unfortunately, we have to be like the rest of the country and hope we are going to be blessed with good news.' He pulled the curtaining away, to look out at the orange sky again. His lips tightened for a minute. A sigh escaped. 'Of course, it may not be the munitions' factory at all.'

Charlotte nodded and quickly looked away, when the sound of rattling cups reached her.

Sophie pushed open the door with her elbow, the hinges screaming in the silence of the room.

Jack tutted as he stepped forward and took the tray from her. His heart was drumming hard in his chest. 'You were supposed to give me a shout, not struggle by yourself.' He gasped, as pain gripped his chest. He struggled for breath as he laid the tray on the coffee table. He flopped into the armchair and tried to take a couple of deep breaths, until the pain began to subside.

Sophie raised her eyebrows. 'I'm not as helpless as you two think I am.'

'No one thinks you are helpless, Ma, we just don't want you slipping and hurting yourself.' Charlotte sighed as weariness washed over her.

Sophie smiled. 'Hmm, well anyway, I've brought some cake as well, Victoria Sandwich, because I have a feeling it's going to be a long night.' She glanced at her daughter.

'Don't give me that look. I'm not going to bed until I know Molly's safe.'

The clock ticked away the minutes, and then the hours. The tea sat cold in the cups. The cake remained untouched. The three of them sat in silence, locked in their own thoughts. For the umpteenth time, Jack took his gold fob watch out of his waistcoat pocket and ran his thumb over the gold scrollwork that covered the top of it. He stared down at the treasured gift from Emily and George Wyatt, which they had presented to him when he started working in her father's accountancy company. He sighed. It all seemed another lifetime ago now. He had been more than grateful at the time, for the job they had given him. Jack hadn't fully understood the importance, or the meaning, of the little black book he'd handed over to them at the time. He only knew they were grateful, and offered him a job. All that was about fifty years ago, and now he had to answer questions about things he knew nothing about. He rubbed the top of his left arm, before flicking open the lid. Molly should have been home hours ago. Perhaps he should visit the hospitals, but something told him to stay put. Pain gripped his chest again. His hand came up and clutched at his shirt. He gasped for breath. Was it too late to tell his family he loved them?

Chapter 19

Victoria climbed over the smouldering debris of the fire. Bricks, stone and wood made her way hazardous. A pain shot up her leg as her foot slipped. Her eyes squeezed shut as she bent over, clutching her ankle, biting down on her bottom lip, until the iron taste of blood seeped into her mouth. She finally looked up to see Alice pulling up her dress and ripping her petticoat into shreds. Had she found Molly? Victoria tentatively took a couple of steps, careful not to make any sudden movements. The heat from the fire took her breath away, as she stepped nearer to Alice. 'Have you found Molly?'

Alice glanced across, shaking her head. She bent over and used one of her petticoat strips to tie a tourniquet around a woman's leg, to stem the bleeding. She looked down at the pale skin covered with dust and ash. She wiped some of it away from her eyes and mouth. 'You're going to be all right. I'll let the ambulance people know you are here, and they can take you to hospital.' She stood up, straightening her back, before running her hands over her face and shouting out. 'Molly.' Nothing came back from her friend.

The woman groaned. 'She was... still in there... when I left.'

Alice and Victoria stared over at the fire, still billowing; there was no sign of it going out. They couldn't get any nearer to it. Neither of them spoke, as the helplessness of the situation took hold.

A tear caused a rivulet through the dust on Alice's face. 'Come on, Victoria, we have to try and help the people we can, at least until someone arrives.'

A child screamed out, nearby. Victoria's head jerked as she looked around, trying to figure out which direction it came from. 'I think it's from over here, somewhere.'

They both took a few steps towards the crying child and looked around. Alice coughed as the acrid smoke hit the back of her throat. It was hard to see through it, but they kept moving forward. The heat was burning her skin and singeing the hair that had escaped from her hat. 'I can't tell where it's coming from.' The crying got louder.

Alice and Victoria simultaneously looked down. Were they standing on him? Without a word, they both stepped to one side and started clawing at the rubble. The crying slowly faded away and only the occasional sniff could be heard. Victoria uncovered a foot and immediately moved to what she thought would be the other end of the body, and frantically began moving the bricks, stone and burning wood that lay in her way. Her mind flashed back to her parents. Was anyone there to help them, when their train crashed? She truly hoped they hadn't died alone. She worked quicker, ignoring the pain and blisters that were already forming on her hands, where the heat had burnt through her gloves.

'Oh my goodness, thank god,' Victoria screamed. The boy's eyelids fluttered for a couple of seconds, before deep blue eyes stared up at her. 'Thank god you're alive.' Tears rolled down her face, as she leant over and kissed the boy's forehead. 'Thank god.' She gave him a watery smile. 'Try not to move and we'll soon have you out of here.'

They carried on removing the rubble. Alice looked over at the boy. 'I know you'll have bruising, but does it hurt anywhere.'

The boy shook his head.

Victoria removed the last of the stone away from him.

Alice ran her hands down his legs and arms. 'Are you sure?'

'Yes, miss.' The boy moved his hand to wipe his face, coughing as he did so. 'Can I get up now?'

As he spoke, a grey haired man in his fifties stood over them.

Alice looked up, taking in his uniform. 'Thank goodness.' She beamed at him. 'I'm an ambulance driver too, but I didn't want to make the decision that it was all right to move the boy. He says he's not in any pain.'

The man nodded and repeated what Alice had already done. 'The name's Albert, but I only answer to Bert.' He frowned as he stared down at the boy. 'I think he's safe to move.' With that, he picked him up and whisked him away, over the rubble, every step more sure-footed than their nervous attempts.

The girls stood up and shouted out again. 'Molly.' Their voices were lost in the noise of more glass shattering and falling to the ground.

Alice frowned as she watched Bert move further into the smoky haze. Panic ran across her face. 'Bert,' she yelled out. 'There's a lady over there, with half my petticoat wrapped around her leg. I think she needs urgent attention.'

He turned and looked in their direction. 'Don't worry, I'll find her.'

'She's not far from where you're standing now, just over a bit, I think.' Alice pointed, as she shouted to him.

Men could be seen fighting the fire, but it was battling hard; doing its best to stay alive.

Victoria allowed the tears to finally roll down her cheeks. 'Molly's gone, hasn't she?'

Alice stared straight ahead. 'We can't think like that. We have to keep hoping she got out.' She paused, before lowering her tone. 'It's all we have.'

Victoria ran her hands over her face, wiping away her tears. She sniffed. 'I was so harsh with her, telling her she would lose friendships if she kept working here, and now I may never get to... I just can't bear the thought of...'

'We can't think like that.' Alice turned to Victoria. The fight she was having with her own thoughts was written on her face. 'My father once told me I had to keep the faith, and Freddie would return, and he did. That's what we must do now. Keep the faith.' She looked back at the raging fire. 'We have hope, and that's what we have to cling on to. Pray for her safe return to us.'

Victoria nodded, sniffing at the thought of what could be ahead of them. Poor Mr and Mrs Cooper. How would they cope without Molly?

'Come on, the best thing we can do is keep busy.' Alice turned her back on the fire and looked around at the devastation surrounding them. 'There are lots of people here that need help.'

Victoria nodded and followed Alice. Stepping carefully over the rubble, she had long forgotten the pain in her ankle.

They stopped and helped mainly women and children, where they could, using their petticoats to stem any bleeding. Alice and Victoria spent the night guiding people to the Salvation Army and the YMCA first aid stations, where they could get help, along with a hot drink and something to eat.

Victoria looked around her. 'Such devastation. Where would all these people sleep tonight? There must be hundreds of them. It looks like even the church hall has been flattened.'

A lady wearing a Salvation Army uniform approached them. 'Here, girls, have a hot cup of tea.' She passed the mugs over to them. 'You've been here for hours, and no doubt you have helped to save many lives.'

Alice and Victoria tentatively wrapped their sore hands around the cups, having long since taken off their gloves, for ease of touch. 'Thank you,' they chorused.

The lady nodded towards the water. 'It seems the fire has spread over the river.' They all stared in silence at the fireball on the other side of the Thames. 'I hope no one is hurt.'

'You wouldn't think it could travel that far.' Victoria couldn't take her eyes off the orange flames, mushrooming up into the sky. 'I hope there are no more casualties or deaths.' She turned and gave the lady a weak smile, wanting to describe Molly to her, but deciding not to. 'It's been a long night. What will happen to all these people? They've lost everything.'

The lady looked around her. 'We'll find church halls and temporary homes for them. I think most of them are just glad to be alive, although some are having trouble finding family members.'

Alice sipped the strong hot liquid, glad for it to remove the dust from her mouth. 'We came here hours ago to meet our friend from work, and got caught up in it all, but we still haven't found her.'

The lady frowned. 'I can't say for certain how many, but there are a lot of people unaccounted for, so don't give up hope.'

Victoria gulped at her tea, not caring that it burnt her throat on its way down. At least it would take her mind off crying again. She handed the cup to the lady. 'Thank you, I think it's safe to say we needed that.'

Alice followed suit. 'Thank you.'

A blood-curdling scream rang out in the eerie light of the fire. Alice and Victoria looked towards the figure of a woman dropping to her knees. They stared at each other. Was that Molly?

The girls ran towards the woman screaming into the night. There was no mistaking the grief that exuded from her. The woman knelt on the burning embers, with no thought for her own safety. There was no desire in her to keep on living.

Alice's eyes filled with unshed tears, as the woman's grief erupted into another scream. She briefly wondered how they could help someone who was so distraught, but kept moving towards her. The smell of sulphur was more potent, now they were nearer to the blaze.

Victoria grabbed Alice's arm, holding her back. They both stood and watched the tear-stained face of their friend contort in agony. The happiness at seeing Molly alive soon disappeared. Her skin had a yellow tinge to it, and was smattered with dust. As they stepped nearer, they could see her arm was red raw. It was hard to tell if her dress was scorched, or just dirty in places. Alice and Victoria gripped on to each other, as they took a tiny step forward.

Another scream tore through Molly, like shards of glass. 'Anndreew.' It was a raw, terrifying sound. Her knuckles tried to break through the skin.

Alice and Victoria flinched as they moved to stand either side of Molly, to heave her up onto her feet.

Molly looked at them for the first time. 'I… I can't find Andrew.' She gulped for air, her lungs burning, as smoke filled them. 'I can't leave him.' The pain wrenched from her heart. 'I have to find him.'

'Sshh,' Alice soothed. 'We'll look for him, while you have your burns looked at.' She nodded to Victoria and they both pulled her up.

'Nooo, I can't leave him,' Molly cried out. 'I can't, don't you understand, I love him.' She covered her face with her hands. 'I can't do this again, I just can't.'

Victoria blinked quickly. 'We'll find him, I promise.'

Alice's eyes snapped in her direction.

Victoria shrugged her shoulders at her, before lowering her voice. 'We have to get her out of here, so she can have some treatment.'

Alice nodded. 'Come on, Molly, we promise we'll look for him.'

Molly looked at them both, through desperate, watery eyes. 'I can't leave him, I just can't.'

Victoria lifted her arm and put it around her friend, trying to give comfort, but fear of hurting her made her drop it to her side. 'I promise we'll find him. Please trust us.'

Molly sniffed and gulped for air. She opened her mouth to speak, but shut it again. She looked heavenward and clasped her palms together. 'Please God let him be alive. Please, I beg of you. I never told him I love him with all my heart.' The tears gathered dust as they rolled down her face, her voice dropping to a whisper. 'Please, please, let him live.'

Alice looked upwards. Her lips moved, but nothing could be heard above the noise of buildings collapsing all around them. 'Come on, Molly, we'll find him, I promise.'

Molly gasped as she moved to stand up. Her hands splayed as she stumbled.

Victoria caught her by the arm. They both saw Molly's blistered hands for the first time. They took a deep breath, choking as they breathed in the smoke around them.

'Lean into me,' Alice instructed, trying to take shallow breaths. 'You're exhausted. I'm not even sure you can walk.'

Molly did as she was bid. The bottom of her skirt stuck to her legs, as she slowly put one foot in front of the other. She made no attempt to pull it away. Every couple of seconds, she stopped and looked over her shoulder, searching the horizon for Andrew, but he wasn't there. Her red-rimmed, bloodshot eyes gazed at her friends, as she gulped for breath. 'You will look for him, won't you?'

'Yes, yes,' Victoria gasped as Molly's trembling body shivered next to hers. She tried to concentrate on her footing, so she didn't take them all down with her.

Molly looked over her shoulder again. 'You promise.'

Alice moved her arm under Molly's. 'Yes, we promise.' She frowned at Molly. 'You need to concentrate on getting better yourself, otherwise you won't be any good for him, when we do find him.'

Molly's eyes welled up again. 'I know.' Her throat tightened as she tried to hold back the tears. 'He told me he loves me, but I never said it back.' The dam broke and her body convulsed with grief. 'He doesn't know how much I love him.'

Without a thought to any injuries, Alice pulled her into her arms. 'Shh, we will find him, I promise.'

Molly lifted her head. 'I have been such an idiot, and now—'

'Don't think like that.' Victoria rubbed her back with one hand, while wiping away her tears with the other. 'Stay positive. He's here somewhere, just waiting to be found, and we won't give up looking.'

Alice looked at Molly. 'Come on, let's get you to the ambulance, or at least the first aid station.'

Molly didn't move, her eyes set on the fire and rubble behind her. 'You know, he gave me a book of love poems by William Wordsworth for Christmas, and I didn't even thank him for it.' Her eyes welled up again, stinging from the fire and smoke.

Victoria patted her shoulder. 'Come on, the sooner we get you looked at, the quicker Alice and I can carry on looking for your man.'

Molly nodded. She looked around, as if seeing it all for the first time, before whispering to herself. 'What a mess, there are going to be so many homeless people tonight.'

Alice took a deep breath; relieved that Molly's attention had been moved to the many people affected by the explosion. 'A lady from the Salvation Army told us they would be put up in church halls, until they could be found somewhere to live.'

Molly nodded. 'But they've lost everything, all their treasured belongings, things that can't be replaced.' She sighed. 'It's terrible. Was it a bomb?'

Victoria shrugged her shoulders. 'I don't know.'

Molly stopped walking, her mind just catching up with everything. 'Wait, what are you two doing here?'

Alice smiled at her friend's confusion. 'We were on our way to meet you from work.' She shook her head. 'We hadn't seen you since before Christmas and wanted to find out how you were. Obviously, we weren't expecting this, but I'm really pleased we were here, although the explosion did scare us half to death.'

Victoria frowned. 'It was terrifying, but it must have been worse for you. To be honest, we just wanted to find you, and when we couldn't, that frightened me more.'

Tears rolled down Molly's cheeks, as she looked from one to the other. 'I'm sorry, you could have been killed.'

Victoria gave a small smile. 'You've nothing to be sorry about. We're just glad you're all right.'

The lady from the Salvation Army came to meet them. 'Here, drink this, my lovely.' She handed Molly a cup of water, her voice soothing away any anxiety. 'Come with me and I'll get you looked at, then you can have a cup of tea.'

Molly took the lady's arm and stepped forward, before looking back at her friends. 'Don't forget, his name's Andrew Greenwood.'

The lady turned to the girls. 'If you're still looking for someone, they have taken a lot of people to Poplar Hospital. I believe it's on East India Dock Road, if that helps.'

'Thank you.' Victoria raised her eyebrows and turned to Alice. 'Perhaps he's already there.'

'Molly.' Alice flinched and looked around before lifting her voice to be heard over the clanging of falling metal behind her. 'Were the two of you together, when the explosion happened?'

Molly eyes darted from side to side. She shook her head. 'No, I blacked out for a while, but I don't remember seeing anyone when I came round.'

Alice nodded. 'A lady told us you were still in there when it exploded, so we did fear the worst.'

Molly gasped. 'Was that Grace or Flo?'

'I don't know.' Alice shrugged her shoulders. 'At the time, she was hardly conscious and I was too busy, trying to stop her bleeding to death.'

'I think she's been taken to the hospital for further treatment.' The lady held on to Molly's arm quite tightly. 'I heard someone say the use of the petticoat probably saved her life.'

Alice's lips tightened for a moment. 'Let's hope so. Molly, go and get some treatment, while we look for your man.'

Molly nodded.

Alice and Victoria watched her walk towards the waiting ambulance.

Victoria kept her eyes focused on Molly. 'Do you think he might have got out of this alive?'

Alice turned to her. 'I don't know. I must admit, I was beginning to think the worst about Molly, but she's here, so let's hope for the best.'

Victoria breathed in deeply. 'I do hope he's alive. She won't be able to cope a second time.'

Chapter 20

Exhausted, Alice and Victoria walked along East India Dock Road, towards Poplar Hospital. The building had a grand air about it, with its large sash windows on the upper floors and arched windows on the ground floor. As they approached, dawn was just breaking through, and its many chimney pots decorated the skyline. From a distance, it looked like a fortress, although there were no cannons on show.

Alice yawned. 'I hope Freddie isn't too worried about where I am, only I've never stayed out all night before.'

Victoria wanted to laugh, but her body objected to her using that much energy. She ached from head to toe. 'He's a policeman and so is your sister, and mine come to that, so I'm sure between them they'll be able to work it out.'

Alice's steps got slower and shorter. 'I'm so tired.' She ran her hands over her eyes, forgetting about the dust that was smeared all over them.

Victoria took one look at her and laughed.

'What's so funny?'

Victoria gulped for air, in-between each surge of laughter. 'Your face was a mess before, but now you've added yet another layer of dust and god knows what else, it looks even worse.'

Alice looked down at her clothes. Part of her white petticoat was dangling below her skirt, where she'd ripped it to help the lady who had a river of blood running from her leg. 'I hadn't given a thought to the way I look. I suppose we should have gone home and changed before we came here.' She smiled. 'Mind you, if I'd gone home, my bed would have been beckoning me, and I don't suppose I would have fought it very hard.'

'Hmm, that's true.' Victoria gave her friend a wry smile as she took in her appearance. 'But they'll probably keep you in, thinking you were caught up in it.'

Alice laughed. 'No chance, I have my son to get home to, and anyway, you don't look much better.'

Victoria's laughter died on her lips. 'I hope we find Andrew Greenwood here. What are we going to tell Molly, if we don't?'

Alice pushed her hand through her friend's arm. 'I'll tell you what we are not going to do, we are not going to think about it.' She sucked the cold air deep into her lungs. 'He must be here, the alternative doesn't bear thinking about, and I for one can't go home and tell Molly we couldn't find him.'

Victoria nodded. 'No, that's news I definitely don't want to be the bearer of.'

They both stepped through the hospital doorway, to be greeted by an overpowering smell of antiseptic. Groans came from various directions around them. The dove-grey corridor was overcrowded with men, women and children, their faces blackened with soot and hair covered in white and red brick dust. Some were lying on trolleys, while others slouched in chairs. Those that were able, stood, making soothing noises to their loved ones. People turned and stared. Their eyes were bereft of expression. These were people that had lost everything. All hope had been ripped away from them. Nurses in their long blue uniforms, covered with a white apron, strode purposefully from one place to another. Their soft-soled shoes didn't make a sound on the tiled floor. The strain of the long night was etched on their faces.

A young, red-eyed nurse spoke as she approached Alice and Victoria. 'If you need to register for treatment, the desk is over there.' She half turned and indicated to the far end of the corridor.

Alice couldn't resist the half smile that played on her lips. 'No, despite the way we look, we've come looking for someone.' She paused and looked around her, realising the hopelessness of the situation. 'Mr Andrew Greenwood. Do you know whether he has been admitted? We were told the injured were all brought here.'

The nurse nodded. 'That's true, but we've either sent some home after treatment, or moved them on to Charing Cross or St. Thomas' Hospitals.' The nurse frowned as she glanced up the corridor. 'As you see, we are rather pushed for space.'

'Alice, Victoria.'

Both the girls turned around and looked towards the entrance, trying not to gasp at the ashen features, or the fear, in the wide eyes of their friend.

Alice's jaw dropped for a moment. 'Molly, what are you doing here? You should be at home, resting.'

Molly took the couple of steps towards them. 'You two look dreadful, and by the look of it, you should be at home resting.'

Victoria wrapped her arms around her friend, hugging her tight. Molly's heart pounded next to hers. 'We promised to find him, and that's what we're trying to do, although without success so far.'

'Mind you, we've only just arrived,' Alice quickly cut in, stepping forward to hug Molly.

Molly pulled away from Alice. 'Is he here?'

The nurse smiled at the three girls. 'I'll go and check.' She turned to walk away.

Molly called her back. 'I'm sorry, but could you also check for Grace Fairchild and Flo, sorry Florence Attwood.'

The nurse nodded and moved away, to check the records.

Alice frowned. She moved to grab Molly's hand, quickly pulling back as she remembered the horrific burns. 'You should be at home; you've had a terrible shock.'

Molly's lips thinned into a straight line, before she took a deep breath. 'Do you know how hard it is to sit and do nothing? Exhausted as I feel, I wouldn't be able to sleep. Every time I closed my eyes, I'd be reliving the explosion. As it is, I'm constantly struggling to work out where everyone was at the time. I'm driving myself mad, trying to figure it out.'

Victoria nodded. 'I can understand that. I went through a similar thing when my parents died, and I wasn't even there. It must be difficult for you, because you have the shock to deal with as well.'

Molly shrugged her shoulders. 'I don't know about that, I just can't sit and do nothing. It makes me feel so helpless.' Molly looked at the many people around them. 'All these people, and probably a whole lot more.' Tears pricked at her eyelids. She blinked rapidly, trying to prevent them from falling. It was too soon to ask how many had been injured or killed. She couldn't bear the thought of Andrew being one of them.

Alice followed Molly's gaze around the room. 'Do you recognise any of them?'

Molly shook her head. 'I wonder if Flo and Grace survived it.'

Without a word, Victoria gently rubbed Molly's back.

'There's the woman I tore my petticoat for.' Alice chirped up, pointing to a woman lying very still on a trolley that was pushed up against a wall. 'I'm so glad she made it here.'

'Oh my goodness.' Molly took a step forward, before looking back at Alice. 'It's Grace.'

Molly rushed over to the trolley, with Alice and Victoria in pursuit. Molly called out. 'Grace, it is you, isn't it?'

Grace slowly turned her head. Her face was yellow from the sulphur, and when she spoke, her voice was hoarse. 'Molly, you're all right.' She coughed. 'I think a woman asked me about you.'

Alice smiled. 'I'm not surprised you don't remember, as I was tying half my petticoat around your leg at the time.'

Grace gave a faint smile. 'Thank you, apparently you saved my life.' Her eyes became watery as the tears threatened to flow. 'Flo didn't make it.'

Molly shook her head and fought the urge to wrap her arms around Grace. 'I don't know what to say, except I'm so sorry.' She paused. 'We've been looking for you all, but haven't had much success, until now that is.'

A tear tripped down the side of Grace's face. 'Maybe it was a blessing. I think she was following Nora.'

Molly's lips thinned for a moment. She looked at her friends and forced a faint smile, before looking back at Grace. 'Thank goodness you're all right. How long are they keeping you in for?'

'I don't know.' Grace grimaced, as she tried to move her leg. 'But probably not long. There's not enough space for all of us. My father has been in. He said our home's been flattened, but at least everyone's alive. The house doesn't matter.'

Alice sucked in her breath. 'It's not good, Grace.' She shook her head. 'Everywhere was flattened. Did your father tell you where they were staying?'

Grace tried to laugh, but it was a croaky sound. 'That's why he came in.' She took a breath. 'He has a cousin in Kent, so they are going to stay with them until this war is over.'

Molly's finger tips stroked Grace's hair away from her face. 'Grace, you must come and live with me.'

Grace opened her mouth to speak, but nothing came out.

'I insist. When they discharge you, I'll take you home with me.' Molly laughed. 'There'll be no privacy, and my mother will dote on having someone to look after. I can tell you that, after a week of them, you'll be running away, but it will give you a roof over your head and a chance to work things out.'

Grace squeezed her eyes shut and nodded, before gripping Molly's bandaged hand.

Molly winced, as the pain shot up her arm.

'Sorry.' Grace frowned. 'Are you all right? I didn't think, I just—'

'Everything's fine, don't worry.' Molly forced a smile to her cracked, blistered lips.

Victoria glanced from one to the other. 'Right, so now we only need to find Andrew.'

Grace's eyes flew open. She stared hard at Molly. 'Andrew?'

Alice glared at her friend, but it had been a long night and it wasn't over yet.

Molly lowered her eyes and straightened the sleeve of Grace's top. 'Victoria means Mr Greenwood. I've been fretting whether everyone's all right.'

A man's pained voice called out further down the corridor. 'Nurse, nurse, can you help us please?'

The nurse that was heading towards them immediately changed direction and sped towards the voice. The girls turned to look in the direction it came from.

Molly sighed. 'We're in the way here.' She looked at Alice and Victoria. 'These people need her help more than we do.'

Both girls nodded, but kept looking in the direction the nurse had gone.

The nurse looked up and beckoned them.

Molly took a deep breath. 'Don't leave the hospital, Grace. I'll be back later, to take you home.'

'Have you seen me?' Grace tried to laugh. 'Do I look like I'm going anywhere?'

Molly chuckled. 'That's a fair point Grace, but I meant what I said.' Without waiting for a response, she stepped forward.

The girls were close behind her. Was this going to be the moment of truth? Trembling as fear trampled on her bravado, she pulled back her shoulders and lifted her chin. None of it mattered. She just had to know the truth. Had she lost the man she loved?

The bedraggled girls were hungry, tired and forlorn, as they stood outside St. Thomas' Hospital, staring up at the formidable red brick building. Their breath was creating grey, wispy tendrils in the cold air. The ground was covered with a sparkling silver frost and the early morning light glinted off the sleepy River Thames. The boats chugged silently up and down, causing the water to ripple along the riverbanks. It was business as usual for most people, as London came to life. Grey smoke billowed out of chimneystacks, disappearing into the low clouds. Children's voices began to filter through to Molly. The memory of the children playing war games, and the white feather, bombarded her mind all at once. She had no idea what it all meant. She didn't care whether he was a coward, a conscientious objector or anything else. All Molly knew was that she loved him and she would deal with the rest, if she had to.

Victoria cleared her throat, breaking the silence between them all. 'I know it's probably inappropriate, but I could murder a cup of tea.'

Molly swung round to face her friend, noticing for the first time how grey and gaunt she looked. Her eyes were bloodshot and her face was still black with dust. 'I'm sorry, I've been selfish.' She took a deep breath. 'Why don't you both go home and get some sleep.' Her gaze moved to Alice, who had raised her eyebrows. 'You both look dreadful, and I promise I'll be fine.'

Two elderly women walked towards them, deep in conversation, their voices carrying in the still air.

'June, did you feel the earth move last night?'

The lady tied her blue floral headscarf into a bow, under her chin. 'Haha, I haven't felt the earth move for years, Doris.'

The two ladies hooted with laughter.

Doris's smile faded. 'No, seriously, I hear that explosion last night was really bad. Somebody said the munitions' factory has been flattened. I hope the girls got out before it happened.'

June shook her head. 'I can't imagine everyone got out. They say it destroyed everything around it, as well.' She pulled on her woollen gloves.

The two women noticed the girls for the first time, studying them for a few seconds, before lowering their gaze. Without a word, they increased their pace to get past them.

Victoria and Alice glanced at each other, before shaking their heads and speaking in unison. 'No, we're in this together.'

Victoria laughed. 'But I could still do with a cup of tea.'

Molly threaded her arm through hers. 'Then you shall have one.' She glanced up at the building in front of them. 'But first we have to go in, and ask if Andrew is here.'

Victoria gave a playful groan. 'Then you promise I can have a drink?'

'Promise.' Molly bounced from one foot to the other, twisting her aching neck from side to side. 'I know I'm being mean, but I won't be able to concentrate or enjoy the tea, if we don't ask first.'

Alice scraped her tongue along her dry lips. 'Well the sooner we do this, the sooner we get to have a drink, so come on let's get on with it.'

'Right.' Molly's chest puffed out, as she took a deep breath, immediately regretting it when her scorched lungs objected. She squinted, as she stepped into the bright entrance of the hospital. Women and children sat in silence, patiently waiting to see a nurse or a doctor. A baby could be heard crying. A woman cradled a small child, asleep in her arms. Her eyes drooped, but the fear of missing her spot jerked her awake. The walls needed painting, where the trolleys had scraped along them, gouging out the plaster and leaving black marks in their wake. 'Hospitals are such sad places.'

Alice nodded. 'They can be, but on the other hand, most people do come out better than they go in.'

'That's true.' Molly cast her eyes around. 'I suppose, with you driving an ambulance, you see the other side of things.' She wrinkled her nose. 'And they all seem to smell the same.'

Alice smiled. 'It's cleanliness, probably soap and disinfectant.'

Molly forced a smile, before sighing. 'I know, but I can almost taste it.' She walked over towards the desk, stopping just short of it, and looking over her shoulder. Colour drained from face. Her mouth dropped open as she stared across the waiting area. 'Ma?'

Alice and Victoria followed Molly's line of vision and gasped, before frowning at each other.

Molly shrilled. 'Ma, what are you doing here?' Many startled patients stared at her, looking around the room for the person in question, but she was oblivious to them. Her legs wobbled, as her mind went into overdrive. 'Has something happened to Gran?'

Charlotte jumped up, her chair knocking against the wall. Tears began to flow. She swiped the loose tendrils of hair from her face, revealing the lines entrenched in her forehead.

Molly's legs were weak as she ran over to her. Her chin trembled. She straightened her lips. She had to be strong. 'What is it Ma? Is it Gran?'

Charlotte shook her head. She rubbed her face with a handkerchief that she's been twisting in her fingers for hours. 'No, it's not Gran.'

Molly's skin became ashen, as her legs buckled from underneath her. Alice and Victoria reached out to grab her, before she hit the floor.

'Sit down, Mrs Cooper.' Alice looked around. 'We need to find a chair for Molly.'

'I can stand, in fact it'll do me good to.' Charlotte stretched out her arm and stepped aside. 'Sit her down here.'

The girls lowered Molly on to the chair. Alice knelt down in front of her.

Victoria looked around for someone to help. 'I'll see if I can get her a cup of water.' She took a step towards the nurse's station.

Alice nodded as she patted Molly's hand. 'It's probably shock. She's had one helluva night.'

Charlotte bit down hard on her lip for a moment. 'Is Molly going to be all right? Is she hurt? I've been worried sick about her.'

Alice moved away as Victoria approached with a small cup of water. 'Molly, sip this.' Victoria held it to her friend's lips.

Alice squeezed Charlotte's arm. 'I think she'll be fine, it's just been a terrible night.'

Charlotte nodded. 'We felt the explosion at home.' Her lips trembled. 'I thought we'd lost her.' Tears flowed freely down her face. 'We didn't know what to do, so we stayed put, but then Jack, Mr Cooper, got pains in his chest, so we came here.' She sniffed. 'But that was hours ago.'

Alice stared at Mrs Cooper's grey features. She had aged overnight, but then she guessed she wasn't alone.

Memories of her own mother being rushed to hospital flooded her mind. 'I'll see if I can find anything out.' She put her arms around Molly's mother, squeezing her tight, before marching away from her. She remembered Molly had taken control for her, when she hadn't felt able, and now she needed to do the same for her friend, whatever the outcome.

Molly looked up at her mother. Her eyes filled with pain; first Andrew and now her father. When was this dreadful time going to end – and how?

Sophie wanted to pace around the small dining room in Carlisle Street, but her legs wouldn't allow her to pace. The best she could hope for was a hobble. She picked up the previous day's newspaper, for the umpteenth time, staring at it without reading a word. She had too many questions swirling around her head, like a whirlpool. Was her son-in-law going to be all right? Was her granddaughter even alive?

Sophie edged herself forward until she could push herself out of the armchair. A groan escaped, as she tried to straighten up. She had willingly sat there all night, alone for most of it, in case there was any news of Molly. A thud at the front door caused her to jerk round. Was this it? After a few seconds, the letterbox squeaked as it was pushed open.

'Mrs Cooper, Mr Cooper, is anyone in?' a woman's voice yelled into the hallway.

Sophie shuffled forward, shouting towards the front door. 'I'm coming.' She gradually moved forward, gripping the door jamb as it got within arms' reach. Stopping to catch her breath, she yelled out. 'Don't leave, I'm coming.' Shaking her head, she mumbled to herself, 'It's these damn legs of mine, they just don't want to work any more.' Sophie took another tentative step forward, grimacing as her feet touched the floor. She shook her head again; she should have got up and moved around more in the night.

The letterbox flew open. 'There's no rush, it's only Lily, Alice's sister.'

Alarm bells rung in Sophie's head. Hadn't Molly told them she was a police officer, these days? Her eyes filled with unshed tears. Perhaps she'd come with news of Molly. She sniffed and roughly wiped her hand over her eyes. 'Come on girl, you're nearly there.' Her hand reached out and grabbed the door handle, slowly turning it to allow the door to swing open.

Lily stepped forward. 'Hello, I'm Lily, Alice's sister. We've only met a couple of times, but that was many years ago.'

Sophie forced a smile to her tight lips. 'Yes, I remember.' She half turned, while gripping onto the door jamb. 'Have you come with news of Molly?'

Lily followed the silent invitation to enter the house, as Sophie hobbled back to the front room, breathing in the lavender scent that filled the hallway. 'Are you here by yourself? Sorry, I don't remember your name, you've always been Molly's gran.' Lily gave a nervous laugh.

Sophie turned to gaze at Lily. She was a pretty slip of a girl. 'Just call me Sophie.' Her eyes clouded over. 'Do you know whether Molly's all right? That explosion last night travelled through the house, so I'm assuming it was a bomb or something, but Molly hasn't been home since yesterday morning.'

Lily gazed across at the old lady, only deciding then not to mention the destruction of the munitions' factory, or the properties close by. The news hadn't sounded good for Molly, or any of the others that would have been nearby. Lily immediately became the professional policewoman, placing her hand under Sophie's arm. 'Let's get you sitting into a chair.' Her voice softened. 'I'm sorry, I don't have any news about Molly, but Alice and Victoria didn't get home last night, so I'm making the assumption they are together.'

Sophie shook her head. 'I keep telling myself no news is good news.'

'That's true, bad news always travels quickly.' Lily paused as Sophie lowered herself into an armchair. 'Are Mr and Mrs Cooper not here?'

Sophie's eyes filled with tears. 'No, Jack got rushed to hospital, by the doctor.' She sniffed. 'They think it's his heart, but I haven't heard from them either. I hope he's not...'

'I'm sure the doctors and nurses are looking after him, and they'll be home soon.' Lily studied Sophie's translucent skin. Her face was drained of colour, apart from the dark lines under her eyes. 'If you don't mind, I'll make you some tea, and maybe a bit of breakfast.'

Sophie shook her head. A tendril of grey hair freed itself from the bun at the nape of her neck. 'I can't think about eating, at a time like this.'

Lily lowered herself in front of Sophie's chair. 'I know it's a difficult time, but you need to keep your strength up, for when they all come home.' She paused as she clasped Sophie's hand in hers, stroking the soft wrinkled skin. 'You don't want them worrying about you, on top of everything else, do you?'

'No, of course I don't.' Sophie closed her eyes for a split second.

Lily didn't take her eyes off Sophie, as she stood up. 'How about I make us a pot of tea, and maybe some toast or a boiled egg for you?'

Sophie's eyes slowly opened. They were full of sadness and bright with unshed tears. 'I'm sorry, it should be me offering to make the tea.' She blinked rapidly. 'Charlotte would never forgive my bad manners.' She edged herself forward in the chair.

'No, I'm afraid I won't hear of it.' Lily rested her hand on Sophie's arm. 'I shall stay a while.' Lily laughed. 'Now who's showing bad manners? But only on the condition I make the tea.'

Sophie nodded.

Chapter 21

Molly frowned as she stared after Alice, following a nurse down the corridor. The tapping of her heels was lost among the clatter of the trolleys, being pushed by the hospital porters. Molly bit down hard on her lip. Pain and the taste of blood, mixed with dust, jolted her back to reality. She ran her dry tongue over her sore lips. 'I'm sorry, Ma.' Her troubled eyes turned to focus on her mother, squeezing her hand, before glancing at Victoria. 'I'm sorry, but I want to see Pa for myself. Victoria, will you stay with my mother, while I catch up with Alice?'

Victoria nodded. 'Of course.'

Molly stared at her mother's grey features. 'I won't be long, Ma, but I must go.'

Charlotte's body began to tremble. Beads of perspiration were visible on her forehead. 'I can't go, I'm too—'

'I know, Ma, I know.' Molly gripped her mother's bony hand and leant forward to kiss her cheek. 'I won't be long, I promise.'

'Go, I'm fine.' Charlotte's eyes filled with unshed tears.

Victoria placed her hand over Charlotte's, as she spoke in low tones. 'Go, we'll be all right. I promise I won't move until you come back.'

Molly sprung out of her chair. 'Thank you, Victoria. I don't know how I'm going to survive this, with two of them—'

'Don't fret, just go.' Victoria waved her hand at her.

Tension was etched on Molly's face. She hesitated for a moment, before turning and almost running down the corridor.

Alice turned to enter a doorway.

Molly shouted, as she almost drew level, 'Alice.'

Alice turned back at the sound of her name, trying to raise a smile for her friend, but failed.

Molly gasped for breath, stopping dead as the smell of cleaning fluid hit the back of her throat. She coughed to clear it away. 'I couldn't wait. I have to know.'

'Would you rather go in alone?'

Molly's lips trembled. She shook her head.

Alice stayed silent, taking Molly's clammy hand and guiding her through the doorway. 'Are you ready for this?'

Under the dust from the explosion, Molly's colour drained away. She took a couple of breaths. Her mind was racing, wondering what they were going to find. She squeezed Alice's hand, before giving a curt nod.

Molly stepped through the doorway first. A nurse was standing at the foot of the bed, looking at Jack Cooper's notes, blocking Molly's view of her father. The grey, metal-framed bed dominated the narrow room. A small wooden cabinet stood next to the bed. The pale green walls were bare.

The nurse's gaze jumped between the two girls. 'Miss Cooper?'

Molly stepped aside, her eyes fixed on her father. His eyes were shut. He looked peaceful. Was she too late? She stared hard at his chest, checking for movement. Was he dead? Her throat tightened. Lowering her lashes, the tears began to fall.

Alice draped her arm around her friend's shoulders.

The nurse hung the clipboard on the foot of the bed. 'Your father is going to be all right. He just needs to rest. I'm sorry the doctor is unable to come and speak to you at the moment, but I'm afraid the munitions' factory explosion last night has kept us all busy.'

'You… you mean he's not…'

'He's asleep. It seems exhaustion has finally taken over. Well that, and the couple of tablets we gave him, to help him relax.'

Molly nodded, stepping forward to take her father's hand in hers. His fingers twitched as she stroked his hand. Thankful for the movement, which confirmed the nurse's words, she gazed down at his clean fingernails and the callous free hands that told everyone he wasn't a labourer.

'He should be able to go home later, but he needs plenty of rest, and if possible, no worry, for the time being at least.' The nurse studied Molly. 'By the look of you, I suspect you were caught up in last night's explosion.'

'Yes, I didn't know my father was here,' Molly gasped. 'I came here looking for someone who's missing.'

'Have you checked at the desk?'

Molly shook her head, looking across at the nurse for the first time. 'I had to see my father first. My mother is outside waiting, ageing by the minute.'

The nurse pulled a chair towards the bed. 'She is welcome to sit in here with her husband.'

Molly nodded. 'Thank you.' She leant over and lightly kissed her father's forehead. 'I'll bring her along.'

The nurse nodded. 'If you take me to her, I'll do it, so you can ask about your missing person.'

Molly turned to leave the room, but stopped to look at her father again. 'Are you sure he's going to be all right?'

The nurse nodded. 'Most definitely.'

Molly breathed a sigh of relief as the three of them left the room and marched along the corridor. Her mother made for a lonely, fragile figure as she stared down at her clenched hands. Molly quickened her pace. 'Ma, he's going to be all right. He's going to be all right.' She wrapped her arms around her mother's slender body. Their tears flowed freely.

'Thank God for listening to my prayers,' Charlotte gasped.

Molly stepped back.

Charlotte's fingers whisked across her face, wiping away her tears. Colour started to replace the ashen fragility.

'Ma, the nurse here will take you to see Pa.' Molly noticed the panic race across her mother's face. She took her hand in hers. 'Ma, it's nothing to worry about. Pa's asleep, and he should be able to come home later. He's got to take it easy from now on, so we need to protect him, instead of him worrying about us.'

Charlotte nodded. Slowly, she stood up, arching her back. 'Go and find Andrew.'

Molly's mouth dropped open.

'Victoria told me, so go and get on with it.' Charlotte's no nonsense tone was back. 'I'm sure this lovely nurse will look after me.'

'I don't know if I can do this.' Molly looked over her shoulder at her mother walking next to the nurse. 'What if Andrew isn't here?'

Victoria grabbed her hand and gave it a little shake. 'Then we'll move onto another hospital.'

'But what if we can't find him?'

Alice folded in her lips for a moment. 'Stop it, we're going to find him, but we have to find out whether he's here or not, before we go somewhere else.' She paused and looked over at Victoria. 'Why don't you both wait here and I'll go and ask about him.'

Victoria nodded.

'No.' Molly took a small step forward. 'I have to ask. I have to know.' Staring straight ahead, she walked over to the desk. 'Good morning, I'm looking for a man that may have been brought here from the Silvertown explosion.'

The lady behind the counter looked up at her and gave her a kindly nod. 'Do you have a name?'

'Andrew Greenwood.' Molly held her breath.

The lady ran her finger down a list of names in front of her, before pulling back her shoulders and shaking her head. 'We have no one here by that name.' She spoke with some authority. 'Although, we do have some people we can't identify.'

Molly's eyes immediately filled with tears. 'Is that—' Her voice was low, as the words fought to come out.

Alice put her arm around Molly, holding her tight. 'Is that because they are unconscious?'

'Mainly, but no one has listed an Andrew Greenwood as being brought here.'

Molly's body folded inwards. Alice used all her strength to hold her upright, as the grief took hold. Molly shivered. Fear and pain froze her insides, her heart refusing to accept what her head was saying. She prayed Andrew would still be alive, and know that she loved him with all her being. Her legs wobbled. But how could he have survived?

Victoria stepped forward. 'Is there anything we can do, to help identify him?'

The lady behind the desk blinked quickly, as she tried to hold back the tears. She looked at the three of them. 'Does he have any distinguishing marks that would help to identify him?'

'He has a birthmark,' a subdued voice came from behind the girls. 'In the shape of a strawberry, at the base of his neck.'

The girls all turned at the sound of the woman's voice, immediately recognising her from Café Monico'. She lifted a manicured hand and stroked Molly's arm.

The lady behind the desk nodded. 'We do have a man with that birthmark, but I need to be sure.'

Molly gasped for breath and gave a silent prayer. Please god, let this woman be Andrew's sister, and not a lady friend she didn't know about. She shook her head. None of it matters, as long as he's alive.

The elegant lady sighed. 'If it helps, he has a small scar that is to the side of his stomach.'

The lady behind the counter smiled at her. 'And you are?'

'My name is Elizabeth Penney.'

A lump in Molly's throat restricted her breathing further. Her chest tightened. She couldn't stop her chin from wobbling, as her trembling hands clasped tightly around her body. She wanted to run away, but stood rooted to the spot.

'I'm his sister, and this,' Elizabeth glanced at Molly, 'is his girlfriend.'

The lady behind the desk nodded at Molly and Elizabeth. 'Only two can go in at any one time, and at the moment, you can't stay for longer than half an hour. Doctor's orders I'm afraid.'

Molly's dull red eyes widened, as her head jerked round towards Alice and Victoria.

Alice squeezed Molly's arm. 'It's all right, we'll wait here for you.' She smiled. 'Maybe we'll grab a cup of tea from somewhere.' Alice looked across at Elizabeth Penney, who was watching the three of them. 'That is, if you don't mind Molly going in with you?'

Fear flitted across Molly's face. 'No, no I—'

'I would appreciate it, actually.' Elizabeth frowned, as she let her gaze settle on Molly. 'I hate hospitals; there's something about them that bothers me. Silly I know, but there you are.'

Molly looked at her for a minute, taking in her fine clothes and coiffured hair. Elizabeth Penney seemed too confident to be bothered by hospitals, or anything else for that matter. 'I can wait, I just need to know he's all right.'

Elizabeth dabbed at her eyes with a lace handkerchief. 'Please.'

Alice tried to hide her smile, as she caught Victoria's glance at her.

Molly looked to her friends, who gave encouraging nods, before she looked back at Elizabeth and bowed her head slightly, in acceptance. Molly's stomach somersaulted and nausea washed over her. She took several deep breaths, hoping not to pass out, looking at her friends through worried eyes. 'Why don't you go home and get some rest. Not surprisingly, you look worn out.'

Her friends looked at each other, before Alice spoke. 'I think we should wait, in case you need us.'

Elizabeth cleared her throat. 'I don't mean to interrupt, but I have to say, you all look as though you've had a rough night. You look exhausted.' She smiled at Molly, before looking back at Alice and Victoria. 'I'll look after Molly, if you wish to go home and get some rest.'

Molly frowned at them all. 'I appreciate everyone's concern, but now I know Andrew,' she lowered her eyelashes, 'Mr Greenwood is alive, I'm sure I'll be fine.'

Victoria glanced at Alice. 'It would be good to have that cup of tea, before getting cleaned up and getting some sleep.'

Alice nodded. 'All right.' She wrapped her arms around Molly. 'I'll come back to your house later, to check up on you.'

Molly nodded, breathing in the dust that lay on her friend's skin. She coughed. 'Sorry.' Pulling back, she put her hand to her mouth. 'You're not wearing your best perfume today, it caught in the back of my throat.'

Alice and Victoria smiled. Molly was back. They each gave Molly a hug.

'It's lovely to meet you.' Alice smiled at Elizabeth.

Victoria followed suit and nodded at Elizabeth. 'Take care, both of you.'

A nurse arrived to take them to the ward where Andrew was, her long uniform rustling, as she walked in front of them. Molly walked with Andrew's sister, turning in time to see her friends leave the hospital. She fought the urge to run after them. Elizabeth's heels clipped the tiled flooring, the noise bouncing off the walls and disturbing the silence, as they walked down endless corridors.

The nurse came to an abrupt standstill and pushed open the door, for them to enter, studying their faces as they stared at the man lying still in the bed. 'Is this the man you are looking for – Mr Greenwood?'

Elizabeth's eyes welled up, as she stared down at the only bed in the room. The red welts on his face made her gasp. His hands were lying flat, on top of the blankets. She nodded at the nurse, who proceeded to write his name on a piece of paper.

A groan escaped from Molly's throat. Her legs began to buckle. Her hands reached out and gripped the metal footboard of the bed.

The nurse acted quickly, pulling up chairs for them to lower themselves onto. 'A lot of what you see will heal nicely. 'They're minor cuts and grazes. He does have some burns on his body and we are treating those. The doctor's main concern is that he hasn't come round, since he was admitted. I understand he called for Molly, just before he passed out, but that's as much as I know.'

The girls sat in silence, staring at the man they both loved. Molly willed him to open his eyes, but nothing happened.

Without taking her eyes off her brother, Elizabeth spoke quietly. 'Is there any idea how long it could be before he comes round?'

The nurse shook her head, before realising the women weren't looking at her. 'No, unfortunately we don't. I've heard it said it's good to talk to an unconscious person, but I have no idea whether that's true or not.'

Molly turned to look at the nurse. 'Thank you.' She reached out to touch him, before pulling her hand back, to sit in her lap. She gripped it tightly, ignoring her own pain. Her whole being ached to touch him, to tell him how much she loved him.

The nurse smiled. 'You can touch him. Just try to be careful of his cuts and burns.' She turned to leave. 'We don't want him getting an infection, but feel free to talk to him; it might help.' Her soft shoes were silent as she walked out of the room.

Elizabeth and Molly sat in silence for a few minutes, each staring at the patient, lying so still.

'I hope he's going to be all right.' Elizabeth's voice was barely a whisper. 'He's already been through so much.'

Molly pulled her gaze away from Andrew and looked across at his sister. 'He told me about your mother and father dying. It's terrible.' She sucked in her breath. 'My friend, Alice, drives an ambulance and was called to the explosion outside the Lyceum Theatre. I'm so sorry. The German's have a lot to answer for and it'll be a good thing when the war is over with.'

Elizabeth met Molly's gaze. She opened her mouth to speak, but shut it again, quickly looking left, then right, before looking across at Molly. 'Thank you.'

Molly's chest lifted as she took a deep breath. 'You do know I'm not Andrew's girlfriend, don't you?'

A smile formed easily on Elizabeth's face. 'Well if you're not, you will be when he wakes up from his sleep.'

Molly didn't answer, but turned her gaze back to Andrew.

Elizabeth followed her lead. 'My brother and I are very close, you know. Even more so, since this damned war started and,' she paused for a second before glancing across at Molly, 'everything we've been through has made us realise that family is the most important thing in life. Nothing matters, if you have no one to share it with.'

Molly shook her head. 'I do love him, but I've messed up.' Tears rolled down her face. 'None of that matters now. I just want him to be well.' Pulling a handkerchief from her pocket, she wiped her face.

Elizabeth nodded. 'He's made of stern stuff and won't give up.' She shrugged her shoulders. 'Six months ago, I might have said different, but now he has his life in front of him.' Elizabeth wrung her hands together on her lap. 'He has plans for the future, and I can't just let him fade away in this bed.'

Molly nodded. 'If you don't mind, I'd like to visit him. I can read and chat to him, just in case the nurse is right.'

'That would be good. Come as often, and for as long, as the hospital allows you to. I'm sure when he wakes, he'll want to see you.'

'Haha, I wouldn't count on that.' Molly twisted the handkerchief between her fingers, before glancing down and mumbling. 'I haven't been very nice to him.'

Elizabeth reached over and patted Molly's hand. 'Well you don't seem to have deterred him. Those plans I spoke about include you. I know he loves you too much to not win this battle, and from what I've seen, there's no point kidding yourself about how much you love him.'

Molly nodded and gave a weak smile in Elizabeth's direction. But what about Grace?

The time spent gazing at Andrew, and chatting to Elizabeth, flew by and it wasn't long before the nurse appeared to chivvy them out of Andrew's hospital room.

'Can I give you a lift home?' Elizabeth stopped and studied Molly. 'You must be exhausted.'

Molly was tempted. Exhaustion had set in and she had no idea how she was still standing. Then she remembered her ma and Grace. Travelling across London didn't seem possible to her any more. Her feet felt weighted. Looking down, she expected to see lead plates instead of her feet. 'As lovely as that would be, my father was brought into the hospital last night and my mother is, I'm assuming, still sitting with him.' Molly shook her head, wishing she'd asked Alice and Victoria to check on her father, but her brain was fogged with exhaustion. 'I have to get them home, and then I have to collect Grace from Poplar.' Molly gave a mirthless sound. 'My mother doesn't know yet, but I've offered Grace a roof over her head. Her home was destroyed in last night's explosion. Of course, all of that was before I knew my father was ill.' Molly gave a little laugh. 'It looks like I've messed up again.'

Elizabeth put her arm around Molly. 'No you haven't. You were being kind, in someone's hour of need. That's not messing up.'

Molly stepped away. 'You shouldn't touch me. Your clothes will end up ruined, with all this dust.'

'Do you think I care about that?' Elizabeth pulled her back. 'Some people have lost everything. Until a while ago, I thought I'd lost my brother, and that thought is unbearable.'

'Sorry, I didn't think, I was just thinking of your—'

'I know.' Elizabeth smiled at her. 'We're the lucky ones here, so it's right that we give comfort where we can. Let's see if we can take your parents home first, then we'll search out Grace.' She thrust her arm through Molly's and pulled her along the corridor.

Their steps got slower as they walked along. The clatter of wheels, together with the groans and whispered voices, swirled around Molly's head. The invisible band around it tightened. Her eyes hurt as she squinted ahead. She was sure Elizabeth was almost holding her up when they walked into her father's room.

Charlotte looked up. Her eyes widened, as she sprung out of her chair. 'Sit down, Molly, before you fall down.'

Molly didn't hesitate to do as she was told. How long had it been since she had been in her bed? She reached out and touched her father's hand.

Charlotte gazed lovingly at her husband, before whispering, 'He hasn't stirred.'

Elizabeth eyed the man in the bed. 'He looks peaceful.'

Molly's head jerked round. She had momentarily forgotten about Elizabeth.

Charlotte frowned in her direction. 'I'm sorry; I don't believe we've been introduced. I'm Molly's mother, Mrs Charlotte Cooper.'

'Sorry, Ma, this is Mr Greenwood's sister, Elizabeth Penney. We found Andrew. He's unconscious and they're concerned because they don't know how long it will take him to come round, but his wounds should heal.' Molly looked back at her father. 'Elizabeth has kindly offered to give us a lift home.'

'I'm sure that's very kind of you.' Charlotte hesitated, turning her attention to her daughter. 'You look like you should be in a hospital bed, and yet I understand you have to go back to Poplar Hospital, to bring a woman back to stay at our house.'

Molly nodded. 'Her name's Grace.' She gave a weary sigh. 'I know I should have discussed it with you first, but she has nothing. Everything was destroyed in the explosion.'

'You have a kind daughter, Mrs Cooper. She does you proud. I certainly don't know what I would have done without her today.'

Molly gave a faint smile; the charm obviously ran in the family.

'Thank you, Mrs Penney.' Charlotte beamed as she nodded her head.

'Please call me Elizabeth. Mrs Penney is my mother-in-law.'

Molly's gaze shifted between her mother and father. 'How did you know about Grace?' Her eyelids lowered themselves slowly.

'Alice told me. She came back to see me, before she left with Victoria.'

Her mother's voice drifted through the fog that her mind had created.

'They were worried about leaving you, but I told them I would get you home. That's when they mentioned you'd been to Poplar Hospital, trying to find... people.'

Molly ran her dry tongue over her cracked lips, biting down on the blisters that had broken, and the loose skin pricking her mouth. 'Hmm, I must remember to thank them.'

Charlotte placed her hand on Molly's shoulder, giving it a gentle squeeze. 'Anyway, Alice and Victoria are going to come back for me, so you can go and collect Grace.'

'That's very kind of them.' Elizabeth ventured to join in. 'I think everyone is right to be concerned about you, Molly. After all, you've not slept for god knows how many hours, and you've been through a horrendous experience.' She paused as Charlotte nodded. 'The sooner we get you home, the better.'

Charlotte interweaved her fingers in front of her. 'All of that aside, your gran has been on her own for most of the night and must be worried sick about us all.'

Molly stood up. 'Ma, are you sure you'll be all right?' She frowned as she rested her hand on her mother's. 'I don't like the idea of leaving you here.'

'I'll be fine, now I know your father will be coming home later.' Charlotte chuckled. 'Once he's home, I'm not going to allow him to move.'

Molly reached over and kissed her mother on the cheek. 'Please take care.'

Charlotte's eyes welled up, as she wrapped her arms around her daughter. 'Elizabeth, please make sure you look after my daughter. She's very precious to her father and me.'

Elizabeth could feel the tears pricking at her eyes. 'I will. It's clear that she's precious to quite a few people.'

Charlotte nodded.

Molly bent down and kissed her father on his forehead, before turning away.

❧

Chapter 22

Molly and Elizabeth stepped through the doors of Poplar Hospital. Molly shook her head. It didn't look like anything had changed since she was here looking for Andrew. People were still lying on trollies, pushed against the scuffed grey walls. She wrinkled her nose, as the smell of antiseptic and carbolic soap assaulted her. Placing her hand in front of her mouth, she coughed, to clear the taste from the back of her throat. She looked around. Maybe they were different people, but they had the same desperate look about them.

Molly immediately looked to where Grace had been lying when she last saw her, but an old man had taken up that position. Her gaze darted around, trying to search, until she saw her sitting in a chair, with her eyes shut. Molly turned to Elizabeth. 'She's over there.' She pointed over to her right. 'Let's get her out of here.'

Half an hour later, the three of them were safely tucked in the car, each lost in their own thoughts. The silence was only broken by the car's engine spluttering, as it drove through the London streets, the driver expertly manoeuvring it around the horses and carts. Elizabeth's car finally came to a standstill, outside the terraced house in Carlisle Street. The driver jumped out and opened the car door for Elizabeth, who stepped out in one fluid movement.

Molly watched, in awe of her elegance, before stepping out of the car herself. The cold breeze winded her.

Grace took a couple of breaths, the wispy spirals floating up into the grey clouds. She placed her hand on Molly's arm, before leaning heavily on her. Elizabeth rushed round to the other side and placed her arm around her waist. With their help, Grace limped up the path to Molly's front door. 'Does your ma know I'm coming?'

Molly frowned. Her eyes clouded over, as she searched her memory for that conversation. She felt sure it had taken place. 'Everything will be fine. My mother will love having someone to fuss over.' She lifted the letterbox, to pull at the string, but before she could reach the key, the door startled her by opening. The creaking hinges went unnoticed by her. Her tired bloodshot eyes widened. 'Lily.' Relief spread across Molly's face, before it was quickly chased away by the realisation she could be there as a policewoman. 'Wait, is Gran all right?'

A tired Lily stood smiling in front of her. 'Your gran is going to be very pleased to see you. She's been worried sick about all of you, and wouldn't go to bed. Thank god you're all right.'

The corners of Molly's lips lifted slightly. 'I don't know how you came to be here, but I'm truly thankful you are.' Her eyes became full of mischief. 'It's going to be lovely to see her too. Do you think we can come in out of the cold?

We're gasping for a cup of tea and Grace is a bit of a dead weight, leaning on me.' She turned to Grace and smiled. 'Sorry, I didn't mean that, as bad as it sounded.'

Colour rose in Lily's cheeks as she stepped aside. 'Yes, of course. Sorry, I was just so relieved to see you, I didn't think.'

Between the three of them, they managed to get Grace through the front door and into the dining room, before lowering her onto a chair.

Sophie looked up from the newspaper that was crumpled on her lap, and eyed the three of them quizzically, before a high pitched scream filled the room. 'Molly, thank goodness you're alive.' She stretched her arms out. 'Come and give your gran a hug.'

Molly rushed over and wrapped her arms around her, squeezing her tight.

Tears filled Sophie's eyes. 'I've been so frightened for you, and felt so helpless. Thank goodness Lily stayed with me.'

Molly pulled back and stared at her gran's face. This had been a bad night for her too. She looked over her shoulder at the three tearful faces staring back at her. 'Thank you, Lily, you probably saved my gran's life.'

Lily nodded.

Molly pulled away, to walk over to her. 'Are you all right? It's been quite a night.'

Sophie tugged at Molly's arm. 'I don't suppose you've seen your mother and father, have you?'

'Yes I have, and Pa is going to be fine, but he's got to take it easy from now on.'

The tension in Sophie's face drifted away. 'Thank goodness.' She lifted a handkerchief and dabbed at her eyes. 'Lily here has been lovely. She's sat with me for hours on end, making me cups of tea, and making sure I had something to eat.'

Molly moved to wrap her arms around Lily. 'Thank you so much, it was a lovely thing to do, especially as you were probably worried about Alice. She should be at home now. She and Victoria stayed with me all night.'

Lily's gaze travelled over Molly's face, as they pulled away. 'I'd guessed that's where she was, especially when you weren't here.' She raised her eyebrows. 'You look like you need to go to bed, and not get up again for at least a week.'

Molly nodded, squeezing her lips tight. 'I'm sorry, I've been very rude.' She stepped back. 'Let me introduce you to Elizabeth Penney, Andrew Greenwood's sister, and the invalid is Grace, who I work with.' She sighed as she extended her arm, indicating which one was which, and raised her eyebrows. 'Although, maybe that should be who I worked with.'

Sophie bowed her head slightly. 'It's lovely to meet you both. Shall I make some tea for you all?'

'No,' they all chorused.

Molly took a step towards the doorway. 'I'll make it.'

'Actually, tea making is my job.'

Molly jerked round, to see her mother and father standing just inside the room. 'Thank goodness you're both home.' Tears flowed freely down Molly's cheeks.

Alice and Victoria smiled at the scene in front of them, pleased they had managed to fulfill their promises and get

Molly's parents back home to her. Lily joined them, and without a word, they quietly left the house.

Charlotte and Jack moved as one, to wrap their arms around their daughter. They clung to each other, as the tears flowed.

Molly pulled back a little, to gaze up at them both. 'Thank goodness you are both all right. Come on, Pa, let's get you seated, and later we will talk about what will happen in the future.'

Jack raised his eyebrows, as he studied his daughter's dirt-smeared face. 'I don't know what that means, but I'm too tired to worry about it now. You're alive, and that's all that matters to me right now.'

A lump formed in Molly's throat and her eyes welled up. 'I feel exactly the same, Pa, exactly the same.'

Sophie beamed as she looked around. 'Lily made some soup for when you all came home, didn't you?' She peered round, looking for the young girl.

Molly laughed. 'I didn't know you could make soup, Lily.' She turned round. 'Where is she?'

Elizabeth smiled. 'I think she left with your friends.'

Charlotte pulled back and looked around. 'We owe those girls a lot, and your good self. You have all looked after us so well. I can't thank you enough.'

Molly nodded.

'We all have to do what we can to help each other, during this dreadful time.' Elizabeth paused. 'Your daughter has walked all over London, looking for my brother, and she wanted to give Grace a home until things settle down.' She dabbed a handkerchief at her eyes. 'I have done very little by comparison. You have a daughter to be proud of.'

Molly turned away, as the colour started to rise in her cheeks. She tightened her hold on Jack's arm, as he took the couple of steps towards the armchair and sunk down into it, closing his eyes for a split second.

Charlotte pulled back her shoulders and stood tall. 'Thank you for saying so. She has a very independent spirit, does our Molly.' She smiled in Molly's direction. 'Right, it seems, thanks to Lily, there's some soup we can all have. I don't think there have ever been so many people in this tiny room, but hopefully, there should be enough to go round.' She ran her hands down her creased black skirt. 'So, tea and soup it is, although I'm not taking responsibility for the soup.'

Laughter spread around the room.

Elizabeth smiled at Charlotte. 'How kind. You know, that's exactly what my own mother would have done. She always said it was a welcoming gesture, and I think she was right, but then mothers usually are, aren't they?'

Molly smiled. The family charm came shining through again.

'Let me help.'

Charlotte raised her chin.

Molly knew the signs. She was about to refuse Elizabeth's offer.

'Please.' Elizabeth gave her best smile. 'Your daughter and I have been sat around most of the day, so it will be good to actually do something.'

Charlotte nodded.

Elizabeth followed her out, through the dining room door. 'I'm sure Grace must be parched. It's very good of you to offer Grace...'

Molly gasped, as the voices faded along the hall.

Sophie frowned at Grace. 'Are you comfortable sitting there? You can always sit in the armchair.' Her head nodded over to one side. 'Molly will help you move. Unfortunately, I'm no use to man or beast any more.'

Grace forced a smile. 'I'm fine. My leg is throbbing, but at least I'm still here.'

Sophie nodded. 'We've been worried sick. We felt the tremor, sitting here, so god knows what it was like at the factory.'

'It's been awful, Gran.' Molly flopped down on one of the dining chairs. 'They say Alice's quick action saved Grace's life. I don't know how many bodies were under the rubble. Everything has been wiped out, not just the factory, but also the houses, the church and the fire station, from what I hear. It's been a nightmare.'

Sophie studied Molly, as she stared into the distance. 'And Mr Greenwood?'

Molly jerked back to the present. 'He's unconscious at the hospital, but at least he's alive.' She closed her eyes for a moment.

Grace looked from one to the other. She opened her mouth to speak, but said nothing, as Elizabeth came in, holding a loaded tray.

'Here we go.' Elizabeth placed the tray on the dining table. 'This is just what the doctor ordered.'

Charlotte placed a terrine and ladle on the table, along with some soup dishes. 'I have some vegetable soup here for you all.' Charlotte placed a ladle of the hot liquid into each bowl, and handed them out.

Grace sniffed the green liquid, with lumps of carrot and potato just visible. 'It smells delicious, Mrs Cooper.'

'Please call me Charlotte, I can't have you staying here and keep calling me Mrs Cooper.' Charlotte smiled at the young woman, who looked worse for wear. 'May I call you Grace?'

Grace nodded and gave her a smile.

Elizabeth smiled her approval at what she guessed could have been a sticky situation. 'Well I must also take my leave, but I would like to thank you for letting me help.'

Molly put the breakfast tray on the wooden floorboards, which creaked under the weight, before knocking lightly on the bedroom door. The room that used to be her gran's many years ago, before her legs refused to climb the stairs. It had taken some doing, but she had managed, with the help of the banister, to get Grace upstairs and into bed the previous evening.

'Come in,' Grace's muffled voice came from the other side of the oak door.

Molly twisted the squeaking wooden handle and pushed the door open. The small bedroom was in darkness, but rain could be heard drumming against the window. She picked up the tray and sidled into the room.

'Morning, Grace, did you manage to get any sleep at all?' Molly walked past the foot of the bed and the large oak chest of drawers and wardrobe that dominated the room. Old photographs of her parents sat on the thick oak mantelpiece, over the ornate Victorian fireplace.

Grace tried to pull herself upright. A groan escaped, as she moved in the single bed. 'Once I had managed to find a comfortable position, I wasn't too bad. It's the throbbing that's getting me down.'

Molly nodded. 'It must be awful for you.' She put the tray on the bedside cabinet and moved towards the window. 'As you can see, I've brought you up a cup of tea, a boiled egg and a slice of bread.' Molly pulled the soft black material away from the window, before opening the dark green curtains a fraction. 'It's pretty grey out there, and as you can probably hear, it's raining again.'

'Thank you for the tea and the breakfast.' Grace's lips thinned, as she struggled into position.

Molly quickly stepped forward, clenching her hands in front of her. 'Can I help? I'm afraid I've no experience of nursing anyone before.'

Grace grimaced. 'Don't worry, you and your family are doing so much for me already, and if I'm honest, I'm not sure I deserve your kindness.'

Molly shook her head. 'Don't talk nonsense. You would have done the same for me.'

Grace gave a humourless laugh. 'But you weren't horrible to us, in fact you did nothing to deserve the way I treated you.' She shook her head. 'I've had all night to think about it, and as much as I don't want to admit it,

I was jealous of you. Yet you were still willing to teach me to read and write. Your family has taken me in, a complete stranger. Your friend saved my life, and I'm not sure I deserved to be saved.'

Molly moved to sit on the edge of the bed, but remembered Grace's leg, and turned to pull up a rickety old wooden chair. 'I will not listen to that kind of talk.' She stared at Grace for a moment, before reaching out and resting her hand on hers. 'I want you to feel at home here, and with you living here, not able to get out, we can do more of the reading and writing. The first thing you need to do is stop with all this nonsense talk, then write to your brother so he knows where to send his letters, and to your father so he knows you are safe.'

Grace nodded. 'I'm sorry, Molly, I want you to understand that you didn't deserve what I did.'

'You didn't do anything.' Molly laughed. 'You were mean in the way you spoke to me sometimes, but that's all.'

'Sometimes, I was jealous.'

'I've had those feelings. I think that's what probably brought me to the munitions' factory in the first place. I was convinced I didn't fit in with my friends. I was riddled with guilt for persuading someone to enlist, and had the desire for more in life.' Molly gave a feeble smile. 'Thing is, I was wrong about everything.' She placed her hand flat on her chest. 'Underneath the finery, we're all the same and it's what's inside that counts.' Molly shrugged her shoulders. 'Anyway, I guessed it wasn't about me, but had something to do with your time in domestic service.'

'It might have started off that way. I was accused of stealing something, and lost my job. I've never stolen anything in my life. I'm not a thief.' Grace stared hard at the breakfast tray.

'I'm so sorry.' Molly frowned, as memories of her father's mother trampled into her mind, always telling them to be honest and work hard.

Grace shrugged her shoulders. 'Anyway, I later heard they found it, but the toffs didn't say they were sorry, and I didn't get my job back.' She looked up and smiled at Molly. 'Just as well, cos the governor was a bit handy with the women, if you know what I mean.' Grace shook her head. 'But, I'm ashamed to say I was also jealous of the way Mr Greenwood remembered your name, and then it just grew and grew.'

'What?'

Grace laughed. 'He never remembers any of our names. I always thought it had something to do with what happened to him on the front line, but I was clearly wrong about that too.'

Molly's mouth gaped open for a minute. She tried to digest the information Grace had let slip. 'What happened to him?' Molly picked up the blue floral cup and saucer from the tray, passing it to Grace. 'Drink your tea before it gets cold.'

'I have no idea.' Grace held the cup to her lips and sipped at the dark brown liquid. 'I heard talk he was badly injured, and that's why he's always on at us to work harder.' She replaced the cup onto the saucer. 'He likes you.'

Molly shrugged her shoulders, before standing up and moving to look out of the window. The street was an array of coloured umbrellas as people scurried along, trying to avoid each other, and the puddles that scattered the pavement.

'Flo told me about seeing you both together in Hyde Park.' Grace paused.

Molly closed her eyes and lowered her head, as the memory of that day brought colour to her cheeks.

Grace raised her voice. 'I know you love him, so you should tell him.'

Molly shook her head. 'That's not possible.'

'Why not?' Grace frowned.

Molly lifted her head and jutted out her chin, before taking a deep breath. 'Because... you love him, that's why.' She took a step nearer to the bed. 'Now eat your egg. They're hard to come by, these days.' She looked at Grace. 'It's up to you whether you come downstairs, or prefer to stay in your room until your leg heals—'

'Stop about the egg, and the damned leg, we're talking about your future here.' Grace glared at Molly. 'I'm not going to stand by and let you throw it all away because of me. This is the least I can do for you, and him.'

Molly flopped back down on to the chair, closing her eyes.

'You do know he doesn't love me, don't you? He only just knows who I am, and truth be known, I probably don't love him. I don't really know him, so how can I love him? He was just a distraction in this god-awful time we are living in.' Grace stared at Molly for a few minutes. 'Look at me.'

Molly opened her watery eyes. 'I don't want to talk about this.'

Grace's voice softened. 'I know, but we need to. You know, when Flo told me about you two together, I didn't feel any jealousy. She didn't get the reaction she wanted. You are both lovely people and deserve to be happy, so you must go and tell him. I don't want to be responsible for your unhappiness. Does he feel the same?'

Molly bit down on her bottom lip, ignoring the pain that shot through her. She nodded. 'He doesn't know I love him. I couldn't do that to you.'

'Well, you now have my permission to do so, not that you need it, but you are a lovely person, so go and fight for what you want.'

Molly stared at her.

'Well, what are you waiting for? I'll stay here until you get back. In fact, if you get me some paper and a pen, I'll have a go at writing my letters.'

The hospital room was bare of any niceties. The pale green walls were devoid of beauty and character. A jug of water stood on the bedside cabinet, next to a cup and a bowl. The usual clatter and voices filled the hallways, but the room was eerily quiet.

Molly stared down at the unconscious figure, lying in the hospital bed. Her stomach lurched. She had been there for three hours, trying to smile, while rambling on about her friends and family, but there had been no sign of consciousness. Ignoring the pain of the burns on her own hands, she stroked his arm. His dark ruffled hair gave his unshaven face a boyish charm, despite being almost covered with red welts from the fire. His hands looked sore as they rested on the bed covers. Her eyes filled up. She shook her head. No more tears. He's alive and that's all that matters right now. Molly bent forward and kissed the top of his head. She ran her fingers through his hair, moving the fine soft strands away from his face. Dust clung to her fingers, reminding her why he was lying so still. Molly dragged the chair nearer to the bed and sat down, leaving the unopened newspaper she had brought with her on top of the bed covers. She carefully pulled at the coarse grey blanket, to straighten it. She sat very still, watching him, enjoying the freedom of sitting with him, touching and gazing. She looked for signs that he was waking up, but there was nothing.

'Andrew, I don't know if you can hear me or not, but it's time I said I'm sorry for being such a fool. I hope, one day, you can find it in your heart to forgive me.' A tear tripped over her lashes and she wiped it away with her fingers. 'I love you, Andrew, with all my heart. I think I always have.'

A whispered voice came from the doorway of the room. 'I'm sorry to disturb you, but I just need to check Mr Greenwood's dressings.'

Molly flushed with colour, wondering how much the young nurse had heard. She nodded. 'Would you like me to leave?'

The nurse glanced down at the tray she was carrying, before giving her a sympathetic smile. 'No, that won't be necessary, unless of course you would like to have a break.'

Molly shook her head. 'No, I'm fine. I just don't want to be in the way.'

The nurse stepped further into the room, her soft-soled shoes not making a sound on the tiled flooring. There was a rattle from the tray, as she placed it on the cabinet and began checking Andrew's dressings and taking his pulse.

Molly couldn't take her eyes off the nurse's hands, as they deftly changed dressings and examined Andrew. 'Is he going to be all right?'

The nurse didn't stop work or look up. 'He's healing nicely. It's just about him waking up now.' She picked up the tray and, with only the rattle of the scissors for company, left the room.

Molly couldn't take her eyes off Andrew. How she wished it was her lying there, rather than him. She cleared her throat. 'I met your sister yesterday.' Laughter erupted from her. 'I would have liked to have met your parents, as it's obvious that charm runs in the family.' She looked down at her hands for a moment. 'Elizabeth is lovely. She was very kind to me and my family.' She chuckled. 'You'll be pleased to know that Grace is staying at my house for the time being but, and you may not agree, it's a good thing. It was her who told me to let you know my feelings. She said it was obvious to her how much we loved each other. I don't know if that's true, because it wasn't obvious to me for a long time.' Molly tightened her lips and looked up at Andrew. 'I thought I'd lost you yesterday. It was unbearable.' Her vision blurred, as the memories flooded her mind. 'The thought of you not being in my life is unthinkable, but if that's my punishment for you to survive, then so be it.' Tears ran down her face. Molly swiped them away angrily. 'Your life and happiness are much more important to me than mine.' She took her handkerchief out of her pocket and dabbed at her eyes. 'This is much harder than I thought it would be.'

Molly stood up and, with clenched hands, paced around the room, her footsteps echoing back off the walls. She looked back at Andrew. 'My father was in this hospital as well, yesterday. It was a suspected heart attack, but he's home again now, under strict instructions to take it easy.' She dropped herself back onto the chair. 'I need to go home and talk to him, to try to get him to stop working, but suspect that will be an argument I probably won't win. They will worry about money, but I can get another job and look after the three of them.'

The clipping of heels jolted Molly out of her meanderings. She looked round, in time to see Elizabeth coming into the room.

'Hello, Molly, how are you feeling today? To be honest, I'm surprised you're up and about so soon.' She looked at her brother, lying so still in the bed. 'Has there been any change?'

'No.' Molly turned to look at Andrew. 'I've been chatting to him, but I'm not convinced he can hear me.' She turned back to Elizabeth. 'It's harder than you think, talking to someone who can't respond in any way.'

Chapter 23

Molly's winter coat weighed heavily on her shoulders. Her body ached, with every step she took away from the hospital. When she had arrived that morning, there had been hope that Andrew would have woken up at the sound of her voice, but that hadn't happened. Molly's throat tightened. She wanted to be there when he did come round, but no one knew when that would be. It could be hours, days or even weeks. Elizabeth had insisted she went home to rest. She longed for a cup of tea, and the warmth and comfort of her bed. A sigh escaped, as she pushed the front door shut. The lavender scent of the plant in the hall calmed her a little. She closed her eyes and leant against the inside of the door, the hard wood making its mark on her forehead.

'Molly, are you all right?'

Startled, Molly jerked, banging her head on the door.

'Sorry, are you all right? I didn't mean to alarm you.'

Grace's voice drifted in, from behind Molly. She stepped back, rubbing her forehead, before turning to face Grace. 'That's all right, it wasn't your fault.'

Grace was sat on the stairs, midway between top and bottom. 'How's Mr Greenwood?'

Molly shook her head. 'There's no change.' She sighed and began unbuttoning her coat. 'I've been talking to him for hours, but there's no sign he can hear me.' She slipped out of her coat and hung it on a hook, frowning back at Grace. 'What are you doing out of bed?'

Grace laughed. 'Your mother came up with another cup of tea, but it's not right her running up and down stairs waiting on me, so I asked if I could come downstairs.' She looked down at the pink tulip-style dress and smiled. 'I hope you don't mind, but she found me this dress to wear. I expect it's yours, sorry.'

Molly smiled. 'Don't be. I hadn't thought about what clothes you'll need. If we can manage to share for a few days, then I'll go shopping to get you some bits.' Molly took a step forward. 'Let me try and help you down these stairs.'

Grace gripped the edge of the step. 'I can manage, thank you. It's not very ladylike, but I've got this far by sliding down on my bottom. Watch.' She bit her lip, as she demonstrated her technique. She giggled as her bottom thudded onto the next step. 'As I said, not very ladylike, but I'm getting there.'

'Be careful, I don't want you getting any splinters.' Molly laughed. 'Because if you do, I won't be getting them out.'

Grace chuckled, before wriggling down a couple more and stopping to take a breath. 'I'll probably need help getting from here to the dining room, though.'

Molly nodded. 'I'll wait.' She glanced towards the dining room doorway. 'Did my mother say if she was going to work?'

Grace shook her head, before lowering herself to the next step. 'No, but I got the impression she's looking after your father.' She looked up, letting her gaze rest on Molly. 'She was telling me how she's in domestic service.'

Molly's eyes became hooded. 'Yes, I've been trying to get her to give it up. She deserves better than cleaning up after other people, but she won't have any of it.'

Grace nodded. 'Your mother's a lovely lady; it's clear she worries about her family.' She frowned. 'And I'm sure her experience isn't the same as mine.' She thudded down to the last step.

'As far as I know, Ma has only worked for people Alice's family know.' Molly stepped forward and put her arm under Grace's. 'Right, hold on to the banister and, on the count of three, lean on it and pull yourself up.'

Grace nodded and reached up, to grip the hard wood. 'Ready?'

Grace took a deep breath and nodded again.

'One... two... three.' Molly heaved, as Grace pulled herself up. They both giggled. 'Well done. Now let's get you into a comfortable chair so you can put your leg up.'

Grace leant on Molly and hobbled into the dining room.

Sophie looked up from her armchair and beamed at them. 'It's good to see you both up and about.' She watched Molly lower Grace onto the chair and move a small table, for her to rest her foot on.

Grace smiled. 'Thank you; Molly was up and about early this morning. I've been spoilt, with cups of tea in bed and a boiled egg.'

Molly looked up and studied her gran. 'How are you, after the worry of the last few days?'

'I'm fine.' Sophie laughed. 'I think you all aged me by about ten years, which I don't think I had to spare, but now you're all home safe and sound, all is good again. I can't ask for anything more.'

Molly beamed. 'I'll go and make some tea, I'm gasping.' She looked up as she heard crockery rattling together.

'I've made the tea.' Charlotte put down the heavy tray. 'I've even managed to scrape together the ingredients for a sponge cake. It may not be as sweet as usual, because I'm afraid there wasn't enough sugar.'

'Thanks, Ma, I'm as dry as a bone.' Molly turned the china cups over and placed them on matching saucers. 'I'm afraid I can't swallow cake, until I've had at least one cup of tea.'

Charlotte smiled. 'That's fine, it'll keep.' She turned to Grace. 'Please tell me you'll have a piece?'

Grace flushed with colour. 'If you don't mind, I'd love some.'

Charlotte giggled. 'Of course I don't mind. This is a celebration, of sorts.'

Molly couldn't hold back the smile, as she passed Grace a cake fork and the tea plate, holding a large slice of sponge. 'It looks delicious, Ma.'

Charlotte beamed at her daughter. 'I must save some for your father. The doctor said he needs to rest, so I don't want to wake him.'

The thud of the knocker hitting the front door caused everyone to look towards the hallway. 'Sit down, Ma, I'll go and see who it is.' Molly walked towards the front door.

Charlotte shouted into the hall. 'I'm not expecting anyone.'

The creaking of the hinges told everyone the door was open.

Molly beamed as she moved aside. 'Alice, Victoria, come in, oh and Arthur. How wonderful.'

Victoria smiled. 'I hope it's all right for us to just pop round, but we were worrying about you all.'

Molly's smile lit up her face. 'I think Arthur is just what the doctor ordered.' She bent down and kissed his forehead. 'He's got so big.'

Alice laughed. 'He's nearly eighteen months old now.' She leant on the handle and pushed the pram into the hall, filling the space. 'If it's all right, I'll take him out, but he will keep us on our toes.'

'My mother will love him.' Molly grinned. 'As indeed we all do.' Her smile faded away, as she looked from one to the other of the girls. 'I don't know if I've told you both how grateful I am for all that you and Lily did for me and my family. My gran would have been out of her mind with worry, here by herself, so she probably saved her life. It never occurred to me that she would have been on her own.' Molly shook her head.

Victoria leant forward and wrapped her arms around Molly. 'You do know we are all family, so what affects you, affects us as well. I know I for one couldn't have sat at home and done nothing.'

Alice enveloped them both in a hug. 'I definitely couldn't have done, and nor could you in our position.

I'm just glad we were there when the explosion happened, otherwise we may not have known about it, in time to help.'

Arthur yelled out for his mother's attention.

Alice smiled, as she turned to release him from the pram. 'I want to ask you about Andrew, but I'll wait until we've said hello to everyone, and have more time to speak.'

Molly's lips thinned. 'There's nothing to tell you. He's healing, but still unconscious.' She sighed. 'But he's alive and that's all that matters at the moment.'

The front door clicked shut, holding back the cold January air. Molly breathed a sigh of relief, pleased to see her friends and Arthur, and her mother had been over the moon, but Molly was desperate to talk to her father. She ran up the stairs, not worrying about the creaks of each step, unlike her first day at the munitions' factory. Pausing outside his bedroom, before moving in closer, Molly pressed her ear against the hard wood of the door, listening for movement. Stepping back, she knocked lightly and waited.

'Come in.'

A slow smile spread across Molly's face as her father's voice rang out loud and true. Her eyes looked heavenward, as she let out a huge breath and gave a silent prayer. Twisting the handle, she pushed the door open. 'It's only me, Pa.' The distinctive antiseptic smell of carbolic soap greeted her and made her want to retch, as it rushed to the back of her throat. She swallowed hard several times, in a bid to remove the taste.

'It could never be "only" you.' Jack chuckled.

Molly laughed, as she stepped inside. The grey sky invaded the room, giving it a gloomy feel. 'How are you feeling? You sound on fine form.' She stood next to the bed, studying him. 'You do look better than you did at the hospital.'

Jack pulled at the blankets and the bedspread, straightening them, as he sat up a little. 'Come.' He patted the edge of the bed. 'Sit with me, I want to talk to you.'

Molly grimaced. 'You're not cross with me for not coming home, are you? I had to find Andrew.' Her eyes welled up. 'I had to know, you must understand that.'

'Stop worrying yourself.' Jack took her hand in his.

Molly's eyes widened, as realisation dawned on her. 'I wasn't the reason you ended up in hospital, was I?'

Jack shook his head. 'You know as well as I do, I've been under an enormous strain lately, so I expect it was more to do with that.'

Molly stood up and began to pace around the room. The green and brown carpet was worn under her feet. The walls were pale grey in colour. Embroidery hung in frames from the picture rails, all treasured possessions, as they were hand sown by her grans. Many family photographs sat on the wooden mantelpiece, above the wrought iron fireplace. She wrung her hands together, trying not to get distracted by it all. 'Pa, I wanted to talk to you about all that.'

'Stop pacing, Molly. Come and sit with me. I want to talk to you about the future. It's important.' Jack patted the chocolate brown woven cotton bedspread.

Molly moved around the double bed and perched on the edge, near to her father. She looked down at her hands, clenched tightly in her lap. Her heart pounded in her chest. Nausea rose in her throat.

'I have something to give you.' Jack paused. 'I've thought about it long and hard, and with everything that's been going on, you know, me being taken to hospital like that and everything that has happened to you, it's just reinforced that I need to sort things out now, rather than wait.'

Molly shook her head and her vision became blurry. 'Don't, Pa, I can't bear to think about you not being around.'

Jack leant forward and wrapped his arms around her. 'I have no plans to go anywhere yet, but that doesn't mean I shouldn't put my house in order.' He pulled away from his daughter and lifted her chin. 'You do know you're very precious to all of us, don't you?'

'Pa, you're scaring me.' Molly sniffed as a tear spilled down her cheek, leaving a salty residue on her lips.

'I'm sorry, don't get upset, everything is fine.' Jack arched his eyebrows and gently thumbed away her tears. 'I intend to be around for a long time yet, but when you have a scare, it makes you think about things differently.'

Molly nodded. Her mind immediately jumped to Andrew, lying so still in his hospital bed. 'I can understand that.'

Jack pulled open the bedside draw and rifled around, before finally pulling out an envelope. 'Don't tell your ma, but this should have been put in the bank years ago.' He chuckled, almost to himself. 'Me ma used to say keep fings and people that are important close.'

Molly laughed as her father feigned an exaggerated cockney accent.

'That's better.' Jack smiled at his daughter. 'I don't like seeing you unhappy, especially when I have a gift for you.' He put the envelope face down on the bed. 'It's a gift that will look after you forever, if you act wisely.'

Molly frowned. 'I don't understand, Pa.'

Jack laughed. 'You will in a minute, but I'm enjoying painting a picture for you.' He picked up the envelope again. 'Right, I'll get on with it.'

Molly swallowed hard, but didn't take her eyes off her father. She shook her head, before reaching up and rubbing the base of her neck. This wasn't going the way she had planned.

Jack opened the envelope and pulled out several large pieces of paper. 'Molly, look at this.' He passed the printed pages to her.

Molly took them, but laid them on the bed, keeping her gaze fixed on her father. 'Pa, I want you to stop working for the Gettins.' Through her eyelashes, she tried to gauge his expression. 'I can earn enough to look after us all, if we're careful.'

Jack smiled and reached over to cover his daughter's hands with his own. 'As soon as I stop work, we lose this house.'

'You're more important than any house.' Molly glared at her father.

Jack arched his eyebrows at his fiery daughter. 'Look at the papers I have given you.'

Molly looked down at them. Her eyes scanned over them, but she didn't understand what she was reading. 'Pa, what is it?'

Jack laughed. 'Molly, you own a house in Percy Street, not far from Victoria's home.'

'What? How? I don't understand.'

'I always knew that when I stopped work, or died, the family would lose this house, because it came with the job. Therefore, I wanted to make sure you weren't forced to marry because of your circumstances, or worse, living off the street or in a refuge somewhere.'

Molly frowned at her father. 'That wouldn't happen, Pa. I can work.'

Jack chuckled. 'You're so independent.' He shook his head. 'It's unbelievable. When Henry and Lilian Gettin died, William wanted to sell his parents' house, so I asked to buy it. Luckily, Emily and George helped me to sort everything out.' Jack chuckled. 'At the time, you were a tiny bundle of joy, but they felt they owed me everything, because of a little black book I found, so they let me buy it for a good price. I put tenants in there, and that has covered the payments. That house is, and has always been, in your name. I put myself down as acting on your behalf.'

Molly shook her head. 'So you have gone without all your life, just to make sure I'm looked after.'

It was Jack's turn to shake his head. 'We haven't gone without. Remember, if I hadn't rescued the book from an awful man, who Emily's father wanted her to marry, goodness knows what I would have been doing. We had nothing, so this house was a palace to us.'

Molly sighed. Sadness engulfed her. Her father's words echoed her mother's, when she told Molly off, all those weeks ago. 'Pa, you should have enjoyed your earnings more, taken pleasure in some of the finer things in life.'

Jack let out a belly laugh. 'I don't expect you to understand, Molly, but I took great pleasure in knowing I would still be looking after you, when I was gone.' He sighed. 'Don't be angry because we love you. I've also managed to save a very nice nest egg for you, which if you were careful, you could live on.'

Molly stared at her father. 'I don't know what to say, except it does explain a lot. I could never understand why we had everybody's furniture cast offs, and why you lived so frugally, when you earned a good wage.'

Jack smiled for a moment. 'Your ma and I have always been in agreement that what we were doing was right, and both your grans thought so too.'

Molly shook her head. Staring down at the paper, she tried to take in what her father was telling her.

'You must understand we wanted you to have a better life than us.'

With watery eyes, Molly looked up at her father. 'You could have had an even better life if you'd spent your wages, instead of saving them for me.' She shook her head. 'No wonder ma thought I was ashamed of where I came from. I feel terrible now, for wanting more.'

Jack put his arms around his daughter and squeezed her tight. 'Don't feel bad. We all wanted more for each other. Both your grans ran away from brutal men, so they understood how hard life could be. We all wanted more, or maybe a better life, for you.'

Molly pulled back from her father. 'It all falls into place now. I always thought you were disappointed in me, because I wasn't interested in marrying a man and becoming a kept woman. I never wanted to be owned, I just wanted to be loved.'

'Be sure, none of us ever wanted you to marry for anything other than love, but the house and savings were there in case a dowry was ever needed.' Jack paused. 'We didn't want to let you down either.'

'Perhaps Alice and I aren't so different, after all.'

The strong smell of antiseptic no longer made Molly nauseous as she walked, almost on her toes, down the corridor in St Thomas' Hospital. Her head was swimming with new information. There was a lot to take in and, gradually, the penny dropped on many of the conversations she'd had in the past, with her parents. Molly fleetingly wondered if Alice knew about the house. Her grandfather must know. If she did, why hadn't she said anything? Colour began to fill her cheeks. She felt foolish. She kept her eyes forward, not wanting to see the patients lying on the trollies, or hear the murmurs of comfort people were trying to give each other. Molly pushed open the door to Andrew's room. Her shoes clipped the tiled floor as she stepped inside and stopped at the foot of the bed. Nothing had changed. She had so wanted to be there when he came round, but more than anything, she wanted him to wake up and smile at her. She wanted to tell him she was sorry, and loved him with all her heart, but Andrew was still lying in the same position he was in when she left, all those hours ago. Sadness wrapped itself around her.

'Evening, Molly.'

Molly jerked. She had been so intent on watching Andrew, she hadn't noticed Elizabeth sitting at the end of the bed, hidden by the open door.

'Hello, Elizabeth, sorry, I didn't see you there.' Molly began unbuttoning her coat.

'I thought I'd sit where I'm not in the way of the nurses coming in, to check on Andrew.' Elizabeth looked from Molly to her brother. 'Nothing's changed. I started off talking to him, but it's surprising how quickly I ran out of things to say, so I read your newspaper to him, several times.' Elizabeth grimaced. 'I could probably tell you what article is on which page, should you ever wish to know.' She chuckled. 'Not that I can ever imagine anybody would.'

Molly grinned. 'It's hard, isn't it? Much harder than I thought it would be.' She placed her folded coat at the foot of the bed.

'How's Grace?' Elizabeth touched the pearl drop earrings that were just visible below her hair.

Molly smiled. 'She's settled in well; it's going to take time for her to heal properly, though.'

Elizabeth nodded.

'The one thing I didn't think about yesterday was clothing.' Molly raised her eyebrows. 'Grace has obviously lost everything, so I need to do some shopping for her.'

'Of course, I didn't think about that either.' Elizabeth tapped her finger against her lips. 'Don't go shopping yet. I'm sure some of my clothes could be altered, to fit Grace. I'll have a look when I get home.'

'That would be very kind, thank you.' Molly frowned. 'But please don't feel, because I've mentioned it, you need to donate something.'

Elizabeth shrugged her slender shoulders. 'Trust me when I say it would be helping me, to let some of it go.'

Molly gazed at her new friend. 'Just as it helped you to not go in the hospital room by yourself?' She laughed. 'You've been lovely towards me, a complete stranger and you can't begin to know what it all means to me.' She pulled up a chair, to face Elizabeth.

Elizabeth smiled. 'That's just it, Molly, I've heard so much about you, you're not a complete stranger. My brother loves you, so that makes you family, even if you don't end up getting married.'

Colour rushed into Molly's face. She looked down at her hands, resting on the bed. 'I'm not sure Andrew will want me, once he wakes up, but that's not important now. I just want him to be all right.'

Elizabeth reached over and clasped Molly's hand. 'You've spoken like someone who is truly in love, and I know he feels the same about you.'

Words failed Molly and she found herself nodding in Elizabeth's direction. A comfortable silence sat between them for a few minutes.

The stillness was broken, when a clatter came from outside the room, in the corridor. Both girls jerked round, to face the doorway. Raised voices followed the clanging of things being picked up and placed on a tray.

Elizabeth looked over at Molly. 'Sounds like someone could be in trouble.'

'Do you think we should go and see if everything's all right?' Molly frowned as she leant over a little. 'Mind you, I'm not sure what help we could be.'

'I agree, we probably would be in the way, but it does sound like it's all sorted out now.'

Molly nodded.

Elizabeth giggled. 'So what do you think of the beard?'

Molly stared down at Andrew. 'I don't mind it.' She paused for a moment. 'I think I prefer him without it.'

Elizabeth smiled. 'Most definitely. I'm not a lover of beards.'

Molly looked back at Elizabeth for a moment, wondering where her husband was. Should she ask? Unknowingly, she shook her head. She had no desire to rake up painful times for anybody, least of all Andrew's sister.

Elizabeth's voice was flat, when she spoke. 'My husband is away on the front line somewhere.' She paused. 'Andrew won't talk about the war, because he knows I worry about David. I know I'm no different to every other woman, where that's concerned. You worry about whether they will live through it, and whether he will come back the same loving man that went away.'

It was Molly's turn to reach out and clasp Elizabeth's hand, soft against her own dried blistered skin. 'Alice told me once you have to have faith. If David can get back to you, he will.' She hesitated. 'The war has ripped families apart, in more ways than one. There are the men at the front, then there's the likes of Grace, that are now homeless, injured, with no money. Keep believing he will return.' Molly studied Elizabeth for a moment, taking in the dark circles under her eyes that seemed to have become a new fixture to her English rose complexion. 'You look tired. Why don't you go home and rest for a few hours, while I sit and try and find things to talk to Andrew about.' She turned and carried on staring at Andrew, willing him to wake up.

Elizabeth stood up and arched her back. 'I'm so stiff. These aren't the most comfortable chairs I've ever sat on.' The scraping of the chair screamed in the silent room.

Molly gasped. 'Did you see that?'

Elizabeth followed Molly's gaze and rested on Andrew's face.

'His fingers twitched, when the chair scraped across the floor.' Molly's face lit up. 'He must be able to hear us.' She pulled her chair closer to the bed. Elizabeth promptly sat back down.

'Do you think he can?'

Molly grinned across the bed at her. 'He must be able to, mustn't he?' She looked back at the man she adored. His beard had grown. She tipped her head to one side. He looked different with hair on his face, but it didn't change anything for her. Her body tingled, as blood rushed through her veins. She was suddenly glad to be alive.

'Perhaps we should just sit here and talk together; the sound of both our voices in the same room might scare him into waking up.' Elizabeth giggled.

Molly chuckled.

Chapter 24

Elizabeth and Molly's smiles faded, as they silently stared at Andrew, eagerly watching for any indication he was about to wake up. The air in the room was stuffy, but neither of them said anything. A child could be heard screaming further along the corridor; the sobs lessened within seconds.

Molly pushed her blonde hair away from her face, before breaking the silence in the room. 'He looks so peaceful, doesn't he?'

'He does.' Elizabeth glanced across at Molly. 'Perhaps we should scrape the chairs across the floor again. That seemed to cause movement, before.' She gave a nervous giggle. 'Mind you, it might bring the nurses rushing in to see what's wrong.' Elizabeth arched her back. Straightening up, her hands ran down her skirt, smoothing out her ankle length, dove-grey dress. She slipped her feet out of the matching shoes and wriggled her toes, resting them on the cold floor tiles.

'Maybe I imagined the movement, almost willed it to happen.' Molly sighed and threw herself back into her chair, the hard slats of wood bruising her back, causing her to pull forward a little. She frowned, her hands clenched tight in her lap. 'It's frustrating isn't it? Especially when you think it could go on for months.' Molly fidgeted in her chair and the folds of her navy blue skirt partially covered her white knuckles, which were promising to break through the skin, should the opportunity arise.

Elizabeth nodded. 'It won't though, I'm sure you didn't imagine it.' She didn't let her gaze stray from her brother's face. 'He's already been through so much, and survived.' She glanced across at Molly. 'You know, he's riddled with guilt, because he was the only one to survive a German assault.' Elizabeth took a couple of gasps of air. 'I say survived, but he had shrapnel injuries and, thankfully, because he can't bend his trigger finger, he can never go back.' She shook her head. 'You know, someone had the nerve to give him a white feather. I was so angry, when I saw it in the hall. He nearly died, for goodness sake, and yet he insists on keeping it as a reminder.'

'It makes you wonder how something so beautiful and soft can be used to represent cowardice.' Molly's throat tightened. 'I've seen it on the console table. Why does he keep it as a reminder?'

Elizabeth's eyes blazed with pent up anger. 'God only knows. It's probably guilt, because he survived and his friends didn't.' Tears tripped over her lashes and she quickly swiped away with her fingertips. 'He won't leave me on my own, or you. He loves us too much.'

A lump formed in Molly's throat; it ached with unspent tears. She swallowed hard, hoping with all her heart that Elizabeth was right. Her mind was foggy, as she tried to digest what she'd just been told, while searching for something to say, something to reassure Elizabeth, but words were lost to her. Molly's eyes were tired, as they darted from side to side. She wanted to break the silence.

The squeak of wheels turning made them both look round.

A young nurse handed them both a cup of tea and a plain lincoln biscuit. 'I hope it's all right,' she whispered. 'I'm not meant to give anything to visitors, but you've been here for ages.'

Elizabeth smiled, taking the offered cup and saucer. 'Oh I won't tell, thank you, I'm parched.'

Molly followed suit. 'Thank you, it looks lovely and strong.'

The nurse beamed. 'Leave the cups on the bedside cabinet and I'll be back for them later.'

The girls nodded, answering as one. 'Thank you.'

Molly lifted the cup to her dry cracked lips, sipping the steaming, dark brown liquid. 'That's incredibly hot, and I must admit it did sting my lips, but it's a welcome cuppa.'

Elizabeth smiled. 'I might let mine cool for a bit, then.'

Molly nodded. 'That sounds wise. You know, Grace has been learning to read and write. She managed to write a letter to her father and brother.' Molly forced a smile. 'They will be shocked, because they don't know she's been practising.'

Elizabeth looked wide-eyed at Molly. 'What a wonderful surprise for them.'

'Her father went to stay with family in Kent after the explosion, and her brother is away fighting somewhere.'

Molly raised her eyebrows. 'Her brother writes to her all the time, even though he knows she can't read, but I think it's his way of letting her know he's still alive.'

Elizabeth smiled. 'How wonderful for them to receive a letter from her.' She shook her head. 'I never think about people not being able to read and write, these days. I just assume everyone can.'

Molly nodded. 'I know what you mean. It took a lot of courage for her to admit it, and to let me help her, but on my part, it's been lovely to help someone with something I love. I can't even begin to know what it must be like to not be able to read all those books. I told her I'd buy her Pride and Prejudice, then she'll understand what she has been missing all these years.'

Elizabeth gave a faint smile. 'Ahh, Mr Darcy.' She had a faraway look, as she travelled down memory lane. 'Jane Austen weaves a wonderful story.' She giggled.

Molly smiled at Elizabeth's expression, before glancing back at Andrew and lowering her voice. 'Yes, it's what we all want, our own Mr Darcy.'

Elizabeth followed Molly's gaze. 'Perhaps that's your calling, to be a teacher. It must be very rewarding.'

Molly nodded; keeping her eyes fixed on Andrew, unable to think about anything else but him, no matter how hard she tried.

Andrew's fingers twitched.

Elizabeth squealed. 'Did you see that?'

'Yes, yes I did.' Molly beamed. 'Thank God I didn't imagine it.' She leant over and caressed the top of his hand, careful to avoid the bright crimson welts that were slowly darkening as they healed. 'Andrew, if you can hear me please let us know you are all right. I've met your lovely sister, who's here with me now. I have to say, you could have told me the lady I saw you with at Monico's was your sister, then we might not have got into such a mess.' She sighed, her eyes becoming watery. 'Listen to me, having a moan. I didn't ask, but just assumed, so we're equally at fault. I have always loved you, and nothing we say or do will ever change that.'

Elizabeth leant forward and stroked Molly's arm. 'It's not about blame.'

Molly looked over at her and gave a faint smile. A tear fell onto her cheek. 'It is, if he doesn't come round.' She looked back at Andrew. 'I love you Andrew and I'm so sorry for everything.'

Both women sat in silence, watching the man they loved lying so still.

'Don't be.' A quiet rasping sound came from Andrew. 'We're both to blame.'

Molly jumped in her seat and quickly glanced at Elizabeth, before looking back at Andrew. His eyes were still shut. 'Did he speak? Did he?'

Elizabeth nodded. 'Yes, yes, yes he did.'

Molly swivelled in her seat. 'Should we fetch someone?'

Both girls sat staring at him, waiting for his eyes to open.

His singed eyelashes fluttered. His fingers curled slightly. His mouth tightened, as the pain from the burns took hold. Andrew slowly opened his eyes.

Elizabeth and Molly gasped.

★

Grace carefully placed the tip of her teaspoon into the soft, boiled egg. The bright yellow yolk began to creep over the edges and down the shell. She ran her finger up the already congealing yellow river. Licking off the stickiness, she glanced up at Molly. 'I can't let any of it go to waste.'

Molly looked up and smiled, before biting into her egg-covered bread soldier. She ran her tongue over her teeth, removing the soft dough from around her mouth. 'I'm sorry I haven't been here much lately.'

Deciding to change tack, Grace placed the spoon on the tea plate and picked up the lightly buttered slice of bread. 'That's all right, your ma and gran have been really kind to me.' She smiled over at Sophie, sitting in her usual position in the armchair, with her knitting needles and a ball of wool on her lap. 'Anyway, it should be me saying sorry. I was mean, when I knew nothing about you, and yet you've been nothing but kind to me.' She paused, staring into her egg. 'I'm sorry and don't deserve your thoughtfulness, or your family's.'

Molly picked up her cup and sipped the strong, hot tea. 'Things are difficult for everyone at the moment and we could all do with some kindness in our lives, don't you think?' She replaced the china cup onto its matching saucer.

Grace shrugged her shoulders. 'You're right.' She looked up and frowned. 'I'm guilty of not thinking about what other people are going through.' She paused. 'Does that make me an awful person?'

Molly reached across the table and lightly touched Grace's hand. 'No, we all have stuff going on, and are just trying to survive.'

Grace nodded, glancing down at their hands. 'How are your burns now? They don't look as sore as they did.'

Molly consciously snatched her hand away and rested it on her lap, letting the folds of her black skirt cushion and protect it. The burns were drying up, scabs forming, as the skin repaired itself. 'No, I was lucky compared to others, especially you, Flo and Mr Greenwood.'

Grace frowned, as she picked up her teaspoon again. 'How is Mr Greenwood?'

Molly's face immediately flushed with colour. 'He's awake, thank goodness.' She giggled. 'It's funny seeing him with a beard.' She picked up her cup again and mumbled into it. 'I left him with Elizabeth, last night.'

They sat in silence for a few moments. Grace stared into her egg, intent on finding the answer to her unasked questions. 'Are you going to see him today?'

Molly jerked, nearly spilling her tea. 'I don't think so.' She didn't look at Grace. 'Now I know he's going to be all right, I shall leave him in Elizabeth's capable hands. I think they have a lot to talk about.'

Grace dropped her spoon, jumping as it clattered on to her plate. 'And what about you, don't you have something to say to him?'

Molly gripped her cup. 'I have a lot to do today. I've neglected my family and friends, over the last few days.' She sighed. 'If nothing else, I've learnt there's nothing more important than the people you love.'

'They'll understand. You're precious to them, and so is your happiness.'

Molly gulped the remains of her tea. 'Mr Greenwood needs to heal and get stronger, without any extra problems to deal with.'

Grace gave an impatient shake of her head. Her eyes widened. 'Is that how you see yourself, a "problem"?'

Sophie tilted her head, but didn't look up.

Grace raised her voice. 'Is it?'

Silence screamed across the table for a few minutes.

'I don't believe this.' Grace folded her arms across her stomach, as she stared at Molly. 'I know you love him; so you need to stop thinking he can't possibly love you. You're a good person.' She raised her eyebrows and thrust her hands up in the air. 'My goodness, he even wore our overalls, so he had an excuse to see you.'

Molly chuckled at the memory.

Grace laughed. 'You know, for a clever person, you really are quite stupid when it comes to you.'

Sophie picked up her knitting needles, smiling as she tried to look busy.

Molly mumbled. 'I know.'

The clunk of the doorknocker had Molly scraping back her chair. 'I wonder who that can be, so early in the morning.'

Sophie looked up. 'It's not that early. You two were late starters this morning, your ma will be home from work soon.'

Molly glanced over at the clock on the mantelpiece, just as it chimed half past eleven. Her lips tightened. 'I need to get a move on. I want to pop into Foyles today, and go shopping for Grace.' She carried on walking into the hall, her heels clipping the tiles, as she stepped towards the front door and opened it. The wintery air rushed in, filling the space around her.

'Hello, Molly.' Elizabeth looked sheepish, as she tightened the navy blue woollen scarf around her neck. 'I must apologise for coming without an invitation, but I've brought some clothes for Grace.'

'Come in out of the cold, I'll make you a cup of tea.' Molly shivered, as she stepped further back into the hall. 'That wind feels biting today, and I've only stood here for a few minutes.'

Elizabeth picked up the two shopping bags by her feet, and stepped over the threshold.

Molly quickly shut out the cold, damp air, not noticing the inevitable squeak of the hinges. 'I hate this bitterly cold weather.' She turned round to face Elizabeth. 'Tell me that's not all for Grace, is it?'

Elizabeth laughed. 'I'm afraid so. I told you I had plenty of clothes I could give her, but whether they fit or not is a different matter.'

Molly beamed. 'I'm sure between us we can manage some alterations. I believe Grace is a good seamstress, as indeed are my mother and gran.' She took one of the bulging bags from Elizabeth, leading her towards the dining room. 'I'm sorry, we are a little slow at getting ourselves organised this morning.'

'I wouldn't worry about that. You've had a very worrying few days, and I suspect you needed the rest.

Morning everyone.' Elizabeth announced herself, as she walked into the room.

Sophie beamed at their guest. 'How lovely to see you again, Mrs Penney. How is your brother?'

'Please call me Elizabeth.' She grinned, as her gaze touched everyone in the room. 'He is doing fine. His burns are not good, but they are healing slowly. The doctors are saying he can go home soon, as long as someone's there to look after him.' Her eyes focused on Molly. 'And of course, there would be.' Elizabeth took a deep breath. 'It's all good news.'

Grace's words kept coming back to Molly; she hadn't been to the hospital today. A voice shouted in her head. *You mean, since he came round. What are you afraid of?*

Elizabeth turned to look at Sophie. 'I'm sorry to barge in on you, but I have some clothes for Grace.' She peered down at the bags. 'I shan't be offended if you don't want them, but I thought they may do you a turn, especially until you can get work again.'

Grace's mouth dropped open at the sight of the large packed bags.

Elizabeth blushed. 'It looks more than it is, because there's a winter coat in there, so that takes up a lot of space.'

Molly raised her eyebrows. 'I never even thought about a winter coat. I was just concerning myself with dresses and shoes.'

'I don't know what to say.' Grace looked up at Elizabeth. 'You've all been so kind and generous to me.'

'I'm not sure what will fit, but you are welcome to all of it, and alter it as you must.' Elizabeth smiled.

Grace's eyes became watery. 'Thank you.'

Elizabeth giggled. 'Don't get too excited; you haven't seen any of it yet.'

Molly laughed. 'Take a seat, Elizabeth, and I'll go and put the kettle on. Maybe Grace can try some clothes on, and we'll pin where it needs altering.'

Charlotte quietly pushed her front door closed. The laughter coming from the dining room drowned out the squeaks of the hinges and the thud of the lock closing. She rested her head against its hard paneling for a moment, closing her eyes. Her work in domestic service was more than it used to be. She was starting earlier and finding it harder.

Molly and Elizabeth's melodious laughter travelled towards the hallway, making Charlotte laugh out loud. She smiled to herself, as her fingers deftly undid the buttons of her coat, and then removed her hat. The lavender plant on the console table caught her eye. It looked a little sad, and not as fragrant. With everything that had been going on, she had forgotten to water it. The house had come alive in recent weeks, with the constant stream of visitors. She bent down to pick up a letter that was lying on the floor. She turned it over; it was addressed to Grace.

'My goodness, some of these clothes are going to need altering quite a bit,' Elizabeth trilled.

Molly giggled. 'Yes, it's not very flattering on you, Grace, but I'm sure it will be, once we've made the alterations.'

Charlotte stepped into the room and glanced around at the smiling faces, and resting on Grace. 'Blimey, that's going to take a bit of altering.'

Elizabeth stood up, her small gold drop earrings swaying slightly with the movement. 'Hello, Mrs Cooper, I hope you don't mind, but I've brought some clothes in for Grace.' She cast her gaze towards Grace again. 'To be honest, I thought we were similar in size, but apparently not.'

Charlotte laughed. 'Hello, Elizabeth, it's lovely to see you again.' Charlotte walked around Grace, scrunching bits of the soft blue material around the waist and shoulders. A rose fragrance drifted from the fabric. 'Not to worry, it looks like it can be taken in without too much trouble.'

Elizabeth giggled and shook her head. 'It's shocking. I can't believe it. I truly thought we were about the same size, but that clearly isn't the case.'

Grace smiled as she hobbled over to a chair and sat down. 'I'm very grateful for them, regardless.'

Molly smiled and stood up, as she looked over at her mother. 'Sit down, Ma, you look tired. I'll go and make some tea.'

Charlotte rested her hand on Molly's arm. 'No, I think you need to rest. It's been a terrible few days for all of us, but particularly for you girls.' She smiled as she turned away. 'Besides which, I like making the tea. Oh, I almost forgot, there's a letter for you, Grace.'

'Thank you.' Grace beamed, as she took the letter from Charlotte.

Molly sat down again, as Charlotte left the room. Murmured voices came from just outside the door. Was that her father she could hear? She leant forward for a moment, tilting her head to listen.

Grace looked around the room.

Molly turned to watch her. She smiled, before turning the envelope over in her hands.

Sophie nodded her encouragement. It suddenly got too much and Grace ripped the envelope open. The paper rustled as she pulled it out. Her eyes travelled across the page.

Molly watched Grace's finger slowly move, under each word. Her lips mouthed each word silently. Time seemed to stand still as Molly waited to see if she was needed, to help read the letter.

Grace giggled, looking over at Molly. 'It's from my father, well, he didn't write it himself, but it's from him all the same.' She looked down again, turning the single page over. 'When I'm well enough, he wants me to move down into Kent with them. Apparently, I can work on the land, whatever that means.'

Jack strode in and gave Grace a smile. 'I would imagine it involves growing things, or looking after animals of some sort.'

Grace laughed. 'I don't know anything about growing things or looking after animals.'

Molly chuckled. 'But you can learn, and it's got to be better than turning yellow, in a munitions' factory.'

Grace's lips formed a straight line for a moment, but then she nodded. 'You're right, Molly, especially after everything that's happened. It's got to be worth a go.'

Jack looked around the room. 'Good afternoon, Mrs Penney, it's lovely to see you again. I hope your brother is on the mend. He's a real gentleman, and it's been an honour to make his acquaintance.' He gave her his best smile, before taking in the clothes, strewn across every possible surface. 'What's going on here, then?'

'Thank you, Mr Cooper; hopefully he should be home soon. They are just keeping an eye on him, thank goodness.' Elizabeth started to gather up the pinned garments that had been left around the room. 'I'm sorry about the mess. I'm afraid I'm to blame, because I brought the clothes over for Grace.'

'It's all right, Elizabeth, Pa doesn't mind. He's used to being surrounded by women, aren't you Pa?'

Jack raised his eyebrows at his daughter. 'Yes I am, but it would be nice to be able to sit down.' He frowned, as he glanced across at Elizabeth. 'You know, it costs a pretty penny to stay in hospital.'

Elizabeth nodded, her eyes clouding over. 'Apart from my husband, Andrew is the only family I have, so the cost isn't important. I will find the money, regardless of the sum.'

Molly glanced from one to the other, before standing up to move the pile of skirts and dresses off the armchair that was designated as her father's. 'Sorry Pa, we weren't expecting you home yet.' She smiled, indicating to his chair.

A smile crept across Jack's face. 'If I'd known there was a party going on, I wouldn't have gone to work in the first place.'

The thud of the doorknocker stopped the conversation. Jack turned on his heels. 'I'll get it.' His soft-soled shoes were silent on the tiled flooring in the hall.

The front door whined as it was opened. The curtains in the dining room fluttered in the breeze that found its way into the room. Molly shivered.

Everyone looked towards the doorway, waiting to see who Jack was talking to. The creaking hinges and the lack of cold draft, told Molly the door had been closed. She stared hard, concentrating on the mumbled voices. Footsteps moved along the hallway, towards the best room, at the back of the house. She wondered if anyone would say anything if she got up and peeked into the hall, but she knew that was not acceptable, and would have to wait. Was it the man in the trilby hat again? She would wait a few minutes, then go and find out. The last thing she wanted was her father in hospital again.

Chapter 25

Molly strained to hear the conversation from down the hall. Her father wasn't raising his voice. She couldn't hear the man with the trilby hat either. Had her father been taken ill again and collapsed? She looked around the room and watched everyone laughing and talking about the clothes that had to be altered. Surely no one would notice if she left for a few minutes. She stood up and skulked out of the room on tiptoes. The soles of her shoes squeaked on the floor tiles, as she moved stealthily down the hallway. Molly looked over her shoulder, knowing she was desperate to hear any conversation that was taking place. She hesitated, standing in front of the closed door. Her gran's voice shouted in her head, repeating words Molly had heard many years ago when, as a child, she got caught listening in on a conversation. *Nobody ever 'eard anyfink good about themselves by eavesdropping.* Molly shook her head and raised her hand, rapping her knuckles on the door a couple of times in quick succession.

Jack's voice bellowed through the closed door. 'Come in.'

Molly took a deep breath, wondering what she was going to say, when her father showed his displeasure at being interrupted. She turned the handle, which squeaked its disapproval at being disturbed. Molly forced her brightest smile to her lips and walked in. 'Pa, there's tea...' Her eyes widened, as the man in the armchair stood up. 'Andrew, what... how... your sister...' She looked over her shoulder and pointed to the hallway.

Andrew's lips lifted slightly. 'They were only keeping me in hospital for observation, so they agreed to discharge me last night, on the understanding that I return every couple of days, to have my dressings changed.' He looked sheepishly from Molly to her father, and back again. 'Yes, Elizabeth will be cross with me, but I wasn't resting properly and I had things I wanted to say and do.'

Jack nodded. 'There's no better place than your own bed, but you need to be careful you don't overdo it.'

Molly blinked rapidly, as tears began to form. She was fighting for the words she wanted to say, but failing. Her voice was barely audible, when she did speak. 'What brings you here?'

Andrew stared at her pale features for a few minutes. He cleared his throat and glanced across at Jack. 'A couple of things.'

Molly gathered herself together, wondering whether to offer to leave the room, but decided against it. They would have to order her out.

Jack looked at Molly, who immediately looked away. He raised his eyebrows. 'Well take a seat and we can chat. Would you like some tea?'

As he sat down, Andrew's gaze was drawn back to Molly. 'No, thank you, one of the things I wanted to talk to you about was the man that paid you a visit. A stocky man wearing a dark suit and a trilby hat.'

Jack slowly lowered himself into an armchair. His hands gripped the wooden arms, until his knuckles were white. 'How do you know about that visit?'

'That was my fault, Pa. I was worried and didn't know what to do about it, so I mentioned it to Andrew.' Remembering the comfort of Andrew's arms carrying her into his office, Molly's complexion flooded with colour. She never did get to the bottom of what was wrong with her that day.

'Mr Cooper, Molly was right to be concerned. This man is apparently known to the police and, when I last spoke to them, he was about to be arrested.'

Jack paled. 'You mean he wasn't the police?'

'No sir, he was a blackmailer. I believe he tried it on with a number of people, and eventually with the wrong person.' Andrew crossed his legs in front of him. 'I believe he posed as a policeman, to get information on people.'

Molly flopped, unladylike, on to a chair. 'We thought he was the police, and so did Frank.'

Andrew nodded. 'Yes, I know.'

'He wanted to come in.' Stunned, Molly spoke in a whisper. 'When Pa was at work, but we wouldn't let him.'

'Good job too. From what I understand, he's a nasty character.' Andrew's gaze darted between father and daughter. 'I've spoken to Frank. He came to see me in hospital this morning and we talked about Mr Trilby Hat, and how he was fishing for information all the time.'

'I kept telling him I knew nothing.' Jack jumped up and paced around the small room. 'I'm not privy to the information he was asking about, that's if it existed at all.'

Andrew watched Jack thrust his hands into his trouser pockets. 'Well, you can stop worrying now, because Frank told me the man in the trilby hat is going away for a long time.'

Jack stopped and stared out of the window, looking at the small yard that was their garden.

Andrew slowly stood up. 'There's something else, sir, which is not related to Mr Trilby.'

Jack pulled back his shoulders and jutted out his chin, before turning to face Andrew Greenwood. 'What is it?'

Colour crept up Andrew's neck and he kept his eyes fixed on Jack. He took a couple of deep breaths. He cleared his throat. 'I, er, I would like your permission to ask for your daughter's hand in marriage.'

Molly gasped for air. The room began to spin.

Jack's face lit up for a second, before frowning at his daughter. 'Well, Molly, you wanted to stay in this room. What do you think? Should I say yes or no?'

Molly's heart was pumping hard in her chest. She closed her eyes and took a couple of long breaths.

Jack turned back to Andrew. 'The thing is, I always promised myself that Molly would marry who she wanted, as long as he was law abiding. I have made provision for Molly, so she doesn't have to get married to live a happy life. She can be free.'

Andrew nodded. Beads of sweat formed on his forehead. He licked his dry lips, wishing he'd taken the cup of tea that had been offered. 'I understand, sir, and I'm sure I would take the same stance in your position, but you must understand that I love your daughter, and I can promise you no harm will ever come to her, while I'm around.' He looked across at Molly, who looked like she'd seen a ghost. 'I know we have had a rocky start, but that's because your daughter has fought it. I know she loves me. She can deny it as much as she likes, but why else would she have spent the night looking for me.'

Jack smiled. 'I know Molly loves you too. What concerns me is whether Molly knows she loves you, and whether you will both love each other, regardless of what life throws at you.'

Molly walked the once daily route from her home in Carlisle Street to Charing Cross Road. The cold licked at her face. Every breath was a white vapor, spiralling up into the grey sky. She raised her gloved hands and pulled up the collar of her heavy black coat, as the wind whipped around her neck, trying to find a way in. She was thankful it hadn't snatched the hat off her head. Her ankle boots clipped the pavement. She was relieved the earlier snow flurries hadn't amounted to much, but the frost was still evident on the pavements. Excitement coursed through her body. Her stomach churned. Had Andrew really asked for her father's permission to marry her? It wasn't long before the large white letters, spelling out Foyles Bookstore, came into view. Molly couldn't resist smiling at the sign above the door, advertising novels at 3d. She shook her head, wondering why she had ever thought it was a good idea to leave. Ahh, but then she would never have met Andrew. She shook her head. Her smile didn't fade, as she stepped into the comfort of Foyles Bookshop.

The familiar smell of books wrapped itself around her, like a warm blanket on a cold day. The dust and smokiness of the second hand books fought against the cleanliness of the pristine unsnapped spines of the new ones. Molly glanced up and down the maze of shelving that was stacked high with dog-eared books. She removed her gloves and ran her fingers down a couple of the spines; they were books that had been read, and probably loved, many times.

'Hello, Miss Cooper.'

The familiar deep voice behind her, made her snatch her hand away. She smiled to herself; nothing had changed. 'Hello, Mr Leadbetter.' She turned around to face the tall grey haired man, who was once her manager.

'You look well.' Mr Leadbetter paused for a moment. 'When I heard about the explosion at the munitions' factory, I worried for your safety, so it is good to see you here.'

Molly nodded. 'I was one of the lucky ones. Some people not only lost loved ones, but they lost their homes as well. They've lost everything.'

Mr Leadbetter shook his head. 'I must admit I was thankful, when Mrs Leybourne came in and told me you were safe.'

Molly nodded. 'It was a long night, searching for people. Alice and Victoria risked their lives, digging people out from under the rubble. If it hadn't been for Alice's quick action, a friend of mine would have died.' She sighed as the memories flooded her mind. 'I was at the hospital, when I found out my father was taken there that same evening.' Colour filled her cheeks. 'Sorry, I'm talking too much, as always.'

Mr Leadbetter stared at the young girl in front of him, knowing instinctively she wasn't the same person that had left Foyles, just a few short months ago. 'Not at all, you carry on.' He smiled. 'I'm listening.'

Molly shrugged her shoulders. 'There's not much more to say, except I'm trying to get him to stop working, but he has it in his head that he needs to provide for me.' Sparks flew from her eyes when she looked up at Mr Leadbetter. 'You know, he's at work now.'

Mr Leadbetter frowned. 'I expect he feels it's his responsibility. I think that's called being a parent.'

'I know, but I don't want him working himself into the ground.' Molly sighed.

Mr Leadbetter straightened his shoulders and clasped his hands behind his back. 'What will you do about work now? Can you go back to the factory, or is it closed?'

Molly loosened her scarf from around her neck. 'I don't know. Part of it is still open, but they obviously won't need all of us, so I probably won't be going back.' Her gaze darted around, as she tried to think of what to do next.

'I meant what I said to you on the day you left here.' Mr Leadbetter smiled, as Molly gave a puzzled look. 'There will always be work for you here.'

A smile spread slowly across Molly's face and she tilted her head slightly. 'Really? I thought you were just being polite, because I was leaving.'

Mr Leadbetter's bellowing laugh filled the space around them.

Molly looked sheepishly at him. 'I thought you would have been glad to see the back of me, especially as I was always getting into trouble.'

'You were never in serious trouble, you just liked to chat too much.' He ran a hand through his hair, before a smile lit up his face. 'So what do you think? Have you missed us?'

Molly smiled up at the gentle giant in front of her. 'I must admit, when I walked in here, it did feel like I was coming home.'

'Well, that's it then.' Mr Leadbetter grinned from ear to ear. 'Let me know when you are ready to come back, and I will make all the necessary arrangements.'

Molly nodded. 'I might need a week or two, before I can come back.'

'That's fine, just let me know when you are ready.' He chuckled. 'I expect you want to have a chat with your friends.' He pulled out his gold fob watch from a pocket in his dark blue waistcoat and flicked the lid open. 'It's pretty close to lunch time, and I have a feeling they are not working this afternoon, so you might as well wait for them, if you'd like to?'

Molly nodded. 'Thank you, Mr Leadbetter, I'll come back a better person than I was last time.' She smiled.

'Not too much, I hope.' He laughed. 'Now get on with yer.'

Molly smiled and turned to walk towards Alice's counter.

Alice was serving a young soldier, his cap tucked under his arm. The khaki uniform stood out amongst the shoppers in the store. Alice handed him a book and smiled at him. He nodded and moved to turn away. Alice's face suddenly lit up, when she spotted Molly standing a short distance away. She ran around the counter, wrapping her arms around her, in a bear hug. 'Shall we go to Monico's, it's been a long time?'

Molly tucked her hands through Alice and Victoria's arms as they walked along in a row, turning sideways to let people pass them in the street.

Victoria smiled. 'I've decided it's time I sorted through my parents' things. I've let it drag on for too long.' She looked down at the pavement ahead of her. 'There are loads of letters and personal papers to go through, but I think it's time to let go and get on with it.'

Molly squeezed Victoria's arm. 'I know you've been threatening to do that for years, but were waiting until the time was right.'

'I'm going to do it. It's time I moved on with my life.'

They all stepped forward in silence, wondering if Victoria would finally be able to bring closure for herself and her family.

Alice laughed. 'This is like old times.'

The cold wintry air was forgotten, as they travelled back in time, blowing their breath out like a smoker does when having a cigarette.

Molly smiled. 'We used to do this when we were children, and remember how we held our fingers, as if we were holding a cigarette.'

Victoria chuckled. 'And didn't we get into trouble for it.'

The girls giggled as they strode along.

Victoria frowned, as she glanced across at the girls stepping forward. 'It's not quite the same; Molly isn't one of us Foyles girls any more.'

Molly giggled. 'Hah, that's what you think.'

The girls stopped dead, yanking Molly back, as she continued to walk forward.

'What?' they called out in unison.

With a smile, Molly pulled them both forward. 'It's a wonder I have any arms left.' She rolled her shoulders. The three of them turned into Regent Street and the pyramid shapes of Monico's came into view.

The light touch of butterflies was flying around Molly's stomach. She knew her friends would be happy with her news, but she had to delay it for a few more minutes.

Victoria squeezed Molly's arm. 'Come on, out with it, what did you mean?'

Molly laughed. 'I have a lot to tell you, but you have to be patient, because I'm not saying anything until we've sat down and ordered chocolate cake.'

Victoria opened her mouth to speak.

'No, Vicky, we have a tradition and I'm not going to be the one to break it.'

Victoria's mouth instantly straightened into a thin line.

Molly giggled. 'Don't get angry, Victoria, I'm only playing with you.'

Alice laughed. 'See, it is like old times.'

Molly pushed open the glass door to Monico's. A couple of customers looked towards them, their conversation and food momentarily forgotten. The warm interior invited customers to stay. The strong aroma of coffee mingled with the inviting smells of the hot food that was being served. There was no hint of a war slowing down this business. The marble pillars and the arched windows gave the room elegance, while the potted palms, reflected in large ornate mirrors across the room, transported you to another time and world. A waitress walked serenely towards them. 'Can we have a table for three please?'

The waitress nodded and led the way to a table by the window.

'Thank you.' The girls spoke as one.

The waitress turned to walk away, but Victoria called her back. 'Sorry, we know what we want. Three teas and three slices of your best chocolate cake, please.'

The waitress smiled and walked away.

The girls unbuttoned their coats and pushed the scarves into their sleeves, before hooking them onto the oak coat stand, near their table. Molly pulled back her chair and sat down, quickly followed by the other two.

Molly chuckled. 'I don't think we've ever ordered so quickly.'

Victoria poked her tongue out at Molly.

Alice and Molly roared with laughter.

'Well, that's because I want your news, and you weren't going to tell us until we had sat down and ordered.'

Molly gasped in between breaths. 'Well, we have come a long way, haven't we?'

Victoria's mouth dropped open. 'I've a good mind to throw something at you.'

Molly tilted her head. 'Have you both missed me at Foyles?'

Alice frowned, as she glanced across at Victoria. They both looked at Molly. 'Yes,' they said in unison. 'Of course we have, it's not been the same without you.'

Victoria's eyes narrowed. 'Are you coming back?'

Molly beamed at her friends, nodding frantically.

Alice jumped up. 'Oh my goodness, I'm so happy, this is the best news I've had in ages.' She enveloped Molly in a bear hug. Her floral perfume mingled with Molly's rose fragrance.

Victoria leapt out of her chair and ran round the table, throwing her arms around Molly and Alice. 'I'm so thrilled. It hasn't been the same, without you causing havoc around us.'

Molly raised her eyebrows. 'Charming.'

The girls both sat back down at the table, smoothing out the crisp white tablecloth they'd taken with them, in their rush to give Molly a hug. The waitress came over, carrying a tray weighed down with tea things and three slices of chocolate cake. They sat in silence as the waitress laid the table setting, for each of them in turn.

'Thank you,' Molly said, as she turned to walk away. She looked back at her friends. 'I need to find something to do for the war effort, something I can do around working at Foyles.'

Alice leant forward. 'I'm sure we'll think of something.' She beamed from ear to ear, as she clapped her hands together a couple of times. 'This is so exciting. When are you coming back?'

'I don't think it will be for a week or two. I need to let Mr Leadbetter know, when I've sorted it out.'

Victoria chuckled. 'Oh, Mr Leadbetter, is he? What happened to old Leadbetter?'

Molly shrugged her shoulders. 'I don't know; it just doesn't seem appropriate any more.'

The girls nodded somberly.

Alice smiled, unable to resist holding her tongue. 'I've always said he was a nice man, but you never believed me.'

'You did.' Molly smiled. 'But I always thought he didn't like me, because I was always in trouble.' She picked up the silver cake fork, letting it balance between her thumb and forefinger. 'I have something a little more serious to talk to you about.'

'It's not Mr Greenwood, is it?'

Molly sighed. Victoria was always so impatient. 'No.' She shook her head and put the fork down on her tea plate. 'It... It seems I own my own house.'

'What?'

Molly glanced from one to the other of her friends; their mouths were gaping open. She smiled. 'It's shocking, isn't it?'

'Are you sure?' Victoria was the first to find her voice.

Molly laughed, but there was no humour in the sound. 'No. I've seen the paperwork, but I don't know if it's real or not. To be honest, I can't believe it.'

'No.' Alice found her voice. 'But if it's true, it's a good thing. Where is it?'

Molly shook her head and looked across at Victoria. 'I don't know what house number it is, but apparently it's not far from Victoria's.'

'In Percy Street?' Alice thought for a moment. 'It's not Henry and Lilian's old home is it?'

Molly smiled. 'When my father told me, I wondered if you knew about it, because of the family connection, but then I wondered why you had never told me.'

Alice shook her head. 'I didn't know about it, but in all fairness, if I had, I wouldn't have told you because it's not my news to tell.'

Molly and Victoria nodded.

'I expect my grandfather knows, because his father would have been consulted in selling his parent's home.' Alice picked up her teaspoon and lifted the lid off the teapot. 'It doesn't matter how it came about, it's wonderful news.' She stirred the brown liquid vigorously, before tapping the tea leaves off her spoon and replacing the lid.

Victoria reached across the table and clasped Molly's hand. 'You must be happy about it, surely.'

'Of course, it just takes a bit of believing.' Molly shrugged her shoulders and glanced from Victoria to Molly. 'When my father told me, so many things suddenly made sense. I do wonder what he'd done for the Gettins, for them to feel so indebted to him, though.'

Alice laughed. 'Don't look at me, I only know your father saved them from a huge embarrassment. He apparently saved them a lot of money, and that was always the driving force for Henry and William Gettin.' Alice smiled. 'We will never know the detail, and it was such a long time ago, I'm not sure it matters any more. Instead of worrying, we should be celebrating.'

'That's true.' Victoria beamed as she picked up the teapot and began pouring the tea into their cups. 'We could be neighbours; how exciting is that? I assume you're not going to sell it, are you?'

'No, I'm trying to get them to stop work and move into the house, but at the moment, I'm losing that battle.' Molly sighed. 'It seems their frugal ways have meant they've saved up quite a lot of money, and they want me to have it. They say I have choices now, either to use it as a dowry, or not worry about being on the street because I'm not married. But I would rather they spent it, so they could have a better life, and that's the argument at the moment.'

Victoria laughed. 'They're just trying to look after you. Don't forget that.'

'I know, but they are so stubborn. It's frustrating.'

Alice smiled warmly at Molly. 'Well, that's two pieces of excellent news. I wonder what the third will be. I wonder if it will involve Mr Greenwood.'

Molly immediately looked down at her slice of cake, as her cheeks began to flush.

Victoria giggled. 'Something tells me it will, but let's eat the cake and drink the tea before it goes cold. Remember, tea and chocolate cake solves everything.'

Acknowledgements

The encouragement and support I've had since my debut novel, The Foyles Bookshop Girls, was published has been unbelievable.

Firstly, I would like to thank my wonderful family, there are too many to name, for being so proud that I achieved my long held dream. I also want to thank the many readers that have sent me messages, saying how much they have enjoyed my writing and are looking forward to the next book, and here it is. It has all meant a lot to me. A special mention needs to go to a lady named Beverley, only her first name because I don't wish to embarrass her. She is very supportive of many authors, despite the ups and downs that life is throwing her way. Thank you, Beverley.

On a personal note, I've always known about the suffragette movement but researching the home front of World War One has brought home to me how these women changed the way women would be treated in the future. Through their endless hard work, they gained respect, and eventually the vote. I have the utmost admiration for them.

A big thank you must go to the tutor and students of The Write Place Creative Writing School, always there to offer advice and guidance. Writers, editors and agents are a special breed of people and I have been fortunate to meet quite a few on my journey. They are happy to share experiences, good or bad, offering guidance and advice, which I much appreciate. Many of these I met when I joined the Romantic Novelists' Association and the Society of Women Writers and Journalists and started attending their events. I am lucky to be a member of such supportive organisations and would like to thank them for their endless encouragement.

A huge thank you must go to my editor, Lucy Gilmour and the team at Aria, who are publishing this second book in The Foyles Bookshop Girls series. They have believed in me and fine-tuned my novel. They have been a pleasure to work with. I truly hope everyone who reads The Foyles Bookshop Girls At War enjoys it.

Hello from Aria

We hope you enjoyed this book! Let us know, we'd love to hear from you.

We are Aria, a dynamic digital-first fiction imprint from award-winning independent publishers Head of Zeus. At heart, we're avid readers committed to publishing exactly the kind of books we love to read — from romance and sagas to crime, thrillers and historical adventures. Visit us online and discover a community of like-minded fiction fans!

We're also on the look out for tomorrow's superstar authors. So, if you're a budding writer looking for a publisher, we'd love to hear from you. You can submit your book online at ariafiction.com/we-want-read-your-book

You can find us at:
Email: aria@headofzeus.com
Website: www.ariafiction.com
Submissions: www.ariafiction.com/
we-want-read-your-book
Facebook: @ariafiction
Twitter: @Aria_Fiction
Instagram: @ariafiction

Printed in Great Britain
by Amazon